# CROSSROADS OF CANOPY

# CROSSROADS OF CANOPY

## THORAIYA DYER

*A Tom Doherty Associates Book*

NEW YORK

CROSSROADS OF CANOPY

Copyright © 2017 by Thoraiya Dyer

All rights reserved.

Map by Jennifer Hanover

A Tor Book
Published by Tom Doherty Associates
175 Fifth Avenue
New York, NY 10010

www.tor-forge.com

Tor® is a registered trademark of Macmillan Publishing Group, LLC.

The Library of Congress Cataloging-in-Publication Data is available upon request.

ISBN 978-0-7653-8592-5 (hardcover)
ISBN 978-0-7653-8593-2 (e-book)

Our books may be purchased in bulk for promotional, educational, or business use.
Please contact your local bookseller or the Macmillan Corporate and Premium
Sales Department at 1-800-221-7945, extension 5442, or by e-mail at
MacmillanSpecialMarkets@macmillan.com.

First Edition: January 2017

Printed in the United States of America

0  9  8  7  6  5  4  3  2  1

*For Melissa Freeman*
*Friends for the journey*

# *Acknowledgments*

This is my first published novel. Along this tortuous path I've left many beta readers broken and crying behind me (Shout-out to David Fenwick-Mulcahy! Who could have guessed that the were-platypus novel would be buried by another ten full novel manuscripts as well as various detritus left by the raising of actual children?), or something. In short, if the thought of my naked gratitude makes you squeamish, look away now. Or you'll go blind! You have been warned.

Most immediately and in regards to this specific book, I must thank my agent, Evan Gregory; my editor, Diana M. Pho; plus everyone at Tor involved in production, publicity, etc (thanks again for the beautiful artwork, Marc!). Next, my faithful and, necessarily, slightly cruel manuscript readers Anna Tambour, Jenny Blackford, and Kaaron Warren. Sofia Samatar, your owlish feedback was hugely appreciated, and to Rowena Cory Daniells and Jason Nahrung, for helping wrestle the stupid series proposal into shape, you have my eternal thanks. During the editing phases, kudos to Cat Sparks for the burgers, Rivqa Rafael for the tea, and Zena Shapter for the ferry rides.

Moving further back in time, I have to thank the Australian spec fic writing community at large, too huge to name, but anyone who has been snapshotted in the last decade, you rock and I couldn't have done this without you.

Sincere thanks to all my small press and magazine editors and publishers, Australian and international, for teaching me not only about the industry, but to trust good people who know what they're doing, and about my own strengths and limitations. Special indebtedness to Tehani Wessely, who believed in me from the time she pulled my very first published story out of the *Andromeda Spaceways* slush.

To anyone who has helped me with critiques and/or research, whether for this manuscript or earlier ones, your patience and advice was much appreciated; to Mark Brothers, who helped with sailing; Warren Keen with rock climbing; Graeme Stockton with Scots; Peter Holz with dasyurids; Andrew Harrison with helicopters; David Dyer with the air force; Simon Petrie with chemistry; Chris Large with geology; Dirk Flinthart with bone flutes; Christopher Bobridge with the superstructure of ships; the books you helped with may someday see the light, but in case they don't, at least I'll have thanked you here. Because I couldn't have written this book without first writing those ones.

Thanks to my WoT Clan, Shen an Calhar (Look at me! I wrote a Tor book!) and other WoT players (hi, Mathias!), my Raymo board pals, and my PotBS Society, Les Condamnes. Not to mention my archery club, my Sydney Uni vet friends, my bemused coworkers at Port Stephens, and my Singo school pick-up and library book club posses. Your encouragement was fuel in my writing tank. Sunshine on my solar cells. The tide in my tidal generator, etc.

Thank you to Juliet Marillier, mentor and role model (Margaret, you get major brownie points for introducing me to her work), to Nancy Kress, who gave me hope, and to the legendary Ursula K. Le Guin, whose writing has irrevocably shaped mine.

Finally, to my friends Melissa, Sarah, Kelly, Danielle, Morgan, Fiona, and Jessie, and to family members of the Dyer, Bousaleh, Frankcombe, and Dillon persuasions, it is my privilege to know you. Until I find copies of books that have been signed to you in Lifeline and Salvos stores. Then I'm putting you in the next book as monkey poo collectors. XXOO.

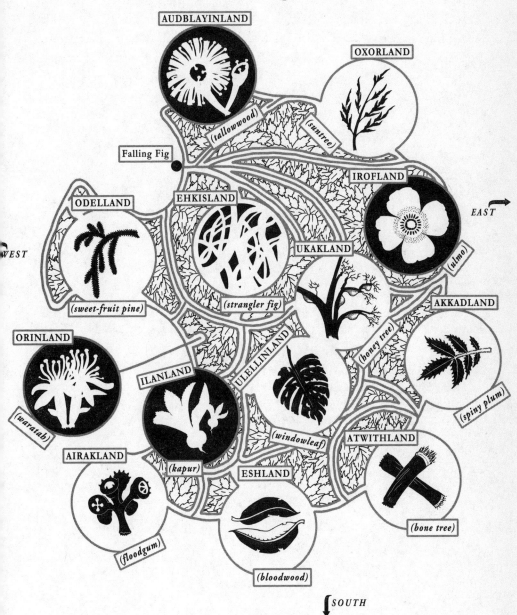

NORTH (to the ocean)

AUDBLAYINLAND

OXORLAND

*(tallowwood)*

*(suntree)*

Falling Fig

IROFLAND

ODELLAND

EHKISLAND

UKAKLAND

WEST

EAST

*(sweet-fruit pine)*

*(strangler fig)*

*(ulmo)*

ORINLAND

ULELLINLAND

AKKADLAND

ILANLAND

*(waratah)*

*(honey tree)*

*(spiny plum)*

AIRAKLAND

*(windowleaf)*

ATWITHLAND

*(kapur)*

ESHLAND

*(floodgum)*

*(bone tree)*

*(bloodwood)*

SOUTH

# TEMPLE EMERGENTS OF CANOPY

# CROSSROADS OF CANOPY

# PROLOGUE

Unar lies as still as a twelve-year-old can lie.

Eyes shut tight, anticipating her mother's pleased and surprised reaction to her day's work, she breathes, deliberately and deeply, with intent to deceive, in the wreckage of the cot that belonged to her sister. A curtain divides the cot from the rest of the hollowed-out, one-room dwelling. The corner twitches. Tickles her foot. Father checking on her.

Unar's bent arm is her pillow. She keeps her legs curled so they won't dangle over the splintered edges. The cot bars have been broken off to burn for fuel but the body remains whole.

Father thinks she's sleeping. She's never been so wide awake. He lets the curtain edge drop.

"It's time to sell her," Unar's mother says from the other side of it, dashing Unar's excitement to dust. Unar can't remember if she was breathing slowly in or breathing slowly out. She can't breathe. She doesn't want to breathe.

And then her old friend anger finds her. Anger heats and eases open her lungs, letting in the steamy, mould-smelling air.

Father says in his soft, befuddled voice, "Wait a little. She'll marry. We'll have a dowry."

"A slave price is more than a dowry." Mother is as merciless as splinters.

"Your belly's speaking, Erid. Eat these."

Unar smells nut oil. She hears the rattle of cooked grubs being shaken out of a gourd. Surely, now, Mother will show surprise, will take back what she said about selling her only remaining child.

"What are they?" Mother asks, though she must be able to see what they are. "Why so few?"

"She grows too heavy for the highest branches," Father says. "Besides, she spends the mornings helping me."

Today, in search of prey, Unar trespassed over the border of their niche, into the Kingdom of Oxorland. She loves climbing into the mango-coloured sunset sky on the uppermost arms of the great trees of Canopy. Hugging the smooth, cool, powdery barks of gobletfruit and floodgum, she had pressed her ear to the wood, listening for the grind of grub jaws. Pried the fat, white gnawers out of their little tunnels with her bore-knife.

"She's fit only for the block," Mother says, voice muffled, mouth full.

In Oxorland, the suntrees, smothered in gleaming, poison-nectared flowers like copper bracelets weighing down a rich woman's wrist, host many more grubs. They have softer wood, besides. Unar's bore-knife went into them so easily.

"What's the use, Erid? You'll spend it all at once if we sell her. I know you. A lode of metal. A fine gown for begging from high-borns."

"No! We'll keep it. We'll make sure it lasts till the end of our days."

As evening approached, from her seat in the wind-tossed suntree crown, Unar saw a woman with midnight hair bound in a yellow-feathered head-dress walking lithely along a branch path. Light-footed, the woman wore nothing but two slim cloths over hips and breasts, her moonset skin covered in sunburst patterns as though gold metal had been somehow pressed into her flesh. Merchants and slaves on the path had scattered hastily out of her way. The biggest man that Unar had ever seen, holding a wooden shield and bronze sword, walked in front of her, and six Servants in hooded honey-coloured robes walked behind.

It was the incarnation of the sun goddess, Oxor.

"And our family?" Father despises his fortuneless family. Except when trying to claim a distant ancestor who saved the life of a god in disguise by sharing wood for a fire. "My blood?"

"Your blood will go on. You said yourself just now that she's almost old enough to breed. They'll feed her. They'll let her lie with whom she pleases. She'll be happier a slave, Uranun. Happier than stricken and starving."

Unar has never heard a crueller lie. She half expects the tattered blue curtain that curls around the cot to be thrown back, for her mother to seize her and insist that her father take her to the market at once.

She thinks, *I can't be a slave. That's not what I'm for.*

This conviction shines in her mind; she turns it like a coal on a fire. What is she for? Cutting dead branches for others to burn? Digging grubs?

Unar shivers on the broken cot in the dark behind the flimsy curtain and thinks of the proud poise of the sun goddess.

*I wasn't born a goddess or a god, and there's nothing I can do about that.*

She raises her callused hands to cover her mouth, to keep the sobs inside. But then her eyes open, and she stares at her hands.

Maybe they *are* the hands of a goddess.

*How would anyone know if they are or not? Mighty souls don't always choose wealthy bodies, so Teacher Eann says.*

The soul enters the body at first breath. Anybody can be chosen. Usually a baby that takes its first breath close to the place where the old body died, but not always.

*More than one goddess is missing from her Temple. Ilan, goddess of justice and kings. Irof, goddess of flowers. I could be one of them, not yet discovered.*

That would teach her mother a lesson for wanting to sell her. If Unar had the mighty magic powers of a goddess, oh, how her mother would regret her careless selfishness!

The monsoon is over. The paths are open. Unar resolves to go to the closest Temple. How do they test for goddess souls? Does it hurt? It can't hurt more than having a mother who hates her. The Temple lies in the crown of the biggest tallowwood tree, one of the emergent trees that rise even higher than the canopy and are always bathed in strong, full sun. Unar's never dared dig for grubs there, because the biggest tallowwood is the sacred emergent of the goddess of birth and life, Audblayin, Waker of Senses.

*At the Temple, they'll know how to tell.*

When her parents try to sell her as a slave in the morning, to have the sigil of obedience burned into her tongue forever, she'll already be gone. Goddess or no, she won't come back to the hovel.

As soon as she makes the decision, Unar's heart races. The smell of quince blossom and wood fern fills her nostrils. Something inside her chest, like a seed sending out a tiny root, begins to grow there. No idea she's ever had has felt so right, yet the sensation is distressing; she clutches at her rib cage. Had she eaten a grub that somehow survived and is squirming around in there? The seed-feeling stops.

Unar thinks the thought again, deliberately: *I will go to Audblayin's Garden.*

Her whole body thrills with it. She hasn't swallowed a live grub; it feels more like she's swallowed a thousand candles. Hugging herself only makes it pulse harder. A second heart she didn't know she could have. She almost cries out to ask her parents what's happening, but stops herself in time.

This isn't a thing of axe makers or woodcutters. It's a thing whispered about in the school or the square.

A thing of Temple Servants and gods.

*I'll wait until they're sleeping, and I'll go.*

Until now, the Garden seemed a place of dread. Life-sized carvings on the Gates show soldiers and spell-casters, victorious, defending the Temple in a hundred battles. They say there's an invisible wall around it that keeps out wrongdoers, and in Unar's world, wrongdoers means have-nothings, so that she, a have-nothing, can't help but be a wrongdoer.

Yet when Unar sets out, the humming seed inside her seems to put out an added leaf whenever she takes the correct turn. The lower branch roads aren't lit. Bats scream about their fruit-feasts, and Unar startles an owl. She carries only her bore-knife, heavy at her waist, and the night is cold and damp through the holes in her knee-length, knotted tunic. She sleeps in her father's castoffs, too shameful to be seen by daylight.

When she finds the Great Gates, takes a deep breath, and approaches them, she stares up at the flickering strings of lanterns for so long that she almost trips over a skinny boy, about her age, sitting with his arms around his knees on the abandoned platform before the Temple.

"Too late," he says softly. "The Gatekeeper's already locked it for the night. We have to wait until morning."

"We?" Unar's shoulders stiffen about her ears. Why are they being quiet? Do sleeping monsters guard those tall wooden walls with the Garden's pointed pavilion roofs and curling passionfruit tendrils showing over the tops? "Why are you waiting here?"

"Why do you think? I'm not trying to get pregnant, am I?"

Disappointment drops Unar's shoulders. Is that what the Garden is for?

"I think you're mean, and you look hungry. Are you going to rob the first Servant who comes out with a night soil bucket?"

The boy's face falls. His bare arms are brown as bear hide in the lamp light. He's lanky and long-faced with short, sun-bleached hair, and he carries nothing. Under the loose tunic and short waist-wrap that barely covers his loincloth, it's easy to see he hasn't so much as a knife or a coil of rope on him.

*Wrongdoers. Have-nothings.*

"I didn't mean to be rude to you." He holds his knees tighter. "Forgive me. I misspoke. My brother died in the monsoon. He drowned only three days ago."

"I'm sorry." Unar takes a deep breath. She kneels next to him. It's easier to whisper. "I'm sorry I was rude to you, too."

His smile is hesitant.

"They keep their night soil in the Garden. It's good for the plants."

"Oh."

"My brother died because my parents defied the goddess. The rain goddess, I mean. I'm from Ehkisland. My parents died, too. I've come to serve Audblayin, the goddess of life, not just because I want to live, but because it's the right thing to do." He rubs his temple with his left hand. "Submit to them. Serve them. Why else are we here? What else are we for?"

*I can't be a slave. That's not what I'm for.*

"How do you know?" Unar asks. "Whether you can serve the goddess or not, I mean?"

"There's a tree growing out of a tree." The boy's hands relax. They rest by his sides. "The night-yew, I mean. It's the first tree, the beginning of the forest, but it's a parasite, like all babies when they're new. It grows out of the host tree. When Audblayin's a goddess, like she is now, it flowers at night and is the night-yew. When Audblayin's a god, it flowers in the day and is the day-yew. It wakes up the magic, if you have it. And if you have it, you can serve."

"I have it," Unar says at once, her certainty making her louder than she would have liked to be. *Magic.* That's what she has, and she has it without even visiting the tree that grows out of the tree. Does that mean she's something better than a Servant? Does it mean she really could be a goddess of her own? She remembers how Oxor glowed. How the seed in her chest tugged her towards the Garden. "I saw some Servants in Oxorland. Six women and a fighting man."

"I suppose the fighting man was Oxor's Bodyguard. Deities in male bodies each have a female Bodyguard. The ones in female bodies have male ones. My grandmother told me that my brother drowned and I lived for a reason. She said I felt drawn towards Temple service because the deathless ones had a use for me. I'm not so sure. There's nothing special about me. How could there be? I was a twin. There was always a spare one of me."

Unar stares at him. His eyes are wide, searching her face for some sort of reassurance, but she's barely seeing him; she's thinking about what he said.

*When Audblayin's a god, it flowers in the day and is the day-yew.*

*Deities in male bodies each have a female Bodyguard.*

*I felt drawn towards Temple service because the deathless ones had a use for me.*

Possibilities branch in all directions.

*Audblayin is a goddess now, but in her next incarnation, she could be a he.*

*Maybe I'm to be the Bodyguard of the god of life.*

The seed in Unar's chest bursts into vibrant, thrumming tangles that fill her from fingertips to toes. The smell of quince and wood fern comes again, stronger than ever. It startles her afresh. Twitches her. Sinks from her feet into the platform of living wood. The first smells are washed away, replaced by the scent of turned-over, month-old mulch and pungent tallowwood sap. The boy stares, drawing back slightly, as though he can feel it, too.

Slowly the smells and sensations fade. Unar can't find any trace of the seed inside her. Bats still screech and owls still hunt, but everything is changed. The goddess of life has called to her. Marked her out. Pulled her close, filling her with the belonging and warmth she has rarely felt in her mother's presence.

Saved her, but not her sister, from her parents' neglect, for a reason.

"Why don't you want to serve Ehkis, then?" she asks the boy, as though nothing unusual has happened. The seed is gone, but the memory, the powerful conviction that she is on an ordained road, remains.

The boy's mouth makes a flat line, and his wide nostrils flare.

"The rain goddess drowned my brother," he says. He rubs his skinny left shoulder with his right hand. "He punched me in this arm, the last time I saw him alive. It went numb and then it hurt for the rest of the day. I wish I could still feel it hurting."

So. He might say he wants to submit, but not to the rain goddess. Not yet.

Unar almost tells him about her baby sister, Isin. She almost shows him the indents in her skin from the cot she lay in, tells how it smells of emptiness and death, and how her cold mother thought nothing of making her sleep in it.

After Isin fell.

Instead, she sits down cross-legged beside the boy. Together, surrounded by the sounds of falling water, whining mosquitoes, and musky night-parrots making small branches creak and crack with their weight, they wait for the break of day.

# PART I

*Dry Season*

# ONE

MOONLIGHT HAD followed Unar in the hours since she'd slipped out of the Garden, and now, as a shadow on a branch resolved into a rain-silvered silhouette, she realised something else had followed her, too.

Unar wanted to ignore the crouching outline above and to the left of her. Barefoot on her own broad bough in loose leaf-trousers and a red Gardener's tunic, she was impatient to see if she could reach the thing, several body lengths below, that she'd come for. There, barely discernible in the dark, a cloth-wrapped bundle was stuck in the fork of the next lowest lateral branch, tantalising her, but half-heard myths of the Understorey kept her gaze fixed to the silhouette.

She gripped her bore-knife. It had proven useless in her descent through the mighty forest. This was a gap-axe tree and couldn't be bored into by any means short of magic. The knife should puncture a lung easily enough, though.

"Who's there?" she called defiantly.

"You climb well," a man's low, amused voice replied. "For a Gardener. But you're trespassing. You crossed the border many minutes ago."

"Which border?"

"Both of them."

Unar had been aware of it even before she reached the crossroads. She'd felt the Garden's power shrinking as she crossed horizontally from the realm of the birth goddess into the realm of the rain goddess. Then she'd felt queasy in her gut as she'd climbed lower and lower, crossing the vertical border from Canopy into Understorey.

Here, none of the Canopian gods or goddesses held sway. All the magical gifts of Unar's mistress had faded completely. Only Unar's physical strength and stamina mattered here.

"You've crossed the border, too," she said. "Who are you?"

The man leaned forward out of the tree's moonshadow. A lined brow suggested he'd seen at least twice as many as Unar's sixteen years. Water dripped from his glossy, tousled hair. Raised, charcoal-rubbed scars in the shape of tears streaked down cheeks that in daylight would be dark brown, naming him neither Understorian, nor slave, but a Canopian dedicated to the rain goddess, Ehkis. The tears of her Servants were said to have terrible powers, but below the magically defended border, they could do nothing but mingle harmlessly with the rain.

Unar relaxed her grip on the bore-knife.

"I'm Edax," he said. "Bodyguard of the Bringer of Rain. Shall I tell you her birth name while she's sleeping?"

"You're not her Bodyguard," Unar said, shocked. "If you were, you'd be with her, watching her." As if the rain goddess's Bodyguard, her most trusted, feared, and beloved, would betray childhood secrets from a time before the nature of her soul became apparent.

"She sleeps in the bottom of a lake. Who can harm her there? Meanwhile, I'm cursed with a Bodyguard's sleeplessness."

"It's a gift."

"You think you want that gift, little adept from the Garden Temple? You think you want to be a Bodyguard to the next incarnation of your goddess, when she is reborn a god? And what if she is a woman, again, and then another woman, and then a woman a third time? Mulch for brains!"

"You're the mulch for brains if you think you can guess the next gender of the one I serve."

The goddess that Unar served, Audblayin, the birth goddess, had been a woman for three incarnations. She was old now, so old. Surely she would take a turn at being a man. She must be a man. Then she would need a woman Bodyguard, and Unar would be waiting, ready to take the power that being a Bodyguard would bring.

*To never need sleep!*

"You have bigger problems than the next incarnation of Audblayin. Staying out after dark, for one thing. Will the Great Gates of the Garden not be closed to you forever, little Gardener?"

Unar raised the rain-speckled bore-knife higher as Edax came closer again. She realised as he moved along the underside of the branch, with a brazenness only a chimera should have owned, that he must be what he claimed to be. With utter certainty, she knew she couldn't fight him and live.

But he didn't know everything. The Great Gates were already closed, of course. Unar had climbed them. Edax eased himself down to the final branch between them. The flaps of a sodden, silver-star-embroidered, indigo jacket hung loosely over his black tunic. Also hanging were the paired hems of a calf-length skirt, split up the sides to give him freedom to climb while still appearing formal when he stood on a flat platform. She couldn't see if he was barefooted like she was or wore boots.

"I came for that," she said, indicating the bundle below them with her knife tip, not looking away from him.

"And what is that, exactly?" he asked.

"I felt it. When I was higher. I felt new life on the brink of being extinguished. Audblayin shares that power with all of us. So we can tend the Garden."

He dropped suddenly, suspended by clawed toes in front of her, upside-down with his skirt hems held in one hand, loincloth and concealed throwing knives showing, grinning, making her gasp. It wasn't right, to have feet like that. Unar had heard rumours that those who served Orin, goddess of birds and beasts, were permanently changed in size and shape, but nobody had ever mentioned to her that the Bodyguard of Ehkis had the grey toes and talons of a sooty owl.

"Shall I fetch it for you?" he asked whimsically.

"Yes," she said at once.

"What will you give me in exchange?"

"What do you want? I have nothing but what you see, and what you see is owned already. Audblayin gives no gifts to the Servants of her rivals."

"She owns you while you're in Canopy," Edax said salaciously. "Just as my oaths keep me celibate while I, one who walks in the grace of Ehkis, find myself in Canopy. This is Understorey."

Unar cursed.

"This is Understorey," she agreed. "Your goddess-given abilities to walk sideways and upside down won't work here, will they? Your tears will melt neither bones nor iron bars. Why did you offer to fetch it when you can't reach it? You're a liar. You're wasting my time." His owl talons were able to encircle the smaller branch that he hung from, but they couldn't penetrate the bark of the gap-axe tree.

*New life on the brink of being extinguished.* That bundle stuck in the tree fork could be the baby, Imeris, only fourteen days old. Unar had never met the baby's father, the merchant, Epatut. Imeris had fallen some ten hours ago. Everybody was looking for that baby, though. Epatut had offered a huge food reward. He'd even paid the Servants of the death god, Atwith, in order to learn that the child's spirit had not yet passed under their master's eye.

Unar didn't know Epatut, but she admired him for so desperately seeking a child who was probably far out of reach and alone in the dark, with death only a matter of time.

*Except that I have surely found her.*

Edax continued to grin and watch in silence while Unar stubbornly roped the wet, lichen-dappled bough of the great gap-axe tree. It was slippery, dangerous work. The tree was taller than seven hundred men standing on each other's shoulders, and falling wasn't the only risk. Understorians could be lurking anywhere in the gloom.

Worse, the longer she stayed below the border of Canopy, the more the arcane aura faded from her skin. By morning, the unseen magical barrier she'd passed through so easily would no longer admit her back to the high stratum that was her home.

Ten hours since the baby had fallen. Perhaps Imeris's aura was gone already, but Unar had to try. Nobody had tried to get Unar's sister back a decade ago when Isin had fallen.

*Isin.*

Isin had fallen during the monsoon. Unar paused with her fists tangled in rope, remembering. The rain had seemed to hang, fixed like spiderwebs. Water ran off branches unpredictably. There had been dry patches in odd places. Puddles in others. A man screamed that his dried fruit storage room was flooded and his fire was out, blaming the external stair tacked on by a neighbour.

All of that fell away when Unar, six years old, saw the open door of the hovel. Lacewings filled the black hole of it like flies in a dead animal's mouth. Her first, stupid thought: *Our fire is out, too. Mother will be mad.*

Father had halfheartedly called her name. That was how she knew she'd pushed ahead of him, teetering precariously on the path. The broken lock was gone. Stolen. It had contained a minuscule amount of metal. Faint light from the excuse for a window showed the empty crib.

*Mother has taken Isin to the forge.*

Mother had never taken either of her children to the forge.

*Isin is taken*, little Unar had thought, horrified. *Isin is stolen, like the lock.*

But, no. The ashy, wet smears on the splintered floor told the story. Isin had climbed over the railing and fallen into the wet ashes of the fire here. She'd crawled there, to get cooked grain from the cold wooden bowl with both hands, leaving ghostly, glutinous handprints here. Footprints there, where she used the bars of the crib to pull herself up. Landed on her bottom. Maybe she had cried.

She'd crawled to the open door and fallen into the dark.

Drips slowly, inexorably carried the ash and sticky grain residue over the edge. Unar had shrieked Isin's name.

And what had Father said?

*We'll get another.*

Another lock? Another child? Unar was afraid she knew which one he really meant, and when he tried to gather her, to push her inside, she bit his hand.

She didn't run away. Not then. Not yet. Not until years later, when she heard them talking and knew they intended to make her a slave.

"Your rope is too short," Edax observed, bringing her jarringly back to the present.

Unar wanted to cry. The man who claimed he was the Bodyguard of the rain goddess was right. She could return to the Garden for more rope, but by then it would be too late.

When she turned back to Edax, he stood beside her on the bough.

"Take my ankles," he said. For a moment, she simply stared up into his face. He couldn't be Ehkis's closest and most loyal Servant. Nobody with such grave responsibilities would be so rash.

Matching his impulsiveness, she wrapped her arms around his knees. Together, they toppled, face-first, the rope tied tight to Unar's climbing harness. It jolted them as they reached the end of it. Unar's grip on Edax's knees slipped to his feet. She managed not to recoil from them, even as the long owl-toes flexed, keeping the sharp talon-tips turned inwards. His hands grappled with the bundle.

"I have it," he shouted.

"What do we do now?" Unar cried as they swung in a pendulum arc, crashing into the gap-axe's smooth, unyielding trunk. But Edax, serpent-like, doubled back on himself, scaling the rope with the cloth-wrapped burden tucked under his arm, and with both of Unar's hands freed, she was able to climb up after him.

"Here," he said, breathing heavily, handing the bundle to her.

When Unar unwrapped it, her hands still shaking from the chance she'd taken, she found not a baby, but a bag of half-rotten blue quandong and white satinash fruit. Some of the seeds had germinated but withered in the absence of light.

"New life," Edax said. "Are you going to save it?"

Made mute by the deepness of her disappointment, Unar spread her hands, spilling the seeds and the wrappings into the blackness below.

# TWO

THE GARDEN Gates were high and glittered in the moonlight with inset metals.

Elaborate carvings provided purchase for Unar's fingers and toes. It was probably sacrilege for her bark-encrusted bare soles to soil the life-giving lips of the engraved goddess, but she didn't care. All she could think about was the baby who had fallen and the smirk on Edax's face as she'd let the seeds scatter.

At the top of the Gate, the wards interrogated her memory, invading her mind.

*Have you stolen food?*

*Have you stolen the sovereignty of another's body?*

That question irritated her. If she'd been made a slave, as her mother intended, she could have been sold to the Garden and her bodily sovereignty stolen daily. But the Garden cared only for the sanctity of free Canopians.

*Have you stolen human life?*

"None of those things," she whispered, clutching her head as images of everything from her sister Isin's cross-eyed baby face to the withered seedlings flared and died. At last, the wards permitted her to drop down from the lintel into the Garden.

The Garden grew in the hollowed-out trunk and crown of a lopped-off tallowwood two hundred paces in diameter. It was the tallest tree in the niche of Audblayinland, one of thirteen sovereign kingdom niches that comprised the great city of Canopy, and despite losing half its leaves in the lopping, it was kept alive, growing, and malleable by the birth goddess's power.

Delicate suspended bridges connected the two dozen smaller gardens, planted in lopped lateral branches, to the central circle of the main garden. Soil was cultivated in the hollows, providing foundations for ferns and flowering miniature trees from Understorey and Floor. Open to the sky, except in the places where peaked pavilions stood, the Garden was watered by rain during the monsoon. In the dry season, slaves carried water from pools in the crotches of leafy lower laterals by screw pumps and buckets on chains.

At the very heart, surrounded by a moat filled with rainbow-hued fish, stood the egg-shaped Temple of Audblayin, Waker of Senses, the birth goddess, sometimes a god, carved of a piece from the lustrous white sapwood and pale yellow heartwood of the tree.

Unar hoped that the lone sentry, the sleepless Bodyguard of the goddess, would be hypnotised by the beauty of the moon this night and fail to spot the miscreant Gardener who crept back towards her hammock in the loquat grove. Unar had seen the goddess only once. It was the morning after an assassination attempt by a pregnant woman who had hoped to gain Audblayin's soul for her imminent child. The Bodyguard hadn't been with Audblayin when Unar saw her. Whispers said he had gone to punish the woman's family. It was he who had foiled the attempt itself, tossing the perpetrator out of one of those crescent-shaped windows to break her neck on the steps below.

Audblayin had emerged from the Temple at dawn to reassure her Gardeners and Servants. Her many-layered robe of eggshell-white and frost-green had a high, constrictive neck. It held her aged face in a receptacle like a benevolent, overripe aubergine. She'd made no motion to aid the growth of any tree or vine, yet all green things in close proximity had sent new growth creeping towards her. Out of season, luminous blue flax lily fruits burst into being on the ends of long black stems, and flowerfowl came nervously out from among the possum-paw plants and golden guinea-flowers to lay their eggs at her feet.

Later in the morning, when the goddess had gone back into the Temple, Gardeners and slaves relished the eggs and fruit. Only Unar stared at the crescent-shaped window and wondered whether Audblayin's Bodyguard was short or tall, educated or unlettered, born an internoder or born stricken, a superior warrior or a superior mage.

Memories faded. Right now there wasn't time for Unar to stare at the window, not when she feared the Bodyguard might be staring back. She'd wasted enough of the night on her futile mission without being caught and punished as well.

As she skipped across a slender bridge that chimed gently and swayed under her weight, she barely avoided a collision with a slave.

The woman was cloaked and hooded. Dirty hands flew to her face an instant before she fell to her knees. White hands looked unfinished to Unar, like portrait outlines on parchment waiting for the mixing of the colours. Unar's friend Oos had made portraits on monkey-vellum upon arriving in the Garden. Those portraits, added to her manner of speaking, earned Oos the instant enmity of the other candidates. Plenty of them would have, prior to their calling, enjoyed a few extra animal skins, the source of the vellum, for warmth. They resented the vizier's daughter who wasted them on trifles.

"Forgive me, Warmed One," the slave said. She lowered her hands, revealing a bleached, hawkish face, and gazed up with white-lashed, watery, pale eyes.

Unar had noticed this particular slave before, one of five ageing beauties that had been left as a tribute at the Temple before Unar was born. They were the purchase price for the fertility of a Canopian princess, and in two decades, the five women had grown expert in tending plants.

Unar examined this one closely for the first time. The woman had the baby-sick skin but not the deep forearm scars of Understorian warriors with retractable "claws" for scaling trees. She couldn't be a slave taken in war, but instead must have been born a slave. Nobody had set the snake's teeth in place at puberty to form a grown fighter's magically grafted climbing spines.

"What are you doing?" Unar asked.

"Gardening, Warmed One."

"By moonlight?" Unar demanded, even as the rain clouds that had been covering and uncovering the moon all night cloaked it once again. Though the monsoon was over, there would be a few final, intermittent showers. "Is this Understorey superstition passing for true magic?"

"No!"

"Then explain what you're doing."

The slave looked everywhere but at Unar.

"One of the other women from my previous household." The dirty hands clenched on the slave's knees. "The oldest one. She can't work as she once did. She couldn't turn the crank handle to bring up water, so I did it for her. It took me all day."

"So?"

"So I was left with no time to prepare the soil and plant the seeds that were given to me to complete the spiral pattern. I buried them in a single hole. Now I have to dig them up again, loosen the earth, and plant them properly before morning, but I can't find where I buried them. I need a lantern, or when daylight comes, they'll find out about the old woman. They'll push her off the edge of the Garden."

Unar had been raised to hate slaves. If they were dark-skinned slaves, Canopians who had been sold by their families to settle debts, they were weak and deserved to starve, and if they were pale Understorian slaves, they deserved to be pushed off the edge of the Garden for being enemy raiders or the descendants of enemy raiders.

But before she could turn away in disgust, she heard her mother's voice, saying that Unar was fit only for sale at the block. She remembered her sister, Isin, who had fallen, and the missing baby Imeris. It was too late for either of them to return to Canopy, but if they had somehow survived the fall and been found alive by the denizens of Understorey or Floor, she would wish for strangers to show them forgiveness. Kindness, even.

She felt for, and quickly found, the strength of the life force in the seeds and their yearning to grow tall and strong. Inside the other woman was the unfurling of potential life; the slave was ovulating. The smell of earth and pulpy red arils filled her nostrils.

"It's that bed over there. That's where you buried them," she said.

"Yes, Warmed One."

Unar led the way off the bridge and over to the raised bed. She began digging, and found the seeds almost at once. The slave gave a small cry of relief. Smooth, shiny shapes filled Unar's palms. She lifted them, sniffed at them, using her goddess-given gift.

"These are gap-axe seeds," she observed.

"Yes, Warmed One. Planted here in the Garden, watered by rain, they will grow to only ten paces tall. There's something about having their roots in Floor that makes the great trees grow to one thousand paces and more."

"I know more than you about the great trees!"

"Yes, Warmed One."

Unar didn't feel particularly warmed at that moment. She dwelled in abundant sunshine that rarely reached Understorey, it was true, but she shouldn't have boasted about having more knowledge than a slave.

"Go to sleep," she said. "I'll plant the seeds in the spiral pattern. With magic, it won't matter that the soil hasn't been loosened. I'll lend them the strength to push through compacted ground. I'll even germinate them, so that all can see the work was done."

Unar saw from her hesitant expression that the slave woman didn't believe her, and didn't care. Were there Understorian gods? If so, they must be pathetic and powerless compared to those of Canopy, but maybe they had eyes to see; maybe they would recognise the tribute that Unar paid to them by protecting one of their own.

And maybe they would watch over a helpless, fallen girl child in recognition of Unar's tribute.

# THREE

THE HAMMOCKS were tied between loquat trunks.

Unar stopped at the paired, hollow-trunked, deciduous prison trees at the grove entrance to return the unknotted ropes of her climbing harness to the store. Fallen leaves were beginning to make paired, patterned circles around their bases. Leashed tapirs were sometimes kept there, when the wealthy brought their foliage-fattened livestock for tribute. The meat of the docile animals, captive bred and accustomed to being farmed in treetops, was a rare treat. It was generations since troublemaking slaves had been sealed up inside either of the swollen, stumpy prison tree trunks, but Servant Eilif had threatened to do it to Unar the last time she was caught out of her hammock by moonlight.

On that occasion, Unar had been trying to sprout the seeds of the night-yew, despite knowing that it was forbidden for there to be more than one night-yew tree in the Garden. And when Unar had asked why there could be only one, Eilif's answer had been that there could be only one incarnation of Audblayin at a time, which seemed irrelevant, but Unar hadn't tried again.

The scent of loquat nectar in fuzzy, still-furled flowers and the sound of snoring drew Unar along the dirt path towards the hammocks. Layered, petal-like eaves of the Gardener's Gathering pavilion sheltered the sleepers from light rain without blocking afternoon sunlight. Streams of water, diverted from the pavilion's peak over the edge of the Garden nearby, connected the higher platform with one of the pools below. Oos said she hated the waterfalls, because they made her need to pee, but Unar appreciated their ability to mask murmured midnight conversations.

Midnight was well behind her now. She'd spent an hour planting, and her mind was numb, all the magic bled out of her by the task of germinating the gap-axe seeds. In hindsight, it had been a little ambitious, but Unar was accustomed to having a deeper well to draw on than most.

"Did you find the baby?" Oos asked sleepily, invisibly enfolded in her hammock, as Unar tried to climb into the one beside it.

"No."

Unar's arms felt like logs. She slipped back to the turf, rested a moment, and then tried again to drag herself, headfirst, into the hammock.

"It was good of you to join the search, Unar."

"It was stupid of me," Unar said, her voice muffled by blankets. "Nobody lives who falls."

"Did you go into Understorey?"

"Yes."

Oos caught her breath reverently.

"What was it like?"

"Dark." Unar struggled to turn over, to lie on her back and look through the gap of her cocoon at the underside of the red-painted roof. The hammocks came from Ukakland, where the insect god imbued them with the ability to repel night invaders, but the soft silk lining was something Oos had sewn for her. "The rain was mostly stopped. The moonlight too."

"Did you meet anybody? Any wild slaves?"

"I met a liar. His name was Edax."

Oos guffawed.

"He was a liar if he said his name was Edax. That's the name of the Bringer of Rain's Bodyguard. Nobody else is allowed to take that name."

Unar was taken aback by the instant recognition, but she had no energy to ask questions. What did she care, or need to know, about neighbouring gods and their Servants, anyway? Her place was here in the Garden. As a Gardener, she could sense struggling life and strengthen it. Soon enough she would be a Servant and germinate more than just plants; she would help to kindle human life. When she finally became the Bodyguard, the only one to have direct contact with the deity who stayed inside the egg-shaped Temple at all times, she would be able to ask: Had her sister, Isin, been reborn?

For just as the death god dreamed the names of those who passed into the ether, Audblayin dreamed the names of those who returned to be born again.

Oos, in contrast, hadn't come to the Garden with ambition. She was fifteen years old. Only a year younger than Unar, she was delighted, like a child, by flowers, the feel of soil, and the sight of fish swimming. The daughter of a king's vizier, she had an extensive knowledge of politics, astronomy, and religion. She'd come to the Garden in pursuit of beauty.

Unar's mother was an axe maker, her father a fuel finder. Both were stricken, which meant they were free, but just barely. They didn't own houses, like citizens. They were certainly not internoders, who owned whole sections of trunk between two branches, nor were they crowns, who owned the tops of entire trees. They were neither royalty nor gods.

*They still should have found the food somewhere. Somehow. They should have paid tribute to the god Odel, the Protector of Children, so that Isin could live.*

Unar would find Isin. New body or old. They would be together again.

As she relaxed in the hammock, she let images of her family's hovel surround her. Unar's earliest memory was of a cramped room: a wooden hollow all yellow lamplight and sooty shadow. The rocking and the creaking of the tree sometimes seemed to possess Mother. Her rocking and creaking with baby Isin in the chair moved in time with the great tree, as if their unity was something that might calm the tree in the storm. Little Unar knew that agreeing with Mother, mirroring her, sometimes calmed Mother.

Perhaps Mother thought rocking and creaking would calm the rocking, creaking room. Unar, blanket-wrapped, had crouched by the kettle and ashes a few paces away, mesmerised by the baby's bright eyes and the puzzlement on the small, unformed face. Isin's doughy cheek slumped against Mother's right shoulder like dropped, unfired clay.

Baby's puzzlement deepened. She vomited a splash of white breast milk onto Mother's dark shawl. Then her little furrowed brow relaxed. All was well with her. She might as well have laughed with relief. Unar had laughed.

*Is something funny?* Mother shouted. *Are you laughing at me? Here. Take her.*

Unar took Isin while Mother rinsed the corner of her shawl in a bucket. Isin's head wobbled and her inturned, useless feet fell out of her wrap, dragging near the rough, splintered floor. Unar was five years old, almost six, barely tall enough to hold her sister out of the dust. They stared at each other until Isin went cross-eyed and Unar had to bite her tongue to keep from laughing again.

*We'll laugh together,* she thought. *When you're big enough. We'll laugh at all the funny things.*

A few months later, though, Isin had fallen, and Unar felt like she would never laugh again.

Oos's voice, insistent, brought Unar back from her dark recollections.

"Unar?" Oos ventured.

"Mmm?"

"Did your oaths bind? While you were in Understorey? Could you have broken them?"

"There's nothing out there that I want to steal," Unar said scornfully. "And nobody I want to rape. I have no enemies to murder."

"One who walks in the grace of Audblayin was only asking," Oos replied, too quickly. "One only wanted to know how it felt. Did it feel like it did before? Before you came to the Garden, I mean. Could you care about things that weren't birthing or sprouting? Could you think wicked thoughts?"

"I don't know what you mean," Unar admitted, her eyes closing as she slipped into sleep. "All my thoughts are wicked."

# FOUR

By morning, the Waker of Senses was dead.

The high-pitched harmonising of trumpet fruit roused the Gardeners from their hammocks. Oos emerged gracefully, slipping the red woven shirt she'd adjusted to flatter her form on over soft, knitted, seedpod-down undergarments, but Unar, barely having slept, tipped drunkenly out of hers, only to have the breath punched out of her by the ground.

"What's that racket?" she croaked, palms pressed to her ears, the direct sunlight blinding. She blinked rapidly up in the direction of what she thought was Oos's indulgent smile. Oos was taller than she was, curvier, and surrounded by a sweet-smelling cloud, the coconut oil she combed through her tresses. Her long hair leaped straight up like a black flame in the dry season and curled down like wet vines in the monsoon; Unar half suspected her of using magic on it. Thick, black eyebrows framed Oos's enormous, guileless eyes, a smooth, broad nose, and bee-stung lips the carmine colour of cut tamarillos.

But Oos wasn't the only one looming over her.

"It's the transition call," said a calm male voice from even higher up than Oos's. "Audblayin has gone into the ether. By sundown, he or she will be born again, though we won't find him or her for another twelve or thirteen years."

Aoun. The lanky boy who'd waited with Unar at the Gates. They'd rarely spoken since. Aoun spoke rarely to anyone. There *had* been the incident with the fish. And the bulrushes. Only crazy people from Ehkisland who lived by the side of lakes could eat fish or the nauseating, glue-paste-tasting roots of bulrushes.

"Why don't you lecture me for twelve or thirteen years, instead of helping me up off the ground?"

"Aoun doesn't touch the flesh of mortals," Oos teased from somewhere behind Unar. "He thinks he's a god."

"I don't think that," Aoun said. No, Aoun didn't think he was a deity. Unar had hoped she was, once, and been disappointed to learn she was unusual, yes, but not extraordinary. Which was why she could never tell Oos about her ambition to be the Bodyguard. Oos might look at her in a pitying way, the same way Aoun had looked at her when he found out about her mother wanting to sell her as a slave, and she couldn't stand being pitied. Better her friends looked at her with admiration when she succeeded.

When Unar and Aoun had pledged their lives to the Garden together, he an orphan and she a short step ahead of the slave block, he'd been shorter than she, his face pimply and his voice reedy. Four years later, he towered head and shoulders above her. His curls, once sun-bleached, stayed black these days, and he spoke as deeply and ponderously as a tree bear.

His hand, where it grasped her forearm, was as big as a tree bear's, too. He lifted her easily to her feet, where she swayed and made whimpering noises, still covering one ear against the wild music. It was normally so quiet. Singing and the use of instruments in the Garden were forbidden.

"We've got to go to the Temple, Unar," Oos said, giggling, pulling Unar along behind the other Gardeners. "This way."

"I forget what happens."

"Isn't it exciting? I can't wait to see the inside of the Temple."

"Wait. Is this the part where we take our clothes off and swim through the fish to get purified?"

The fish incident. Unar tried to contain her shudder. After a teaching exercise where they'd sprouted purplepea saplings from seed under the watchful eye of Servant Eilif, Unar had pulled out her tree and put it on the woodpile as instructed, but both Oos and Aoun had mysteriously vanished with their saplings.

When Unar sneaked after Oos's light sandal-prints, she caught her friend extracting dye from the flowers to make blue ribbons for braiding through her tall, magnificent hair. Unar left Oos to follow Aoun's prints and found *him* using the purplepea leaves to stun fish in one of the smaller pools. His mouth was full of the raw flesh of one he'd stabbed after it floated to the surface. Unar had been repulsed.

Aoun had wordlessly offered one of the gasping, scaly abominations to her. Its horrible mustaches were like slug feelers, and a row of spines stuck up on its back. Unar hit Aoun's hand away from her so hard that the fish sailed off the edge of the Garden.

Now she would have to get naked in the water with them.

Oos, meanwhile, rapturously shaped the Temple interior in the air with her slim hands, made smooth by wasting her time rubbing rough skin off with sandpaper fig leaves. "My father said the inside of the egg shape is spiralled and segmented like a snail shell. It has marble steps and banisters of purpleheart. He said everything leaving the safety of the staircases, passing into the centre, becomes weightless. Great living artworks of white sky-coral cross the empty spaces, and birds build their nests upside down, but the eggs don't fall out of them."

"Oos, I can't swim. And I hate fish. They're creepy."

"Your magic will hold you up. Do you feel sick?"

The question was obsolete by the time Oos had finished asking; Unar made it to the other side of a hanging bridge before stumbling to her knees. She vomited into a stand of bulrushes at the edge of the small lily pond where the spoonbills nested. They were the same bulrushes whose roots Aoun once roasted for supper. He'd known the trick of pulling them out without cutting his hands on the sharp-bladed leaves. And then he'd eaten them laden with fish.

"But I don't have any magic." Unar would have eaten a hundred bulrush roots to avoid swimming through the fish. "I need to wait for it to grow back. I used it all up. That's why I'm sick."

Oos knelt beside her and whispered, "You mean you used it up when you were looking for the baby that fell?"

"Yes." Unar wasn't about to admit she'd been helping a slave.

"It'll grow back very slowly, now that Audblayin is dead."

"I didn't know she was going to die today!"

"I'm a good swimmer. I'll help you. Quickly. We're falling behind."

The loquat grove and the petal-like pavilion were well behind them. Three bridge crossings later, they stood at the edge of the main tallowwood trunk that supported the widest part of the Garden with the Temple at its heart. On a platform at the edge of the moat, cracked halves of toucan eggshells held the precious mother-of-pearl powder given as tribute when the deity died, to beg for a speedy return.

Unar wasn't sure that she really believed in the ocean. She thought the mother-of-pearl, pulverised and waiting, might come from stones hidden in the muck in the foul, reeking depths of Floor. Nobody alive could claim to have seen such a terrifying thing as the sea. The moat at the centre of the Garden was terrifying enough for Unar.

"I'm heavier than you," she said to Oos. "What if I drown us both?"

The morning sun turned the surface of the water to molten gold. Aoun stood on the platform, stripping off his woven shirt and untying the drawstring of his trousers. For some reason, Unar didn't hear whatever reassuring reply Oos made. She couldn't take her eyes off Aoun as slaves began brushing the mother-of-pearl powder over his smooth chest and naked flanks.

Something was wrong. Unar searched uneasily inside herself for the power of the Garden, the power of the goddess.

Oos had asked her, *Did it feel like it did before? Could you think wicked thoughts?*

Unar couldn't tell whether it was wickedness or curiosity that drew her eyes to the reddish-brown organ, like a tapir's trunk, nestling in the curls of Aoun's pubic hair.

She must have had a hundred opportunities to look at Aoun naked before. She hadn't cared. She hadn't tried. What was different now?

Audblayin's absence. Unar's forbidden excursion beyond the barrier into Understorey. Had she broken something, some vital connection, forever? No amount of enjoying the way Aoun suddenly looked to her could be worth that!

Then Aoun turned his back to her and Unar realised slaves had helped her to take off her own clothes and started brushing her busily with the powder. She obediently raised her arms just as Aoun dived from the edge of the platform. Shards of sun from the widening ripples interfered with her ability to watch him. Squinting, she saw his wet head surface in the middle of the lake, the purifying powder washed away, left behind in the water as a tribute to the deity.

Fear paralysed her limbs in the face of her own imminent dive. More and more Gardeners leaped carelessly from the platform. Aoun already stood on the distant steps that led to the oval doorway in the egg-shaped Temple.

"You've done a poor job, slave," Oos admonished, taking up the brush herself and drawing it lightly across Unar's inadequately dusted breasts, her pupils widening as she did so. Unar noticed she was holding her breath.

"You have a secret," Unar said.

Oos dropped the brush.

"It's the death of the goddess," she breathed. "The oaths we took are weakest while she has no bodily form."

So. That explained why Unar had become so conscious of Aoun. The magic enforcing her promise of chastity was falling away, as it had done when she'd ventured into Understorey. And now Oos's eyes were glued to Unar's breasts the same way that Unar's eyes had been glued to Aoun.

"You must go, Warmed One," the slave said. Unar recognised the middle-aged hawk-faced woman she'd helped the previous night. "The others have all gone."

"What's your name, slave?"

"It's Ylly, Warmed One."

Oos tried to take Unar's hand, but Unar pulled away sharply.

"I'm going to be sick again," she said.

Tears filled Oos's dark eyes and ran down through the mother-of-pearl dust. She looked as though Unar had stabbed her with a bore-knife.

"No," Unar said shortly, angry with herself for being too consumed by her terror of the fish to consider Oos, but also angry with Oos for thinking so poorly of her. "Not because of you."

Oos blinked, relieved. She dusted over the tear trails with the powder. Unar retched over the grassy end of the platform. Then she turned, straightened, and ignoring her shaking knees, took the hand she'd shaken off just a moment ago.

"Ehkis give me courage," she said, naming the rain goddess.

"You shouldn't swear by other gods!" Oos said, scandalised.

"I can if I want. When my goddess is dead, anyway. Ehkis holds sway over fish, doesn't she? She can keep them away from me!"

They jumped off the platform's watery edge together.

# FIVE

THE WATER was cold, like death.

Like slow falling.

Unar's arm jerked in its socket. Oos was trying to pull her up towards the surface. Unar imagined there were slimy fish all around her. She sucked water into her lungs. White lights burst behind her eyes. She curled her body and tried to cough.

Something powerful uncurled her. It was water weeds, in the grip of Oos's magic. Just as Oos was able to coax seedlings up towards the light, she was able to form a floating, moving mat of weeds that drew Unar up and flattened her, belly-up, on the surface of the lake.

"Relax," Oos said soothingly by her ear. Unar found her chest full of air again. The urge to choke and thrash was gone. Streaks of powdered mother-of-pearl dripped from Oos's hair.

"I don't know why there isn't a bridge."

"It's so we can be reborn by passing through water."

"I don't want to be born again. Once was enough. Please get me out. I'm scared of the fish."

"You really should have thought of that before you gave yourself to the Garden."

They climbed out together beside the others, who had already been robed in red by waiting slaves. Twenty-eight Gardeners ascended the ivory steps into the egg-shaped Temple they'd pledged themselves to but had only ever seen from the outside.

Sunlight penetrated the translucent white walls, making them glow, making Unar's eyes widen in awe. Inside, the promised white-and-purple banisters spiralled up to a ring-shaped platform that rested against the widest circumference of the egg, halfway up the sides of it.

But the sky-coral and the birds had fallen. Broken shells, yolk-matted feathers, and honeycomb-structures made an ugly mess on the floor. The power of the goddess had held them suspended.

*The goddess is dead.*

Unar climbed the staircase at the end of the single-file procession, combing her wet hair back from her forehead with her fingers, pulling stray weed strands away, treading barefoot in the little drips left behind by the others. Soon, she saw the white-robed Servants standing in a semicircle on the annular platform, most of the men grey-bearded, the women white-haired. They'd served a long time. This incarnation had been long-lived. Gardeners had come and gone without the opportunity to be promoted.

Until now.

Unar was one of the youngest, but she knew the magic was suited to her nature. Ambition, desperation, single-mindedness, and strength; these were all the qualities of unborn life. Her mother had cursed her for selfishness, for striving above her station, but striving was the basic nature of a seed and selfishness the basic nature of a newborn child.

Her magic was powerful. Perhaps the most powerful of all the candidates.

*I will be chosen. I must be chosen.*

She bowed her head with the others as the old goddess's Bodyguard came up the other staircase, carrying a white-shrouded body in his thickly-muscled forearms. Unar studied him intently. At last. Her chance to see him up close, to speculate on the qualities Audblayin's Bodyguard must cultivate.

The man had wide shoulders and a tree-trunk neck. A broad nose like a bracket fungus. A potbelly that he actually rested the weight of the corpse on as he walked. He wore an open, elaborately embellished jacket over a tunic and long, split skirt, the same as Edax had, but his were white instead of black; pristine, as though he'd never left the Temple.

And perhaps he hadn't, since the foray that had separated him from Audblayin the one and only time that Unar had laid eyes on her living goddess.

Unar was utterly dismayed. This man was nothing like the skilled, athletic Edax. She chastised herself for not realising what was obvious: Why should the Bodyguard of Audblayin leave the Temple when the deity did not? He was never required to fight. Even if the Understorians staged a raid and penetrated the local niche, how could warriors hope to pass by the wards that protected the Garden?

This Bodyguard had spent his tenure watching from the high, crescent-moon-shaped windows, and when he didn't watch, he ate. Food was the most common tribute to the gods, and how much could one little old woman, imprisoned in an egg, possibly eat?

He looked up from his burden and met her gaze blackly, as though he knew what she was thinking. When he opened his mouth, she expected to be chastised, but instead, he said, "Our Audblayin has gone at last to Atwith, as Atwith must go to her when he is born. Her body will remain in the Temple until we find her—or him—again."

He took a step back and, with his magic, lowered the shrouded shape through the central hole in the platform. It floated gently down to rest upon the shattered corals and ruined nests.

One of the Servants stepped forward. Unar recognised the Gatekeeper of the Garden, even as the old woman set the heavy bronze lantern and red-and-green stole of her office down by the hem of her white robe, relinquishing the role.

"I will join you in the search," she said. Five others mimicked her, stepping forward, saying the words. Six ex-Servants would leave the Garden with the ex-Bodyguard, making a total of seven. They would make note of new babies that had been born, even though the incarnation wouldn't reveal itself until puberty. They would wander, without magic, naked as when they were born out of respect for the birth goddess, living from charity, speaking only to each other, for ten or fifteen years, watching the children from afar as they grew.

Some of the searchers, Unar realised, would die of old age before the new god or goddess was revealed.

In the meantime, the Servants who remained in the Temple would train the seven new ones to be raised. The new Servants would learn to perform everything from the subtlest hidden magics to the most blatant and most powerful. Many spells would be effective only within the Garden, but Unar yearned for mastery over them. She could already do things her parents could never have imagined.

The Bodyguard came to stand before her, his palm hovering over her heart.

"Your magic is weak," he pronounced. "You will not serve."

Unar's eyes blazed. She bit her lip so hard that she tasted blood. Her magic was weak because of her efforts germinating seeds the previous night. Couldn't he divine it? Didn't he sense the sign that the goddess had given her, the first time it occurred to her to seek out the Garden, the seed of power that had sprouted in her chest and the smell of quince and wood fern that had surrounded her? She had to tell him.

She couldn't tell him. The candidates must respect the silence of grief. The silence was enforced by the magic of the Servants; Unar could feel it. She suspected that even if she opened her mouth to object, the words wouldn't pass.

"You will serve," the Bodyguard told Oos.

The glance that Oos gave Unar was frightened, not pleased. Unar didn't know why. Was Oos frightened of her? Of her anger? Or frightened for her? Frightened of what punishments might be meted out if Unar publicly rebelled?

"You will serve," the Bodyguard told Aoun.

Unar had time to think about ways in which she might rebel. She might leap off the edge of the platform and die in a broken, bleeding mess on top of the corpse of the goddess. That would show them. What could they do about that?

They might catch her with magic and prevent her from falling. How could they not know her destiny? How could they not sense that she was greater than Oos, greater than Aoun, greater than all of them?

The ones who had been chosen separated themselves from the ones who would go back to the Garden. Oos and Aoun received white robes from the ex-Servants who would shortly pass through the Gate on their way to examine every cradle from beggar's to queen's. Unar couldn't bear to raise her eyes to them. She stared down through the hole at the lifeless shape below.

*Audblayin, hear me.* She moved her lips without sound, invoking the birth god inaudibly. *I'll prove myself to you, I swear. I'll show them. I'll be the one to find you. I have an advantage! I already know you're reborn a man.*

A hand seized hers in a brushing of robes. It was Oos on her way back down the stairs, white-robed in the company of Servants. Her eyes locked with Unar's, begging for forgiveness, and for patience.

Then she was gone.

Unar's new conviction wavered as she realised she'd have to face the moat alone. She wondered if she might drown herself and be eaten by fish, polluting the purifying moat with her death. But the returning Gardeners were permitted to wade through the shallow part of the moat, the ford where women seeking enhanced fertility were allowed to cross and enter the Temple, and she couldn't drown where she was able to stand.

She couldn't drown. She had to show them. She would teach herself. She was like a seed.

Ambitious. Desperate. Single-minded. Strong.

# SIX

UNAR SLEPT early and woke when it was still dark.

Unfamiliar shapes snored in the hammocks to either side of her. Newly admitted Gardeners. Unar hated them. Oos hadn't snored. The fresh arrivals' magic hadn't been wakened yet. She could have put seeds in their nostrils and germinated the shoots into their brains.

Scowling, she climbed out of her hammock and left the loquat grove, only to find the pasty-faced slave woman, Ylly, beating clothes against a rock by the waterfall to clean them. Dirty water fell through empty air down to one of the pools. Tiny, chirping, insectivorous bats flew through the edges of it, snatching mouthfuls of water on the wing.

"I suppose this is the old woman's work, too?"

Ylly shrank back, folding herself into an uncomfortable bow with her forehead in the moss.

"I'll accept your punishment, Warmed One," she said. "If not for me, you would have been chosen to serve today. When I saw you didn't have enough magic to swim through the moat, I knew the disaster that would fall on you. The young gap-axe trees were knee-high in the morning!"

"Sit up. It wasn't your fault. It was their fault. They're stupid. How can stupid select for smart? Can a monkey choose a checkers player?"

Ylly sat back on her heels and risked the suggestion of a smile.

Unar remembered another woman sitting back on her heels in that spot. Another hesitant smile.

The vizier's daughter, beautiful and haughty, had clutched a wooden rod in her right hand and the rim of a wide, evil-smelling glass bowl in her left.

She'd also had a black eye that Unar knew was payback from the other Gardeners for some decision the king of Audblayinland had made two generations ago. Having received more than her share of beatings in life, Unar wouldn't have cared about one black eye on a rich girl; only, she'd expected a vizier's daughter to run to her superiors at the first sign of trouble, and this one had not. She'd taken the punishment with unusual equanimity.

Inside Oos's bowl had been half a dozen handfuls of fresh, scarlet poinsettia leaves and something that had once resembled a lopsided, misshapen man's tunic. The red tunics handed out to the Gardeners were sometimes made of leathery, stitched-together leaves, and sometimes the wispy, white wool inside seedpods. This one was the latter.

Oos had altered it to a slim-fitting woman's shirt that crossed over in front, tied with ribbons, and boasted a roomy bust and tight waist. Unar had seen the vizier's daughter working on it under the eaves of the pavilion during their break for midday meal.

*They don't mind which style we use, so long as the colours are correct,* she had said shyly. *One who walks in the grace of Audblayin thought it would better glorify the goddess if the colours didn't fade, too. This mordant was gifted as tribute in the Temple. Servant Eilif said one who walks in the grace of Audblayin could use it.*

*What is it?*

*Green vitriol. It is of iron and the milk of mudwasp stings. One of my minderwomen used to make it.*

*I've never made anything like that before,* Unar said, wrinkling her nose. *But I have mixed leaves and mud to make a poultice for bringing bruise swellings down.*

Unar had helped Oos with her swollen eye. Oos had offered to treat Unar's red Gardener's shirt so that the colour wouldn't fade. And that was the last involvement with laundry that Unar had had, because it was slave's work.

Until now.

"I'm almost finished," the slave woman said.

Unar came closer to the baskets of clothes. They were the dirty slept-in clothes she and the other Gardeners had shucked off by the moat the previous morning. She picked up a shirt. It was Aoun's.

He wouldn't need it again. He wouldn't return to the Garden to toil with his hands again; only to toil with his magic. The sleeve was worn over the upper arm on the left side. He still missed his brother, the one who had drowned.

*We used to fight all the time,* he told Unar once when they'd been given the job of finding some escaped flowerfowl together. *My mother kept a great sack full of all the wishbones from every fowl she ever ate, and we'd snap a dozen*

*a day, deciding who would get a new shirt or which of us would have a bath*
*first and which would get the dirty water.*

He'd gone shirtless while they climbed after the foolish, easily frightened
birds that day, and Unar hadn't bothered to look. As a Servant, he'd be
wrapped up tight in a white robe all the time; now, when it was too late,
was when she wanted to look?

Unar sighed. She wet the shirt and began beating it, hard, against one of
the rocks that protruded into the stream of falling water. It felt good. Like
she was beating the fat Bodyguard.

"Forgive me, Warmed One," Ylly said, "but you shouldn't strike so hard.
You'll distort the weave."

"Oh. Sorry."

They beat clothes together in silence for a while. Ylly wrung them out
and placed them in another basket. When the shirts were done, she brought
out the red robes that the Gardeners had worn to the ceremony, their hems
feathered and pale with mother-of-pearl dust.

Unar sighed again as she remembered the sight of a glittering Aoun diving into the water. It was a new and strange sensation, being so fixated on
his beautiful form, on the slabs of muscle that covered his once-skinny ribs,
on his bulging arms and the shadow of a man's growth deepening the darkness down his throat. How long would she have to wait before all such
urges were repressed once again? She had no time for distractions if she was
to meet her destiny. Hopefully this wouldn't go on until Unar brought Audblayin back to the Garden.

"Ylly," she mused, to distract herself. "It's a funny name. I never heard of
it before."

"It was my mother's name, Warmed One," Ylly said. "Her only gift to
me, other than the gift of my life. We of the Understorey believe it's good
luck to have names that sound the same forwards and backwards. Warriors
should be able to travel up and down the trunks of the great trees."

"Do you really think that if your name was Unar, you'd be able to go up
trees but not down again? That is just as stupid as the Bodyguard."

"Whatever you say, Warmed One."

"You know what else is stupid?" Unar went on, feeling her face become
heated. "Pushing old women off the edge of the Garden when they're too
weak to wash clothes. Surely there's other work she could do, elsewhere.
Cooking. Caring for children."

"She cannot be sold elsewhere, Warmed One. She knows the secrets of the Garden."

"What secrets?" Unar said scathingly. "She doesn't know any secrets."

*Neither do I,* she thought. *But I'm going to discover them. Somehow.*

They lapsed into silence again as they cleaned the thicker, heavier robes. Unar found Oos's robe, smaller than the others and, like the shirts, more fashionably tailored, and wondered if her friend would enjoy sleeping in the feather beds of the Temple, and whether she'd get fat from an oversupply of food tributes, too.

"Ylly," she said at last when the laundry was done and they bent to lift the heavy baskets and take them to the drying bushes, "what would happen to a baby who fell from Canopy? If your mother's people found it alive, would they care for it?"

"An adopted fallen baby is even luckier than a good name, Warmed One. But I must tell you that they rarely survive. If the babe's bones were not broken by branches, the child's cries would call demons before warriors."

"Demons?"

"The predators that your gods and goddesses keep away from Canopy, Warmed One. The old woman tells tales of them. Spotted swarms. They snatch a bite of flesh each with their needle teeth and leave nothing but bones behind. Embracers squeeze the life from sleeping women and men. Dayhunters take possums from their nests and children from their cradles, and longarms, who hunt in packs of five, pull monkeys and men by their heads and limbs into five bloody pieces."

Unar shivered.

"And of course," Ylly continued calmly, leading the way with the heaviest basket, "there are chimeras."

Unar followed behind her. "Chimeras aren't real."

"When I belonged to the princess, I accompanied her to the Temple of Odel, Protector of Children. There was the skin of a preserved chimera there. I saw it with my own eyes, Warmed One."

"Is it still there?"

"I suppose so."

Unar couldn't have explained her sudden need to seek it out. It was something to do with the legend of the creature laying two eggs into its own mouth as a female, transforming into a male, and then fertilising the eggs. One of the eggs became male; the other, female. And then the two of them merged into a single offspring. Something about the Temple of Audblayin being shaped like an egg. Something to do with Unar's conviction that Audblayin would change from female to male in this next incarnation.

*The chimera will be a guardian spirit to me,* Unar decided, *watching over and helping me in my quest to find the god.* The fact that the skin was in the wrong Temple, the Temple of a rival god, was no deterrent.

"I'll go to see it," she said. "Tomorrow night, I'll go to see it. You'll tell me the best way to go."

Unar had asked for directions to Odel's Temple before. If she closed her eyes, she could still see it. A day speckled by sun, a month before Isin fell. Beams of light roved over the hovels of the poor only three or four days a year. Maybe it was the crack of sunlight on the ledge that had enticed Isin out of her crib.

Most babies in Canopy didn't have cribs. *Cages—it's a cage,* little Unar had thought, *like a cage for laying fowl.* Most babies stayed tied to their mothers morning and night. How else to be certain they wouldn't fall, if the parents were too poor to pay tribute to Odel? Wide sashes with holes for arms and legs were popular at the local market where Mother wed her axe-heads to smooth, polished handles and Father sold his stacks of fuel. Unar's parents pooled their meagre earnings to pay rent to their internoder landlord for the one-room hollow with its ill-fitting, west-facing door and single window wide enough to admit pythons but not a grown man's arm.

Isin slept in the crib, for Mother couldn't keep a babe close to the forge fire in the stone-lined workhouse three trees over, where she sweated over costly metals. Nor could she leave her work mid-shaping; she must ignore her baby's needs lest the steel cool and the tempering fail. And who, in similarly drastic circumstances, could spare the time to look up from their own drudgery to wonder why a child's hungry cries sometimes leaked from the locked door beside or below their own?

Unar didn't like to go with her father, searching for fuel, leaving her little sister behind, but she wasn't grown; she couldn't strap the baby to her own body. She might lose her balance and kill them both. That day, the day the sunlight touched the window, Unar and Father had returned to the hovel for lunch, just in time to see Isin pull herself out of the crib and fall, headfirst, onto the floor.

There was blood. Unar had been frightened. Could babies break? Was her new sister broken? Father had picked Isin up, holding her high so that

Unar couldn't see her. There was just his head brushing the ceiling, his sandals in the blood, and the snake-sound of shushing. Isin hadn't died.

Not then. Not yet.

*I'll tie you to me,* Unar had whispered to the baby, days later, and she had tried. Isin had cried at Unar's attempt, and Mother had seen, and taken the baby, and beaten Unar until she'd lain senseless on that rough, splintery floor. Mother made those axe handles so beautiful and smooth. Why not polish the place where her own children must set their cut and blood-crusted feet?

*If I fixed the floor, foolish girl, do you think we'd be allowed to stay here?* Unar remembered her mother growling the season before. *The owner, the internoder, could charge twice as much then, and where would we be? Out there in the monsoon!*

Mother was always growling. Unar was always wrong. Despite being wrong, and foolish, and all the rest, Unar was afraid of what would happen if Isin got out again. She asked Father which was the way to the Temple of the Protector of Children. She'd found a ring of rare mushrooms and gathered them carefully in the dirty cloth that held back her hair.

Father had laughed and shaken his head, refusing to answer. He'd taken the mushrooms and put them in his tea. They simmered into a broth, which he ate where Mother couldn't see. Unar had looked on, helpless and silent.

She opened her eyes, returning to the Garden of the present.

He wasn't there to steal from her anymore. Audblayin knew where he was. Unar didn't care if he was dead or alive.

She dumped the basket of laundry down beside the bare black briars that would bear white flowers later in the dry season but which, for now, made convenient clothes-hanging places. Her arms ached. She found herself rubbing her left shoulder with her right hand, mimicking the habit of Aoun's.

It was too late, now, for offerings. Too late for Isin to be saved by Odel. But Unar still, unaccountably, craved the sight of that old demon skin.

"I will try to remember the way, Warmed One," was Ylly's weary reply.

# SEVEN

UNAR FINISHED pulling weeds.

Smudging her brow with the back of her hand, she washed in the irrigation channel before lowering its wooden lid into place and setting off for the kitchens to collect her supper rations.

Sunset painted the wooden terraces of the vegetable garden surrounding the store circle, turning the weathered grey timbers to bronze and making the fruiting oranges and apricots look more orange than they truly were. Unar took a small leaf-bowl of seed porridge and a strip of smoked monkey meat and went to sit by herself on the edge of one of the terraces.

"Can I join you?" one of the handsome new Gardeners asked her.

"No," Unar answered brusquely; the man half scrambled away before he could settle down beside her. She needed to think. Not chatter with new arrivals. Her magic was still weak. How would she trick the Gate into letting her out, into thinking she was a seed blowing on the wind?

She would have to open it, walk through it, but how to get the key? The Gatekeeper carried the key, but there was no Gatekeeper right now, was there? They couldn't have had time to choose a new one yet. Some other Servant must have temporarily picked up the lantern. Unar would have to wait and see who came to lock the Gate at dusk.

She slipped out amongst the slaves, ducking behind bushes when fellow Gardeners came past. She dashed furtively over bridges, so swiftly they were left swaying crazily behind her.

The Gate had a thicket of black-trunked tree ferns growing behind it. Unar concealed herself behind the luminous, lime-green fronds until the bobbing of a lantern in the gloom betrayed the lone Servant's approach.

It was Aoun.

Unar's mad plan to somehow pickpocket the key away from the Servant died instantly. She showed herself in the centre of the path before Aoun could reach the wide-open Garden entrance.

"You should be at the loquat grove," he said, but Unar thought she detected an amused quirk at the corners of his mouth. She hadn't cared about his mouth before. In fact, the sight of it stuffed with fish flesh should have been enough to turn her off it forever. But now she noticed the fullness of his lower lip and the thinness of his upper one, the long lines connecting it to his nose, and the way his stubble grew between the lines, and outside of them, but not on them.

Stupid things to notice.

"I should be with you and Oos in the Temple," she said. "It isn't fair."

"That's why you're waiting here to ambush me? You want me to intercede for you somehow?"

"No! I don't need you! That is . . . I need you to lend me the key to the Gate."

Aoun's eyes bulged.

"You need me to lend you the key?"

"So I can get past the wards. The Gate looks innocent, doesn't it? It looks like just anybody could walk out. But not the slaves. And not me."

"You chose this. We both did. Where do you want to go?"

"To Odel's emergent."

"The Temple of a rival god? No, Unar!"

"Listen, Aoun. My sister fell because my parents didn't go there. I want to go and say a prayer for her. Your parents went there for you. They went there and gave gifts to the Protector of Children. They kept you safe."

In the year of Aoun's birth, the king of Ehkisland had ordered all the citizens of that niche to reserve their tributes solely for Ehkis. The goddess Ehkis's incarnation had not been found, the rains were late, the trees were dying, and the king's subjects were forbidden to waste their worship on other gods and goddesses. All efforts must be focused on bringing the rains.

Aoun's parents had defied the king and been executed for that defiance, but their final act had protected him.

"They kept me safe. My brother wasn't so lucky," he said. His right hand, holding the upraised lantern by its bronze handle, tried to creep across to his left shoulder, but the sway of the lantern made the candlelight flicker and his hand stilled. "Odel's power kept us from falling, but it didn't stop him from drowning."

Executed for refusing to pay tribute to Ehkis. And after they had died, one of their sons had drowned in a flood caused by excessive tributes to the rain goddess. There was no justice outside Ilan's niche. Aoun was crazy to think that obedience would keep him safe when disobedience was sometimes imperative.

"You lived," Unar said. "You didn't drown. You didn't fall. Even orphaned. Even alone. Please let me out. Just this once. I'm asking you respectfully. I didn't try to hit you over the head and steal the key."

Aoun rubbed his temple with his left hand ruefully.

"The key is magical, Unar. There is no physical key. You know that the Garden rewards those who are true to themselves, and it's in me to be law-abiding since my brother died. I've learned my family's lesson. Don't defy the goddesses and gods." His face was open. Earnest. He rattled the lantern a little. "Servant Eilif determined that I was best suited to carry the secret of the key. It was my first lesson today."

"Oh," she said, feeling stupid.

He tilted his head and considered her for a long silent moment.

"Go on, then," he said at last. "I've opened it for you. Go through."

"What?"

"Go through. Go to Odel's Temple. Say a prayer for your sister. It's far away. You won't be back until a few hours before dawn. I'll come back to open the Gate for you."

"Oh. You don't have to do that. I can climb back in." Getting out required Unar's knack of magical disguise, because the wards were designed to keep slaves, Servants, and Gardeners safely inside. Getting in, however, required only that a person be innocent of the three crimes that the wards probed memories to find.

Aoun looked incensed.

"Climb over the Gate, like a raiding Understorian? Like a thief seeking tributes? Have you done it before?"

"Maybe."

"Oh, Unar." His mouth flattened. "This explains why you weren't chosen. You haven't given your heart to this goddess."

"He will be a god this time," Unar retorted, stung. "You think you'll be his Bodyguard, Aoun, but you won't. That's not why I wasn't chosen. It's because—"

Aoun didn't argue; he pushed her through the Gate. Without so much as putting a hand to it, his magic giving him the strength of ten ordinary men, he closed it in her face.

# EIGHT

The paths of the city followed the flat tops of interwoven branches.

Unar trotted along with her head down, muttering Ylly's directions under her breath to keep from forgetting them. She wore a green, sewn-leaf jacket over dark red tunic and green trousers that identified her as a Gardener, as she had when she'd trespassed into Understorey, but it would only give her protected status within the boundaries of Audblayinland, her own goddess's rainforest niche.

The directions took her along the lower roads where stricken, slaves, and out-of-nichers tended to walk. Citizens and internoders urinating and defecating off the edges of the higher paths were a hazard of the lower roads, but the only likely hazard for Unar. Robbers had no incentive to accost the poor, and slaves couldn't be sold without birth or capture carvings that matched the magically embedded sigils on their tongues.

Lower roads were safer, even at night. Even without the torches set at intervals along the high roads and kept bright by the cold fire of Airak, God of Lightning.

"Cross the border of Audblayinland at the Falling Fig," Unar repeated again in a whisper. The Falling Fig wasn't actually falling, but it formed a great crossroads, with the widest spread of any of the great trees. Its root-curtains fell like waterfalls towards Floor in five different, intersecting niches.

There was no rain this time but no moonlight, either. By touch, Unar climbed a ladder woven from lianas, emerging through maidenhair ferns and orchids onto a walkway that led to a small slave's gate. It was little more than a hole bored through one of the fig's many trunks, with a small plate over the archway to indicate she was passing into Ehkisland.

She couldn't read it. Despite Teacher Eann's good intentions, she'd never learned. But her sense of direction was good, and she'd been into Ehkisland quite recently, albeit by a higher and grander gate. Her awareness of the Garden diminished as she crossed. She startled a crowded stricken family that had built a cooking fire in the shelter of the Gate, not expecting anybody to pass at this hour.

"The snake path, to Odelland?" Unar asked the woman, who stood gawping, holding two birds that she'd charred in their feathers.

The woman told her the way, the same way told by Ylly, and Unar paid her in dried monkey meat she'd been given for her supper.

"Ehkis bless you," the woman said.

"And you," Unar said, squirming a little. She should have named Audblayin. Maybe Aoun was right, and she hadn't given her heart to her master. Then she heard the *nyaaa!* of a newborn baby and froze where she was on the branch. "You have a little one?"

"He's my grandson. Born this morning. His mother sleeps."

Unar stared at the baby's blotchy, puckered face as it turned towards the fire in what must have been his older sister's arms. Unar had been an older sister like that. She'd squeezed little Isin so tightly.

"What's his name? I'm going to Odel's emergent. I'll pay tribute for him."

The girl that held the baby told Unar his name.

"Don't let him fall," Unar said.

"I won't," the girl said fiercely.

"He might be a god."

The woman who had given directions squawked a laugh.

"A god? Don't be putting ideas in her head. Gods don't walk among the stricken."

Unar took one last look at the baby. It was too early. She couldn't search for him yet.

The wind was cold, and the snake path beckoned.

# NINE

ODEL'S EMERGENT was a sweet-fruit pine.

It was a softwood, and Unar climbed the spiraling plank stairs that had been hammered easily into the upper trunk of the great tree. The Temple, shaped like a yellow carp standing on its nose, fluked tail to the sky, and eyes the open doors through which the worshippers walked, was abandoned at this hour.

Inside, on a raised platform, the embers of a bonfire died in a bronze dish that floated in a shallow pool. Around it, food tributes had been set carefully, some on priceless platters, others on fresh-picked leaves.

Unar unwrapped her barely touched seed porridge and put it beside the other tributes, bowing her head and uttering the name of the boy she had met along the way. Then she went looking for the chimera skin. Ylly said it was outside The Temple proper, in a tunnel that went through the heart of the tree and emerged at Odel's Test. Long ago, the wealthy had boasted of their patronage by throwing their children off the balcony there and watching them float in a bubble of Odel's protection.

The practice was frowned on in Unar's time, but the tunnel remained nearby. Unar had brought her machete, ropes, and bore-knife, in case branches had broken or passageways had been strangled by vines in the years since Ylly's visit. She climbed into the undamaged crown of the tree until she had a good view of the Temple surroundings, and sat cross-legged on a branch to look and to think. She was tired, physically and mentally, but the lure of the chimera hadn't faded.

Then she saw somebody walking on a branch road towards the Temple, carrying a lit taper that made the smallest possible amount of light. The figure was pale. A naked slave—no, a man clothed completely in high-necked, long-sleeved robes, a tunic and waist-wrap of pale pink. The colour of dawn, the colour of the orchid mantis, the colour of women's parts he'd never see or touch, for gods and goddesses swore the same oaths of virginity as their Bodyguards.

He stopped on the path beneath her and looked up. His square face was middle-aged and kindly.

"You don't look like a killer," he said, raising the taper in his gloved hand. Whenever Odel ventured into the thick of the populace, he had to keep his skin covered. Like other incarnated deities, he could only be touched by sunlight and rain. It would be a shame for his Bodyguard to have to toss some innocent down to their death because of an accidental skin-to-skin contact.

"My god," Unar gasped.

"No." Odel smiled. "I see that I am not, in fact, your god, and even if it weren't for those clothes, you have the smell of the Garden on you. You serve Audblayin, who has died this day. Have you come looking for newborn babes?"

"No!" She didn't know what to do. She should stay where she was. She shouldn't approach a god without permission. But she was higher than he was. It was disrespectful to be higher than a god.

"Sensible of you. There are no women here, after all, but my Bodyguard, and she will carry no children. She mustn't be made vulnerable by their potential to fall."

Unar tried to look everywhere at once. There was no sign of the Bodyguard.

"Where is she?"

He ignored the question.

"I recognise you from a long-ago dream. You had a sister who fell."

She gazed at him helplessly. For a moment, she couldn't answer. Finally, she said, "It wasn't your fault, Holy One. They didn't come. My parents."

"No. They didn't."

"Did you think I came here to kill you, Holy One?"

"Many attempts are made." Odel shrugged. "Sometimes they wish to release my soul from this body. Their own offspring are almost ready to draw their first breath, the breath that brings the soul into the body, and they would have a god's soul in the ether, waiting. Others wish for revenge."

Unar shifted in her seat and realised the weights of her valuable boreknife and machete were gone from her belt. Twisting, she saw them only an arm's length away, unsheathed in the grip of a beautiful, naked woman whose amputated breasts allowed her to press, flat as a lizard, against the bark of the tree.

"Those are mine," Unar cried.

"Give them back to her, Aurilon," instructed the god, and the Bodyguard, quick as a hunter spearing a snake, drove the weapons back into their sheaths, making Unar cry out wordlessly again.

The Bodyguard fitted her fingers back into leather gloves tipped with claws as long and keen as knives, which had clung by themselves to the bark while she stole the tools, and tightened the leather wrist-straps in their black-painted buckles with her teeth. The back of her body from nape to heels was criss-crossed with raised scars to look like the brindled bark. In the dark, still naked but for the clawed climbing gloves, she was all but invisible.

"Chimera claws," Unar blurted out. "They are real. You have a chimera skin here. I came to see it."

"That old thing?" the god called up to her. "It's rotted away. But why should you want to see it?"

"I have to see it. I'm losing belief in Audblayin. I'm losing hope. I need the proof that female can turn to male. I need to see that she can return to us a man, if she chooses."

"Come down here," Odel said. Unar was afraid to come close to him, and he must have known it. He stepped back, still smiling, to give her room. She hated herself for trembling, for feeling like bursting into tears. She bowed to him, deeply, and didn't rise.

"Were there not elders in the Garden," he asked quietly, "Servants of Audblayin, whom you might have gone to for guidance?"

"I hate them," she whispered.

"Why?"

"I wasn't chosen."

Her heart pounded. Why was she telling him this? She was wicked; she'd always known it. She hadn't obeyed her parents. In the end, although they'd given her life, the most precious commodity of Audblayinland, she hadn't loved them. Grub gathering as a child, by crossing the border of Oxorland, she'd thought to be rewarded by her mother's love, but instead had been rejected even more harshly. Failing to learn from this, she had crossed the barrier into Understorey where, instead of finding the fallen baby, Isin, she'd weakened the Garden's hold on her, wakening something she feared might be desire.

As incapable of obeying the Servants' laws as she was of obeying her duty to family, she'd treated the Great Gates like streams to be stepped over instead of walls to keep her safe, and now she stood in another niche insulting one god to another. He'd have her thrown down, one thousand paces into darkness, to break in the boneyard of Floor as her baby sister had broken before her.

She raised her eyes to his face, briefly, expecting scorn, but found only understanding.

"I can't see the future," Odel said. "Not yours, anyway. It's only the deaths of children that I see. Since I turned sixteen, whenever I close my eyes, it's little children falling who fill my dreams. I am the forty-fourth incarnation of Odel, and I will find no peace until I die. Here's a thing that I have learned, little Gardener. Sometimes, it's best to not be chosen."

# TEN

Once she returned to the Garden, Unar burrowed into her hammock.

She fell into a nightmare sleep of broken children being eaten by demons, a tiredness so deep that when morning came, she resisted being awakened. The new Gardeners carried her across the shallow part of the moat to the Temple. Some part of her was aware of entering the great egg's shade.

She woke in a dim room with Oos's cool hand on her forehead and the sensation of being fully refreshed.

"It worked," Oos exclaimed in delight.

"Is this a dream?" Unar asked.

"You're a fast learner, Oos," a hooded old woman—Servant Eilif—said with satisfaction, ignoring Unar, before turning to leave the room. It was barely three paces across, with only a bed and a chair to furnish it. Bird droppings littered the sills of the three circular windows, which let in light but had no visible way to close them.

"Where are we?" Unar wanted to know.

"One of the treatment rooms," Oos said. "Oh, Unar, I wanted to speak to you after the ceremony, but we couldn't—"

"Treatment? For what? I'm not sick."

"You were. One who walks in the grace of Audblayin cured you." By that, of course, Oos meant herself.

"You cured her of tiredness," said Aoun sombrely. He'd been sitting on the floor, below Unar's line of sight. When he stood, his dark hair brushed the curving outer wall of the small room.

Unar's heart fluttered. Aoun had been waiting for her to wake.

"Are you still angry, Unar?" Oos wrung her hands. "Are you so upset by not being selected that you haven't slept since?"

"How did you do it?" Unar asked. "How did you cure my tiredness?"

"By opening channels in the mind with magic. It's like opening channels in plants to help them draw water. Watch, I'll show you—"

"No, you won't," Aoun said sternly.

"Will you punish her if she does?" Unar sat up sharply. "Will you throw her off the edge of the Garden like a slave too old to work?"

He hadn't been waiting out of concern for her, then, but so he could berate her.

"Oos isn't a slave. Disobedience here is punished by a draining of magic. Any two Servants can perform this upon a third. There's no need for citizens to fall."

Neither Oos nor Aoun had reacted with shock to the notion of throwing slaves to their deaths. Of course not.

"You've learned many things in just one day," Unar observed, glaring at them in turn. "Many things that Gardeners aren't permitted to know. You've changed. I don't know you."

"You know us," Oos protested, and Unar pressed her momentary advantage.

"What's this room for?" She waved her hands around at it. *Here I am in the Temple at last, but not the way I wanted.*

"The women who pay tribute, who come to have their fertility enhanced. They're treated in the rooms."

*Worse. I'm in the room for noninitiates.*

"Can I see where you sleep?" Unar sat up and swung her feet over the edge of the bed, struck by the fact her feet were clean. She was wearing a clean red robe. Who had changed her? Aoun? A thrill went through her before she realised it had to be Oos. The long sleeves had been taken in to fit Unar's arms. Only a few quick stitches, but nobody else would have noticed or cared.

"I don't—" Oos said breathlessly, darting a glance after the departed old woman, at the same time as Aoun rubbed his temple and said with exasperation, "No!"

A fantail flew into the room by the open door and departed by one of the round windows. Able to move freely where Unar was not.

"The women don't mind the bird droppings?" she asked jealously.

"Birds are beloved of the goddess," Oos said. She sat on the bed next to Unar and put her hand consolingly in the small of Unar's back, as if Unar were a decrepit crone in need of support.

Unar knew about the beloved bloody birds. One day separated them, and Oos was already treating Unar like some empty-headed supplicant.

"Oh, great teacher!" Unar said. "Wiser than Eilif already!"

Oos's chin jerked upwards.

"One who walks in the grace of Audblayin admits one's nervousness about one's ability to convey the desires of the goddess—"

"He's a god, now," Unar said, and Oos took her hand away as if burned.

"How can you know that?"

Oos and Aoun both stared at her as if she'd added her own shit to the neat piles of bird droppings.

"Trust me," Unar said stubbornly. "I just know."

# ELEVEN

IN THE afternoon, Oos came out of the Temple to give the new Gardeners a lesson.

Unar would have gone to sleep early, but Aoun came to the loquat grove to tip her out of her hammock and tell her she was needed in the grass plot, that she must undo the blow she'd delivered to Oos's confidence.

"I'm still recovering," she answered, made hostile by guilt, sprawled on the ground and gazing up into his carob-brown irises, which gleamed under the pronounced shelf of his brow. Somehow, her hostility lessened. She didn't want it to.

She wanted to make fun of him for turning out so hairy, not be made breathless by the sudden, masculine smell of him mingling with the perfume of the grove.

"You're recovered," he said calmly, offering his hand, which she didn't take. "Oos saw to that."

"I still don't have any magic. It hasn't grown back."

"Have patience. Watch. Listen."

"In the Temple, you were worried about me. You waited for me to wake up."

For someone who had just advised patience, Unar found the manner in which Aoun lifted her by the shoulders and set her on her feet rather impatient.

"You don't seem worried by how Oos will feel if you don't bother going to her lesson."

Remorse made Unar snap her jaws shut midyawn.

"Fine. I'm going." She was of a mind to push him out of her way, but by the time she fixed her hair, found a jacket, gobbled the lumpy, cold, ant-infested seed-porridge portion she'd dumped in a branch-fork and filled a leaf-cup with water to gargle in, he was gone. Unar crossed five bridges to reach the grass plot, which graced one of the eastern arms of the Garden.

The exotic plot was filled with rare blue and bronze-coloured grasses from the places where Floor met the edge of the forest. A messy hedge of maroon guavas, interspersed with purple sugarcane thickets, formed a semicircle around the western boundary. A family of purple wrens peeped a warning as Unar stepped off the bridge. Maroon hummingbird hatchlings were almost too big for their falling-apart nest in the jacaranda tree that formed the centrepiece of the plot. It had flowered during the wet and would drop its lush, ferny leaves at the very end of the dry.

The other Gardeners clustered by the jacaranda, waiting in silence. Unar should have known all their names but didn't. Oos had chided her for not knowing the intimate life histories of Servants who should have been her role models, but Unar didn't care for role models; at least, she hadn't until she'd met that Bodyguard of Odel's.

What was her name?

"If you're quite ready for the lesson to begin," Oos said.

Oos stood at the focus of the loose semicircle of Gardeners, the snowy pistil to their bloody stamens. She'd procured a white hat-peak, complete with white ribbons, to lace into her white-beaded hair. She always wore hat-peaks, even in the shade, in the belief that it would keep her skin smooth and soft. Unar wouldn't have been surprised to see Oos wearing one in the dark. She'd heard that at internoder balls, the dancers wore hats indoors.

"Sorry," Unar said with as much sincerity as she could gather. Oos was her friend. She didn't deserve to be punished for the stupidity of the other Servants. Unar didn't really want to ruin her first day as a teacher.

"Today we'll learn to determine," Oos said, raising her voice to reach all of them, smoothing the perfect folds of her white robe, "whether a seed will give rise to a plant showing mostly the character of the plant that contributed the pollen, or the plant that contributed the ovum. In the case of self-pollination, we'll still be able to predict indicators relevant to our interests, such as leaf blade length or the sweetness of fruit."

And then Unar, who had fully intended to be attentive and courteous, found herself irritated beyond her ability to hide it.

She didn't care about the sweetness of fruit, but she cared that the vizier's daughter's belaboured, noble-born speech had reasserted itself so strongly with her promotion.

*O great teacher!*

Oos's fingers stilled on her robe. Her eyes narrowed, and Unar realised she had spoken out loud.

"One who walks in the grace of Audblayin begs your pardon, Gardener Unar. Perhaps you would like to teach the class."

"Teaching is for Servants only."

"Rightly so." Oos's arms, straight at her sides, clenched handfuls of her robe. "Do you have any other questions, child?"

*Child.*

Unar's anger blazed up, as Oos had no doubt intended.

"Yes. I do. Why are the plants allowed to breed, and the slaves, and the birds, but not the Gardeners or the Servants? Because I think you and Aoun might breed a sort of perfect hat-wearing offspring with his boring seriousness and your dim-witted conceit."

Oos could have struck Unar, could have given her the same black eye that the other initiates had once given her. Instead, she lifted her chin and swallowed hard. When she spoke again, her voice became shrill, but, shockingly, she answered the question.

"Once, long ago, it was the duty of Gardeners and Servants to give up their wombs or their seed for the use of worshippers who could get no children of their own. That practice faded as our skills improved. But the tradition of magically enabled freedom from lust was adopted by all deities of Canopy once it became clear that such freedom reduced split loyalties between blood relatives and service to the Temple."

Unar stared into Oos's eyes. How many times had they puzzled over this matter, in their hammocks in the loquat grove? All of Oos's questions would be answered, but none of Unar's.

*Tell me more,* Unar begged silently with an open expression of longing. *Tell me everything you know. I belong with you.*

Oos's large, liquid eyes softened with sympathy.

Then she turned away. She plucked a disc-shaped, hanging seedpod from the jacaranda tree. In her hand, it darkened from brilliant green to very dark brown, and split, first into a wide frog grin and then into separate halves, revealing the papery-winged seeds inside.

Unar barely felt the magic that Oos had used. She was still exhausted by her effort on Ylly's behalf and the slowed recovery caused by Audblayin's death. Something tiny and bright did seem to unfold in Oos's breast. Unar couldn't tell if the smell of sweet rot and crushed jacaranda flower in her nostrils was from the magic or the actual tree, and she certainly couldn't discern the qualities the seed had gained from either contributor to pollination.

The place inside her where her magic lived was hollow, and it ached.

Instead of dwelling on it, she remembered how her whole body had thrummed, like a hanging bridge in high wind, at the thought that Aoun might have undressed her.

*Freedom from lust,* she thought. *It's not working for me, but I don't care. When I have the ear of the god, I'll put a stop to that tradition. Or at least change it so that those within the Garden can be with one another. There'll be no split loyalties then.*

For Unar might have become newly, uncomfortably aware of Aoun, but worried about her or not, he was incapable of becoming similarly aware of her. Despite all his working parts, magic made him impotent, and although they were both have-nothings, only Unar was a wrongdoer; Aoun would never willingly weaken his bond with the Garden, never break any of its rules.

*It's in me to be law-abiding.*

Wait.

He had broken a rule, after all. He'd let Unar out of the Garden. Why make an exception for her? There was no good reason.

Unless.

Abruptly, the emptiness where her magic should have been didn't hurt quite so much. Suppressing a smile, Unar arranged her face into an expression of interest.

*Have patience,* Aoun had told her. *Watch. Listen.*

DAYS AND nights passed slowly while Unar waited for her magic to regrow.

*Watch. Listen. If you say so, Gatekeeper Aoun.*

By trial and error, she discovered a place directly across the moat where she could best position herself, hidden by painfully prickly pomegranate bushes. There, she could listen for snatches of conversation to float out through the windows of the treatment rooms at the side of the Temple and across the fish-filled water.

It wasn't enough. She couldn't hear anything worth hearing, couldn't eavesdrop with magical ears on whispered incantations nor see, with her magical sight, how the patterns were performed.

She had to get closer.

While she waited for a new plan to come to her, she performed her usual

duties. Unar weeded, harvested, planted seeds, separated clumps of colourful grasses, slept at midday when she should have been mingling with the
other Gardeners at luncheon, and spent the hours after sundown helping
Ylly with her ever-increasing workload. There was no Bodyguard to spy on
her out the crescent windows anymore.

"You said you were named after your mother, Ylly."

"Yes."

"Where is your mother now?" Side by side at the same waterfall that had
once made Oos want to pee, they scrubbed metal racks that had been used
for roasting afterbirths, considered a prized offering to Audblayin and eaten
only by Servants. Unar hoped they tasted terrible. She hoped Aoun had
choked on his.

"The princess," Ylly said, "my former mistress, pushed my mother over the
palace wall when her bladder became weak and she began to smell of urine."

"Did you see her fall?" Unar demanded, outraged, then worried she'd spoken too loudly and woken someone in the nearby grove. She paused,
straightening with her fist full of soapleaf, and listened for the warning calls
of roosting lorikeets. They could be disturbed by human weight shifting in
hammocks, and Unar shooed them out her own hammock-trees for that
reason.

Nothing. Her little living alarms stayed silent. Unar bent back over
the racks. Ylly shuffled past her, setting the rinsed, dripping racks along the
pavilion wall to dry. The water trickling from them watered the moss that
grew beneath the wooden foundations.

"No, Warmed One. I was playing with kittens by the kitchen herbery.
When I found out what had happened, I was so angry that I threw one of the
kittens out of the princess's window, into the setting sun. The kitten belonged
to the princess. She ordered my legs to be broken. I was seven years old."

Unar stopped scrubbing.

"Ylly. That's terrible."

Ylly held the last of the dirty racks before her, her body in the shadow of
the pavilion. Unar couldn't see her face, but her hands were steady. Her voice
floated on the wind, disembodied.

"The king was furious that my promise of future beauty had been ruined.
He had me taken to Eshland for my bones to be repaired. That's why you
can't tell. There aren't even any scars."

"This king who was father to the princess who owned you. Was he the
king of Audblayinland?"

"Of Odelland." Ylly still didn't come out from the shadow of the pavilion. Unar bent her head back over her task.

"You must have thanked all the goddesses and gods when you were sold away from that place."

"I cursed them. I was heavy with the king's child. They argued about whether to let me live. One of the viziers told them to cut me open and send the child-making parts inside of me as tribute to this Temple."

Unar felt her gorge rise.

"The law doesn't permit the torture of slaves!" She got up and slammed the rack under the waterfall to rinse it.

"Kings enforce the laws they choose, in their own niches."

Unar took the last dirty rack from Ylly's hands, swapping it for the clean one she held. Was Ylly hiding in the shadows because she was crying? Oos had always liked to be held when she cried. When she'd been separated from her silver bells, there'd been plenty of crying and holding involved. But Unar rarely wanted to be touched when she was upset. And Ylly didn't sound upset.

She sounded resigned. Distant.

"I've been so wrong," Unar said. "I've ignored slaves. I've failed to see them."

"They've seen you. They've feared you. I still fear you, even now."

Unar wanted to pull Ylly by the wrist out of the shadow, but Ylly had spent a lifetime being forced to do things she didn't want to do. She wasn't Oos.

"You're brave. You've taught me much about slaves."

Ylly took a few slow steps to set the rack to drip with the others. She shook her head.

"No. I've taught you about myself. You've learned a little bit about a woman called Ylly. That's all. There are no slaves. There are no citizens. Only the living and the dead."

Unlike Unar, Ylly couldn't hide in the bamboo thickets and doze during the day. Sleep deprivation was making her say things that didn't make sense, Unar decided uneasily. She changed the subject.

"Do you know how to swim, Ylly?"

"No."

"I must learn." Unar tried not to think of fish. Slimy fish and spiny fish, moving in darkness, in water she couldn't see through. "If I don't learn to swim, I'll never learn the magic of the Servants."

Ylly snatched up the drying cloth at Unar's feet, betraying anger.

"Do you think to earn my trust by giving me power over you?" Her voice stayed calm. "By confessing to wrongdoings? Nobody listens to a slave. Nobody rewards a slave for betraying her betters."

"What can I give you, then?" Unar asked, surprised. "What can I do to earn your trust?"

The cloth flew over the wet racks, and now it was Ylly's turn to throw caution aside, stacking them together with a crash that brought a few sleepy whistles from the roosting birds.

"Protect my grandchild, only fourteen days old. The father is a thatcher who came nine months ago, wanting to be a Gardener. He was turned away, but on his way out, my daughter showed him the moss garden. If you want to earn my trust, take an offering to Odel's Temple and whisper my grand-daughter's name."

The moss garden. It was sheltered by small-leafed myrtles whose dark green foliage turned to buttercup, persimmon, and blood-tinged hues after the monsoon. Over the myrtle trees stood spiny plums whose jagged-edged fronds interlaced like flat fingers warming themselves over a fire.

The mosses made beds even softer than the silk lining Oos had sewn for Unar's hammock. In that forever-warm, wind-sheltered hollow, water wicking into clothes hardly mattered.

It was the perfect place for conception, in the old days Oos had spoken of, when Servants served in other ways.

Unar shoved the image of Aoun's muscled arms out of her thoughts.

"You didn't think to mention this before," she demanded of Ylly, "when I asked for directions to Odel's Temple?"

"I didn't think you would really go."

"I went." Unar threw her hands up in the air. "The chimera skin was all rotten!"

"Yes. You told me."

"If I go there again, if I do as you ask, then what?"

"Then my daughter will do as I ask." Ylly's tone brooked no argument. "She's an accomplished diver. Her work is to unclog the water-carriers. Other-wise, they fill with leaves and sticks. So do the bottoms of the pools that surround the Temple, and rot pollutes the water. She can teach you to swim."

"Is this daughter the child of the king of Odelland? Why doesn't your daughter help you with this awful work, this old woman's work, which you've taken upon yourself?"

"I'm confined to the upper levels of the Garden," Ylly explained. "Sawas is confined below. We haven't spoken in fifteen years. Trained birds carry our messages."

She set the last dry rack atop the others, bending her back to lift the entire stack. The work was done. Unar should have returned at once to her hammock, to try to get an hour or two of rest, but she drifted after the departing slave.

"And did a bird bring you a message to tell you your grandchild's name, fourteen days ago when your daughter gave birth?"

Ylly stopped walking and turned so that Unar could see her smile deepening.

"Indeed. The child's name is Ylly. My mother's gift lives on, though we're powerless to protect this latest namesake. You'll see that she's protected. You and Odel. I trust you to be truthful on this matter. And then Sawas will teach you to swim."

# TWELVE

Two NEW moons later, the evening came when Unar had enough magic to fool the wards on the wall.

As she climbed, the light, inner touch of the magic reached her senses, smelling like turned earth and life but also a male presence, and she recognised that maintenance of the spell had been Aoun's. The magic was as muscularly built and unadorned as his naked body had been the day of Audblayin's death, and the feel of it set Unar's heart fluttering, her nipples hardening, and her cheeks flushing; the deity's dampening effect upon her urges had never fully returned, or perhaps it was simply her age and attainment of a woman's full growth and capabilities.

"I am a seedpod," she whispered to the wards. "A seedpod borne on the wind."

The wards allowed her to pass, since she carried the seeds inside of her that all young women carried, and she dropped down on the other side, triumphant. She didn't need Aoun and his key. With her magic regrown, the Garden knew her. The Garden was part of her.

*The Garden is mine.*

She'd eaten supper to give her stamina for the journey, but food was not what she had in mind for the tribute that would keep baby Ylly safe. The season had changed. The three-month dry-season winter inexorably followed the short, one-month autumn. Slaves were allowed to lie in with their newborns for a season, but now was the time when Sawas, the baby's mother, would be required to return to work. Baby Ylly would be learning to move, struggle, escape from the confines of cradles and tree trunk hollows.

The other baby, Imeris, who had fallen in the autumn, the one that Unar had futilely searched for with her goddess-given senses, was all but forgotten by the searchers once keen to claim the reward. Wife-of-Epatut had come to the Temple to seek enhanced fertility and the conception of a new child.

Unar, despite being excluded from the lessons of the Servants, through her friendship with the elder Ylly now had access to slaves' gossip. It was said that Wife-of-Epatut had dropped her daughter at the silk market. The beewife who had bumped her was imprisoned at the palace of the king of Ehkisland.

Unar sought a different palace tonight. The story of Ylly and the princess of Odelland haunted her. Should such wickedness go unpunished? Perhaps an Understorian could be ignored by the gods and goddesses of Canopy. Perhaps the fate of an enemy's descendent was not the concern of higher powers. But the elder Ylly was Unar's friend now.

Ylly was hers to protect, as she would one day protect Audblayin.

*To protect or to avenge.*

Canopy's roads were crowded, both high and low. The fruit harvest had peaked and the season of nuts and seeds was waning. Though it was past sunset, slaves and citizens alike carried baskets brimming with macadamias or windgrass grain, green oilseeds and orange oilseeds, some for eating and some for burning, some for leaching of their toxins to make them edible and others for pounding into sealant or adhesive. Several hours passed before Unar reached the crossroads of the Falling Fig, and several more before she'd squeezed through the press of bodies along the snake path and found her way into Odelland.

It wasn't Odel's emergent, the sweet-fruit pine, which Unar sought first, this time.

She went to the palace of the king of Odelland, and stared for a long while at the parapets from which Ylly's mother had been pushed.

The palace, built in a blue quandong tree, swayed in the stiff winds like a giant bird's nest, polished timber after polished timber placed in a seemingly unstable fashion. Though the breeze bent the boughs that the building rested on, not a plank fell out of place. Hidden dovetails and dowels held snowy sweet-fruit pine branches snugged tight to scarlet bloodwood. The steep roofs of fresh, grey windgrass thatch, highly valued as insect-repellent bedding and for driving the foul flavour from cooked monkey meat, not only trumpeted the king's wealth but completed the image of Odelland royalty as colourful toucans nesting where fruit would fall on them like rain.

Yet they had killed a woman for the crime of growing old. Perhaps the death god, Atwith, approved of such things, but Unar didn't, and Atwith was not her god.

Unar sat where the trunk of the adjacent floodgum obscured her from the guards who watched from crooked towers at the corners of the ever-swaying structure. Ostensibly kicking her sandalled feet out in a pose of relaxation, she felt for defects in the path, and in a moment when all human traffic was moving away from her, she swung herself underneath it, hanging like a sloth from ropes of torn floodgum bark.

Hand over hand, wary of the scorpions, biting ants, and tarantulas that called the cracks and bark curls home, Unar made her way to the place where floodgum branch met quandong, directly below the palace.

There, she began to scale the walls in darkness. Nothing could have been easier. The untrimmed ends of the artfully stacked timbers would have given purchase to a child. Soon, she was so high that not even the light from lamp-carrying merchants below could show her the contrast of her fingernails against the fine finish of the multicoloured woods.

Her magic was faded this far from the Garden, but it was still strong enough to inform Unar whether there were any women in the princess's apartments before she climbed into them. A screen of fragrant smoke filled the window, to keep the insects out, and Unar felt a beetle abandon the back of her jacket in a panic as she passed through the smoke. She had known these west-facing rooms would be the princess's, but she hadn't known how a royal daughter would sleep: on a pink, orchid-shaped mattress floating above a lily-pad-shaped platform of pale bone.

How had the royal family traded for such a thing from Odel? Unar hadn't realised the gentle god owned any powers besides keeping children from falling. Then again, Audblayin could make sky-coral and her Bodyguard float; why not all the goddesses and gods? Unar tried to examine the mattress with her magical senses, but her link to the distant Garden was too strained. She couldn't see the threads of power holding it in place, nor could she smell anything arcane.

The ostentatiousness of the bed and the sound of Ylly's voice in her head made Unar want to burn it and its feather-filled pillows. That would make a fine smell, but she'd come for one thing—an object suitable for tribute to Odel, to keep Ylly's granddaughter safe from falling—and she mustn't become distracted. She must escape the palace without any alarms having been raised.

Gold combs and charmed anklets covered the dresser with its opal-studded silver mirror, but every item was stamped with the toucan crest of the king of Odelland, and soldiers would be summoned if she offered any such thing at a Temple. The goblets and pitcher on the mantel were the same. Even the iron pokers by the smoke-producing braziers were marked with the symbols.

Her attention was caught by railings that had been plugged into place by the bed and by the armchairs. She threw back the veil surrounding the squat, where the covered hole for piss and shit to fall through had a sort of harness in place, suitable for an old woman whose knees wouldn't hold her weight while she squatted.

The princess was old. Much older than Ylly's mother had been at the time of her demise, Unar would wager. It made her blood boil. Without magic, this room would probably smell of urine, too. The beautiful bed no longer seemed a girl's flight of fancy, but a hag's need for the bed to rise in order to roll herself out of it.

Unar had wasted too much time. The decrepit princess could retire to her apartment any moment. Unar expanded her tenuous ability as far as she could, her nostrils filling with the smell of sweet-sour quandong fruit, bitter kernel and clean, fresh crushed leaf, in the hope she'd be warned of women approaching.

Instead, something hidden in the floor under a silk carpet tickled her mind.

Unar threw herself to the floor. She peeled back the carpet. A hexagon of bloodwood pulled out of place like a puzzle piece. Inside a small, revealed hollow lay bundles of something black, cool and supple to touch, but difficult to see; as Unar lifted the edge of the cloth, it rippled to brown, taking on the colour of her hand.

*Chimera skin.* It changed colour, like a chameleon's, even after the animal's death. There was something inside. Bits of old bones. She shook them out of the cloth.

Then Unar stuffed the cloth into the front of her jacket, making a false paunch above her belt, before putting the piece of bloodwood back in place and smoothing out the carpet. She leaped for the window, but the smoke solidified, throwing her roughly back.

Stunned, Unar waited for her dizziness to clear. She tried to make sense of the swirl of sound that had thickened around her.

*You are a thief,* the window had accused her.

It was something similar to the wards around the Garden.

Unar climbed to her feet. She went to the window and laid her fingers tentatively on the sill. The smoke buzzed angrily.

"I'm no thief," Unar told it softly, trying to link her mind to it the way she linked her mind to the Garden. "The five pieces of cloth I've taken are payment for the life of a murdered woman."

*It is too much,* the window said. *That cloth can buy a thousand slaves.*

"But never replace a specific one who has fallen. Slaves aren't all the same! You could buy a thousand slaves and yet not find another like her. Read my thoughts. See my truth. I'm taking this cloth to protect a great-grandchild that the murdered woman is not alive to protect. I am no thief!"

*You are no thief,* the smoke conceded, parting.

Unar climbed through the window, triumphant, to begin her descent of the swaying, bird's nest castle.

# THIRTEEN

Unar yawned as Ylly tried to wake her.

"Warmed One," the older woman said urgently, "they've come to question you."

Unar swayed in her hammock, resenting Ylly's insistent hands almost as much as she resented the sunlight shafting through the loquat trees onto her upturned face.

"Who? Who has come to question me?"

"Soldiers from Odelland. They've been sent to every Temple in Canopy. They say something was stolen from the king that only a Servant of a deity could have stolen. Warmed One, what have you done?"

Unar's mood changed from sullen to satisfied at once. She sat up in her hammock, gripped the edges of it, and gave a smug little laugh.

"Every Temple in Canopy? That king thinks he's a cockerel, but he's a dumpy, featherless duckling, and I'm the one who cooked him."

Ylly's eyes went wide and her hands covered her mouth. They were alone. In the Garden, her beloved Garden, with her magic renewed, Unar was capable of plotting the position of every man and woman within the walls. She sensed clusters of men by the Gate, heavy on the soil and the underlying tallowwood. Elsewhere, men and women who had to be Servants massed slightly apart from the younger demographic of the other Gardeners. Unar smelled the vitriol in one of the robes that brushed the earth; that one was Oos. They were attended by almost all of the slaves, who were also mostly young-smelling and trod lightly but held no magic, at the moat's shallow ford by the Temple doors.

"I went to Odel's emergent," Unar said. "I did what you asked."

Ylly lowered her hands.

"My grandchild is safe?"

Unar took her hands and squeezed them.

"Your grandchild is so safe that the Servants combined couldn't cast her down if they tried. I paid for her safety with five lengths of chimera skin cloth."

Unar laughed again, remembering, and let Ylly go.

"How did you take such riches without the king seeing you?"

"I didn't take the cloth from the king. I took it from the stupid old princess who murdered your mother. Her window still faces the setting sun. You serve the Garden now. I would have it that the Garden serves you."

"Don't say such things," Ylly breathed. "Warmed One, you've kept your word, you're great of heart, but you're also young and made moon-mad by your anger at the friends who left you behind. The Garden serves Audblayin. They will come to find you if you don't join them right away."

Part of Unar wanted to recline in the hammock with her hands behind her head, smiling and waiting for them to come. Yet some wiser part of her set her pulling on the clean clothes Ylly had brought, rinsing her mouth and slicking her hair back with water from the waterfall, wandering down to the Temple to find her fellow Gardeners.

She still hadn't bothered to learn their names, but she stood by a serious-looking, shaved-headed girl that she recognised from barrow-repair duty and tried to assume a similar expression of deep gravity. The girl had dirty hands. They all did. Obviously they'd been up and working for some hours before the soldiers had arrived.

Unar's stomach growled.

Before she could sneak over to the blueberry bushes and stuff some of the ripe fruit into her mouth, the twenty-eight Gardeners were forming a single line, and the fourteen Servants were moving along it, led by Servant Eilif, who asked questions about who had seen what.

Unar lined up by the shaved-headed girl. Soon, she could see Oos, Aoun, and the five others who had been raised ahead of her. With her magic, she felt inside their bodies, seeking some identifying aspect of their magic, of their capability to reproduce, that would allow her to not only follow the movements of others in the Garden, but know exactly who they were. The shape and scent of Aoun's magic, she recognised well enough, but what about Oos? Her femaleness felt like a pod bursting with peas under a tracery of Unar's fingers, but the clothes-dye aroma seemed to disguise whatever else might have been beneath.

Somebody else's magic cut off Unar's breath and sense of smell at the same time, like fingers pinching her nostrils shut. She stifled a snort and with-drew.

"Impertinent!" Servant Eilif said, glowering. That one smelled of worm-wood and fig fruit dried to dust.

Unar bowed deeply and said nothing, but Servant Eilif stood before her and didn't move on down the line.

"The others say you've been slow to wake, Unar of the Garden. They say you're barely coherent at breakfast, use your magic for tasks that can be accomplished by hand, and fall asleep during the day."

"I haven't slept well at night since Audblayin's death."

"Do you think yourself my equal?" the Servant thundered.

Unar couldn't answer that question truthfully and avoid punishment. She remained bowed.

"Forgive me. I haven't slept well since Audblayin's death, Warmed One," she repeated dully.

"Did you leave the Garden last night? Did you steal from the king of Odelland?"

Unar straightened and looked the white-haired Servant directly in the eye.

"I am no thief, Warmed One. I stole nothing. The Garden is my home. If I'd stolen from the king of Odelland, I'd still have been standing outside the Great Gates when the soldiers came."

The old woman turned, looking for Aoun; she found him, and they shared a glance.

"The wards hold," Aoun said mildly.

"And just as well," Oos chimed in. "The Odelland king's soldiers are mostly murderers. Some are rapists. A few are thieves. One who walks in the grace of Audblayin senses only one or two who could pass through the Gate, even if you invited them, Servant Eilif."

"You must never invite out-of-niche soldiers into the Garden," Eilif said. "Listen. All of you. Even our own king's men should set foot inside the wall only as a last resort, should the wards fail and Understorian warriors breach our sanctuary. As for the Temple itself, it must remain pure at all costs. The Garden is for women, male Servants and Gardeners who have given them-selves to Audblayin, and male slaves who have been given as tribute."

"Yes, Servant Eilif," Oos and the other Servants chorused, but Unar turned the stricture over in her mind. She could see no good reason for women being seen as safe. They were no less dangerous than men. She thought of Odel's Bodyguard, the scarred woman who had taken her machete and bore-knife without her knowing.

"Our own king's soldiers come at last," Eilif said, turning abruptly away from Unar, heading for the Gates. In the absence of an explicit order to remain behind, Unar and the mass of Gardeners and slaves followed along behind her, crossing bridges and traipsing over stepping-stones, avoiding flowering groundcovers and fragile, brightly coloured fungi.

The Gates stood wide open with Odelland soldiers clearly visible on the other side. They wore scarlet leaf-skirts over leather loincloths, pale yellow bracers and shin guards, and lacquered breastplates studded with beetle carapaces over peach-coloured tunics that bordered on trespassing on their god's reserved colour.

"Your people lack discipline in the absence of your goddess," their leader called to Servant Eilif as she approached the invisible barrier.

"The person you are looking for," Eilif said with conviction, "is not among my people. You have my oath. Now you must leave."

"We'll question your people ourselves."

"Our king's men are close."

"You think one who walks in the grace of Odel cares about your king's men? Your king is weak. The magic of this niche is faded. You'd better do as our king demands, or who will protect you in the raids when they come? You'll be begging us for help."

"The Garden will not admit anyone who has taken a life."

"Is that so?"

"Try to step through the Gate."

"Save your tricks for the raiders."

"The Garden doesn't admit thieves any more than it admits murderers. You could have saved yourselves the trip, soldiers of Odelland."

"We're not stupid, old woman." The leader let his frustration show. "We learned as schoolboys in the leaf hut that the Garden Temple favours women, as the death god's Temple favours men. But we have orders from our king. If we can't get in, you'll have to come out."

"Look there," Eilif said, but a scout had already rushed forward to tug at the lead soldier's tunic.

On a barely visible branch path to the east, the brown-clad soldiers of Audblayinland advanced in an orderly centipede formation, moving two by two, left-handers with right-handers, so that weapons could be wielded on both sides. Citizens pressed themselves to trunks to keep out of their path, and children emerged from their hollowed-out houses to point and cheer.

"I won't flee before fighters made inferior by their godlessness," the leader said.

"Do not flee," Eilif suggested. "Go to meet them. Tell them you've realised your error. That the Garden is incapable of sheltering thieves."

It galled the man to do as she said, but Unar could imagine no alternative. The Odelland soldiers turned to leave, and the Gardeners fell into each other's arms, soothing one another. Unar caught Aoun gazing flatly at her.

As their eyes met, her heart thudded. Had she ever thought he was too tall, that his jaw was too long, that his soulful eyes were too deep-set, too serious? He was stunning. Did he think the same about her? No, of course not. He was wondering if, despite the wards, despite everything, she really had stolen from the king of Odelland.

Insolently, knowing that nobody else was watching, she gave him a slow smile and the briefest, barest nod of her head.

# FOURTEEN

Unar licked the last of her seed porridge from its leaf-bowl.

She let the bowl fall off the edge of the Garden and washed her hands and mouth in an irrigation channel. With the sun setting, she turned towards the slave quarters, intending to find Ylly and claim her reward, her first swimming lesson, but a lofty figure in a white robe and red-and-green stole stepped out from behind the closest pavilion.

It was Aoun.

"Come with me, Gardener," he said.

"As you wish, Warmed One," Unar answered instantly. She followed him with foreboding across a series of bridges, wondering whether other Servants would be waiting at the Gate to expel her from the Garden forever.

There was nobody else at the Gate. Unar and Aoun stopped together by the black-trunked tree ferns, the fronds forming a tangled roof above their heads, staring at the empty space where soldiers had milled like angry ants that morning.

Unar's skin prickled. She stood, poised, on the balls of her feet with her knees bent, smelling nightflower honey, the reek of bats, and the powder of moths. Would he simply and silently throw her through that empty space? He'd pushed her through it before, but her magic had been weak then. She would resist him, if he tried to cast her from the Garden.

"Watch," he said.

"It's too dark to see anything. Where's your lantern?"

"Watch."

There was nothing in the doorway and then there was a seed, the size of a human heart, formed from light that only a Gardener's eyes could see. It throbbed like a heart, and with every pulse, it grew larger, sending out shoots above and roots below, until it filled the space between gateposts, smelling like rain.

Unar's mouth was dry. He wasn't casting her out. He was breaking the rules for her again, and Aoun did not break rules.

"The key," she whispered. "I am dreaming."

"You're not dreaming."

"Why have you shown me the key?"

"I'm showing you that the Gate is locked. Now, show me how to go through, Unar."

"No! That is, I don't know—"

"If you can discover a way through, our enemies might discover it, too. Show me, please."

"So you can strengthen the wards?" Hope turned to dismay. For a whole minute, she'd thought he was helping her, training her, maybe a little in love with her. She thought he'd escaped from the anti-lust magic after all, but all he wanted was to strengthen the Garden, faithful as a fourth-generation slave. "So you can cage me?"

He laid his hand lightly on her shoulder, and she felt that she was melting. It wasn't fair, that he could do this to her but not she to him.

"Pay attention. I've given you the key."

She'd forgotten.

Of course. After what she had just seen, the Garden would never be closed to her again. Her emotions were in turmoil. Joy warred with terror; the ground scarcely seemed solid. Surely he couldn't just show her the key. Maybe he still planned to throw her out afterwards.

"Am I not the enemy?" she asked. "I've rebelled against a king. Against the natural order."

"My parents rebelled against that order."

"And now you rebel against it?"

His hand fell away.

"No. We knelt together on the same day, Unar, but we aren't alike in this. You know I came here to submit to their will. But you must learn greater discipline—"

"We aren't alike? You showed me the key! That's not allowed, is it?"

"I swore never to lock the Gate in front of anyone, except in the advent of Audblayin's reincarnation, my own mortal wounding, or in defence of a Garden under imminent threat."

"Is the Garden under imminent threat?"

"You've breached wards that have been impenetrable for four hundred years, Unar. I can't imagine a true disciple of the Garden would ever do such a thing."

She blinked back tears, wounded by his disapproval. Shouldn't the fact that she had found a way through four-hundred-year-old defences prove to the Servants that she was fit to join them? Shouldn't Aoun be awed? Full of praise instead of chastisement?

He was as stupid as the others. He could leap off the edge of the Garden for all she cared. Audblayin was reborn a man.

*And I'm the only one fit to be his guardian.*

"You want to go through?" she said at last. "You guessed that giving me the key would be the only way to convince me to show you. Very well. Your turn to pay attention."

She could have done it gently. Instead, she lashed out with a whip-crack of power that tightened around his testicles, finding the seeds beneath his clothes, beneath his skin.

*He carries new life,* she said to the wards, while Aoun's pupils dilated and his breathing quickened. *Do you see them? Do you see that he is only a seed, blowing on the wind?*

She gave him a push in the direction of the Gate. Aoun went awkwardly through the wards, bent at the waist, his legs wide apart, and groaned when he found himself on the other side.

Unar let go of him. Her anger died.

"Aoun," she said, "I'm sorry."

He tried to come back through at once, made inattentive by pain, and was repelled. Unar studied the structure of the seed at the centre of the lock, and saw instantly how to sow a piece of it inside Aoun, to grow it so that it filled him, so that the Gate would confuse his body with part of itself. She mentally traced the patterns with magic as they occurred to her, knowing from the rich earth smell in her nostrils that life-power was flowing through her and into them, half remembering the flowering that had brought her to the Garden four years ago, half making it her own, hardly noticing that what she did was visible to him, too.

When he came back through, he was still panting, open-mouthed. He stared at her the way he'd stared that morning when Servants and soldiers had been all around them hunting fruitlessly for the thief who served a deity.

"You could destroy everything," he said. "All of it. You could unmake it. I could almost believe that you are the goddess reborn. Only banishment to Understorey could make you safe."

"I am a Gardener," Unar said stiffly. "We knelt together on the same day, Aoun."

She was frightened into doing something else she hadn't known she knew how to do, and that was to conceal her strength from him. She felt him probe for the leaves, branches, and glowing stem of it, until he was satisfied that opening the Gate for him had cost her most of her strength.

She wanted to feel his real hands on her, and not just the brush of his magic, but he stayed a respectful step back from her.

"You are a Gardener," he agreed. "Make sure you don't fall behind in your work. Your own work, assigned to you. Have an early night. Get some rest."

For once, she didn't dare disobey.

# FIFTEEN

THE OLD slave woman, whose tasks Ylly had taken on, was called Hasbabsah.

They stood in the kitchen garden, with bean-covered trellises forming a labyrinth around them. The trellises caught every sparkle, every glint of full sun.

"Stand straight," Unar said. "I can't see your face."

"I am standing as straight as I can, Warmed One," Hasbabsah replied drily. She was puckered and toothless. Her balding head was spotted, and her toenails were like claws. Unar had never seen such an old slave.

She'd never thought to wonder why, before.

"Show me your arms."

Hasbabsah pushed back the sleeves of her coarse winter robe. At intervals along the blades of her forearms, blunt bone-coloured nubs showed where her warrior's climbing grafts had been snapped or filed off.

"Why do you attack us?"

"I have served for fifty years, Warmed One."

"No, I mean why do your people, Understorians like you, attack Canopy?"

"There are bones the size of the great trees in the soil of Floor, Warmed One, if you ever cared to dig to find them. They are the bones of the Old Gods, huge and fierce animals with the intellects of people. Before they were slain by the thirteen gods and goddesses of Canopy, they ruled us, all of us, wisely and well. Humankind was not divided into three. We were one."

"What a disgusting notion," Unar said, fascinated and repelled. "Do you seek revenge on our deities?"

"Some of the learned of Understorey believe that if the thirteen are cast down together, between sunrise and sunset of a single day, the Old Gods will rise again."

Unar laughed.

"That can never happen. The most your attacks have ever achieved is to capture one god, and he was rescued by his Bodyguard. Understorians are too few."

"But of course we are few," Hasbabsah said. "We are denied the light. We are denied the toucan's share of the fruit of the great trees. We are prey to demons. We have no magic to keep our children from falling."

Unar wished she hadn't laughed.

"I'm sorry, Hasbabsah. I don't blame you for coming to kill Audblayin. But she was gentle, wasn't she? She was kind?"

Unar was only guessing. She had never met the goddess face-to-face.

"I did not come to kill Audblayin, Warmed One. I was captured in Odel-land. I came to kill Odel, not knowing that his incarnation had not even been found, that the empty Temple was a trap."

"Hasbabsah and my mother were taken together," Ylly said, setting her basket of beans on the ground. "Luckily for us, as of today, she's been assigned to the lower branches of the Temple to care for my new grandchild while Sawas is diving."

"That is lucky," Unar said. "I think Aoun knows I've been working with you at night. He said something about doing my own work, work assigned specifically to me."

"That is the name of the Servant, the Gatekeeper, who told me this morning to go below," Hasbabsah said. "He changed the mark in my mouth. Once I go down, I will not be able to come back up, Ylly."

Ylly's expression didn't change. Unar began to step back, to withdraw so they could show their true feelings in private, but other Gardeners and slaves were around the next corner and she didn't want to rouse suspicion.

"This is farewell, then," Ylly said.

They embraced tightly.

"I thought that the Warmed One might go with you to the lower branches. She could meet Sawas. Perhaps watch her work for a little while."

"And her allotted Gardener's work?"

"Oh, that," Unar said. Turning carelessly to the wall of vines, she reached out to pollinated seeds too small to see, her magic drawing them out from the husks of faded flowers into beans that were brilliant green and a hand-span across. "There. I've done it. Enjoy the picking, Ylly."

"Hasbabsah will need your help on the descent, Warmed One," Ylly said. "I beg you, however she grumbles, not to let her fall."

Unar began to take the old woman's arm, but Ylly's hiss recalled to mind that any assistance was to occur once they were out of sight.

The slave's loose, spotted skin abruptly reminded Unar of how her mother had looked, wasted by illness, on the day she'd come to demand compensation from the Garden for her runaway daughter. That was the first time Unar had climbed the walls of the Garden. She thought she'd recognised the source of the disturbance as a woman she'd hoped never to see again and was horrified to discover she was right.

*I'm old,* Mother had raged at the white-robed figure outside the Great Gate. *I must have what I'm owed. You serve life. Do you want me to die? Because I will die, without silver, without children to do the work.*

Unar had resisted the urge to answer in the affirmative. She'd leaned with one foot against the wooden wall, the other foot braced back against the trunk of a coconut palm, her hands slashed by the sharp edges of the fronds, her ears straining to hear the Servant's reply. Anxiety had twisted her innards. She hadn't been of age when she'd pledged herself to Audblayin. Was it possible that she'd be sent back?

*Give me what I am owed!* Mother had screeched.

And Unar remembered Isin and the broken lock. She said fiercely under her breath, *You are the one who owes us, Mother. You are a murderer, and the Garden will never let you pass.*

Yet the Servants who passed freely through the wards every day had pushed slaves to their deaths; how did that work? Unar had touched them with her magic to find out, and realised that just as the wards could be fooled by her insistence she was a seed, they could also be fooled by the magical sigils on the slaves' tongues into thinking that aged humans were discarded refuse, no more significant to the goddess than the used leaf-plates tossed away once they were emptied of porridge.

"I won't let her fall," Unar told Ylly, grimly.

Delve as she might with her magic, though, she could neither figure out how the sigils were made, nor how they might be removed. She would have to ask Oos.

# SIXTEEN

Unar stood at the woody water's edge.

There were no fish in this pool. These storage hollows, shaped in the clefts where the great branches of the tallowwood met the trunk, were the recipients of carved channels and leaf-nets designed to capture and divert as much rainwater from the lateral branches as possible. Underwater tunnels and tubes with various mechanisms inside them became frequently blocked by debris.

Sawas, submerged, was a darker brown shape against the brown bowl of water. It reflected the sky in some places, the smooth trunk and overhead Temple in others. The bastard child of an Odelland king popped her head out of the pool. She dumped two handfuls of soggy leaves on the edge, where they were swept up by another slave and taken away.

"So." Hasbabsah sat on a blanket with the sleeping baby, not far from the edge. "Why does the Warmed One wish to learn to swim?"

Unar shivered. She didn't wish to. Not really. She had no choice, if she was to grow in magical power.

"Hasbabsah!" Sawas said.

"It's all right," Unar said. "I'm not like them. I don't toss old women from treetops."

"I would like to see them try," Hasbabsah grumbled. "I would take that Servant Eilif down to the forest floor with me."

"Hasbabsah!"

"Down you go again, little duck. Let the Warmed One worry about me." When Sawas had obediently dived again, the old slave indicated the baby on the blanket. "This one is fourth generation."

"She's pretty," Unar said, keeping her distance. Babies didn't really interest her, except for their potential to house the souls of gods. Their screams were high-pitched enough to split heads, and they couldn't do or say anything interesting. A pet bear cub or a trained parrot was more entertaining. Isin had been different. Isin had been her own blood.

"She will never be a warrior," Hasbabsah said, "up here in Canopy."

Unar shrugged. "Can't you teach her what she needs to know?" She hadn't come to chat about the baby. She'd done her duty by it. Odel's protection lay over it. "She's got a good name, right? She'll be able to go both up and down."

It was a sop; baby Ylly was owned by the Garden, and even if someone tried to take her down, it was more likely she would stubbornly float, buoyed by the power of the god. Unar was trying to put a good face on the fact that names were the only inane influence slaves had over their children.

Sawas surfaced with another two handfuls of leaves and sticks. Her breasts, swollen with milk, bumped like clinked goblets on the surface while she pushed the little pile away from her.

"Only if her tongue carries the correct glyph," Hasbabsah muttered, and Unar realised she was thinking of her own demotion, and that she might never see the elder Ylly again.

"Are we talking about tongues, now?" Sawas asked with a sparkle in her eyes. "I heard it was the handsome new Gatekeeper who changed yours, Hasbabsah. I wish he'd give me a kiss and change mine."

"You have done enough harm by kissing, Sawas. Look at the child you unthinkingly brought into the world. Into a life of misery!"

"My life isn't misery." Sawas laughed. "What do you think of Servant Aoun, Warmed One?"

Unar felt the blood rush to her face.

"He was . . . is my friend," she said. "Are the marks on your tongues truly changed by kissing?"

"They can be, if the man is an adept. Perhaps one day he'll come to me. Sawas, he'll say, I cannot live without you! He'll kiss me and carry me up into the Garden proper. Perhaps Ylly will have a sister."

"No!" Hasbabsah raged.

"I think I know why the Warmed One wishes to swim. So she can swim across the moat and spy on the Gatekeeper without clothes on, while he's sleeping in the Temple. He has such fine, fleshy fruit. I would wake it with my marked tongue. I would take it between my thighs. It would reach so far up inside of me!"

"Sawas! One birthing was not enough to sting some sense into your empty head?"

Sawas turned lithely in the water and went under, bubbles of laughter trailing in her wake, while Unar stood, stock-still, trying not to picture Aoun's so-called fine, fleshy fruit. She didn't want to imagine it reaching up inside of her. It was indeed bigger than others she'd seen. She knew that, like monkey's parts, men's grew bigger in preparation for mating. That was a slightly stomach-turning thought. She had sworn to Audblayin not to try it, and she didn't want to try it.

A kiss, though. That would be safe. A kiss would break no oaths. Being held by Aoun might not be too much of a transgression, either. But Unar didn't serve the love goddess, Oxor. This was Audblayin's emergent.

"You spoke of Old Gods, Hasbabsah," Unar said. She hoped her voice sounded normal. She hoped the old slave, behind her, couldn't read her thoughts from her body language. Even if she had, who would she tell? Hasbabsah would never return to the upper levels of the Garden. It was a mean thought.

"I did speak of them, Warmed One."

"You mentioned their bones. When I stole those chimera cloths from the princess of Odelland, there were broken bones inside of them."

Unar had found more bits after she'd left the palace, and had shaken the old, yellowed fragments into the forest. They'd fallen quickly out of sight. Old bones weren't what she'd wanted to give to Odel as tribute. The chimera skin was the prize.

Or so she had thought.

"Chimera skin keeps its magic for many hundreds of years," Hasbabsah said quietly. "I know the cloths you speak of. I was there when my mistress hid them under the floor. The cloth shields magic-imbued objects from one another. She did not want them interfering with the bone-magic of the bed."

"The platform? That was bone? It was too big."

"It was a neck bone of the Old Gods."

"How could something so big be raised from Floor without any enemies noticing?"

"You are young. Understorians do not always raid Canopy. In hungry times, they trade. In prosperous times, they buy back captured slaves. That bed was once part of a Floorian place of worship. Understorians carried it up to Canopy, to purchase the lives of their loved ones."

Unar was astonished.

"I've never heard of slaves being bought back."

"These are not times of prosperity."

"You must have hoped. When you were first captured. You must have hoped they'd bring something like that floating bed and buy you back with it."

"I still hope it," Hasbabsah said.

The baby woke.

"Come, Sawas," Hasbabsah called as the young mother surfaced again. "It is feeding time for baby Ylly." She put her little finger into the baby's mouth to mollify it for a moment. "There are no spells to stop the menstrual cycles of slaves. The Garden can always use more hands. How convenient for them that we multiply."

# SEVENTEEN

THAT NIGHT, Unar climbed down to the pool for her first lesson.

It was different in darkness. She couldn't see its depths. Shapes she thought looked like fish in the moonlight were the long, shining leaves of neighbouring trees.

"Sawas?" she whispered as loudly as she dared.

Streams of dirty wash water falling from the edges of the Garden splashed into hollows that were lined with the purifying pith of fiveways fruit. The pith strained and sweetened the water before it joined the main pool. Unar paced along the path. Somewhere below her, a baby cried.

The slaves slept in small hollows in the branches. Some of them would have smoke holes bored through to the branch-top paths, but Unar couldn't smell any smoke. It was a mild winter and a still evening.

"Sawas," she whispered again.

"I'm here, Warmed One," Sawas said cheerfully, scrambling up from underneath onto the path. "Let's go to the pool."

She had something like a wooden turtle shell on her back. When they reached the water, where an Airak-lit brazier was reflected, blue-white and blazing, Unar saw that the shell was a shallow, smooth, baby's sleeping-bowl, one that could be rocked with a foot to settle a bundled child. Sawas set her clothes beside it.

"Are you cold?" Sawas asked. "Are you going to swim with your clothes on? They won't keep you warm, and they'll grow heavy. It's dangerous."

"Aren't you going to show me some swimming movements first? Can't I practice the movements? Build the correct muscles?"

"You can't build the correct muscles without the resistance of the water."

Unar took her clothes off. There was nobody to see her but Sawas. Had Aoun looked at her, the day she'd woken in the Temple? Or on the day of Audblayin's death? Or had he only looked forward, towards the Temple? She should've only looked at the Temple, too. Maybe then she'd be a Servant, like him.

"Hold the bowl with both hands," Sawas said. "It floats. It'll hold you up. Don't let go. The first action you must practice is kicking. Don't use your magic."

Unar's skin crawled as she slid into the cool water. She gritted her teeth to stop from reaching for the power and found that her body did float without it, after a fashion; feet deep down and flailing, her back bent and her eyes upwards, clutching the wooden bowl to her chest.

"Your teeth are chattering," Sawas observed, laughing. "You must be cold. Look what happens to you, away from sunlight. Gardeners must be a little bit like lizards. You can only move about in the heat of the day."

"It's nothing like that," Unar said. "I feel like I'm falling!"

Sawas swam around her in circles.

"Everybody is falling," she said. "Everybody grows old and dies and is born again. The water will catch you. The water will hold you up."

Unar waited. She floated. The fear ebbed from her.

"I don't like fish," she said at last, to break the silence.

"I've never tasted one," Sawas replied.

# EIGHTEEN

IN THE morning, Unar had barely started work when Ylly flew out of no-where at her.

"They've taken her away to sell," Ylly sobbed, her arms wrapped around Unar's knees. "Sawas and the baby. They must have seen you. She's being punished because of you!"

"Quiet, slave!" Unar hissed, in case anyone was close by, but a quick flick of her magic showed they were alone by the watercress beds. "Nobody saw me with Sawas, Ylly."

Ylly's whole body quaked.

"Hasbabsah sent me a bird with a message. At daybreak, a Servant went below to grow a new room in Sawas's hollow. A separate sleeping room for the baby. Sawas and the Servant spoke. Hasbabsah couldn't overhear them. But then the Servant took Sawas and baby Ylly away, out of the Garden, in the direction of the market. Where else could they be going?"

"Maybe the Servant needed a slave to carry her basket?"

"Then why take the baby?"

Ylly was frantic. Unar didn't know what to say to calm her. Her magic warned her that others were coming.

"Don't shake me," she said. "If anybody sees you, they'll sell you as well. Listen, you said that Hasbabsah couldn't be sold because she knew the secrets of the Garden. Doesn't Sawas know any secrets?"

"No! She's always stayed below!" Ylly released Unar and crumpled to the earth, burying her face in her hands.

"I'll find out what's happening," Unar said in a low voice. "Oos will tell me. My friend. You remember her. She's a Servant, now."

Ylly shook her head.

"Your friend," she repeated huskily, hopelessly, "she was the Servant who took my daughter and granddaughter away. Oos, the vizier's daughter."

Unar grunted. Had Oos been sent on some grim errand to prove her loyalty to Servant Eilif? Or had she thoughtlessly gone to buy glass goblets, jewelled shoes, or other fineries she'd grown accustomed to having in her father's home, enjoying the freedom she had as a Servant that had been denied her as a Gardener? Not that Oos had wanted to leave the Garden, since passing through the Gates.

"How old is this news?" she asked.

"Three hours, by the water clock. Hasbabsah had to find chalk and paperbark. She had to steal grain to entice the messenger bird to come."

"Come with me."

Unar went to the Gate. Ylly followed. The market wasn't far from the Garden. If Oos had gone there, she'd be back soon; Unar bit her lip and gazed at the open archway with the beautiful carved doors thrown back, wondering if she dared leave the Garden in broad daylight.

She'd almost been a slave. Her parents had all but agreed to sell her. The Garden had saved her. It was her home and her shelter. She wouldn't risk being expelled for the sake of a rescue mission that might be completely unnecessary. Not when she had so much to learn, and more to accomplish.

Before Unar could decide on anything drastic, Oos returned, alone, along the steep path up to the Garden Gate. Ylly, rocking on her heels at Unar's side, stiffened at the sight of her but said nothing.

"Unar," Oos said breathlessly, ignoring the crouching slave. "Were you waiting for me?"

"Yes, I was," Unar said, relieved to see Oos pass easily through the wards. Oos had neither stolen, raped, nor killed. Nothing bad could have happened to Sawas. She'd be along, soon, carrying some bought trinket or other. "Where have you been?"

Oos seemed taken aback.

"One who walks in the grace of Audblayin has been to the home of the weaver, Epatut. It grows cooler at night, and the Temple was in need of some new blankets. I took two slaves from the low levels for the trade. They weren't needed here. They're with Wife-of-Epatut, now. She's pregnant again, by the grace of Audblayin, and wanted a wet nurse in waiting."

Unar couldn't bring herself to look at Ylly.

"It has been cooler at night," Unar repeated stupidly.

"I don't need you now, slave," Oos told Ylly. "I'll walk alone with this Gardener."

When Ylly had gone, Oos seized Unar's hand and dragged her into the green shade of the ferns, where they were concealed by a profusion of new fronds.

"What are you doing, Unar?"

"What do you mean?"

"That slave girl, Sawas, came to me this morning. She said you were learning to swim. She said you wanted to sneak into the Temple and make babies with Aoun. You aren't loyal to the Temple, she said, but she offered to report everything you did to Servant Eilif, if only she would be allowed to keep her child with her until it was of age, instead of being at the mercy of the Garden's needs. I had to get rid of her and the child before she could tell anyone else!"

"I don't want to make babies with Aoun!"

"Is that all you have to say? Have you been learning to swim?"

"Just one lesson, Oos. I'm trying to conquer my weaknesses. You know I'm afraid of the water!"

"Don't you have enough work to do?"

"Don't speak to me like I'm a slave. I lied for you, when you made music in the loquat grove. I hid your bells under the avocado tree so you wouldn't be cast out of the Garden."

"And now I've sold two slaves for you."

"She was lying about me," Unar spat, eye to eye with Oos.

"Are your oaths unbound, Unar?"

"No!"

"I think they might be. I think when you went into Understorey, something happened—"

"Nothing happened! I love the Garden. I'm loyal to it. Don't you believe me? Don't you know me at all? If my oaths are unbound, why haven't I bled?"

"Haven't you?"

"I should hate you for that," Unar said, but she knew she couldn't hate Oos, not really.

Ylly's hatred would surely be enough for both of them.

# NINETEEN

ON THE first day of spring, word reached the Garden that Wife-of-Epatut's child was lost.

Ylly no longer spoke at all to Unar, even though they worked together every night by the light of the moon or stars. No longer required as a child-minder, Hasbabsah had been returned to the Garden proper, where she was, as before, physically incapable of doing the work she was assigned. Though Ylly clearly despised Unar, blaming her for the loss of her daughter, Unar fell again into the routine of helping to hide Hasbabsah's weakness in order to keep her alive.

Unar couldn't help but overhear the Gardeners' gossip at mealtimes. Soon after the miscarriage, Wife-of-Epatut came again to be blessed. It was late in the afternoon. She didn't bring Sawas with her to carry her tribute; she carried it alone.

It was a basket of metal-stone fruit from Akkadland. The fruit goddess could cause the great trees to draw up metal through their mighty roots and form it into seed-shaped ingots at the heart of her emergent's stringy, yellow fruit. It was a power that Audblayin didn't have, even during her incarnation's prime of life.

"I must have a son this time," Wife-of-Epatut said to Unar, who had sensed her coming and met her at the Gate. "Please, Gardener. Lead me to the Temple."

Unar tried to take the basket, but Wife-of-Epatut resisted.

"I must carry the offering," she said. "I must show my humility to Audblayin. I couldn't carry the last child that she gave to me. The fault must be mine."

She was a wide-built woman with an unblemished brow, colourful silks woven into her hair to advertise her trade, and a bosom that caused the front of her gown to fall a foot-length in front of the rest of her body.

"It's not your fault," Unar said. She tried to think of a way to ask about Sawas, about baby Ylly, but Wife-of-Epatut's protuberant, pain-filled, expectant eyes, turned in the direction of the Temple, and she began to lead the way towards the shallow ford where penitents crossed the fish-filled moat.

Unar glared at the water that she wasn't allowed to trespass through as Wife-of-Epatut waded awkwardly onward, struggling under the weight of the basket. Aoun came out of the egg-shaped Temple to meet her. He looked even taller than the last time Unar had seen him, and there was two days' growth along his jaw as though he'd been too busy with his new and very important training to take the time to shave.

Wife-of-Epatut allowed him to take the basket.

As night fell, Unar stayed standing by the ford. She should have retreated to the loquat grove, but she didn't care about being reprimanded. Aoun emerged, carrying his Gatekeeper's lantern. He walked across the surface of the water without sinking, his magic more luminous than the lantern. Unar hadn't seen any of the Servants do such a thing before. His sandals were dry.

"Go to bed, Gardener," he said wearily.

She fell in beside him.

"Have you helped her?" Unar wanted to know. "Have you guaranteed a son to her, who dropped one daughter and miscarried another?"

"We've done nothing yet. Wife-of-Epatut gives tribute. She prays to Audblayin."

"Where is Audblayin?"

"It doesn't matter where. She hears our prayers."

"He hears them, you mean. He hears them, even though he's a scream-ing infant. That's ridiculous. We both know he hears nothing until he comes of age."

"What do you want, Unar?"

"Show me what you're going to do to Wife-of-Epatut. How is it that you make a woman more fertile? Is it the same as plants? How is it that you choose the baby's sex?"

"That's for Servants to know."

Unar shot a sideways glance at him as they walked, but his expression was blank. She couldn't tell if his word choice reflected her rudeness to Oos in the grass plot.

"Unless somebody pushes Servant Eilif off the edge of the Garden, I will never be a Servant!"

"Is that something you have considered? Pushing Servant Eilif off the edge of the Garden?"

"Of course not."

He hesitated within arm's reach of the Gate. "Go to bed, Unar. Go on."

She left him, fuming, but she didn't go to bed. Instead, she crept back to her old listening post in the pomegranate bushes, directly across the moat from the treatment room where Oos had once cured her tiredness.

There were voices. Wife-of-Epatut's voice. The words were indiscernible, but the sounds drifted out of the round, open windows in the white egg of the Temple.

Unar stripped off her robe, leaving her loincloth and her breast-bindings in place. She was too angry to care about fish or drowning. She was going to see, at last, the Servants' way. She would be tutored whether her tutors wanted her or not.

The water was icy, as it hadn't been during daylight. So high, and exposed to winds that normally broke against the green roof of Canopy, it was probably the coldest water in all the land; it was rumoured to have frozen, once, many centuries ago, when Audblayin had fallen to Floor but not been killed, so that he was the farthest he could be from the Temple and not have his spirit returned to a body that was closer.

Unar tried to think of a seed in warm earth. It was spring, after all. She convinced her body that it wasn't cold. Using a fraction of her magic, she summoned a raft of watercress to hold on to and floated across, not high and dry as Aoun had done, but neck-deep and gasping.

When she reached the little island, she crouched on the tiny ledge of rotted leaves under the window, arms around her knees, shivering and listening.

"I'm so afraid, Servant Eilif," Wife-of-Epatut said. "And I'm tired of being afraid of my husband's wrath. But if this doesn't work, I don't think I could bear to try again."

"It will work," Eilif said comfortingly. "Lie down, please."

There were sounds of clothes being shifted and feet shuffling. Unar forced her frigid body to uncurl. She had to look through the window if she was to see with eyes of power the procedure that Eilif was about to perform.

When she peered over the edge of the open window, Eilif stood there, waiting calmly. Her eyes met Unar's. Her hood and cloak blocked Unar's view of anyone else in the room.

Unar's rage died. She felt like crying, again.

"Wait only a moment, Wife-of-Epatut," Eilif said without turning. Without blinking. "My assistants must see to a troublesome weed that is growing by this window. Go."

The unseen assistants left the room, but Unar knew who they were even before she saw them wading in the muck, one hand each on the outer wall of the Temple, the other holding their robes away from the rotted leaves that their sandals sank into. She thought about running away from them, but it would only have postponed her punishment.

"Oh, Unar," Oos said, lip trembling in the light that came from the window.

Aoun said nothing.

They slung her arms over their shoulders so that she was between them. It seemed like a group embrace until their combined magic groped around inside of her, seized hers like a weed, and pulled it out by the roots.

Unar did cry, then. She had no strength to speak or to stand. Those she had once called friends supported her weight between them. They walked across the moat without sinking, carrying her all the way to the loquat grove, and laid her down in her hammock. The lorikeets roused, but none of the other Gardeners so much as raised their heads.

She was still crying long after they left her alone.

# TWENTY

Blossoms rained on Unar's bent back that spring.

As the season drew to a close, the first stirring of her magic sprouted up again. She'd spent those months on her knees, weeding the orchid garden, and the sensation was strange enough for her to cradle her midriff, mouth open in surprise and relief. She had wondered if it would ever return, so deep and dark had the empty places seemed.

There was nobody for her to share her excitement with. Nobody to tell. As the weather warmed, Ylly still accepted her help in silence. The other Gardeners had given up trying to get to know her, both in response to her brusqueness and in the full knowledge that she had been drained as punishment for trying to spy on Temple proceedings.

It was just enough magic for her to unlock the Gate.

For the first time in a long time, Unar left the Garden.

Her first thought was to find the House of Epatut, to check that Sawas and baby Ylly weren't being ill-used. Maybe if she brought news of them to old Ylly, she'd be forgiven.

But she didn't know where it was, and she didn't want to draw attention to herself by asking for directions from strangers. Her second thought was to practice swimming by herself. She couldn't do it in the moat, and she couldn't do it in the Garden pools without the slaves seeing.

Ehkisland. The home of the rain goddess received more rain than any other part of Canopy. There were hundreds of pools, claimed by no one.

Unar crossed the border at the Falling Fig.

She found a suitably desolate pool just as a light rain began to fall. It wasn't quite yet time for the summer monsoon, but many dry-season shops and dwellings had been shuttered in anticipation. Some of the drizzle penetrated past the leafy roof over the pool, but most collected on the leaves and fell, slightly delayed, as fat drips, heavy with dust and dead insects.

Very little light came down from the high paths lit by the lightning god, but it was enough that Unar could see the complex and hypnotising patterns formed by the drops. Tiny fish and frogs came to eat the dead insects. Unar made herself look at them with determination.

Eilif had sensed her approach because of her magic. She must learn to swim without it. She was not beaten, would never be beaten.

Unar disrobed, keeping her loincloth and breast bindings as before. She put her toe in the water.

"She's not in that one," an oddly familiar voice said.

Without her magic and without proximity to the Garden, people could creep up on her unawares, but this man, she suspected, could creep up on anyone he wanted to. She looked up and around for him but didn't withdraw her toe.

"It's you," she said steadily. "Edax. The Bodyguard who doesn't sleep."

He walked, upside down, along the underside of a branch too small to form a safe path in its own right. Talons didn't need to dig into the bark. In his own niche, he walked where he wanted. His long black hair hung like moss. The tear-scores on his cheeks bunched as he smiled, turning his brown skin to polished tigereye.

Upside down, the effect of his bared teeth was gruesome.

"It's you," he said. "The little Gardener who wanders away from safe places."

"Doesn't the blood rush to your head?"

"No. This is part of my gift from the goddess. There is no up or down underwater."

"Can you fly, then?"

"Oh, no. I may be owl-footed, but I have no wings. Flying is for the Bodyguard of Orin, Queen of Birds, and the Bodyguard of Audblayin, Waker of Senses."

"I never saw him fly," Unar said scornfully. "Probably because he was too fat."

"Was he fat, then?"

"Oh, yes."

Edax laughed in his low, rich voice. He was much older than Aoun and his face more expressive. His nose was sharper, his cheekbones were more prominent, and he had a shorter, squarer jaw. When he walked to the tree trunk, set his bare bird-foot against it, and pressed, hard, as though realigning himself horizontally, the weapons at his belt and over his shoulders swung vertical, popping out of his clothes like uncurling creepers.

He strode down the trunk, set himself upright on the path beside her and approached with interest. She tried not to look at his feet. They were the only part of him she didn't like, because girls should not be attracted to birds, but the rest of him was so attractive.

"What are you searching for in the bottom of the pool, Gardener? More new life on the brink of death?"

"Who says I'm searching for anything?"

"Many things fall in. Heavy things. Valuable things. Coins. Jewels. Very few can dive deep enough to find them."

"I'm not diving for treasure. I'm learning to swim."

"Where's your teacher?"

Unar started to say that she had none, but then her mood darkened.

"They took her away from me," she said. "She was a slave."

"I can teach you."

"I'm not allowed to learn the powers of other goddesses and gods."

"It's not magic." He put his warm hand on her bare shoulder and stroked down her spine. "It's only movement. A thrilling kind of movement. A secret kind."

Unar grew heated at his touch, in the place, low in her belly, where her magic should have been; she met his laughing eyes and wondered if he was still talking about swimming. She wanted to learn from him but felt too much at a disadvantage here, in Ehkisland, where his powers worked but hers didn't.

"If it's not magic," she said, "you can teach me in Understorey."

"There's a pool close by the barrier," he said without hesitation. "These final few weeks of spring are weeks of relative safety. When the monsoon begins and rivers run down the great trees, the enemy warriors of Understorey are confined to their dwellings. They'll already be confined, in anticipation. But we couldn't stay there for very long at one time, or we'd risk being barred from Canopy forever."

"Would you miss your goddess so very much?"

"She'd miss me. Three men tried to drown her today."

"Did they?" Unar turned so his hand fell away from her lower back. She'd liked having it there. Oos must be right about her oaths. If they hadn't broken by now, when she went with Edax below the barrier again, they would surely tear in two. She'd crack like an egg full of blood.

"I needed only to keep the men under," he said, "after they realised she couldn't be drowned. They tried to let go of her. To give up their attempted murder. I pulled them down and fixed them by their foot bones to the bottom, next to all the others who have tried to harm her. Their finger bones wave in the current like water-weeds."

"They do?" Unar was fascinated. "In which pool?"

"Not this one," Edax said. "In the great fig-pool where my goddess dreams. In Ehkis's emergent, the Temple of the Bringer of Rain. But that's not where we'll go."

# TWENTY-ONE

"I can't help you work tonight, Ylly," Unar said, two weeks later.

She had to shout to be heard over the roaring wind and rumbling of the storm. This wild night belonged to Ehkis and to Airak. The monsoon was very close. The Gardeners wouldn't know for sure until the storm broke. If the rain stopped when morning came, then this storm was but a precursor, and the true storm was still to come. If it didn't stop after a day, they could be almost certain it would continue for five months. Unar didn't even bother to try to stay dry. She'd left her sandals behind at her hammock, along with her waterproof leaf-jacket. It didn't matter. The driving rain was blood-warm.

Ylly said nothing. She'd said nothing since the day Sawas was taken away from the Garden. Unar pressed her seed porridge portion into the older woman's hands.

"Take my supper. You're losing weight. I'll help you again tomorrow."

Ylly took the porridge and turned away.

Unar dashed across the bridge, not worried about being seen. Who but Ylly would be out in this weather? She went to the Gate, locked hours before, and early, by Aoun, and pushed it open a body's width, boring a hole through the lock with her magic and sealing it again behind her with the rich scent of thirsty soil thick in her nostrils.

The water above her, below her, to both sides of her, made her feel like raising her arms, winglike, and swimming through the air. She laughed with the joy of it as she flitted over the slippery, winding paths towards Ehkis-land.

When she came to the lowest branch over the Understorian border, with the pool she and Edax practiced in yawning black and tantalising below, she laid her wet red tunic and green trousers over the peeling bark and stretched her arms above her head.

"Wait for me, Audblayin," she said. "Keep your gifts until my return."

She dived smoothly, several body lengths, down into the pool. Somewhere in midair, she lost her magic, but she was used to that sensation now. It would be there when she came back up to get her clothes.

Thunder seemed to shake the great trees. The myrtle pool quivered, hissing where rain sheeted into it. Unar swam confidently to the edge. She hardly needed Edax now. Only there was something about his gaze on her, about his wiry arms and clever fingers, that drew her back again.

She climbed out of the pool, stood in the warm rain, and waited for him.

For the longest time, he didn't come. A twinge of worry twisted her gut. Had an attempt on the goddess killed Edax instead? Perhaps he'd forgotten this night was a lesson night.

Hands landed lightly on the wet crown of her head, and she looked up, getting rain in her eyes. Edax hung from a branch by his talons, above and behind her. When she turned to him, their lips were level. His hands were at the back of her head now, pressing her forward, so that their mouths met.

She was glad to close her eyes; she couldn't get used to the sight of his upside-down smile. The kiss electrified her, as if she had sworn herself to the lightning god. Like her powers, her oaths had been left behind in Canopy.

He had kissed her before, but this time he didn't stop. Edax lowered himself slowly, sliding down her body like a viper; he kissed her chin and her throat. He unbound her breasts and kissed them, and Unar's stomach plunged as though she was in free fall, diving, a thing she had been afraid of, once, but now thrilled to do.

Her knees felt weak, but to kneel would be to put herself out of reach of his lips. He slid down further, his tongue leaving imprints down her belly, and without removing her loincloth, he encircled her hips with his arms and pressed his face between her shivering thighs.

Unar looked up and saw the deep cuts he'd made in the branch with his unnatural feet. Without the goddess in him, blood must be rushing to his head as it hadn't in Ehkis's realm, but she couldn't think of that; his clever fingers had found their way inside her final wrappings, found it hot and wet as the rain.

She clung to him to keep from collapsing and pulled some leather binding loose by accident. Were his weapons slipping? She didn't want him to lose them. Abruptly, there was his manhood, at the level of her eyes, shockingly engorged, at once ridiculous and mesmerising. Had she been afraid of such a thing?

His feet couldn't hold their combined weight. He lost his grip. They fell into the pool. Unar hadn't had a chance to take a proper breath and water filled her nose. She remembered not to scream; she had screamed underwater in the moat at the Temple, where Oos's magic had saved her.

There was no magic here.

Edax hauled her out of the water. Fingers that had probed her private places now cleared her mouth of her own myrtle-leaf-garlanded hair.

"Are you hurt?" he shouted.

"No!" she managed in return.

He kissed her again, the right way up this time.

"And your oaths? Little Gardener, do you wish to keep them?"

"No," Unar said. She closed her eyes. Not to block the view of his sensuous mouth, when he stood the right way up, but so she could pretend he was Aoun, who would die before breaking those oaths his ignorant childself had made long ago.

# TWENTY-TWO

RAIN, WIND, and thunder still assaulted the Garden upon Unar's return.

Her fingers slipped on the streaming Gate carvings.

*Have you stolen food?* the wards whispered. *Have you stolen the sovereignty of another's body? Have you stolen human life?*

"No!" Unar gasped as she reached the top of the Garden wall. Her ankle caught on one of the carved fruits, and she tumbled instead of sliding, turning her shoulder to take the impact of the ground—only it wasn't the ground that she fell on.

It was a shape, warm, white-robed, well-wrapped, and twice the size of her, smelling of eggshell and lantern oil, burnt wick and wet soil. Unar knew she smelled of sex; impulsively she wanted Aoun to smell it on her—taste it, even.

"Gatekeeper," she said as they struggled to stand, and when he bent to peer into her face, she put her tongue in his mouth.

His body straightened, and he thrust her away, holding her at arm's length.

"Only another adept could do this to you," he breathed. "Break your bonds this way. Who was it? I'll kill them."

"You did it to me, Aoun. Come closer. Keep doing it."

He let go of her completely, backing away.

"Iririn woke and saw your hammock left behind in the loquat grove. Everyone else had moved theirs to the monsoon pavilion to stay dry. She was terrified for you. She thought you must have fallen from a bridge or an edge in the storm. It never occurred to her that you might have left the Garden to meet men."

"Audblayin's bones, who is Iririn?"

"Your fellow Gardener."

"The one who shaves her head?" Unar's fists went to her hips.

"Yes."

"She should mind her own business."

"Are you drunk? Injured?"

"No."

"While Iririn and I searched the Garden for you, we found a slave woman working. Washing clothes in the dark. She said you had given the order. Did you?"

"Of course I did," Unar started to say, but Aoun had put one of his great bear paws to her throat; his hand was huge enough to almost encircle it. Her eyes went wide, and she began to pry at his fingers, even as some magic-working of his inside her chest distracted her. Time ran backwards for a moment; Aoun was forcing her to relive the emotions of the past night, out of order; a sensuous surge went through her as the working brought strongly back to her what she had done with Edax; and then she was feeling pity for Ylly, warm fingers touching cold as she handed over the seed porridge.

No, they weren't her own warm fingers she was feeling, but Aoun's, his hand turning over the soil where her memory-seeds were buried.

"Did you order the slave to wash clothes after dark?"

"No," Unar said immediately, against her will. "Her name is Ylly. She's friends with another slave, Hasbabsah, who's too old to do the work that's given to her. Ylly and I do Hasbabsah's work after nightfall so that Servant Eilif won't throw her down."

Aoun let go of her throat. The magical structure that he had grown in her shrivelled instantly and died. Unar wrapped her arms around herself, no longer aroused, incredulous at what he'd done.

"The Garden will spit you out, Aoun!" she screamed. "You have stolen the sovereignty of my body!"

"In the service of the Garden," he insisted, staring at his palm as though it was someone else's, sounding as shaken as she was. "It is allowed."

"Like killing slaves is allowed? You could have been a slave! I was almost a slave! Would you throw me down if I couldn't work? Is that what you are for?"

There was nothing but the sound of the rain and wind for a long time. Aoun put his right hand through his hair; it settled at last on his left shoulder, trembling. Unar put her back against the Gates, squeezing herself tighter and tighter. Her floating high, the giddy sensations elicited by Edax, had turned to horror and the spectre of death.

"It is the way of the Garden," Aoun said at last, helplessly. "Old growth is cut away to make room for the new. I must tell Servant Eilif in the morning."

Unar ran from him. He didn't follow.

If Hasbabsah was to die in the morning, Unar couldn't wait that long. Sunrise was mere hours away.

Suddenly, she felt tired. Too tired to do what had to be done. Hasbabsah had been given extra days. It was enough, wasn't it? The deception was over, now. The inevitable was coming.

Unar imagined the old woman falling and increased her speed.

"Ylly," she crowed by the door to the wet-weather slave quarters.

It was Hasbabsah who hobbled through the insecticidal smoke that screened the door. Her hair was awry, and her eyes were bloodshot.

"Ylly is sleeping."

"But not you? Has the Gatekeeper been here?"

"The storm makes my bones ache; that is why I am awake."

"Wake Ylly. Tell her to gather all her things, and you must gather all yours. We're leaving the Garden, right now. The Gatekeeper knows we've been doing your work."

Shame heated Unar's cheeks, but in the darkness of the storm, nobody could see them.

"And how can we leave the Garden, Warmed One? Our tongues are marked."

"Maybe you can't cross the wall, tread the walkways, or climb the ladders. Maybe you can't pass through the Gate. But your marked tongue won't hold you up when Eilif pushes you off the edge, will it? We'll go straight down. The wards are weakest that way."

"You do not know what you are doing, do you?"

"Has Ylly lied to me all this time? Isn't your life at stake? Hasn't concealing your infirmity been crucial?"

Hasbabsah sighed, a long sigh. "It has been crucial, Warmed One."

"Then go, get her. I'll be back very soon."

Unar didn't go to the kitchens to steal. There might have been people there. She raided the trees and bushes she'd tended for the past four years. Bent, oozing sugarcanes made a frame for a nest of watercress, which cradled a late clutch of flowerfowl eggs. Unar stuffed the wrung-necked mother down on top of the eggs, her downy corpse still keeping the eggs warm. Limes the length and shape of fingers came next, with a layer of beans to follow, and a few handfuls of magenta cherries for good measure.

Instead of stealing ropes, Unar let herself down by a single-handed grip beneath the wattle-grove garden to strip bark-ropes from the great tallow-wood tree itself. She paused to roll the ropes under a roof of sodden wattle-flowers; the blooms sagged on the ends of their branches like new-hatched yellow chicks with their fluff still stuck to their skin.

She didn't dare go to her hammock in the monsoon pavilion for her meticulously maintained bore-knife and machete, but took blunter, cruder ones from the tool cache in the prison-tree outside the loquat grove.

"I'm not leaving you," she whispered to the Garden. "You are mine, and I am yours. We'll simply be apart for a little while."

She returned to the slave quarters. Ylly and Hasbabsah stood just outside it, shod and loaded with soggy blankets. They would need them, if they were to survive the monsoon away from the Garden. When distant lightning struck and Unar could finally see them properly, they were blanched with fear.

"The waterfall," Unar said. "Where we washed the clothes, Ylly."

They set off for it as quickly and quietly as they could, though Hasbabsah missed her footing on the bridges and had to be carried between them. It reminded Unar of the time Oos and Aoun had taken her between them. Her lips drew back from her teeth; she wouldn't allow them to punish her this time.

She wouldn't let herself fall into their hands. Not until Ylly and Hasbabsah were beyond Audblayin's reach, and perhaps not even then. Unar was too learned, too powerful for them to touch her. If she had to learn from other Bodyguards, spy on different goddesses or gods, so be it. Edax knew her, inside and out, now. He'd help her. And the god Odel had been kind to her.

With the bark-ropes, she secured her own belt to Ylly's and to Hasbabsah's, just to be sure she wouldn't lose them. She left several paces of rope between them, so that they each had room to move.

"Take my hands," Unar said as they prepared to drop into the pool far below. It wasn't as deep as the one in Understorey. Unar would have to use her modestly regrown shoot of magic to cushion them from the bottom and perhaps to raise them to the surface again.

Hopefully, no Servants would be awake to sense it.

They jumped.

# PART II

*Wet Season*

# TWENTY-THREE

Unar fell, a glass bead in the darkness with all the other beads of rain.

But this was not the small, safe fall she'd taken so many times with Edax.

Water caught whatever tiny fragments of light it could. Yellow light from the lanterns of the Garden. Blue light from the lanterns of Airak on the roads of Audblayinland. Light bounced from their wet, flailing arms and legs. Reflected light showed Unar a faint mirror of her feet as they approached the surface of the pool. She was slightly ahead of the others, having jumped a moment before them, and the rope between her waist and Ylly's was taut.

The splash blinded and deafened her. She tried to swim upwards, but the rope, which had held her up, now kept her down. Then it came level. Unar's head broke the surface of the water at the same time as Ylly's. They gasped into each other's faces. Ylly seemed to have trouble breathing; perhaps she'd swallowed some water. It had happened to Unar often enough.

Without words, they struck out for the side of the pool; Unar's feet found a carved ramp close to the end of the screw pump.

Together, Unar and Ylly dragged Hasbabsah out of the pool.

The old woman was clawing at her mouth and bawling. Only then did Unar see blood on Ylly's lips and realise why she was having trouble breathing; the blood was black in the blue light.

"Your slave-markings," she said.

"If you would return us to Understorey," Ylly said around her swollen tongue, "you must do it soon, before we choke in our own blood. There's no path from this level. The ladders will turn to dust if we touch them. You must go up, and pull us by the ropes after you, or we must find a way down."

From above Unar came Oos's impassioned voice. "Go back up, Unar. You must go back up. The ladders will obey me. They will hold you. All of you. Go back up."

*Impossible,* Unar thought, flabbergasted to be intercepted by a once-friend who should have been sleeping soundly in the egg-shaped Temple. Oos stepped out from behind an angled leaf-catcher, white robe sodden, beautiful and shivering and, to Unar's eyes, tortured by the wrong she was complicit in.

"Change their markings, Oos," Unar cried. "Remove them. Help them. The old woman can't breathe."

"Aoun knew you'd try to take them, even though it's not in your power. That's why he woke me. He couldn't watch the Gate and this pool at the same time. He wasn't sure which one you'd try."

"Help us, Oos!"

"I am a Servant of Audblayin!"

"I thought you'd say that."

"What do you want me to say?"

Unar moved closer to Oos as they spoke. Ylly and Hasbabsah, still roped to her, had no choice but to stagger after. Unar looked below the leaf-catcher. There, a new-formed river ran between ridges of tough, hairy, orange-tan bark, down the mighty trunk of the tallowwood tree. It would flow until the rain stopped, five months later at the end of the monsoon season.

"Nothing," Unar said. "Don't say anything. Just take a deep breath."

"A deep breath?"

Unar launched her full weight at Oos, carrying them both into the vertical river. Resistance from the twin bark-ropes jerked her back momentarily before Ylly and Hasbabsah were dragged with her over the edge.

They fell for a minute or two. Audblayin's magic ripped away from Unar's insides as they breached the border of Canopy.

Unar clung to Oos, hoping for a pool; waiting for a pool. When they'd fallen for so long that the light of the Temple and surrounding city was lost from sight and demons howled in the dark, she knew they were going to die.

She'd made a mistake. There were no pools. There were no lateral branches in lightless Understorey. Only the straight trunks of the great trees, separated by hundreds of body lengths.

All four of them would smash to pieces when the river reached Floor.

# TWENTY-FOUR

UNAR PLUNGED down with the river, lungs bursting, still gripping Oos around the waist with both arms.

*I'm going to drown before I can smash to pieces.*

But then her legs were bending up behind her head. Bodies pushed into hers. Something had caught them, was stretching with the weight of them.

*A net.*

Unar heard the cracking of the wooden pegs that held it in place. She felt fish flopping around her face. It was a fishnet. There was air. She could breathe it. She shouted with outrage at the fish-slime on her face and with relief at being alive.

Then the pegs gave way, a hidden lever was sprung, and the net leaped up into open air to one side of the river, holding its struggling, tangled, retching occupants in empty space where predators couldn't poach the fish.

"What have you done?" Oos croaked, somewhere above Unar. "You've killed us all."

"Be still," Hasbabsah snapped. "This is a grass net for barkskippers. If you break it, we truly will die."

"The marking on my tongue is gone," Ylly said with wonder. "The pain and the blood, at least. If we'd known that all we had to do was drop down beyond the barrier, we would have gone decades ago."

"Mine still bleeds," Hasbabsah said. "But then, I have worn it longer. And we could not have known there would be people living here. Understorian towns do not normally lie below the most populated parts of Canopian niches, lest the water be polluted and the turds fall like rain."

They hung, and spun, growing gradually still.

"What is the net attached to, Hasbabsah?" Unar asked.

"Probably a plank inserted into the bark of the tree. One of us should climb up to it, check that it is secure, and then pull the others up, one at a time."

"Oos is on top," Unar said.

"You're the stronger climber, Warmed . . . Unar," Ylly said.

Silence. Ylly had never been free, yet she had eagerly and instantly grasped their alterations in status.

Unar shivered. Silence, and the darkness, were much deeper here than they had been on any of her forays into Understorey. Of course. She was much, much further down this time. The air was heavier. Mustier. It held more murky memories. The smells of fish and mud, human sweat, wet bark, rot, and crushed fungi were less separable.

"Let me untie the bark-ropes," Unar said.

"Will you let a slave tell you what to do?" Oos demanded.

"They aren't slaves here, Oos. This is their home. Their markings are gone. We're their guests."

"Mine is not gone," Hasbabsah grumbled.

"Guests?" Oos protested. "I see neither hearths nor homes!"

"My home was in Nessa," Hasbabsah said. "It lies below the edge of Odel-land. But there can be no leaping between trunks in the monsoon. No crossings from tree to tree, and we cannot stay here for a hundred and fifty days and nights. It may be we will have no choice but to try to return to the Temple."

"I think there are enough fish here for us to eat for a hundred and fifty days and nights," Unar said, shrugging to get them away from her neck as her fingers struggled with knots made impossible to untie by the great strain they'd been under. "Be still, everyone. I need to take out my bore-knife. I don't want to cut the net by accident."

Everybody went limp and silent again, except for the barkskippers, who plipped, plopped, and flopped desperately. Unar strove to ignore the feel of the fish; it was so dark she couldn't even see what colour they were. She used her bore-knife to slit the knots by touch and managed to resheathe it without cutting herself.

"Oos, we need to change places."

"Yes, why not?" Oos answered sharply. "It's what you've been trying to do ever since I was chosen to be a Servant and you were not."

They struggled, crushed together, to turn over, as if they were a single body. Finally, Unar wrestled Oos underneath her. She scrambled upwards, stepping on already-bruised arms and legs, towards the top of the net.

"I may have to cut it," she said.

"There should be a solid ring of metal at the top," Hasbabsah said.

When Unar found it, it was barely the circumference of her hips. She had to breathe out to wriggle through it, and then she was glad for the blackness as her toes rested on the ring. She couldn't feel dizzy with no indication of the distance to fall.

She could hardly fear for the fate of the net when she couldn't see how sturdily it was woven. The rope was rough in the palms of her hands. Difficult to climb without magic. There were no knots in it.

"Audblayin keep me," she murmured.

"Don't you speak her name!" Oos shouted furiously.

"His name," Unar said.

She drew herself slowly and steadily upwards.

Before long, the burn in her muscles turned to warnings; her grip would fail fairly soon. She was light, but the rope was wet and her knees couldn't gain purchase. They couldn't take any of her weight to give her arms and hands a rest.

She wondered gloomily if there was any plank at all. What if the fisherman who had set the trap was a Canopian, and the rope went hundreds and hundreds of paces up into the sky? But there was an occasional glowworm on the great trunk, and something black made a silhouette against them.

Then her hand knocked the underside of good, solid wood, and she whooped as she looped her legs around it and hung there for a moment. Feeling returned to her blistered hands. Once she was upright, crouching on top of the planks, she explored the landing with her feet and elbows. It was three body lengths long, with a coating of something on top like decomposed leaves, which suggested it had been in place for a while. Where it met the trunk of the tallowwood, there was no vibration.

"It seems strong," she called down to the others. "Driven in deep. Who'll come next?"

Oos came next, followed by Ylly. When the three of them were sitting, side by side, on the plank, they helped each other to haul the net up, with Hasbabsah still caught in it with the fish.

"Shall I cut her out?" Unar asked.

"We'll lose the fish," Ylly said.

"I'm not hungry," Oos said petulantly.

"Dayhunters come to the smell of decomposing fish," Hasbabsah said.

Unar cut up the net, throwing it and the fish in the direction of the river, which was ten or twenty paces around the trunk from where they sat; it was difficult to judge from the sound of it, the fineness of the spray and, again, from the absence of glowworms.

"Will we even see the daylight from down here?" Unar demanded.

"Yes." Hasbabsah sounded exhausted. "And it is daylight we must wait for. We can go nowhere in the dark."

# TWENTY-FIVE

WITH DAYLIGHT and the part-clearing of storm clouds came the realisation that the coating on the plank was not decomposed leaves.

"I'm stuck," Ylly said abruptly.

"It is sap glue." Hasbabsah sounded even wearier and gloomier. "For day-hunters or needle-teeth, to stop them from damaging the net or taking the fish. The glue could not set hard until the rain stopped."

The rain had stopped, but only temporarily, Unar thought. The rivers were running. The next time it rained, it would rain longer and harder than before and it would go on until the end of the wet season.

"It's only stuck to your clothes," she said. "You can wriggle out of them."

"No," Ylly said. "It's gone through my clothes. The undersides of my knees and my hands are stuck."

Oos began to weep noisily but her hands were stuck, too, so that she couldn't even wipe her face. "My aura is faded by now. I'll never get home. The barrier will be closed to me. And there's no magic here."

Ylly turned on her, as much as she was able.

"Some wicked force that you can't control is keeping you from the ones you love? Imagine that!"

Unar felt strangely remote from Oos's concerns about faded auras; of course they could get back. Of course there was magic here. Understorians had carried a magic bed to the king of Odelland, after all. There must be rules that were not taught, or properly understood, in Canopy.

"We can wait for a raid to breach it," she said, thinking aloud. "When the barrier is weak. They must be able to come through when the god of the niche is weak."

"She is weak," Oos cried. "She's a suckling babe of six moons! Yet there were no raids this winter past. Gods form alliances for the protection of their niches while they are weak."

"My granddaughter is a suckling babe of six moons," Ylly said, "yet I've never seen her. I pray you never see your goddess again."

"That does not help us, Ylly," Hasbabsah said.

"Are you stuck, too, Hasbabsah?" Unar asked, trying to twist; her skin burned, threatening to tear. "I'm stuck by my buttocks. Atwith take whatever Understorian fisherman slathered glue here!"

"I am stuck too," Hasbabsah acknowledged.

"Should we shout to attract attention?"

"Noise will bring hungry demons. It is unlikely anyone will come to assist us. Most Understorians stay in their well-stocked homes for the wet season. As I said to you, there can be no trunk crossings in the monsoon rains."

"Aren't there any bridges between trunks?" Unar tried to see where the nearest trunk might be, but the meagre dawn light through the forest fog was little better than using a candle in another niche's Temple for seeing the carvings on the Garden Gate. Unar could still barely make out the shapes of her companions.

Hasbabsah made a reproving, sucking sound.

"Would you make a bridge to your door for a demon to cross? If there is one good your barrier has done us, it is that demons can no longer cross from tree to tree by the canopy. All but the chimera must descend to the floor. They have been fewer, and leaner, these last thousand years."

"Fire, then," Unar suggested.

Hasbabsah shrugged. She perched glumly in her woven cloak and robe like a wet wood hen.

"Fire would be a fine thing. It would repel the creatures and draw any curious straggling passersby. But I see no way to make one."

Unar had to admit she saw no way to make one, either, and when the rain began again, heavy and relentless, the point became moot. She passed magenta cherries and beans to the others, poking them into mouths when hands were stuck. They chewed slowly as the light grew bright enough for them to see each others' dripping, despondent faces.

"Perhaps the rain will soften the glue," Unar said.

"No," called a voice from around the curve of the trunk, half drowned out by the rushing of the river. A few moments later, a soft, nasal laugh came from closer by. "The rain will not soften it."

Unar stared at the spread-eagled, sticklike young man who crawled carefully around the circumference of the tallowwood. He was slightly above the level of the plank where they perched and drenched like they were; he wore a plain grey shirt and breeches cut off at the elbows and knees, made of strapleaf fibre designed to hold body warmth and protect from bark friction rather than any attempt to keep dry.

The man's forearms and shins seemed to adhere to the trunk. It wasn't until he moved again that Unar saw the flash of slim white spikes that protruded from his ashy Understorian skin. The huge pack on his back was hung with more ropes and grapples than she'd ever seen in one place before.

"They are not the dayhunter who has been poaching my catch," he said over his left shoulder. "But they have wrecked my net all the same. And their skins are not worth anything."

"Who are you talking to?" Unar asked loudly.

"He talks to his blessed side," Hasbabsah said. "It is what one does, when one is contemplating wrong action."

The man turned his head back to them and smiled at Hasbabsah. He had brown hair and clear grey eyes.

"Welcome home, older sister," he said. "You have fallen far. My name is Esse. I will get you down."

"Up," Oos begged. "We want to go up. Not down."

Esse ignored her. He eased one bare foot down onto the platform where it met the trunk, closest to Unar. The brown glue squished between his shockingly pale toes.

"This may warm your rump somewhat, Warmed One," he said. He took a stoppered gourd from the place where it hung from his pack. Laughing his soft, nasal laugh, he turned his head again, briefly, to his left shoulder. Then he poured a splash of clear liquid from the gourd into Unar's lap. It was not the most expedient place to pour it but clearly he intended to provoke her.

As it seeped through her clothes and reached the edges of the hardened glue, smoke began rising from it and it made a hissing sound. Unar bit her lip to keep from letting out a shriek as heat prickled her skin.

Then, she found she was able to lift herself off the plank.

"Stay still," Esse said, climbing over her with his long spider-legs to pour the fluid onto Ylly, Oos, and Hasbabsah.

"What now?" Hasbabsah asked.

"You will stay with us until the rain stops. Then you can go home."

"You are generous."

"I've never seen Nessa," Ylly said longingly. "Nor met my mother's people."

"There is little to see in Nessa," Esse said, smiling, head and shoulders taller than the tallest of them. "It is very dark. Here, the lopping of the tree branches at the level of the fabled Garden lets a little light down to us, sometimes. Gannak is closer and more scenic. Still, to get to Gannak right now, you would have to descend all the way to Floor, and if it is not already flooded, it will be soon. You would have to swim with piranhas or risk a boat voyage not consecrated by Floorian bone women. They would sink you with wicked words."

"We will go with you gratefully," Hasbabsah said.

"We will?" Oos said incredulously.

"If you wish to jump but are too cowardly," Ylly said, "I can push you."

"You are a grandmother, Ylly," Hasbabsah said sharply. "She is a child. Remember yourself."

"Sawas was my child, and this one sent her away."

"Quiet, now," Esse advised. "The rain and mist screen us somewhat, but I built that net to catch something other than Canopians. The dayhunter who visits this part of the tree has claws longer than that Gardener's leg bones."

Unar looked down at her legs.

"This Gardener will go with you," she said, mimicking his stilted, formal manner of speaking. "This Gardener will do what you say."

# TWENTY-SIX

UNAR SQUATTED to watch Esse work.

How would the five of them go down? He was the only one with the serpent-tooth spines that let him cling to the tree like a spider. Hasbabsah's had been snapped off when she'd first been captured and made a slave. Esse took a sharp axe from his pack, cut away a slab of tallowwood bark that would have done for a sleeping mat, and began to chisel something from the side of the tree above their heads.

It seemed forever before the short plank, pointed at one end and barely wide enough to hold a single person, was ready to be separated from the tree. Esse paused to push his pursed lips into a bark crevice, drinking the rainwater. Unar and the others did the same. They waited, wet and miserable, while he meticulously shaped another five short planks.

Unar thought about Aoun discovering that she and the two slaves were gone. She imagined him having to tell Servant Eilif that he had failed. *It serves him right.* Let him torture himself wondering if she and Oos had died or lived.

Edax, though. Edax deserved an explanation. When Unar failed to appear at their secluded meeting place, he might wonder how he'd offended her, when he hadn't offended her at all. The opposite.

He wouldn't know that she was below the barrier, as he was, but too far away for him to hear her and with no magic to stretch out to him. In fact, the pool below Ehkisland where Edax had taught her to dive, swim, and move with a man in intimate ways might be near the Understorian town, Gannak, which Esse had said was the closest town, if not the town where Hasbabsah had come from, Nessa.

It occurred to Unar that she could have visited Nessa at any time. She'd never thought that news of it might comfort Hasbabsah, or that she might carry a message from the old woman to her folk. That was because un-enslaved Understorians were dangerous and savage.

"Step down," Esse told her quietly.

He'd used his axe to make holes in the tree trunk. Then, he'd wedged the six little planks into the holes to make a sort of suicidal spiral staircase. Unar stepped down until she stood on the second-lowest plank. The others were arrayed behind her, with Ylly on the second-highest plank.

"Pull out the highest plank and pass it down to me, potplant."

"Potplant?"

"An Understorian slave grown like an exotic specimen in the soil of the cursed Garden, are you not?" Esse smiled at Ylly. Unar took hold of the front edge of the plank as it was passed down to her, and Esse hacked another hole, lower down, to wedge the plank into.

In this manner, they progressed slowly and carefully, until, by midmorning, they stood at the river's edge far below the place where Esse had netted them. Unar saw a wooden ramp, narrow and covered with moss and lichen, leading straight into the flow.

"Hold the railing tight," their guide advised. "Yes, you must get wet again, but you will become warm and dry inside. We keep the fire burning for the whole of the monsoon. Do not think I have enjoyed cutting and drying the fuel. Go on. Go past me. I must bring the planks in."

Unar brushed him as she passed. His thin, stick-body was completely unyielding; even his belly was hard with muscle. It was like brushing past a sapling. She stared at the rushing water of the vertical river. The ability to swim wouldn't protect her if she slipped from the platform and was washed down to Floor.

She seized the platform railing and dragged herself through the flow. Her feet left the floor. The weight of water was like hammers on her head. She kicked, hard, and found the platform again, propelling herself towards the tree trunk just as her fingers lost their grip.

The tree trunk was hollowed away. She fell, gasping like a landed fish, into a room lit only by luminous fungi.

Men's boots and cloaks hung from hooks in the circular wall. Shelves held sacks and woven items unidentifiable in the gloom. Wet underclothes were draped over a drying rack, and Unar hesitated before plunging into the black corridor that was apparently the only way for her to go—were there hairy, naked Understorian warriors inside? Esse had said that they would stay with him until the rain stopped, but how many fellow trappers, fishers, and hunters shared his quarters?

She couldn't use her magic to find out. The place where it had been no longer felt hollow. It felt like nothing, like before she'd felt the seed inside her for the first time. Unar knew that if she tried to enter Canopy, the border would throw her back as violently as the princess's curtains had.

Before she could start towards the corridor, Oos and Hasbabsah crashed into her back. They sprawled together on the floor; it was unpolished, and splinters found their way into Unar's face. She stumbled into a pile of sacks and sat there, trying to work the wood out from under her skin, swearing until she remembered Edax's tear-shaped scars and became distracted by wondering if their making had been painful for him to endure.

"I think I will just sleep here," Hasbabsah wheezed, staying where she was, facedown on the floor.

Ylly exploded out of the curtain of river water, spluttering and shaking.

Esse came after her with his arms full of boards. He narrowly skirted the slumped shape of Hasbabsah and leaned the boards against the shelves, shaking his short, dark hair like a wet tapir. He helped the groaning old slave to her feet and led her down the corridor without a word.

At the end of it, he opened a door to a second room filled with heat and light. It smelled powerfully of spices and smoked fish.

Unar was irresistibly drawn with the others, single file, towards it.

"Have we leave to sit at your table?" Hasbabsah asked.

"Our table is yours while the bucket fills," said a deeper, heartier voice than Esse's.

When Unar reached the doorway, she saw a stone hearth bigger than a slave's bedroom. It dominated the far wall. She wasn't sure she'd ever seen so much precious stone in one place. Perhaps they had traded it from Floor. This big room was as dry, open, and bright as the first space had been dark, cramped, and dank. A bored chimney carried away the fragrant smoke from the fire, but not before it passed through three tiers of gutted river fish on iron spits. Crates of dried broadleaves sat to the left of the hearth; dried, wrapped meat portions filled cloth sacks to the right. There were embroidered hangings on either side of the hearth, too, that might have been decorative or covered entryways to other corridors.

In the centre of the room, a coarse cross-section of quandong wood served as a table, its surface broad enough to host a demon sacrifice. The slab held dark, dried blood in its crevices, as though it had been used for butchering before.

Two men sat at the table, at the point farthest from the fire. Thankfully, neither was completely naked; they wore short waist-wraps and nothing else. One was an enormous, red-haired brute with a beard and pale arms patterned with inked beasts. The other was small with a smooth chin, yellow hair, and clear eyes the colour of clouds.

"I said that our table is yours," the brute repeated in a gentler voice, and Hasbabsah sank into a four-legged chair by the fire with a relieved groan. Ylly went to stand slightly behind her, her back to the flames, shaking her wet hair and looking wary.

Oos gripped Unar's hand tightly. They stood, rigid, by the door as Esse closed it behind them.

"Some ugly-looking fish you have caught, Esse," said the yellow-haired man, his expression curious.

"Don't kill us," Oos blurted at once. "We can pay you. Just these two slaves for now, but later, when you take us back to Canopy, we'll pay more."

"I see no slaves here." The yellow-haired man looked amused.

"Don't skin us alive. Don't throw us to demons. The goddess we serve—"

"Girl child," Hasbabsah interrupted, "these three brothers have offered us all monsoon-right by asking that we sit at their table. You answer them with insult. They have pledged to share food and water with you until the monsoon is ended. It means that if food runs low before the rains stop, we will all starve together before they throw you to the demons."

"Your gods and goddesses have no power here," Esse said, opening a bag of fresh fish before the fire.

"I've made no pledge not to throw her to the demons," Ylly said.

"We will not run low on food," the deep-voiced, red-haired man boomed, leaning back from his crumb-covered, empty plate. "Introductions are in order. But not before all are seated."

He turned unblinking brown eyes on Unar and Oos until they shuffled, still hand in hand, over to an empty pair of stools. Then he stared at Ylly until she sat down, too.

"I am Bernreb," he said, "second son of Moonoom."

"I am Marram," the yellow-haired man said, smiling into the silence that followed Bernreb's pronouncement. "Third son of Moonoom. Over there, gutting the fish for your breakfast, is Esse, first son of Moonoom."

"I am Hasbabsah of Nessa," Hasbabsah said.

"I'm Ylly, daughter of Ylly."

Oos squeezed Unar's hand so tight that Unar couldn't feel it anymore and said nothing.

"You don't look like brothers," Unar said, avoiding giving her name. "You all look different. How can you all be sons of Moonoom? You look like you all had different fathers."

Bernreb guffawed.

"Canopy must indeed be a strange and wondrous place. I never heard of three brothers all having the same father."

"Fathers die so quickly," Marram said.

"Moonoom was our mother," Esse muttered, throwing fish guts into the fire.

"Oh." Unar took a deep breath. She reminded herself that the floor her feet stood on was the very same sapwood that the Garden stood on. This was still her place. The heart that beat within the great tree was her heart. "I am Unar of the Garden. This is Oos."

"Then we are all well met," Bernreb said.

"Is there nobody else living here?" Ylly asked.

From some other, unknown place in the home wafted the bawls of a baby crying.

Unar shared a glance with Oos.

"Excuse me," Bernreb said. "I only just put her down. The sound of our voices must have woken her. We try to keep her in the back where the demons will not hear her crying and come to investigate." He stood up from the table, passed through one of the embroidered hangings, and returned with a bundle in his bulging, tattooed arms.

Unar stared at the bundle. The blanket-edge bore the family weaves of the House of Epatut. She hadn't cared about family colours and emblems; hadn't taken them with mother's milk, as Oos had.

But she recognised these.

"Now you have seen her," Bernreb said, "I must clean her. Excuse me."

Ylly stood up abruptly, went to Bernreb, and lifted the baby's fat brown body out of the wrappings. This child had been all but newborn when she fell at the end of the last monsoon, and now looked none the worse for it. Her bared bottom had an odorous, muddy smear across the cheeks, but Ylly ignored it.

"She's from Canopy," Ylly said, with eyes only for the baby, cooing and swishing until the cries turned to uncertain smiles. Bernreb looked bemused, but he made no move to take the baby back. Perhaps he felt that babies belonged in the arms of women. Or perhaps, since it appeared they would all be living together for five months, he simply saw no sense in stopping Ylly from taking on some of his duties. He couldn't know how Ylly had longed to hold her true granddaughter, how she'd kept bitterly silent ever since Sawas was sold away.

"Did you steal her?" Oos asked. "Did you steal those blankets?"

"Oos," Unar said with wonder, extricating her bruised hand, remembering the wrappings full of rotten quandongs and satinashes she'd let fall amidst crushing disappointment. "You know whose baby this is, better than me. She is Imeris, daughter of Epatut. She survived the fall."

"She survived a fall," Bernreb agreed heartily. "We had not given her a name."

"She is Imerissiremi," Ylly said at once. "Issi for short."

"Wife-of-Epatut dropped her in the market," Hasbabsah said. "Not at the Garden. You didn't find her caught in this tree. How did you find her?"

"I found her ten days ago in the mouth of a chimera that I killed," Bernreb said, leaning back in his chair and stretching his hands behind his head, cracking his knuckles. "A chimera's milky saliva nourishes its eggs, passing through the soft shells. Seems good enough for a human babe to survive on at that." His eyes followed Ylly, who had left the door open carelessly as she carried the child towards the entry room. Unar heard bucket handles swing and the splash of water.

"Is she leaving?" Unar whispered to Esse, who was half bent in the act of placing a roasted fish on a dried leaf-plate in front of her. "Is she mad? Is she leaving with the baby?"

Esse paused to glance down the pitch-black corridor.

"She is washing the baby's backside," he said. "We would trust a pot-plant a hundred times over before we trusted you, Gardener. Eat your fish."

Unar ate the fish. It tasted like flowerfowl bile mixed with cactus jelly, but she was so hungry she burned her tongue and her fingers in her haste, pausing only to extricate tiny bones from her mouth and line them up on the edge of her plate.

"You did not kill a chimera," Hasbabsah said, wiping fish grease from her chin with her sleeve.

"Did I not?"

"The chimera is life. Life must come from the ashes of its death, or the curse falls on the family of the one who slays it." Hasbabsah began to cough so uncontrollably that she couldn't speak. Unar worried about a fish bone, but Hasbabsah waved Marram back when he stood up and made as if to assist her.

"Life did come from it," Bernreb said. "The child, from its mouth, as I said. She is lucky, and she is life. We will keep her. We will care for her."

Unar noticed that one of the tattoos on Bernreb's arms showed a sinuous, reptilian shape with flattened ears and claws like knives, long teeth in a mouth that opened up the whole head like a hinge, and multicoloured scales from snout to prehensile tail.

It was fresher than the others, the skin around it still red and puckered.

"Your markings," she said. "They show the demons you've slain."

"I was sent away from Gannak because of this one." Bernreb grinned and sat forward, pointing to a depiction of a man on his biceps; a man whose head with its curving, banana-shaped hat had been separated from his body. "The Headman of Gannak told me I must serve with him, on pain of death, on his fool errand to kill a Canopian god. I did not want to go with him. Nor did I wish for death. Now we three live in exile."

Ylly returned to the hearth room, pulling the door closed behind her.

"What do you feed the child?" she asked. "Issi is hungry."

"We fed her the eggs of the chimera, at first. Now she has nut paste. Fruit mush. Insects trapped in sap and boiled in monkey oil."

Unar sucked on the fish head and waited for Ylly to deplore these barbarian foodstuffs. Babies in Audblayinland were breast-fed until their second birthday. Then again, they didn't have Sawas with them. Breast-feeding wasn't an option.

"She is healthy," Ylly said. "She's bright. Those foods you've been giving her must be good for her. Where can I find them?"

"Let me," Hasbabsah said, but she was bent over by coughing again.

"You must rest, Hasbabsah of Nessa," Marram said. "I will prepare pallets for you. We have already sacrificed our storeroom, in the deepest part of the tree, for the baby's safety and comfort, so there is no harm putting our monsoon guests in there, too. You must put up with her noise in the night, as we do, I am afraid."

"I can help," Oos offered, putting her hand on Ylly's as the older woman passed, but Ylly rounded on her with teeth bared.

"You and your ilk took my granddaughter from me. You'll have nothing to do with this child, do you understand me? You won't even look at her. Not even speak her name. Now go find some sandpaper fig leaves for those soft hands of yours. Your beauty will fade soon enough, but you might find an application for it here, better than in the Garden."

Oos swallowed hard. She dry-washed her hands, looking with fear and awe at Ylly as though seeing her for the first time.

"All of you need rest," Bernreb said, shifting uncomfortably. He tried to catch Esse's eye, but Esse was at the fire, roasting more fish, still seeming amused.

He brought Unar and Oos another fish each.

"Monsoon-right," Esse said to his left shoulder, "is better treatment than these Gardeners deserve. I had thought to feed them on rotted leaves and old bones, as potplant and her ilk are fed. Not as equals. My brother Bernreb is soft."

"He killed a chimera," Unar said. "And made the shape of it in his flesh with needles. You think he's soft?"

"He killed the chimera out of brotherly love. Marram needed the skin."

"What for? To make himself invisible? So that he can creep up on Canopy and kill one of our gods?"

Esse gently touched the collar of Unar's Gardener's tunic, by chance a finer variety, where a green sprouting seed had been worked into the red. Unar watched him do it without shrinking back or slapping his long-fingered hand away.

"Marram could kill a god—or a goddess—if he cared to," he said. "But he does not need to be invisible for that. That is not why he needed the skin."

# TWENTY-SEVEN

UNAR LAY on her pallet in the dark, cosy storeroom, listening to Ylly swish and shush the baby, and to Hasbabsah's terrible coughing.

Despite the disturbances, she should have fallen asleep instantly, but her head whirled with thought. The monsoon would last five long months. There was no way for her to leave the home of the three brothers before then. And why should she leave? Why should she go back to Canopy at all, until the re-incarnation of Audblayin was old enough for her to find?

What would the brothers do with Oos and Unar when the rain stopped? Push them out the front door?

She had no forearm spikes with which to climb, nor skill with an axe. Perhaps she'd better learn. Hasbabsah had said there would be no trunk crossings in the wet, but what about in the dry? How did one travel from tree to tree in Understorey, where there were, apparently, no bridges to bring demons to the door?

Unar would have liked to visit Edax at the edge of their swimming pool, though it must be overflowing by now, rejoining a vertical river like the one outside the three brothers' door. Fish would half swim, half climb with their fins or thin speckled legs up the river to lay their eggs in the upper pools. Then, the following year, the hatchlings would abandon the pool, too big to survive on rotting leaves and insect larvae. Many would end up in nets like Esse's, but others would make it all the way down to Floor.

Was that her way back into Canopy? To fool the barrier at the rain goddess's domain into thinking she was a fish, just as she had fooled the Garden Gate into thinking she was a seed? She could swim. She could imagine a fish's thoughts. By then she would smell like a fish, from eating so many.

Unar bit her lower lip. It wasn't simply climbing and axe-work she would have to learn if she was to persist in her search for Audblayin and prove herself the rightful Bodyguard of the god. She must continue her quest for magical knowledge.

"Oos," she whispered, but Oos was lost in exhausted sleep. Her tears had dried on her face, Unar thought, but there were plenty more where they had come from. Yet here in Understorey, Oos could tell her what she needed to know. How to enhance fertility. How to heal.

How to drain an enemy of power, as Unar had been drained.

She couldn't use her magic now, but it would return to her, and when it did, she wanted to have new information in store. *Have patience,* Aoun had said. *Watch. Listen.*

*Your turn to have patience, Aoun. Your turn to wait for what you want to know.*

"Hush, my beautiful little Issi," Ylly crooned. "My changeling child. Wife-of-Epatut holds my blood in her house, now, but you've been given by Audblayin in exchange. I'll hold you. I'll love you. *I* will never drop you."

WHEN UNAR opened her eyes again, it was to the sound of someone pulling a blade across a whetstone.

Oos, breathing deeply beside her, hadn't so much as rolled over in her sleep. A low-burning candle showed Ylly asleep, too, slumped facedown over the cradle with her arms enfolding it. Baby Issi snored inside it. Hasbabsah's coughing floated into the storeroom from the hearth room beyond the workshop.

The person sharpening the knife was Esse.

"Is it morning?" Unar asked him.

"You slept through the day," Esse answered with a small smile. "It is midnight."

"Is that the only knife you have for gutting fish?" She said it scornfully. Metal blades were valuable enough in Canopy. She imagined they were even more costly in Understorey. Esse might be sharpening his knife over her neck but he hadn't murdered them in their sleep. She was starting to believe Hasbabsah about the sanctity of monsoon-rights.

"It is your knife," Esse said.

Unar realised he was right, even before her hand could fumble at her empty sheath.

"Give it back."

"I have taken it as payment for the net that you ruined."

"I'll mend the goddess-forsaken net."

"Can you use a shuttle and thread without magic, then?"

"Of course I can." Unar kept her voice lowered with difficulty.

"I have already mended it."

"I'll gut fish, then. Give the knife to me."

His smile only deepened.

"Fine," Unar said, folding her blanket on her pallet and standing up beside him. "So you won't give me the knife. Tell me how I can earn it back. I'll need it when I leave."

She noticed that the white spikes which had protruded from his forearms and shins while he was climbing were retracted, somehow, into the flesh. They'd seemed to accumulate no debris, nor become stained by sap. She couldn't imagine how it was accomplished without magic. Then she remembered that Esse had said the party could be sunk by the wicked words of Floorian bone women. She remembered Hasbabsah's talk of the bones of the Old Gods, and the bone-magic of the princess's floating bed.

*Bones hold magic in Understorey and in Floor,* Unar realised, her breath catching. Esse saw her looking at his arm, where only a thin, dark seam marked the place where his spikes had been. He could have been a slave with the spines snapped off, if Unar hadn't seen them moving in and out.

"You will never have those," he said. "They are not for you. I might not need you to gut fish or to mend nets, but there are leaves whose stems must be stripped for fibre. There is fibre that needs to be twisted into twine. If the twine is coarse and clumsy, you will have to untwist it and begin again. But if you fill nine sacks, I will give you back this knife."

"I agree," Unar said at once.

Esse led her to the workshop. He showed her how to pull down the racks layered in dark green, sharp-edged, strap-like leaves. They were different from the wide, waxy, light green leaves used for plates, which were different again from the papery, absorbent leaves used for wrapping and storing the smoked fish. Unar recognised the strapleaves, and the sandpaper fig leaves that Marram and Esse must use to keep their beards from growing and that Oos used on her hands. The others were foreign to her. Perhaps the trees Unar was used to didn't grow nearby and to the great tree size that would make them accessible. Or perhaps the unfamiliarity of the three brothers' harvest indicated that the flowers of their host plants were unbeautiful, or that they came from trees that didn't bear fruit. Only the rarest or most glorious of colours, textures, or tastes found a home in the Garden.

"Here are the leaves. Go to the fishing room and make your toilet. Then I will show you what to do."

"The fishing room?"

"The dark room by which you entered this place. The bucket by the right side of the river door is for filling with water, adding bodily wastes and then tossing back into the stream. Do not confuse it with the other bucket, which is for bringing drinking water into the hearth room."

"Hasbabsah said nobody lived downstream of the Garden because the water was polluted."

"This river is clean. It is the overflow of a pool that you Gardeners use for your own drinking water in the dry. The other side of the tree is foul, I grant you."

"And there's nobody downriver of you that might object to the fouling at this point?"

"Floorians have bone women for the cleansing of water. I am tired of talking to you, Gardener. Go on."

On her way out of the workshop, Unar brushed past a cold forge which reminded her uncomfortably of her mother, ropes and bundled nets in various stages of repair, animal whiskers waiting to be made into fishing line, and bark to be made into bootlaces. In the hearth room, Hasbabsah closed her eyes tight as she coughed, twisting in seeming delirium beneath a blanket she shouldn't have needed so close to the roaring fire.

Bernreb was with her. He wiped the sweat from her forehead and the bloody sputum from her lips with a woven cloth.

"What's the matter with her?" Unar asked.

"I do not know. She bleeds from the tongue. The sickness has spread from there, down into her lungs."

Unar felt stuck to the floor, glued by guilt at the stupidity of her mistake. She'd thought their escape was in the service of saving Hasbabsah from certain death, only to discover that her people's cruelty was more cunning than that; in the old and long-encumbered, the mark couldn't be completely removed, not even by passing beyond the scope of the magic that had placed it there. Ylly had proven recoverable. Hasbabsah was not.

"Oos could have healed her," she said. "Oos *should* have healed her. Couldn't you climb with Hasbabsah, and with Oos—"

"No," Bernreb interrupted. "We cannot pass through the barrier, and by now, neither can any of you. We must do our best for her here, without the working of gods."

"Are there no healers? Herb women? Blasphemers of that sort?"

"Not in the monsoon. Nobody travels in the monsoon."

Unar turned on her heel in frustration. In the fishing room, thin beams of moonlight struck the edge of the river where it flowed over the entrance, making a moonbow overlaid on a soft wall of white. She stopped to gape at it. As she watched, the fleeting moonlight faded, leaving the room cold and dark and wet again.

She filled the toilet bucket with water, then with waste, and finally, wrinkling her nose, she poured it away. She crushed a soapleaf and lathered her hands before rinsing them. Then she cupped the river water directly for drinking.

It tasted a little like tannins, a little like rotted leaves. Not much like rainwater, but at least she hadn't caught any fish in her hands.

As she was backing away from the water, ready to go back to Esse, something came through the entrance, splitting the water—something that she couldn't quite see, which she assumed in a panic was a demon. She groped for her knife a second time and loosed a cry of startlement and fear.

"Hush," said Marram. His voice was higher pitched than Bernreb's, not as coldly menacing as Esse's. "What were you doing? I hope I did not walk in through a tossed bucket of solid waste."

"No," Unar managed, mortified.

Marram pulled something like a blanket away from his head and the dark bulk resolved into his slender, pale shape. He carried a long, curved stave and a basket on his back. A thick coil of sodden rope hung at the waist of his short wrap. Coarse-woven cloth to provide better grip was laced onto his insteps and the tops of his knees, leaving his shins bare with their spikes hidden in the seams. The rope coil ended in a metal spike with a round eye for attachment, and when Marram turned to drape the blanket from a hook, the glow of luminescent fungi revealed that the stave was an unstrung, powerful-looking longbow of three different laminated woods.

The blanket took on the colour of the fungi-covered wall, and Unar gasped.

"Chimera skin," she said. She couldn't help but look into the basket as Marram unstrapped it. "Those aren't tallowwood leaves."

"No," Marram admitted.

"But nobody travels from tree to tree in the monsoon. Hasbabsah said so, and Bernreb, too. Where did these leaves come from? How did you get them, if you stayed only on this tree?"

Marram smiled. "Nobody travels in the monsoon," he said, "because wet bark means that resin glues for sticky-climbing will not properly attach. Spikes may not penetrate properly through loosened, sodden bark to the safety of the wood. And traditional leather skins for gliding hold too much weight in water. The glide cannot be sustained, and the hapless hunter falls to Floor."

Unar glanced at the chimera skin again.

"Traditional leather," she repeated. "Is that why Bernreb hunted a demon for you?"

"It is."

"So you can glide from tree to tree, even in the rain?"

"I am the first one. The only one. Only I can move through the trees during the monsoon."

"You," Unar said, "and your two brothers, you mean."

"No. Bernreb is too heavy, and Esse is a barkclinger; he does not fancy flight. But I do."

Hope rose in her chest.

"Then you can go to this barbarian village, Gannak, or whatever you call it. You can find medicines for her. Save her life."

"You forget," Marram said, shaking his head, "we are exiles. I would be killed on sight if I showed my face in Gannak."

"Let me go, then!" Unar grasped his hand. "Teach me to fly!"

"Flying is the easy part. Flying isn't the difficulty."

"What is the difficulty, then?"

Marram pulled his fingers out of her grip. He raised his forearm, held it vertical high above the level of her eyes for a moment, and then brought it down sharply against the fishing room wall.

When Unar looked closely, she realised he had extended his spikes and driven them deeply into the wood.

"The difficulty," he said, "is landing."

# TWENTY-EIGHT

WHEN OOS woke, she emerged into the workroom where Unar was busily stripping fibres from the strap-like leaves.

Oos's white robe was stained by bark, glue, and fish slime. The beads and ribbons in her hair had congealed with woodchips and pallet-straw into an awful-looking, trussed-up, kicked-beehive shape.

"I'm hungry," she said to Unar in a small voice.

"Go on, then," Unar replied, jerking her head towards the hearth room. "They're in there, the three of them. There's fruit and fish."

Since his return with the leaves via the fishing room, Marram had shrugged off his clothes, dried himself, dressed in a clean waist-wrap by the fire, slept for three hours in the bedroom barred to guests, and then risen, refreshed, as if three hours sleep per day were all that he needed. Bernreb had passed Unar once or twice to check on the baby, Issi, only to find Ylly had everything in hand. As for Esse, Unar didn't think he'd slept at all.

"I don't want to talk to them. I don't want to see them. Can't you . . . ?"

Unar sighed and put the leaf to one side. After six hours or so of stripping, her fingers had blisters aplenty, but there was something soothing in the leaf sap that allowed her to keep working stubbornly through the pain. She needed that knife back. From her sitting position on the wooden floor, she looked up at Oos.

"We wouldn't be here at all if only you'd helped instead of hindered."

"How can you say that? You're the one who dragged us into the river, to death, as far as you knew, but you did it anyway. Besides, how could I turn against the Servants? I am a Servant. I can't turn against myself."

Unar didn't say haughtily that they wouldn't have died because she had a destiny, even if she was the only one who could see it. Aoun knew. Aoun said that the wards had stood four hundred years, that Unar had the power to destroy everything, that she was practically the goddess reborn.

"You can still think for yourself, can't you?" Unar tossed her head angrily. "You can decide which traditions are important and which are needlessly cruel. Is Audblayin a god in want of human sacrifices?"

"Of course not—she is the giver of life!"

"Then you failed her when you failed to give life to Hasbabsah. Can't you hear her, coughing, dying in the other room? You can't fool me, Oos. We were friends for too long. It's not those men you're afraid of, it's watching an old woman die."

They glared at each other for a moment. Then Oos brushed past Unar, kicking her pile of fibre in petty vengeance as she went. Unar scraped the pile together again, silently, on her hands and knees, before moving to where she could eavesdrop on the conversation in the hearth room.

"Is it morning?" Oos's voice sounded timid through the curtain.

"The last dawn that your ex-slave is likely to see," Esse said. Hasbabsah's hacking halted the conversation momentarily.

"If I could send a message up to the other Servants," Oos said into the pause. "Servant Eilif could come down here. She could do something to help."

"No message," Bernreb said. "If the Servants knew we were down here, they would poison the river, or dam it, for a chance of getting rid of us. Parasites on their very own tree!"

"Servant Eilif, as you call her, would not venture where her magic could not protect her," Esse said. "Not for the sake of a slave. Or is it you in need of help? A thousand soldiers could not carry you through the barrier now, even if they left us dangling with our throats cut."

"There must be a way." Oos's voice became so quiet that Unar had to lift a corner of the embroidered hanging. "Hasbabsah came to Canopy from Understorey, once."

"There is a way—" Marram began to say, kindly, but Esse interrupted.

"If Hasbabsah decides to tell you how she did it," he said sharply, "I will not stop her. But we three will not tell you. You had better do everything you can think of to help her to get well."

"Magic is the only thing I can think of!"

Nobody had anything to say to that. There was no magic in Understorey. Or was there?

Unar sat back down on the floor and took a deep breath. She pinched her left forearm with the fingers of her right hand, feeling the two long bones beneath the skin. She closed her eyes and ground her jaw; teeth were bones, too. Focus on the bones. Bones and magic.

Nothing.

Issi started crying in the former storeroom, now guestroom. Unar heard the shuffling sounds of Ylly dragging herself upright, murmuring platitudes over the cot, lifting Issi into her arms. Then there was the pungent smell of soiled wrappings being changed, just as Bernreb pushed the hanging up onto its hook and passed through the workshop. He nodded briefly to Unar before ducking into the storeroom.

"I will take those," Unar heard him say.

"Take the baby," Ylly said. "I'll wash these now and hang them up right away."

"The old woman," Bernreb said. "Her fever has not broken. She takes water, but she will not wake. I do not know what to do."

"Neither do I."

Silence.

Issi complained again, loudly.

"I will feed you, then, little black duck," Bernreb said soothingly. "Getting to be a fat, heavy little chick, are you not? With only a few little fuzzy feathers. It is no good talking to me in the language of the chimera. You are with your own kind now."

"Ba," the baby said.

"Bernreb," Bernreb encouraged her.

"Ba."

"Close enough."

Bernreb took Issi back past Unar to the hearth room, with Ylly not far behind him. They left the curtain on its hook, and Marram's voice floated through the open doorway.

"I think it is the smell of the baby bringing that dayhunter around to this side of our tree."

"Did you see it?" Esse asked.

"I saw scales rubbed onto bark, three and four trunks from here. Claw marks. Long streaks of dayhunter waste with insects trapped in it, only hours old and not set. The same fully grown male animal that left marks around your nets, Esse. It is not afraid to swim from tree to tree down at Floor."

"Surely our pet corpse-lover has better pickings at Floor than at this level.

Surely it remembers that it has never, in its long life, found anything to eat below the Garden."

"No matter how we try to hide the baby's smell in the centre of the river, I think it smells her anyway. Its ancestors spent many centuries plucking bald newborns from hollows in trees. I think even fresh corpses from the fighting at Floor cannot tempt it away from its goal. And Bernreb's weapons will not puncture its hide."

"Tonight, I will reset the traps sprung by the Canopians. Trussing it, weighting it, and drowning it remains our best option."

"I agree."

Esse sighed. "I need sleep. You should put this Burned One to work with the other one, Marram. Idleness breeds mischief."

"Not Burned One," Oos corrected him, her distress obvious. "Warmed One."

"Warmed One," Esse repeated mockingly, his voice coming from higher up as if he'd gotten to his feet. "I put some cockles in the fire. To feast on flesh of Floor. One was cold and one was warm. One placed after and one before. I burned one, I splayed one. I'll turn one, I'll trade one. All by the Old Gods sowed and made, found by me with my trusty spade."

"It is a rhyme," Marram said. "He is not threatening you. Look at me, Servant Oos of the Garden. Forget him and forget the dayhunter. You are in no danger."

"Marram always wanted a wife," Esse said, laughing his nasal laugh.

"Go to bed, Esse."

"Now he thinks he will not have to wait for that squeaky infant to grow up. But the truth is that someone like you can never see him as anything but a slave."

Esse's chair scraped as he pushed it back in to the table. There was silence from Marram and Oos. Unar stripped the fibre, her head bowed over the stems, more slowly than she had at first but still working. Esse thought he knew everything, but he was wrong about Oos. Unar had made a similar accusation, and while it was true that Oos had traded Sawas and her child with as much consideration as she might show a hand of plantains, she'd done it for Unar. She had a good heart. She hadn't known, as Unar had, that those acting, however treacherously, from a place of motherly devotion could be forgiven anything.

That Unar would have battled any demon, sacrificed any dream, if only her mother had wanted her.

Oos would come around, soon enough. She would grow calm. She would feel safe. She would realise that the strata of human life in the Garden were artificial. That her refusal to share knowledge with Unar was wrong. They'd become a team again. Oos would help Unar to first heal Hasbabsah and then find the reincarnation of Audblayin. Aoun would be sorry he'd stayed behind.

"I cannot be your wife," Oos blurted out.

"I am not asking you to be," Marram said. "And if I did, it would be entirely your choice to make." He was silent for a while, then asked, "Is it true that no music is permitted in the Garden?"

"It's true." Oos sounded relieved. "But I played the bells as a child."

"Then let me lend you my thirteen-pipe flute. It is not difficult to play."

# TWENTY-NINE

AFTER SUPPER, when it seemed like time for sleeping, though Unar couldn't guess the hour with the constant falling water sounds of rain and river and gloom of the interior, she lay down on her pallet in the storeroom with the others, staring up at the living ceiling that was connected to the well-tended beds of the Garden.

The wood was oil-rich. It shone a polished yellow-brown, lacquered in places where the sapwood must have oozed for a while after it was cut, until the gum hardened in the air. The dwelling was a shallow one, not penetrating anywhere near the heartwood of the tallowwood trunk, but blessedly free of insects. Unar supposed they had the river to thank for that. Not a single flying creature fluttered near the flames. The candles, true tallow, stuck fast by their bear- and tapir-fat drippings, weren't especially bright, but they seemed brighter against the soot-stained niches where they sat.

Unar's pallet was made up of straw beneath bear pelts, black with yellow circles on them, and she couldn't tell if they still smelled of bear, if the stench was the candles, or if it was her own smell. She didn't want to shed her red Gardener's shirt just yet, though it had gathered rainwater, glue, humus, solvent, fish grease, and leaf sap so far.

While she wore it, she could pretend she was still somewhat part of what she'd left behind.

"Oos," she whispered, not wanting to wake the baby. Nor Ylly, snoring softly on the other side of the cradle, who hadn't spoken a word to either one of them all day. She blamed them for Hasbabsah's state, and Unar couldn't fault her for doing it. "Oos, are you awake?"

Oos's back was turned to Unar, but her fingers tightened on a corner of her blanket.

"No."

Unar smiled. It was like old times in the hammocks in the loquat grove, like their early years in the Garden before Oos was made a Servant and Unar was left behind. Unar had wanted to sneak a look at the goddess, and at her Bodyguard, too, until Oos had reminded her about the moat. About the fish. *Do you think she can fly?* Unar had asked, and Oos had snorted and said, *No.*

"Oos, won't you please tell me everything you learned about healing so we can both find a way to make the magic work and heal Hasbabsah?"

"Are you stupid?" She rolled over angrily. "The magic won't work for you, for me, for anyone, Unar! Maybe not ever!"

"You don't know that."

"And why should one who walks in the grace of Audblayin want to heal Hasbabsah?" Oos's tone had turned haughty. "Why should I care if she dies? She's supposed to die, for betraying the Garden. You and me, too. If there's justice, we'll all die."

"You don't really want to die," Unar said calmly, "or you'd have jumped into the river already."

"I want you to die. You ruin everything you touch."

Unar seized Oos's wrist, keeping a hold on it despite Oos's attempt to pull away.

"Did we betray the Garden?" Unar demanded. "We saved it from becoming stained with slaves' blood. The Garden is still pure. Did we somehow admit murderers, rapists, or thieves?"

"You stole two slaves. You are a thief."

Unar fought to keep from laughing in her face.

"I am a thief if a person is a thing to steal."

"Yes, you are."

"Oos," Unar said urgently, "tell me what you know. Hasbabsah doesn't have much time. Please."

Oos freed herself with a sharp twist. "Never," she said, turning her back again.

Unar listened, but she couldn't even hear any coughing now. Nor harsh breathing. If Hasbabsah died, all her efforts were wasted. The extra chores, which had left Unar unsuitable for selection. The nights and nights of washing clothes by moonlight with Ylly and the lunatic leap from the lip of the Garden.

"If it was your grandmother dying, I'd want to help her," Unar said. "She stood outside the Gates and cried that you were killing her, remember? She said you were the birdsong in her heart and that, without you, her heart would turn black and silent. Like Hasbabsah's tongue, Oos. It's wrong to mark slaves in such a way, can't you see?"

"I remember your mother came to the Garden," Oos said. Her voice was muffled. "I remember her at the Gates. She said she could have sold you for one thousand weights of silver but that you'd run away. She demanded that Audblayin pay for you and cursed us all when the Servants told her it was too late. I wish she had sold you. I wish it was you with a black and silent tongue. Be quiet now. I want to sleep."

Unar sighed.

She gave up the conversation, rolling flat onto her back. Staring at the ceiling again, she imagined the patterns of sap were the shapes of herself and Aoun on that first morning, when they had waited outside the dew-covered Gates for the dawn.

*We're so high up,* Unar had said, staring at the sky. *And so exposed.*

*Look,* Aoun had marvelled, nudging her. *The sun.*

It had risen over the endless forest's distant horizon, first making the trees black and stark, then burnishing their many shades of green. Both children had been astonished by the unfiltered heat of it, even so soon after dawn.

*If they let us stay,* Unar said, *we'll be warm all the time.*

*We'll be Warmed Ones,* Aoun had said, grinning.

The Gatekeeper, the woman with the lantern, had been an indistinct shape in the shadow of the half-open Gate.

*Applicants,* she had muttered. *When we haven't even announced the deaths of the old Gardeners. How did you know to come, fledglings?*

Unar and Aoun had looked at one another. They hadn't known that old Gardeners must die before new Gardeners could be admitted.

*We just . . . ,* Unar began uncertainly.

*Came,* Aoun finished awkwardly.

*Has the plague been through your houses?* demanded the Gatekeeper. *Are you in good health?*

*Yes,* they both said at once. The Gatekeeper put her cupped palm through the gap in the Gate. She held a handful of soil.

*How many seeds do I hold?* she'd wanted to know.

*Three,* Aoun said.

*Three,* Unar said, wide-eyed with astonishment that she should be able to answer such a question, having expected a lengthy, labouring trial period before any testing took place. That way, if she failed to gain entry, at least she would have time to formulate another plan to stay free. *Three,* she said again, *and they are passionflower seeds, and there are fern spores in the soil, but you did ask about seeds and not spores.*

*Yes,* the Gatekeeper agreed. *I did ask about seeds. The pair of you may enter the Garden. Give thanks to Audblayin.*

Unar and Aoun had given thanks, profusely. They'd gripped one another by the hand as they stepped over the threshold, and Unar had felt that sense of smelling deeper than ordinary smell, the one with which she'd scented the seeds, sweep down into her chest and coil behind her breastbone. She felt reassured of that other sense, the one that ordinary people didn't have, and remembered that first fierce prickle of providence.

After the announcement had been made that six Gardeners had died of plague, more applicants came to the Gate. Oos had been among them. Rich crown and internoder girls, robed in silk, giggling, painting their lips with pomegranate juice to make them pink and pretty.

Unar ate a pomegranate on the inside of the Gate, spitting the chewed seeds with hardly a care except to avoid getting them on Aoun, who sat beside her, his eyes closed and his oily, spotty face blissful in the sun.

*They're fools,* Unar observed. *Do they think the Garden needs human flowers?*

*Were we less foolish,* Aoun asked without opening his eyes, *when we stood there, not ten days ago?*

*The Garden needs us, Aoun. The Garden needs this.*

She had taken his hand again. The source of power inside of her, between her breasts, had fluttered, and she felt an answering flutter in Aoun, lower down in his belly, and was startled all over again, for she hadn't been able to feel that, the last time she had held his hand as they passed through the Gate.

And that had been the last time she had deliberately taken his hand. His hammock had been far away from hers in the loquat grove. He rarely spoke to anyone at mealtimes or during lessons, so conscientious was he and so intent on submitting his will to the deity's.

Oos, who could talk happily about anything and everything, had become Unar's only real friend.

Until now.

In the home of the three huntsmen in Understorey, Oos's soft snores joined Ylly's, and Unar stared at the ceiling as if she might, with enough effort, see through the solid, living tissue of the tree to where Aoun might stand, right now, by the Gate, in the monsoon rain.

Had announcements been made that one Servant and one Gardener had fallen from Audblayin's emergent? Were the young and curious queuing already at the Gate where Aoun would test them with a handful of dirt?

Unar thought about how much bigger his hands were now and sighed again. She pictured him, naked and brushed with pearl dust, poised to dive into the moat, and shivered with yearning.

He would not desire her. Not for as long as the magic of the Garden held him. But what if he, too, ventured into Understorey? What if Unar led him to the place where Edax had led her? Beneath her blankets, she tucked one hand between her thighs, imagining it was Aoun's.

She hesitated. It was hopeless even to imagine. He was Gatekeeper, and would not leave the Garden, ever. Not until he died, or was sent, like the prior Gatekeeper, to search out a new incarnation of Audblayin.

But what if he did leave? What if he came into Understorey in search of her?

Unar closed her eyes, the better to imagine Aoun descending on pulleys and ropes to the platform outside the river entrance. He'd wonder who had built it and why it was there. And Unar would sense his nearness. She would appear, wet and gasping, beside him, and he would feel what he'd never felt before, and take her into his arms.

Parting flaps with her fingers beneath the bedclothes, Unar found their inner, silken counterparts already slippery with lust, and felt a brief surge of rage at the Garden, and the Servants who maintained its chastening spells. Was it Servant Eilif who, by casting the magic, had made Unar so disinclined to touch herself or others, ever, that she didn't even know what these parts of her own body were called? Flaps? The only word for women's parts she'd ever heard was "hole," and it was thanks to Edax that she even knew how to find that.

Oh, yes, there it was, secret and tight, unchanged by the stretching that the rain goddess's Bodyguard had given it. Aoun would find it, one day; he would make it his own place; it was where he belonged, only he didn't know it; couldn't know it, until he left the Garden and came to find her.

Unar's breath caught as Bernreb walked, bold and oblivious, into the room.

His bulk blotted out the light from the tallow candles. Unar squeezed her legs together. Hopefully the biggest of the brothers would be too busy checking on the baby to notice what she was doing.

No such luck. He looked at her and his eyes widened.

"You are Unar, is that right?"

"Yes," she whispered furiously.

"Do you need a father for your child?"

"No!"

"I am only asking. Just in case. You did not seem particularly interested in the baby. Not like Ylly. But here you are, obviously frustrated—"

"I'm not interested in babies!" Not unless they were reincarnations of gods, anyway. "And I'm not frustrated."

"As you say." His impudent smile made Unar want to throw something heavy at him. "Women do not often visit during the monsoon. Esse has moonflower, though, when you need it, to soak up and disguise the scent of your bleed. If you change your mind, you know where I sleep."

Unar scowled in his direction long after he was gone. Change her mind, indeed. How could she ever be attracted to Bernreb, with his pinkish, fishmeat-coloured skin? *You know where I sleep? Pah!*

She put her hand under her pillow and tried not to smell her fingers. Moonflower, to soak up and disguise the scent of her bleed. Thanks to the combined controlling nature of her tight-lipped, hateful mother and the unforgiving Servant Eilif, a stupid, bearded brute from Understorey knew more about her bodily functions than she did herself.

It took a long time for Unar to fall asleep. As she hovered on the brink of it, she thought she heard the sound of Marram's thirteen-pipe flute. It was haunting, like wind over hollow bones.

Something like a deep sense of smell stirred inside Unar's chest, but it wasn't quite Canopian magic.

It was colder. Blacker. Lighter.

Like being weightless in a pool with no water. Or floating in an egg-shaped Temple where the light never shone.

IN THE morning, Unar emerged to find Hasbabsah, not dead, but awake and cognizant, out of her chair and kneeling by the fire with an entranced expression on her sagging, yellowish face.

Oos sat up at the enormous table, sullenly prodding pieces of fruit around her leaf-plate, while Marram held open a rotted-looking old palmwood chest. It appeared to be the chest contents that had stirred the sickly ex-slave from her stupor.

"What's in there?" Unar asked.

"My mother's birth-crown," Marram answered. "Moonoom gave it to me when we went into exile in case one of us fathered a child. The crown is part of the ceremony welcoming a life. The newborn passes through it."

Ylly came through the curtain with Issi in her arms.

"Hasbabsah," she cried. "What are you doing out of your blankets?"

"Come and see, Ylly," Hasbabsah said in a slurred, slightly delirious voice, and both Unar and Ylly were drawn towards the hearth to look inside the chest.

Unar had expected something shinier. The so-called crown was a ratty, shrivelled circle woven of the same brownish-green leaf fibre she'd been stripping for Esse. Black-flecked, emerald night-parrot feathers and dried gobletfruit were knotted around the edges. It would barely have sufficed as a stricken man's tribute in the Temple. The chest also contained an assortment of musical instruments, none of which would have been allowed in the Garden at all.

"Ylly," Hasbabsah said, "let these men perform the ceremony to birth you into your new Understorian life. Let them lower the crown over your head."

Marram's gaze flicked between Hasbabsah and Ylly.

"We have the means to make the markings," he admitted after a while. "White clay and orange ochre from Floor. Indigo from Canopy. My mother told—"

"Your mother told you to keep them for your wedding, boy, but these women can help you to get more when—" Hasbabsah's interruption was interrupted in turn by a coughing fit that forced her to let go of the edges of the chest. She covered her mouth to keep the bloody sputum from spraying over all of them. Ylly passed the baby to Oos without a word of acknowledgment and forced Hasbabsah back into her chair, bringing water for Hasbabsah to sip and rubbing her back until the coughing eased.

"I don't think your hand will be steady enough, old woman," Marram said, smiling sadly.

"Your hand will do," Hasbabsah managed, and he gaped at her in sudden distress. She gulped at the water and went on in a rush, "I have heard that in Gannak a man does not paint a woman's face except on the occasion of their marital consummation, but that is not the custom in Nessa."

"I was born in Het," Marram said, but Hasbabsah ignored him, speaking over him.

"Do this for me, Marram, third son of Moonoom. Bring my old friend's daughter to this life soon, today, before I leave it."

Marram, contrite, did as she asked. He mixed different kinds of coloured dirt with oil and traced them on Ylly's arms and face. He combed out her hair. Until then, it had resembled an egret's straw nest tangled with white moulted feathers; when Marram finished winding it tightly around crossed pairs of polished purpleheart sticks, it formed a complex tower of violet and silvery-yellow almost too wide for the crown to fit around. He wrapped her tightly, breast to ankle, in an indigo silk blanket woven with the same white and orange designs he had drawn on her.

Then he stood behind her, his back to the fire. Only the top half of his face showed above Ylly's carefully arranged hair. He lowered the ugly woven thing from the chest around her neck, saying sentences that sounded the same backwards and forwards, and made no sense to Unar at all.

Hasbabsah glowed with contentment, though, and Ylly seemed as shy and pleased as a girl half her age.

Marram blushed deeply when his hands came to rest on Ylly's painted collarbones, but Unar suspected it wasn't over what he considered to be the inappropriate intimacy with Ylly. He wasn't looking at Ylly at all. His cloud-coloured eyes lingered on Oos.

Oos, for her part, had eyes only for Ylly.

Probably just wished she was still in the Garden so she could try doing her hair with those fancy crossed sticks.

And then Hasbabsah slipped back into unconsciousness, and the small happiness brought by the ceremony turned to cheerless deathwatch once again.

# THIRTY

Oos's bleed began before Unar's.

She reacted the way that Unar expected her to react, which was with more crying. It was while Unar was holding the back of Oos's shirt, to keep her from falling headfirst into the river as she washed her red-streaked legs, that they both heard the crack, like a lightning strike, and the great tallowwood tree shook as they had never felt it shake before, even in the strongest winds.

"What was that?" Oos whispered.

"Maybe one of the big branches breaking," Unar said. It happened sometimes. The poor hollowed their homes out of the load-bearing parts of too-thin limbs without regard to structural integrity. Nervously, the two women pressed back against the fungus-covered wall. Unar wondered if they would hear another crash when the branch hit Floor, whether it would be too distant or whether the rush of the river would disguise it. One-handed, Oos pulled on a pair of borrowed breeches, the crotch stuffed with dried moonflowers. Her other hand held the door latch down, keeping it from being lifted while she was still half naked.

"What was that?" Ylly bellowed from the other side of the door, trying to lift the latch.

Unar threw herself to the floor, arms protecting her head, as splinters and spray exploded through the wall of water. The tallowwood shook again, hard. Unar imagined Gardeners on swinging bridges in Canopy being tossed to their deaths. Something blocked the thin light that came through the water entrance. Luminescent fungi went dark in long, black scrapes.

The tree hummed as vibration slowly died. The wet tallowwood beneath Unar's cheek became still.

She sat up. Through the falling water, the trunk of a yellowrain tree protruded far enough into the fishing room that it brushed the door where Oos had held the latch. Ylly shouted and pounded on the other side of the door, managing to open it only a handbreadth before it jammed on the intruding beam. The tree trunk parted the river. Its hard, black, close-pattered bark was blotched with frost-green moss and it led like a log road out into sheeting monsoon rain.

There was daylight out there, glimpsed in a narrow pair of triangles beneath the log, in between its rounded edge and the room's floor. Unar searched for Oos, horrified by the thought that she might have been crushed. Then the silhouette of a heavy-breathing head popped up beside the log, close to the river. Oos's shape scrambled up onto the log, rolling up her breeches so that her bare feet could get a grip on the bark.

Taking a deep breath, Oos then clawed her way, on all fours, through the vertical river, to freedom.

"Oos, wait," Unar screeched. Oos didn't wait. Unar went after her.

The river water was relentless, as if a whole tree-crown had fallen on her. Though only a few days had passed, the weight of water was twice what it had been when they had first come to the three brothers' house. It almost carried her away, but then she was through, and she saw Oos ahead of her, fleeing down a road straighter and longer than any that existed in Canopy. The other end of it, where the fallen tree's roots must have been, was lost in murky greyness.

"Where are you going?" Unar shouted, but Oos didn't hesitate or even turn her head.

Rain, everywhere. Rain and gloom and the river. The trunks of the closest trees to the tallowwood were shadowy giants. The sound of Oos's breathing was already lost in the downpour, and the Servant's shape was indistinct with distance. A mosquito half the size of a sparrow whined at Unar's ear, and she slapped at it.

The yellowrain trunk that she stood on might not be stable. She might get a few more footsteps along it, only to join Oos in the abyss. She was not Marram, to extend her spines and stick like a burr to the closest tree.

But Isin, Unar's sister by blood, had fallen. She couldn't let Oos fall, too. Not her sister by soil, seed, and the Garden. No matter how much Oos liked hats and hair-sticks and wouldn't tell Unar what she'd learned in the Temple.

Unar touched the empty sheath at her waist, which she wore to remind Esse of what he owed her. If she slipped, she wouldn't even have the bore-knife to save her.

"Audblayin's bones," she swore, and dashed through the rain after Oos.

# THIRTY-ONE

WITH HER arms out for balance, Unar sprinted along the fallen tree.

It held her weight without moving, which was encouraging. Though the tree's crown was missing, the occasional lateral branch thrust directly up, forcing Unar to skirt around. She couldn't see Oos anymore through the monsoon, but where else could Oos have gone? There were two options, straight ahead or straight down, and Unar hadn't heard any screams.

Another branch blocked her way, one of a cluster radiating out from the trunk at a node. Unar threw her arms around the vertical one and stepped out onto a horizontal one, only to find Oos resting on the other side, sitting with her back to the vertical branch. She nursed a bleeding scrape along her left arm. Her legs dangled down on either side of the trunk.

"Is this where you're going to sleep tonight?" Unar yelled.

"Better than back there!" Oos yelled back. "Leave me alone!"

"What are you going to eat? How are you going to climb? What were you thinking?"

"You want to know what I was thinking? I was thinking that when Hasbabsah was taken as a slave, she could've tried harder to get away. Before she was marked, she could have tried. Maybe she didn't try because her spines were broken. Her power was taken away. It was easier to do what she was told. Eat what she was given. Sleep somewhere warm, with a fire."

"We're not slaves. Understorians don't have slaves."

"Don't they? How do you know? Have you asked, or were you too busy weaving baskets for your new masters? I'm going home, Unar!"

Oos had pulled her legs up, crouching on the yellowrain, ready to run again, when they both heard the deep, threatening hiss of an animal made invisible by the rain. Unar's heart pounded. She met Oos's fearful glance, hardly daring to breathe.

A skinny figure hurled towards them through the gloom, dark-faced and white-grimaced. A starved adult. No, a child of eight or nine.

"A demon is comin'," the child said, throwing herself at the jumble of branches and clambering over them without seeming to slow. Unar and Oos hesitated. They gazed after the fleeing child, then snapped their heads back towards the approaching menace as the angry hiss sounded again, closer this time, but the source still invisible.

Unar wondered, *Is it a chimera?*

Then she didn't have to wonder. A swinging, hammock-sized head sent mist curling away from pointed, scaly chin and jaw. A forked, pink tongue unfurled and dangled to test the air. The massive forearms that followed were striped gold and dark grey, with crescent-moon claws black and gleaming on top but caked on the undersides with animal fur, bark, and old blood.

*A dayhunter.*

Unar had never seen one, but the striped monitor lizards that sunned themselves in the Garden were smaller versions of this demon. And those claws were as long as her thighbones, just as Esse had warned.

"Go," she shouted, but the back of Oos's shirt was snagged on the upright branch. Oos screamed. Wept. Struggled. The shirt tore.

Unar put her foot to Oos's shoulder and scrambled up the branch. Without thinking, she leaped, using her height advantage to get past the demon's head and shoulders. Landing on its back, she ran down it as though it were a branch path itself.

A warm branch path. Smoothly scaled. Rippling. The wide body preparing to turn.

But the monitor lizards in the Garden couldn't walk backwards, and pulling down, hard, on their tails could trap them against a tree, their claws sunk too deep for them to lift their feet free.

*Audblayin keep me,* Unar prayed, seizing the demon's tail with both hands and swinging down to dangle beneath the yellowrain tree.

She hadn't considered what would come next. Only that she must make time for Oos to get free. The emptiness between trees seemed infinite, deep and dark, around her, all sounds muffled, nothing even remotely near that could save her if the creature threw her off.

*I can't die,* she told herself as her grip on the broad, scaly, dangling tail grew slippery with the rain running down its back. *Audblayin called to me.*

*Woke my magic. Gave me purpose.* She wished she had a bore-knife instead of a purpose. She'd climb up the demon's back as easily as scaling one of Oxor's suntrees. But her bare hands couldn't find purchase. If only she had Understorian spines for climbing. No, that was no use. Nothing could get through its hide, the hunters had said.

Then she remembered Marram's report: *Long streaks of dayhunter waste with insects trapped in it, only hours old and not set. The same fully grown male animal that left marks around your nets, Esse.*

Maybe the fallen Canopians hadn't been stuck to that branch by trapper's glue, after all.

Unar hauled herself up slightly, so that she gripped the dayhunter's tail with one clenched elbow instead of both hands. She reached her right hand around for the creature's cloaca. Her curled fingers scooped up a creamy, cement-like substance. The dayhunter's excrement.

She slapped that hand down on the wet scales, and found she was able to grip like a gecko. Her left hand took a turn scraping at the demon's vent. The stuff smelled strongly of fresh-cured leather, and it burned beneath her fingernails.

*What a mighty story this will make. How the storytellers will sing my praises!*

Unar had no way of spreading the sticky waste any further. She let her knees squeeze and her toes scuffle as best they could. Seizing the protruding scales on the leading edge of the dayhunter's hindlimb, followed by the frilled rim of its rib cage, she struggled up the length of it, expecting its huge head to come curving down out of the dark and snap her head off her neck any second.

Then she was standing on the broad shelf of its skull, making a final, desperate leap for the gap between the lateral branches. The dayhunter lifted its head. It hissed. Unar ran up the ramp of its snout. The forked tongue flicked her heel as she flew forwards.

She landed on the trunk of the yellowrain tree and kept running. There was no sign of Oos.

*I do have a destiny.*

Unar laughed maniacally, running along the tapering trunk, until she crashed into Oos's back.

Oos and the child had been seized by Esse, halfway back to the tallow-wood. How he'd gotten into the fishing room with the tree blocking the door, Unar didn't know. It felt strange seeing them, after the completeness of her isolation only minutes ago, suspended in the forest with the demon. Oos held her tattered shirt to her breasts and shivered in the rain.

Unar would have told them at once how she'd dangled from the demon's tail and then jumped off its head, but they were already speaking.

"What kind of demon?" Esse was asking, shaking the child.

"A dayhunter." The child was out of breath. She wore rags. Her black hair was hacked off close to her skull.

"She's Canopian," Oos said. "She's fallen, just like us. She survived."

The child turned and looked up into her face. "None of us will survive this, lady. Not unless you can fly."

Then both turned away from Esse, towards Unar.

"You're alive, Unar!" Oos blubbered.

"Get between me and the tallowwood, the three of you," Esse ordered. "Go back to the fishing room." Unar wasn't going to argue with him. He'd taken her knife; let him try to fight a demon with it. She'd had enough heroics for one day. They grappled on the narrow walkway, and as soon as they were behind him, he began uncoiling something heavy-looking like a rusted rope. No, not rope. It wasn't woven, but made of multiple metal links that clanked and jangled in the rain.

Marram and Bernreb erupted out of the river, shouting and splashing, forcing the trio to stop short once again. For a second time, the women tangled with the men, who tried to let them past without anyone falling off the log. Bernreb carried coiled rope, nets, and a spear with a long, wickedly serrated metal blade.

Marram carried nothing but his leathery, colour-changing wings of chimera skin. His yellow hair, despite being pummelled by the fast-flowing river, was matted with something the same suspicious consistency as the oily motions that Issi passed after a colicky spell. Unar was the last one forced to grapple with him.

"What's that in your hair?" she yelled, wrinkling her nose as the stench hit her.

"Do not be afraid, Gardener," Marram said with amusement. He paused on the other side of her while they still gripped each others' wrists, holding her, it seemed, so that she would look at him and be convinced by his confidence. "The demon will follow me far from here. I will not allow it to empty our little nest." Then he wrinkled his nose. "What is that on your hands?"

Then Esse called and Marram let go of her, turned, and dashed towards the danger, passing Bernreb, who had stopped to help Esse with the unusual chain. They lowered it around the underside of the trunk and held one end of it, each, in both hands. Esse pulled his end of it sharply, and the tree trunk under their feet shuddered. Then Bernreb pulled his end, and shards of green wood flew everywhere.

"A chain saw," Unar said.

"They gonna cut it in half," the child shouted, grabbing at Oos. "Show me where we can safely stand."

Oos went with the child headfirst into the river that flowed down the tallowwood trunk. Unar watched the men, frowning, for a few moments longer. Marram was the only one who could fly, he'd asserted. How would Esse and Bernreb get back to the tree when they'd sawn all the way through?

Finally, she saw that the rope tied to Bernreb wasn't all coils; a length of dark, twisted fibre led from a hastily tied harness at a steep angle, up towards the same lateral branch where the Canopians had become stuck.

With each step now, the trunk shuddered.

"Go back," Bernreb hollered at her, but he didn't stop sawing. Unar thought she heard Marram's cries in the distance, interspersed with angry hisses, but she couldn't be sure it wasn't the rain and her imagination.

She turned and ran after Oos and the child, towards the tallowwood tree and safety.

# THIRTY-TWO

THE RIVER loomed ahead.

Unar knew, now, why the men had been shouting as they burst through the wall of water; she shouted herself, to help focus her will. She increased her speed and thrust her arms above her head as if diving to try and reduce the downward impact of the river. If she slowed, or lost her footing, and truly did dive in, there'd be no going back.

The river smashed around her ears, a terrible, punishing blow. Blackness. Rushing in her head and around it. Legs still pushing. More kicking.

Then she was in the fishing room. Streaks of green-lit fungi exploded in front of her eyes. Her determination had carried her directly into a wall. Her teeth met the splintered wood, blood and river water in her mouth.

"Unghh," she said, and fell onto her bottom in an undignified way.

"You rode on the back of a demon," the child said. "I saw you. That was treasure, that was."

Unar lifted her head towards a light source in her peripheral vision. Ylly stood, her expression horrified, by the gap where the door had been taken off its hinges, holding a lamp in one hand and cradling a grumbling baby Issi to her chest with the other.

"What demon?" she asked.

"A dayhunter," croaked Oos from a dark corner.

"A big lizard," the child added. "Dunderheaded and dank. It cannot jump or glide, but it crosses Floor and climbs to plunder the nests of nocturnal animals while they sleep."

"We're not sleeping," Ylly said fiercely. "This dayhunter. Does it fear fire? Let's heap the logs from the hearth in the hallway, and—"

"It does not feel fire," the child said quickly, "and its flesh does not burn. We would die before it did."

"Then what are the men doing out there?"

"Marram is distracting it," Unar managed. She spat, hoping no teeth went along with the wood and slime, and added, "The other two are trying to saw through the yellowrain tree. You, what is your name?"

"I am called Frog," the child said.

"An unlucky name in Understorey," Ylly said. "Shall we call you Frogorf?"

"No. This Frog is going in only one direction, and that is up. What is there for me in Floor?"

Ylly seemed taken aback.

"How many monsoons have you, Frog?" Unar asked.

"This is my tenth."

"You're small for your age."

"There is no light to warm me, here, Gardener. No fruit for me to pluck from laden branches. Neither slaves' milk nor wasps' honey."

"Is that why you wish to climb higher?"

"I will climb higher," Frog said, showing her white teeth again in that stark, pantherine grimace. "Startin' right now, if I see that demon's head come in through the river."

Unar looked at Frog's forearms. There were the twin creases where her spines were retracted. If the demon's head came through, would Unar search the dwelling for her bore-knife and escape in the child's wake, or would she stay and try to protect the baby and unconscious Hasbabsah to the death, as Ylly no doubt would?

"Audblayin's bones," she swore again.

Another sharp crack. Another single, hard shudder of the tallowwood tree. Ylly and Oos cried out in unison as the river's flow was disturbed, but it wasn't the head of the giant lizard; rather, it was the yellowrain log tilting, hitting the roof, and then sliding away.

They were all sprayed with water. Then there was only the river as there had been before.

"They did it," Unar said, feeling weak with relief.

"I'm trapped here forever," Oos said with despair.

"Is that your baby?" Frog asked Ylly, already shrugging off the fact they had all faced certain death. Even if they had climbed successfully, they would have reached the barrier to Canopy and then what? The demon could have eaten them at its leisure.

"She's mine now," Ylly said, holding Issi tighter. "Her mother let her fall."

"So did mine," Frog said. "I mean, she did not throw me off with 'er two hands, but she wanted me to fall. She wanted sons. To help 'er, see. She was losin' her sight and knew she would not be able to do 'er job for much longer. Why put all that effort into raisin' the wrong sorta child?"

"That's horrible!" Oos exclaimed.

Frog looked sidelong at Unar.

"She knew I would not be able to do the work," Frog went on. "She already had one useless daughter, and she thought I looked . . . small. For my age."

Unar's face flushed with shame. She'd just told Frog that she looked small for her age. Before she could apologise, Esse and Bernreb swung in through the river, detaching their harnesses from the rope at the required moment, only to stumble heavily into the others. The tiny room was full. Unar heard someone's feet kicking the water buckets and the rattling of shelf contents being upset.

"Move," Bernreb gasped. "Further inside. Go!"

"You're back," Unar said, squeezing out from between Esse's sodden, heaving-chested body and the wall with her tooth-marks in it where she'd come through the waterfall too fast.

"You could win the crown at Loftfol with a cut that quick," Frog said, skirting Bernreb's dripping shape to follow Oos and Ylly down the hall. "Treasure."

"To Floor with Loftfol and its crown!" Esse wheezed. "Where is Marram?"

"Not here," Unar said.

"Do not," Bernreb told Esse, gripping his shirt in a giant fist. "If he did not fall, he will come. If he did fall, you cannot help him. The best place to wait is in front of the fire."

When they were all in the hearth room, Bernreb regretfully moved Hasbabsah's chair back from the fire. She didn't move; hadn't moved for some time, except to breathe. Now there was room for all of them to cluster by the heat.

"That old woman stinks," Frog observed.

"Show some respect, child," Ylly said.

"Whose house is this?"

"It is mine," Esse said. His tone did not invite further conversation, but Frog did not fall silent.

"Have I monsoon-right, then? It seems I am trapped here with you people."

"No," Esse said, at the same time as Bernreb said tiredly, "Yes."

"No," Esse said again.

Finally, there was silence. Steam rose from Unar's Gardener's tunic. She shifted her feet, turning each side to the fire as the other grew too hot. Beside her, Oos did the same thing. Her eyes looked glazed, the skin of her bare feet wrinkled by the water. She smelled of blood, and Unar couldn't tell if it was a failure of the dried moonflowers or the wound along her arm.

Ylly made a meal for Issi. When the baby was full and sleeping, she made a meal for Esse and Bernreb, too. Unar didn't feel like eating, but she scrubbed the last of the demon dung off her hands before making herself chew some dried fruit and sweet gobs of insects trapped in sap. Oos coaxed a little water into Hasbabsah and changed her clothes underneath the blanket. For once, Ylly didn't criticise her, but helped lift Hasbabsah's dead weight.

"You are angry with me," Frog said to Esse at last. "What have I done?"

Esse roused himself. He'd been staring at the wall, as if he could see through it to a place where Marram was napping in a hollow to refresh himself before flying home.

"Somebody cut the crown from that yellowrain tree," he said. "Today. This morning. The cut was fresh. Then they cut the tree again, at the base, so that it would fall. Was it you?"

Frog looked incredulous. "Does it seem to you that I could cut a tree down by myself? If I could, my mother surely would have kept me."

"The top of that tree was in Canopy when the sun rose. That means the person who cut off the crown was there, too. And you have the colour of a Canopian."

"She speaks like an Understorian, though," Bernreb said gruffly. "Like she was raised in Gannak. And she has the snake's gift."

"Too young," Esse said, his eyes sparkling with displeasure. "Who would give them to such a young girl?"

"I am ten," Frog said, glaring at him. "I earned them. I did not climb into Canopy. I cannot climb into Canopy. I do not know who cut down that tree any more than you do. I was with my adopted family on the outskirts of Gannak when the tree fell. I thought I would follow it a little way to visit my friends in the palm-oak. Since the monsoon started, we had received no birds from them. Now I know why."

"The dayhunter," Bernreb said.

"The dunderheaded dayhunter." Tears glistened in the corners of Frog's eyes but didn't fall. "If the demon 'as took your fellow, too, then I am sorry for you, but it is not my fault."

"We never said it was your fault."

"'E will not guarantee my safety." She pointed at Esse.

"He will," Bernreb said. Esse's gaze snapped angrily in his direction.

"Floorians take both of you, Bernreb, I—"

"Make a little room for me by the fire, brother." Marram walked into the room, shivering, teeth chattering, and wingless. He must have left the chimera skin in the fishing room, unheard above all the shouting.

Esse crossed the floor and roughly embraced him.

"Who are you?" Marram asked Frog over Esse's shoulder.

"I am Frog," Frog said, her shoulders hunched defensively. "Will you give me monsoon-right now? Am I forgiven for whatever you think I have done, Heightsman?"

"You are small," Marram said, moving past Esse to stretch his hands out to the flames. He gave Frog a sidelong glance, considering. "Small, and yet you have the spines implanted already."

"Does anyone else wish to insult me?" Frog demanded angrily.

Marram grinned despite his chattering teeth.

"I am not insulting you," he said. "Only thinking. I think I could teach you how to fly."

# THIRTY-THREE

Unar's eyes opened in the instant before the last, guttering tallow candle died.

Darkness filled the storeroom. Unar didn't think it was daylight outside. In the ten days since coming to the hunters' home, she'd adjusted to the strange cycle, sun unsighted, and her stomach, not quite ready to break fast, told her it was a few hours before dawn.

In ten days, she'd filled three of Esse's nine sacks with twine. Oos had surpassed Marram's level of skill on the thirteen-pipe flute. Frog had been forbidden by Esse to learn to fly and spent her days drying fish instead. Ylly spent them washing blankets and clothing, trading funny faces and noises with Issi, and trying to turn the nuts and grains that the brothers had in storage into an edible form of unleavened bread. Esse slept in the day and went out at night, keeping opposite hours to Marram and Bernreb.

Incredibly, Hasbabsah clung to life without waking.

Unar sat up in the pitch-blackness. Was Hasbabsah's spirit leaving them? Was that why Unar had woken instinctively? Hope and dread filled her. Maybe she was adjusting to this new level of the forest, no matter how impossible it seemed. Maybe her ability to detect fading life was returning, which meant Hasbabsah was about to leave them.

Feeling her way with her feet into the workshop, which was also completely dark, Unar lifted the embroidered hanging that led to the hearth room. The coals were banked but the room remained comparatively bright and much warmer than even four sleeping bodies could make an enclosed space. There hadn't been floor area in the storeroom for another bed for Frog, so the brothers had put her pallet in the hearth room by Hasbabsah's chair.

Unar looked down at the curled lump beneath the blanket as she passed it. Frog's breathing was slow and regular. She was sleeping.

Hasbabsah's breathing was erratic and barely detectable. Unar knelt by her chair and took hold of her cold, wrinkled hand.

"Hasbabsah, I'm sorry," she murmured. "I'm sorry for what your life has been like, and I'm sorry for how it's ending. I thought I was saving you. I tried to save you."

She swallowed, feeling the smoothness of her tongue on her hard palate, thinking about the markings the goddess Audblayin had allowed to be placed on Hasbabsah's tongue. Unar had believed her goddess was wholly good, but now she couldn't be sure of that.

No, Audblayin was good. He—she—had to be. It was the Servants who were stupid. The wasteful habits of Servants could be changed. They would change, when Unar returned to Canopy.

"I was stupid," she went on, holding harder to the rough palm. "I made mistakes. I'll do better. Your friend's daughter, Ylly, is free, now, isn't she? I promise I'll do everything I can to free Sawas and baby Ylly as well. I'm sure wife-of-Epatut is treating them well."

Unar paused and shook her head. She couldn't be sure of that, at all. She was being stupid again.

"I wish I could help you." Reluctantly, she let go of Hasbabsah's hand. It felt like she was letting go of her at the edge of the Garden, leaving her to fall to Floor. Frustration crept into her voice. "I wish Esse would let Frog learn to fly, so that she could fetch medicines, or that Oos would teach me what I need to know to heal you."

"Oos cannot teach you," Frog said, and Unar's head whipped around to find the skinny girl kneeling beside her, a strange gleam in her eyes. "Oos does not know. But I do."

Unar reared back from her.

"What are you talking about?"

"Hush! Do not wake them. I have been waitin' for you to come alone. Oos would sense it, the thing I wishta show you, and she must not. She must believe that 'er mind merely itches in 'er dreams, that it was 'er own yearnin' and nothing more that she felt. Lately I 'ave thought the old woman would die while I waited. You are so slow. So dank."

Unar had never considered herself slow. Her powers had woken before she'd even reached the Garden. Every trick the other Gardeners had shown her she'd learned instantly. More, she'd gone beyond them. She'd gone beyond the Servants, those fools who hadn't chosen her. Absolute was her belief that the rules that applied to others didn't apply to her.

*I am not slow. Or dank. Whatever that is.*

She peered at Frog. Their faces were close. Frog reminded her of some-one, but who?

"What do you wish to show me? It had better not be handstands or shadow puppets or any of the things you showed Bernreb."

Frog held up Marram's flute in the firelight.

"Can you play this?"

"I'm going back to bed."

"Of course you cannot play it." Frog's eyes still shone. Her mouth was small and stern. So unlike a child's.

The thought came to Unar: *Desperate circumstances have made this girl into something unusual. Perhaps extraordinary. Just like me.* The child went on. "Music is not allowed in the Garden. They did not tell you why, did they? Maybe they did not even tell Servant Oos."

"Music is the province of Orin, the bird goddess. Music in the Garden would be trespass in the territory of a rival deity."

"That is not why," Frog hissed. "Music is the lifeblood of all magic, but it can be borrowed from the gifted, and Audblayin's Servants would not want that, would they? No! Magic, access to the gods, whatever you wanna call it, is only for them, not for filthy Understorian maggots to have or to use! Their precious barrier blocks the movements of large livin' things, but it does not block music, does it?"

"You make no sense. Calm yourself. There's no magic in music. Green things grow in silence."

Frog thrust the instrument into Unar's hands.

"Play something. I will show you. Play it loudly. Play it badly. I do not care. I know you are not the one who has been takin' lessons, but as dank as you are, I am sure you can put your lips to it and make sounds come out."

"You hushed me only moments ago."

"Now I am tellin' you to play."

Unar narrowed her eyes at the girl, but she put the flute to her pursed lips and sent her breath over the row of pipes.

Nothing. No sounds came out. Unar could hear the soft crackle of the fire, Hasbabsah's faint and irregular wheeze, and water falling in the fish-ing room, but no matter how hard she blew, the pipes stayed silent.

Frog's eyes had lost their light. No, it was that her skull had started glow-ing. The same ghostly luminescence that lit the room under the river outlined the girl's skeleton, shining through her clothes. Unar could see her teeth through her closed mouth.

Then came that same strange, weightless feeling from before, on the brink of sleep. Like her body was dissolving and she was becoming part of the very air.

Startled, she let the flute drop into her lap.

"Do not stop," Frog insisted, the glow fading so that the whites of her eyes emerged from the place where two black holes had been. "The spell is not finished. Play on."

At once frightened and exhilarated—she was right, the magic here was in a person's very bones—Unar took Hasbabsah's hand again, finding it warm and the pulse strong. Greedy to wield her own power, herself, she demanded, "How are you using it? How are you borrowing it from me?"

"Play on, I said. Your friend, the Servant, is stirrin'. This is not for 'er to see. Not ever."

"Why not?"

"I will give no weapons to my enemy." Frog's grimace was back. "Your friend is more a slave than this old woman ever was. Listen, Unar, you wished to heal this one. To help 'er, to repay what your people did to 'er. At least, you said so. I do not think you lied. This is your last chance."

Unar filled her lungs. She raised the flute. It made no sound, no matter what she did with it, no matter how she blew into the thinnest, shortest hollow, the thickest, longest one, or any of the whittled wooden chambers in between.

"Is it morning?" Hasbabsah cried, startling and stirring, unable to open her gummed lids. "Am I blind?"

Unar tried to set the flute aside, but Frog snatched it from her hands.

"It's a few hours before dawn," Unar told Hasbabsah, grasping the old woman by her flailing arms. "You haven't opened your eyes for many nights. I'll bring you water and a cloth."

"Ylly?" Hasbabsah croaked.

"I'm Unar. Ylly's sleeping."

Oos pushed through the embroidered hanging and gasped when she saw Hasbabsah.

"Is she awake? Is she getting better? Unar, what did you do?"

In the corner of her eye, Unar saw that Frog had returned to her pallet, curled under the blanket, breathing evenly as though she'd never left her bed.

"Nothing," Unar said. "I did nothing."

She gazed for a long moment at Oos, wondering why a child who had fallen from Canopy would name a Servant of Audblayin her enemy.

"You tried something," Oos said.

"I try lots of things. I tried to be your friend."

Oos swallowed. Her eyes grew round. They glittered. Her dark hair fell over her shoulder in a loose braid twined with ribbons. Marram must have given them to her. She wore her Servant's robe, which she'd scrubbed as hard as she could, but the stains were still there.

"You saved me from the dayhunter. I never thanked you. I'm sorry. I'm thanking you now."

"You're welcome," Unar said. "That's what friends do."

When Oos had gone, Unar sat on the floor beside Frog, cross-legged.

"You can stop pretending to be asleep. Oos is gone. And I'm curious to know why you called her your enemy but revealed yourself to me. You have magic. You serve a deity."

That brought Frog, ferocious-eyed, out from under her blanket.

"I serve no deity!"

"Then how did you do that? Why did you do that?"

Frog's gaze became unfocused, as if her thoughts dwelled on something distant and unpleasant. She shook herself, coming to a decision.

"We will speak of the how," she said, "but not yet. As for the why, it was the way you jumped onto that demon's back. It should have eaten you. You should have died. You made me think of a mother yellow-bellied glider I found once, in a hollow-tree nest with 'er litter."

"A what?"

"Do you not know them? Do Warmed Ones have no use for furs? Them gliders with the rich pelts, fluffy tails, and wicked ivory claws. They are only so big"—Frog made a circle of her arms, like a pregnant woman's belly—"but they have extra skin for glidin' and the fur stretches to a proper-sized blanket for a grown woman's bed. I tried to take the babies. The mother glider scratched me up, bitin', tryin' to lead me away. I did not want to cut 'er and ruin the pelt, but even after I blinded 'er and cut off 'er claws, she would not stop."

Unar shifted uncomfortably. She'd killed animals before, but never tortured them. Frog, still staring into her past, went heedlessly on with her story.

"I returned to my new mother and asked 'er if she would do that for me.

If a demon came, would she die tryin' to defend me? And my new mother said no, she would not."

Frog laughed quietly, closed her eyes, and shook her head.

Unar thought, *My mother wouldn't have suffered for me, either. She expected me to suffer for her.*

"'Er answer did not please me," Frog said. "I sulked until she told me my birth mother had not loved me more. Did I need proof? She told me where to go. Close to the barrier. Close to the crumblin', worm-ridden branches where my birth mother resided. It was not Oxor's magic that showed me the woman who gave me life, but Akkad's magic, for my new mother knew the truth. My birth mother did not love me, yet I was fruit from 'er tree."

"You saw your Canopian birth mother through the barrier?"

"I heard 'er, first," Frog whispered, her gaze distant once again, hands still beneath the blanket. "Vomitin'. She vomited up 'er breakfast onto a branch below. Mushrooms she must have known were not safe to eat. She was skinny. Starving. And then she and the man who was my father fought to gather up the vomit and to eat it again."

Unar was horrified. She reached for Frog's shoulder, to comfort her, but the girl flinched away. Then something occurred to Unar.

"You called me a Warmed One. You asked if Warmed Ones had any use for furs. If you don't serve a deity, if you don't remember your life in Canopy, if you needed magic to find your birth mother, how could you know I was a Warmed One?"

Frog rolled her eyes.

"A slug with a skerrick of sensitivity would know."

Unar said nothing, hungry to hear more, wanting Frog to say that Unar's greatness shone around her like the halo of light around a lantern. But when the child spoke again, all she said was "I am tired. Leave me alone." She lay back down and pulled her blanket up over her head. "You love your friend. You jumped on a demon's back to save 'er. But she would not do the same for you. Next time, save your sacrifice for someone worthy. Unreturned love is for fools."

# THIRTY-FOUR

Nine bags full.

Unar stood and stretched, knuckling the small of her back.

"Where are you going?" Frog asked.

"To ask Esse for my knife back," Unar replied.

"He is sleepin'. We are not allowed in that room."

"I'm going to wake him." Unar smiled tightly. She'd been looking forward to this moment. With her knife in hand, she could whittle a flute of her own. She could work out what it was that Frog had done and do it herself.

She hadn't been alone with Frog since the night of Hasbabsah's recovery, not properly. Not with Oos slumbering and so insensible to the use of magic. When Unar asked questions, Frog only glared at her, tight-lipped, and made a sleeping gesture; she would not discuss her power or who had taught her to use it until everyone else was asleep.

Unar went into the hearth room, where Hasbabsah lectured a reluctant Oos and an eager Ylly. Issi crawled around on a blanket on the side of the great table that was away from the fire, clinging to chair legs, drooling and biting the wood, occasionally trying to pull herself up.

"Have you two come to join my classroom at last?" Hasbabsah asked drily.

In the wake of her near death, Hasbabsah had taken to teaching the other two women everything she knew about medicinal plants. Her knowledge was not inconsequential; as an Understorian warrior, she had learned field medicine, and once a slave of the Garden, she couldn't help but expand on what she'd been taught. She said that Ylly and Oos would never be warriors, so that they might as well learn something useful to trade in at the little villages where they must soon settle.

Oos still resisted the idea of living in Understorey, but was easily bullied by Hasbabsah, while Ylly's shoulders grew straighter and her chin lifted higher every day. Frog excused herself from the classes, saying she was a hunter and would trade for medicines if she needed them, and Marram and Bernreb looked appraisingly at her but did not contradict her.

Unar knew what had healed Hasbabsah, and it wasn't herbs. She glanced back at Frog.

"Where are you going?"

"To watch you wake up Esse."

Hasbabsah cleared her throat. "As I was saying. If the men had known the uses of this tree, their own home, they could have crushed the tallowwood leaves between two stones and rubbed the liquid on my chest to ease the coughing."

Marram was nowhere to be seen. Unar supposed Bernreb was still busy skinning his latest kill, something large and brown with pendulous arms, in the fishing room.

"Except that the leaves are up in Canopy," Frog said quietly, under her breath. Not quietly enough. Hasbabsah answered her.

"Not all of them. Low lateral branches have leaves, too. As for the tree that you came from, little Canopy-fruit, it is good medicine, too. Have you never heard of yellowrain tea? But all that our brave hunters could think to do with that priceless crown was cut it off and let it fall."

"The crown was already cut," Esse said, emerging from the hanging that led to his sleeping room, rubbing his head and looking out of sorts as always. "And I have heard of yellowrain tea. It is dangerous. Makes a man bleed on the inside. Turns his stool black."

"Am I a man?" Hasbabsah scoffed. "By the bones!"

"You would be better off teaching them how to sand floors and stuff mattresses. That is all they will ever be fit for."

"I will decide what they are fit for."

"They are fit for boiling water. Bring me a full kettle, Gardener. Right now."

Unar stared back at him, fists on hips.

"No. I've filled your nine bags with twine. Right now I want my knife back. You agreed."

Frog chortled softly behind her.

"I am afraid," Esse said, "that I made it into something else."

"What? You had no right! It was mine!"

"It was necessary. To guarantee your safety. You have monsoon-right, do you not?"

Frog stopped laughing. Unar marched right up to Esse where he stood by the embroidered hanging, itching to slap his face. Maybe violence against a host violated whatever rights they had granted. Maybe not. Maybe it would be worth the satisfaction. His chin was prickled with regrowth, and his breath smelled like fish.

"If whatever you made out of my metal really was necessary, you should've told me."

"You would have stopped working. Lazing in the sun is all you know. Meanwhile my brothers and I work ourselves to the bone. You want to see your precious metal? You want proof that it was needed? I'll show you."

He seized her arm and bundled her towards the corridor that led to the fishing room.

"Where are we going?"

"You will see."

"Me too," Frog said, but Esse pushed her out of the way.

"No. You stay. Only your big sister can come with me."

"Big sister?" Frog said. She laughed, a little too loudly.

Unar turned to stare at her. That was why Frog looked familiar. Unar didn't see her own face very often, but Frog certainly could have been her little sister.

Her heart raced. No, it was too much to hope. It was coincidence. Ridiculous. Frog said her mother in Canopy was going blind, and Unar's mother hadn't been blind. Before Unar could offer a different name—Isin?—Esse was dragging her away from the fire.

The fishing room was a horror of blood and stringy multiple stomachs, revealed by the light of a greasy lantern with translucent horn panes. Bernreb knelt on the floor, the broad muscles of his back working, lifting his head with a grunt when the door slammed behind Unar and Esse. There were clots in his beard and the carcass stank of rotten thatch.

"You are awake," Bernreb said to Esse. "Where are you going?"

"Out," Esse said, and shoved Unar, hard, in the back.

She went face-first into the river without time to scream. Monsoon-rights or no, Esse was going to kill her. Frog went right out of her head. She should have seen the warning signs. Esse was unstable. She should never have asked for the knife. She should have bided her time and then murdered him in his sleep.

A wooden railing punched her midriff. She seized it. Her feet fumbled on a platform twice the size and sturdiness of the one she had arrived on. She choked and cursed.

Esse came out beside her, a more controlled arrival, with a coil of rope over his shoulder that hadn't been there before. He shook water out of his hair and eyes. His wet sleeves and trouser cuffs were rolled to elbows and knees.

"The yellowrain tree," he said, knotting the rope into a harness for himself, "took away the old platform. I built it bigger, as if for young children."

"You didn't need my knife for this," Unar croaked. Rain melded with river water on her lips and brow. She hugged herself and shivered. Since becoming a Gardener, she'd spent her monsoon seasons dry, indoors, like other reasonably well-off Canopians, but here she was getting used to the cycle of getting drenched by the waterfall and then drying to a toasted crisp in front of the hearth fire. Esse tied the other end of his rope to the wooden railing and clipped his harness onto it with an S-shaped curve of iron.

"No." He turned his back to her, crouching down. "Not for the new railing. Put your arms around my neck. Make sure you have a strong grip."

Unar blinked, frozen for a moment by the realisation that he intended that she cling to him while he swung down lower into Understorey. He hadn't made another harness for her, nor offered to rope their bodies together, as he and Bernreb had been roped. No. If she weakened and fell, he wouldn't be sorry. It would be, as he saw it, her own fault.

She threw her arms around him and closed her eyes as he kicked back, hard, away from the platform.

Then they fell.

# THIRTY-FIVE

IT WASN'T long before Unar opened her eyes again.

Rain, mist, and falling leaves whirled around her. She sank lower, parallel to the great tallowwood river. Spray from it wet the top of the ropy-barked lateral branch where Esse eventually landed with a lurch.

Unar's arms jolted in their sockets. She made herself wait until Esse found his footing before her kicking feet found the branch, too. It was barely wide enough to stand on, and the top of it was neither flat nor smooth. Not like a Canopian road. The wood god, Esh, held no sway down here to form wood into functional structures.

Fibrous chunks broke away beneath her feet. She raised her arms to keep her balance and opened her mouth to accuse Esse. There were no structures at all here that she could see.

Then she smelled something awful and familiar. Issi's solid waste and whey-like sick, mingled with somebody else's menstrual blood. A smell, she supposed, that was irresistible to dayhunters. Past Esse, she finally saw the hollow in the tree. The smell was coming from there, and she squinted through the gloom, trying to see better.

Only then did she realise the opening into the hollow was too regular to be natural, and that there actually was some sort of structure built above it. Something weighted with a cross-section of tallowwood trunk, with perhaps a crumpled leather chute and several sharpened stakes. It was disguised by a net of leaves and bark, but it was there.

"Is it a trap?" she asked Esse, putting her hand out to his arm, half to steady herself and half to get his attention. "A trap to catch the demon?"

"One of my own invention." He did not sound proud, or excited, or doubtful. He sounded far away as though envisioning what would happen. "Inside the hollow, the bait is suspended by a rope. When the rope is pulled, the door will close. Can you see?"

He pulled Unar close and put her on the other side of him, pointing to the mechanism, and Unar could see. She was impressed by it, actually, but wouldn't give him the satisfaction of saying so.

"The weights will serve two functions. One, to drive the stakes into the holes I have made for them, deeply so that the demon cannot brush the door aside. It can dig out with its claws, given time, but by then the chute will have diverted the river's edge, directing the water into the hole. It will fill to the brim in mere seconds and the demon will drown."

"I'm glad," Unar said slowly, "that if we had to fall into one of your traps, it was the net and glue trap, and not this one. You've kept your word, to keep us safe."

"I am glad," Esse said, "that you see the necessity now."

"Wait. There's no metal in the trap. Surely you didn't use my little bore-knife to make that hollow."

"No." Esse unclipped his harness from the rope. He undid the knots and allowed that end to fall. Unar supposed he would haul it back up when they stood again at the railing. The S-shaped piece of metal, he held in front of her face. "Here is your knife. I lost my other piece when we sawed through the yellowrain tree."

"I see."

He tucked it into his pocket and turned away from her. Then he crouched again, one foot in front of the other on the narrow branch.

"Hold on to me. We must climb back up."

Worried that any sudden moves would send them hurtling to their deaths, Unar slowly eased her weight onto his back. No sooner had her feet left the branch than Esse took a quick skip, hop, and jump to the right hand side of the hollow, away from the river, and there was the soft sound of his forearm spines sliding out of their sheaths.

Then, the axe-biting sound and shuddering impact of Esse embedding himself in the bark of the tree.

Unar tucked her face into the back of his neck as splinters flew. Swiftly and steadily, Esse climbed.

She thought, *How those red-and-yellow puffed-up parrots calling themselves soldiers of Odelland would tremble at the sound of a hundred Understorians climbing their precious king's blue quandong tree.*

And she stifled a laugh.

Had she gone crazy? Whose side was she on? The barrier would keep Esse and his ilk from Odelland. From Ehkisland. From Audblayinland. From all of Canopy. It was trespass there that had seen Hasbabsah made a slave, her spines broken.

Yet the magic bed of the decrepit princess was the neck bone of an Old God, Hasbabsah said. There had to be a way through the barrier.

Unar became aware of the heat and movement of Esse's muscles. His arms and legs seeming untiring. Both his thighs together made up the width of one of hers, yet he didn't labour for breath. When he lifted one knee to stick his shin spines into the tree, she thought again that he had the longest shanks she'd ever seen on a man or woman. Edax had long legs, but not so thin. He hadn't wanted to remove all his clothing, but Unar had made him when they had been together during their lessons. She'd wanted to see all of the non-owl parts of him as clearly as possible by meagre moon- and starlight. There had been knife-scars on his skin, sparse body hair, and very little padding, but several knotted veins had stood out on his calves, and his no-longer-youthful knees had been cracked and saggy.

Unlike Aoun's.

That led her to remember Bernreb's offer with a wince. Since he'd made it, she'd followed Oos's example and bled for several days; it had been horrible, but it was over now, and she knew what to expect next moon. Her soiled bedclothes, taken by Esse, had obviously been used for demon bait instead of left in the river to leach out the dangerous scent.

Unar looked up and saw the underside of the platform by the side of the river. The rope still dangled down. They were almost back at the hunters' home. She saw Esse's upraised forearm, the bone blades gleaming, unblunted by the climb.

*Magic must keep them sharp as well as clean.*

She tried to extend her magical senses to examine them, but it was not even like trying to reach with her hands tied behind her back. It was as if she had no arms. As if she was born a worm or a snake and had never had them, except in her feeble imaginings.

Unar made a small noise of frustration. Frog must tell her more. No more waiting.

"Do not let go," Esse said. "We will go through the river together. I will leave the rope tied to the outside, and secure the other end of it to the inside. It will mean extra chores to keep the water from the fishing room floor, but by next moon, the river will be too strong to pass through at all without the aid of a rope."

Unar didn't answer him. She could guess who would be doing the extra chores. Then they were in the river again, and her arms around his neck were all that held her to the world. The water washing over her while she clung to a near stranger reminded her of the feeling of Audblayin's power washing over her the morning she had knelt with Oos and Aoun before the night-yew in the Garden.

There had been six new Gardeners chosen that day. *Fledglings,* the old Gatekeeper had called them. Not quite Gardeners, but not of the world outside, either.

She, Oos, Aoun, and the three others had worn their crimson ceremonial Gardener's garb for the first time. Red leaf-shirts and green trousers beneath hooded crimson robes. Their knees crushed the leaf litter, and the branches of the night-yew spread over their heads. The yew's tiny white flowers were turned to fruit once yearly by the first rays of the first month of the post-monsoonal sun. They had waited for that dawn to transform them too.

Oos had whispered, *One who walks in the grace of Audblayin can't wait for her powers to wake!*

*I can't wait to eat the fruit,* Aoun had muttered, and his belly had grumbled.

Unar hadn't said anything. She'd thought her powers were already awake. How else had she passed the tests they had given her? How else had she watched the work of the Gardeners and felt like she could do it faster and better? They had been in the Garden for weeks already.

Then the sun had risen over the great forest. It struck the crown of the night-yew first, some thirty paces over their heads. Minutes later, the first minuscule crimson fruit began to fall. The fruit tasted like turpentine—bitter with only a hint of sweetness, exactly the way that the crushed night-yew needles smelled—but Unar had reluctantly eaten a few more of them, anyway. It was part of the ritual. Or it amused the Servants to poison them.

As the light travelled further down the yew, more and more fruit fell, till it pinged off their heads and shoulders like rain.

Aoun had said abruptly, *I don't feel well.*

Then the sun had touched them and something had exploded inside Unar's middle, like another, smaller sun whose rays illuminated the life around her, so that she could feel it without seeing. Not only filling the confines of her body, as before, but sending strings out to tangle with every plant, every creature, and every beating human heart.

As the sensation had washed over them, Unar found her arms around

Aoun's neck and his arms around hers. They clung to each other, as if to keep from being pulled apart by all the unfurling threads.

Threads had crossed from each of them into the other, too. For the space between breaths, Unar had felt what Aoun was feeling. So it was no surprise to her when he hunched over and vomited into the dirt between his knees.

*You ate too many,* Unar said, rubbing the space between his trembling shoulder blades. *You wanted it too much.*

Yet Aoun's wanting was a drop next to the monsoon of her own desire.

# THIRTY-SIX

STILL WET from her passage through the vertical river with Esse, Unar plucked Frog by the collar and dragged her from the hearth room into the dark corridor between the fishing room and the rest of the dwelling.

"Are you my sister?" If she could have used her magic, she would have delved into Frog the way that Oos had delved into the jacaranda seed during her lesson in the Garden. She would have determined at once if Frog was fruit from the same tree as Unar was.

"You are wet," Frog said, her small fists striking Unar's chest. "Get off me!"

Unar only leaned harder on her, so she couldn't wriggle away.

"Are you Isin?"

Silence.

"Answer me!" Unar thought of the story about the man and woman fighting over poisoned mushrooms, Frog's parents, on the other side of the barrier. In Canopy. "They were my parents that you saw. They were starving."

Frog's chin lifted insolently.

"You can imagine them easily, can you not? Imagine this. Imagine them screamin' at each other to go to Audblayin's Temple and collect the silver they were owed for their daughter's service. Imagine the man ravin' that the Garden was not a place for men, that it was the woman who would hafta go. I lost sight of them when they went. I could not follow. But from that moment, I knew I had a sister in the Garden."

"You knew," Unar repeated dumbly, hypnotised by the scene that Frog had painted in her mind, "you had a sister in the Garden."

"Yes. Of course I am your sister. You are so dank."

Unar rallied with the old anger she'd always relied on.

"And you," she said, shaking Frog, "are so small. So good at pretending to be weak, but you healed Hasbabsah with magic. Who knows what else you can do? That yellowrain didn't fall by accident, did it?"

"No." Sullenly. "I cut it down."

"But the crown was in Canopy. You said that the crown was in Canopy. You know how to pass through the barrier. You can take us home!"

"No!" Frog gripped Unar's little fingers and bent them back until pain sent Unar stumbling in retreat. "I sent a bird to Canopy. One of my friends in Canopy lopped the crown for me. It was not a great enough tree to 'ave anybody livin' in it. It was tall enough, though. I knew it could reach here from the place where I was waitin'."

Frog rubbed her shoulders where Unar had pinned her.

"You sent a bird?" Unar recoiled again, but there wasn't much room to move in the corridor. The opposite wall was at her back. "You have friends in Canopy, but not me? Not your own sister? Why didn't you send a bird to me?"

Unar realised she was crying. She couldn't scrub the tears away without Frog seeing. Frog was the child here, not Unar. Frog was the one who couldn't remember her birth mother, not Unar. Frog should be the one crying.

"You were a Gardener by the time I found out your name. A keeper of Understorian slaves. 'Ow could I send a bird to you?"

"Keepers of slaves? Is that why you think Gardeners are enemies, unless they share your blood? That's why Oos is your enemy, but not me? That's why you'll teach me, but not her?"

"I never said you were not my enemy." Frog kicked her, hard, in the shin, but the tears that might have come to Unar's eyes from the pain were already there. "I hadta meet you before I could reveal myself to you. I hadta know. My friends in Canopy know where to get gossip. Erid, Wife-of-Uranun, threw me away because she already had one daughter. She did not need another. She needed sons. What if you were like 'er? What if it was your idea to throw me away?"

Unar was shocked and repulsed.

"My idea? My idea? I hated them because they didn't look for you. Not properly."

"Now you know why they did not look. I was too small." Frog folded her arms. "Small and useless."

"Isin." Unar tried to take Frog's shoulders again, with gentleness and love this time. "Isin. Isin."

"Stop sayin' that name." Frog pulled free. Tossed her head. "That is not my name."

Unar slid down the wall of the corridor until she was sitting, wet and shivering, in the dark.

"Not your name?"

"Come back to the hearth room," Frog said. "Get dry. Tell me about whatever it was that Esse showed you."

"What Esse showed me," Unar repeated hollowly.

"Come this way, broken eggs for brains, jumper on dayhunters' backs. You will feel better in front of the fire."

UNAR DRIED herself in front of the fire.

*What if you were like 'er? What if it was your idea to throw me away?*

Was she like her mother? She didn't know. Had Mother been going blind? It was starting to make sense now. Mother staying home on days she should have gone to the forge. Mother making mistakes, flattening a finger of her left hand. Lashing out in a rage but striking the wall or floor beside Unar instead of Unar herself.

Unar and Frog made rope all day without exchanging another word.

Every now and again, Unar looked up from the wood-and-metal jig that Esse had set up for them—*whose bore-knife did he steal to get the metal for these rotating hooks and pins?*—to fix Frog's solemn face again in her mind.

Not lost by accident. Abandoned with deliberation. Unar wanted to recoil from the thought but forced herself to face it instead. When she thought of their mother, Wife-of-Uranun, her starkest memories were of sudden rages. Now that Unar knew they had been provoked, not by Unar herself but by her mother's terror of an inability to work and subsequent starvation, could she forgive the neglect that had led to Isin falling?

No. Not ever.

Isin could have helped their father, just as Unar had. Fuel finding could have kept them from starving, couldn't it? Only, the wood god, Esh, had been weak that year and the rain goddess, Ehkis, had been strong. The wood was wet and would not dry. Neither Unar nor Father could cut wet wood with a blunt axe.

*Your belly's speaking, Erid. Eat these,* Father had murmured.

*Why so few?* Mother had answered. Unar had thought she sounded cold, but what if it was the hollowness of despair? *She's fit only for the block.*

Unar had run, at last, not knowing that her mother was frightened of the forge because the world had become a blur.

Frog had said, *She knew I would not be able to do the work. She thought I looked small. For my age. She wanted sons.*

How did Frog know that? What messages had she received from Canopy? What spies had she sent to peer into Uranun's rented hovel? Unar wondered if Father had been tempted to send Wife-of-Uranun to Audblayin's emergent to ask for a male child. But what gifts could Uranun have sent to the Garden? He had stolen and eaten his own child's mushrooms. Sacrifice was hardly in his nature.

*He was willing to sell his daughter to put food in his own mouth.* Nothing like Wife-of-Epatut, Issi's mother, who lavished rare metals and costly fabrics on the Servants just for a chance of conceiving again. When Wife-of-Uranun had finally made her way to the Garden, it had been to ask, not for a son, but for a thousand weights of silver.

Unar looked fiercely at Frog's face again. She wanted to give her little sister everything that should have been hers by right. It was a miracle that she lived, that this chance even existed. When Unar returned to Canopy, Frog must accompany her. Perhaps they would live rough for a while, as out-of-nichers, searching, finding food with magic that Unar must keep hidden outside of a palace or emergent. But only until they found the reborn Audblayin and returned him to the Garden. Then all honour would be theirs, all powers returned, and Unar would keep Frog by her side, in sunlight, all the time.

But she didn't dare say anything. Not while she feared being rebuffed.

*Unreturned love is for fools.*

Frog held the triplicate, paired strands of twine apart with her small, loosely splayed hands while Unar worked the handle that twisted them. When the twist in the strings was just short of snapping them, Frog slid her hands away from the weighted end of the rope towards the loose end, and the six lines became a single, fatter one.

Unar pinched the place between made and unmade rope as they moved the completed section beyond the clamping, hanging weight that kept the twine tensioned. When it was fixed, and the three rotating hooks reset with loose continuations of the twine, their lengths coming from six of the bags that Unar had filled, she opened and closed her fingers to uncramp them.

Esse's head poked under the flap. He peered at them, at the rope, and at the candles he had given them to work by. There were dark smudges under his eyes. Since the demon trap was completed, he'd told Marram he would become diurnal again, beginning by not sleeping that day.

"That will do," he said. "Cover the jig. Blow out the candle. Come and eat."

Frog and Unar shared repulsed looks. Whatever the name of the lid-less lizard that Bernreb had caught that afternoon, Unar did not enjoy its sour meat or flaky texture. Hasbabsah said it was good for them, especially the eight eyes, which were thin jellied blobs on beds of bright orange fat.

"Do you know, I liked eating that long-armed-thing," Unar lied. Bern-reb's earlier catch had been tainted with its male musk and practically inedible, but it was tastier than the lizard.

"Do you not listen to the old woman's raving?" Esse said. "Eating that meat more than twice in a moon will grow hair on a girl's chest."

"If only I had known," Frog said flatly. Unar guessed she was thinking of Wife-of-Uranun, or perhaps her Understorian mother, whom she'd showed no signs of missing.

"Frog," Unar said, catching her as Esse's head disappeared and Frog made to blow out the candles.

"What is it?"

"You send birds to Canopy. You have friends there. You must know if Wife-of-Uranun was with child a third time. Did she have a son, in the end?"

Frog blew out the candles. Unar couldn't see her face.

"Our mother fell, Unar," she said. "She was not with child, nor will ever be again."

Another shock. Their mother had fallen? Or had she flung herself down in desolation?

"Was it because she was blind?"

"No."

Unar waited for more information, but it wasn't forthcoming.

"You said you had an adopted family here in Understorey. Were they kind to you? The woman you called your new mother. What kind of woman is she?"

"Later, Unar. We will talk later, when they are all sleepin'."

UNAR LAY on her pallet, feigning sleep.

All but Ylly and Issi had retired to bed, pallet, or chair to sleep. Unar wished angrily that Hasbabsah hadn't forced the flaky lizard down the baby's throat; surely that was what kept the normally contented child screaming this late at night.

Ylly sang a soft, wordless song as she jiggled Issi over one shoulder, but Unar noticed the song had gotten hoarser and even tinged with anger and frustration. Oos's restless shifting on the pallet besides Unar's indicated that she, too, was still wide awake.

At last, Oos sat up.

"Let me help you," she begged Ylly. "Let me take her."

"No," Ylly snapped

"I have nieces and nephews." Oos got to her feet. "I know what to do with babies."

"You know what to do with babies, all right. Sell them, if you need a new ribbon for your hair."

Unar tensed beneath her blanket, her back turned to them. Maybe this would be the moment. Oos wasn't her friend anymore. Not faithful to her anymore. She'd finally confess to Ylly that she'd sold Sawas away because Sawas had tried to tell Servant Eilif about Unar learning to swim. And Ylly would, rightfully, blame Unar for involving Sawas in her determination to break the rules of the Garden.

"Ylly, I'm sorry." Oos's voice was thick with emotion. "I'm so sorry. One who walks in the grace of Audblayin was raised never to look down, but that's no excuse. I should have looked, anyway. I should have seen."

"Yes. You should have. It has been a long time. Since I had Sawas. And she was taken so soon. Weaned so early." Ylly sounded even hoarser. As if she had started crying. Oos moved closer to her, away from Unar.

"When my niece had bubbles in her stomach, my sister would hold her like this. Facing down, along her forearm, with her cheek in her hand. And then swing her. Right. Like that."

For a wonder, Issi's squalling subsided into discontented grunts.

"She is heavy like this," Ylly said with a flutter of a forced laugh.

"Should I fetch Bernreb?"

"No. Let him sleep. Will you . . . will you take a turn?"

"Of course."

Long moments went by while the baby settled. *Hurry,* Unar thought. *The sooner you all go to sleep, the sooner I can join Frog in the hearth room and learn more.* She was so hungry to learn.

At last, her ears detected the sounds of tucking a child into her cradle.

Abruptly, before Unar could turn over and risk a peep through her lashes, there were other sounds. Unar couldn't reconcile them, at first, with what she knew: Ylly hated Oos, and was old enough to be her mother, besides. Kissing sounds were kissing sounds, though. They hadn't been a feature of the Garden, but Unar remembered them from the streets.

She didn't need to roll over to see what was happening. There was nobody else in the storeroom but Unar and the baby, and the women were not kissing the baby. Not like that.

*Get on with it!* she raged inwardly.

No sooner had she had the thought than two bodies thudded onto Oos's pallet beside her. Hands scrabbled to pull the too-small blanket over both of them. Elbows and knees invaded Unar's space. They had to be wriggling out of their clothes.

For her own amusement, Unar would have liked Bernreb to appear just then. He still sometimes checked on the baby. He didn't appear this time, though. And Ylly and Oos didn't go to sleep. After what seemed like hours, the soft, sucking sounds of fingers in fluid-filled places were accompanied by Oos's strangled gasp, and Unar dared to hope that they would fall asleep where they were, collapsed on one another, and she could make her escape.

"The last power of the Garden has finally left us," Ylly whispered with joy.

Oos's new lover obviously didn't know her as well as Unar did. There was nothing Ylly could have said more calculated to make Oos cry. Unar was sorely tempted to leap up and advise Ylly to put Oos facedown along her forearm and rock her until she settled.

Instead, she held herself completely still. Ylly held Oos. The night surely held only a few more hours.

Unar counted silently to a hundred after she thought the other two women were asleep. They didn't stir when she rolled away from them. She crawled through the workshop and, kneeling, peeled back the corner of the embroidered hanging.

No movement in the hearth room. Hasbabsah snored in her chair. Frog was curled in her corner. Unar crawled over to her, hating Oos and Ylly for discovering they didn't actually despise one another. They'd spent so long cuddling that Frog had fallen asleep, but she would surely want Unar to wake her.

Frog's eyes opened before Unar could touch her. Were they Wife-of-Uranun's eyes? Unar didn't know. She couldn't remember. Maybe she didn't want to remember. The Garden was the only place worth remembering.

"The fishing room," Frog mouthed. Unar nodded. Once they stood by the roaring wall of water that would disguise any sounds they made, Frog rubbed her eyes and asked, "What did Esse show you, then?"

"A trap he made to catch that demon."

"Only magic-wielders can catch a dayhunter. 'E wasted his time."

"If you say so. Little sister, will you teach me how to use my own magic now, or must I continue to simply provide my power for your use?"

Frog put her fists on her hips.

"It would serve you right if I never teach you. You still think you walk on high paths above me. Above everyone, with how black you are. But soon you will lose the sun's kiss."

"I never said—"

"Of course not. You do not wanna stay here in Understorey, though, do you? The first thing you wanted to know was how to get through the barrier. You begged me to take you home. But this is my home, do you see? This is *anyone's* home who would fight for justice."

Unar only gazed at Frog. Justice? Why should she care about that?

"I'm not sworn to the goddess Ilan, Protector of Kings," she said carefully, "but to Audblayin, Waker of Senses."

"Yes," Frog answered impatiently, "obviously. If you were sworn to Ilan, I could use you to debilitate my enemies with remorse. Fill them with self-loathin' until they slit their own throats. We would not hafta fight anyone, then."

"Fighting? What are you—"

"If you served Airak, I could use you to strike my enemies down with lightnin'. If you served Atwith, I could make them fall dead by the score, like autumn leaves. Instead, you serve Audblayin. Am I to bring down the kings of Canopy by impregnatin' their wives? Your so-called gift is all but useless to us."

"Us?" Unar waved her hands around in the air. "Who is us? Your adopted family, Frog?"

"I might as well show you. You can always heal the injured. Useful, I suppose, since I have been wounded in battle. Sit down on this crate." Frog nudged one of two crates with her knee. "And don't interrupt me. You look at me and see a child, but *you* are the child."

# THIRTY-SEVEN

UNAR SAT on the crate.

Frog sat on the other crate, opposite her, knee to knee. Unar stared at Frog, childlike and yet not-child, lost and found and yet still lost. Unar could make no sense of her words: *This is anyone's home who would fight for justice.*

The river hissed as it sheeted past. Only Esse's rope, stretching from a fixed shelf into the flow, wicking water along its length to *plip-plop-plip* on the floor, broke the glassy sheen of it in the light of the luminescent fungi. All evidence of Bernreb's butchery was gone.

"Do you know the godsong?" Frog asked. "They do not allow music, but you should have learned the godsong before they locked you up behind those Gates."

"Yes," Unar said. Teacher Eann hadn't been completely ineffective.

"Listen to my voice carefully as I sing the first verse."

"I will."

Frog's singing voice was soft and high.

> *Airak the white with his forked swords of light*
> *stole the gleam from the Old One's eye*
> *while the winged and the furred, the beast and the bird*
> *come when summoned by Orin, or die.*

Unar's lips compressed. Those weren't the words she'd been taught.

"Now you sing it," Frog said.

Unar hesitated, unsure of whether Frog intended to steal the sound from her very throat, as Frog had stolen the sound of Marram's flute, or if Unar would be permitted to hear the words that she sang in her deeper, raspier voice.

*Airak the white with his forked swords of light*
*dances with those who will dare*
*while Oxor is love and her sunshine above*
*pierces mortals and mists with her care.*

Frog had done nothing to alter her singing, Unar thought, unless it was something that she couldn't sense.

"Well?" Frog said.

"Well, what?"

"Could you tell the difference? That you were an adept but not me? That you had the gift and a patron deity, and I did not?"

"No." Unar kept her expression fixed but wanted to slap the incredulity off her sister's face. Frog already knew she couldn't tell. Was this just a reminder of her supposed place? Frog shook her head.

"I had heard power is purposely waked in Gardeners as surely as it is waked here in Understorey, but the effect does not carry across the barrier, it seems. I must do the work of wakin' your bones in the Understorian way myself. Sing again, in the next highest octave."

"Octave?"

Frog grimaced. Even seated, her small fists went to her narrow hips.

"Startin' with this note. Like this. Airak."

"Airak."

"No, no." Frog rolled her eyes. "Match it exactly. Airak."

"Airak."

"Huh. That is not your natural frequency, either. The bones stay quiet. Try again. Airak."

"Airak," Unar squeaked.

"To Floor with Airak," Frog said, baring her teeth. "It is not workin'. Wait. Maybe you need to go one lower than where you started. Find it yourself. I cannot sing that low."

Unar tried, but her voice croaked, dry and useless, and she couldn't make it sound like song.

"Neither can I."

"You must try again!" Frog's fists firmed. "Or stay here, powerless, forever."

Unar stood up. She went to the bucket for drinking water, dipped it into the river, wet her throat, and washed her face and hands. She stood with her shoulders back and her chin lifted, eyes closed. She could do it. She *would* do it! She had never failed at any magical task ever set for her.

> *Airak the white with his forked swords of light*
> *dances with those who will dare*
> *while Oxor is love, and her sunshine above*
> *pierces mortals and mists with her care.*

"Do not stop!" Frog leaped up from her crate. Unar heard the sound of it tipping carelessly onto the floor. Her body felt like it was dissolving in the now-familiar indication of Understorian magic—all weightlessness and no smells. Her eyes flew open. Frog was crossing the floor between them, hands extended, the tiny bones inside them glowing like the bones of a transparent fish. "Sing the whole song!" She laid her hands on Unar's.

> *Atwith the king of the unliving thing*
> *rules a restful, lightless land*
> *while the winged and the furred, the beast and the bird*
> *come to Orin if she lifts a hand.*
>
> *Ukak, he calls the small creatures that crawl*
> *to the lamps that are Airak's bliss*
> *while Odel sets their adored children in air*
> *as soft as a mother's kiss.*
>
> *Esh grows the paths between family hearths*
> *and knits up the limbs of the sleepers.*
> *Irof brings blooms to the humblest of tombs*
> *and wakes up the hearts of the weepers.*
>
> *Ehkis brings rain to the forest again*
> *and rests in the heart of the waters.*
> *Audblayin guards birth and the things of the earth*
> *and opens the eyes of their daughters.*
>
> *Ulellin whose leaves and the stir of the breeze*
> *bring delight to the high and the bidden*

*is no less than Akkad, whose greatfruit can be had*
*for sweetness or seed-metals hidden.*

Unar looked down and saw the bones in her own hands beginning to glow. There was uneasiness in her midriff, too, a feeling like the cramps in a stomach empty for weeks suddenly finding itself full of food. At the same time, her stomach was breaking into floating fragments with the rest of her. She had no body. She needed no body. Only the pure vibration of sound. The glow of her bones strengthened as she sang the final verse.

*Ilan guards rights of the royals, whose heights*
*are not for the stricken unclad.*
*Together, they raise all the meek who give praise*
*to the skies with a green, glowing hand.*

Disembodied, hot and cold at the same time, a collection of motes floating on currents of music, her mote-fingers tangled with Frog's mote-fingers, Unar sensed it for sure.

Frog was her sister.

They had come from the same mother. They had come from the same father.

The song ended. Unar's body solidified as if her soul had been suddenly coated in clay. Frog let her hands drop. She looked at Unar with satisfaction.

"You will hafta practice singin' in that octave," she said. "Your voice is terrible. Not that anyone will know, if you use it for magic. The use of it will render it silent. But remember that your friend Oos has always been sensitive to music. She will feel it. Not the makin', but the usin'. 'Er bones are already awake."

Unar wasn't best pleased to hear that just as she herself had not needed the Garden to wake her Canopian magic, Oos was a natural at musical Understorian magic. But she tried to stick up for her friend.

"Then why keep it secret from her? You said she . . . we . . . couldn't get back up through the barrier. What harm, if she has her magic to help her heal, down here, the same as she did before? She could show me—"

"She will never show you! I am the only one who will show you. I am the only one you 'ave, Unar." Frog's teeth showed again in that characteristic grimace that Unar thought she could grow to love. "The only one who loves you."

Unar closed the distance between them, trying to fold Frog in her arms, but the girl flinched back.

"What's wrong?"

"Hold me when you mean it. Only when you mean it."

"I mean it. I tried to find you, Isin, but I was too small. I tried to find other babies that fell because of you. I went to the Garden because becoming Bodyguard to Audblayin was my chance to find you when you were re-born. Yet here you are, in the same body. You are my sister." Frog allowed the embrace, this time. Her thin body quivered, and she didn't relax into it. Unar sighed. "Oos was my sister too. I wish you could—"

Frog pulled away.

"No. Only me. I am your *only* real sister."

Unar bowed her head in acknowledgement.

"You are my only real sister."

When she lifted her head, Frog had gone back to her blankets. Unar stood there alone, listening to the sound of her own breathing, feeling the tiny increments of Audblayin's birth magic expelled with every vibration, as though the Garden lived inside her.

# THIRTY-EIGHT

THE TEMPTATION to test her new power was almost overwhelming.

Unar listened to Marram and Oos play the pipes in the morning. They each had an instrument now, and harmonised with one another in complex ways. To Unar, it was like watching two painted bronzebacks entwined, one living and one dead, and the living snake looked at her with crystalline eyes and promised to obey her, if she would only give it a command.

Frog ate her breakfast fish fastidiously, lining up the bones, and gave Unar a single, severe, meaningful glance. Ylly and Issi slept late, as did Esse, recovering from the sleep debt accumulated from building the new platform and the demon trap.

Unar and Frog finished making the rope together by midday. Esse woke in time for that meal and made a spicy, oily mush of legumes and orchid bulbs that tasted better than anything Unar had eaten in Understorey so far.

"Is this our reward for finishing the rope?" Unar asked.

"What rope?" Esse replied. "I need a new net. I think I see a way to use glue solvent to make the fibres all but invisible."

"What fibres?" Bernreb grunted. "I'm not killing any more bears for their whiskers. It's wasteful."

"Hookvine spines for strength," Esse said, hardly listening to Bernreb. "Caterpillar hairs for length, I think. You know the ones. As long as my hand. They are so hairy the wasps cannot lay eggs in them. The hairs are orange, but I think I can soak them till they turn transparent."

"I know the ones. You want Marram to go out in the monsoon, risking his life, to collect caterpillars?"

Esse's distracted grey eyes flickered to Marram's amused face.

"Unless he is busy with something else."

"I am not busy," Marram said. "We need more moonflowers for the women. Ylly needs soapleaf for the sheets. Hasbabsah has asked for green leaves from this tallowwood to rub on the baby's chest. Issi is sick, she says."

"That explains all the crying last night," Unar said, rubbing her face, but her tiredness wasn't really because of the baby. She longed to return to bed right there and then.

"Honey might soothe her throat," Oos said, and Unar couldn't help but sense the potential for seeds to sprout in nothing more musical than Oos's ordinary speaking voice. If Oos's bones were awake, too, why couldn't she hear it when Unar spoke? Unar's speaking voice was simply not musical, she supposed.

"Honey is for Canopians," Hasbabsah said. "The tallowwood leaves will do to clear her blessed little head."

"Esse can climb for those," Unar said, looking Esse in the eye. Maybe he would get angry enough to take her with him, out of the warmth and into the rain, and if he climbed close enough to the barrier, maybe she could examine it for weakness, now that she had her magic back.

She had her magic back. That was all that mattered. How could Esse make her angry? Even exhaustion couldn't lead her to lose her temper today. She had known, from that first moment in the hovel, and again at the Gates of the Garden, that she had an important purpose; that she was born to serve a god. Let others lose their magic when they fell. She would never lose hers. Not for long, anyway. She squashed the urge to tell them the baby would be well by the following morning. Frog had promised to show her how to heal Issi by magic later that night.

"You will prepare the extract," Hasbabsah said to Oos. "I know you have memorised the method. It is time to demonstrate what you have learned."

"Yes, Ser—I mean, yes, Hasbabsah," Oos said quickly, colour flooding her cheeks at the lapse, but Hasbabsah didn't comment on it.

Unar thought, *So obedient, Oos. So obedient, my sister, and too stubborn to teach me, but I won't hold it against you. I will take you with me to Canopy when I go, no matter what Frog thinks.*

Then she remembered Oos and Ylly writhing around under their too-small blanket. Maybe Oos wouldn't want to come with Unar by the time she was ready to go. Frog had much to show her before that day of departure.

Perhaps at the end of the monsoon, when all of them would be forced to leave the banished hunters' lair. Yes, that would be a good time to go.

In another room, Issi screamed. Ylly got up from the table to go to her, with Oos right behind her. When Oos sang a lullaby to calm the child, Unar sweated from the effort of not wresting the sound away and sinking it into something just to see it change, just to be sure she was as great as she had been before.

Frog sank the tines of her fork into the back of Unar's hand, and she yelped.

"Watch what you're doing, Frog!"

"Sorry."

"Why don't you go sweep the water out of the fishing room, if you've nothing better to do?"

"And what will you be doin'?"

Unar grunted.

"Making myself some new clothes. Esse keeps reminding me that I'm no longer a Gardener. It's time I put off red and green and put on something darker. More depressing. Better suited to my future life as a . . . what did you suggest, Esse? A floor sander? A mattress stuffer?"

Her bitterness was feigned. Inside, her spirit danced. She was greater than a Gardener now, for no mere Gardener could operate here, divided so sharply from the seat of Audblayin's power.

If Frog's name was a testament to her intent—that she move in a single direction, and that movement towards the sun, in step with an Understorian invasion or whatever it was she planned—then perhaps Unar should take the name Unaranu, because she would not stay down. She would feel that warmth on her skin again.

# THIRTY-NINE

THE RILLS of Oos and Marram's music ran through the room where Unar reclined comfortably on a coil of rope.

It was ten days since she and Frog had crept into the storeroom, stood by Issi's crib, and healed the chill that had taken root inside her. Frog had done it, but this time Unar had been able to watch closely, to see with her second sight what her little sister had done, and she knew now that she could do it again. All parts of the body, it seemed, were potential seeds, not just the ones that came together to make children, and Unar could give them what they needed to grow, and in the growing, to heal over the broken places.

Frog had said sternly, *You must remember to stop them from growin'.*

Unar had asked, *Why? If this much growth recoups her usual strength, would it not be better to make her twice as strong?*

Frog's face had shown panic. *You are a deep well,* she said, *deeper than your friend, deeper than anythin' I have ever seen. With Oos, this warnin' would not be necessary. She has not the strength, but you . . . you would not make Issi twice as strong. You would make 'er misshapen, maybe even kill 'er.*

Unar said calmly, *I thought my powers were useless. I thought you couldn't use them against enemies. Whoever these supposed enemies are. I thought you wanted me to kill.*

*So dank,* Frog had said through clenched teeth. *So dunderheaded. You cannot heal this way without love. Can you not feel it? You love Issi, or you could not heal 'er. Maybe you do not even admit to yourself that you love 'er, but you do, or this would not have worked. The old woman, too, or I could not have used your strength to heal 'er. Do you love my enemies? Can you fall for strangers quickly enough to kill them?*

*You said Oos was your enemy. I love Oos.*

Frog's eyes had narrowed at Ylly's sleeping form.

*You are not the only one. The ex-slave and the young hunter love 'er, too, but they are both fools and so are you.*

In the ten elapsed days, Unar had conferred with Frog twice more, both times by the river in the fishing room. Frog had allowed her to transform Esse's rope from a woven thing to a single, unbreakable strand by growing the vestiges of life deep in the fibres into an interlocking matrix that still made Unar shake her head with awe.

"Does this mean I love the rope?" Unar had asked, somewhat clumsily, hating to appear stupid but wanting to understand.

"You want my advice," Frog said darkly, "do not love anyone. Or anythin'."

"I love you, Frog."

"Lucky for me if I should be wounded and need healin'!" Frog tossed her head and folded her arms. "I do not love you."

"Yes, you do. You told me before that you love me. You found me before I found you."

"I lied." Unar glared at her, but she went on carelessly. "I found you at the Master's bidding, and it is the Master who will teach you what lessons you must learn about love and the kind of magic we use here."

"The Master? Who is that?"

Frog shook her head and refused to answer.

The second time they met in the fishing room, Frog had made the drifting spores of the luminescent fungi burst into life while still floating and unattached. The room had blazed with bright beauty. Unar, with her mouth wide to sing the godsong, had fleetingly, with her mind's eye, placed Aoun in that room, so that his face could light with pleasure as she knew hers was lit—until Frog punched her in the stomach to make her stop singing, anyway.

Now, with her back resting against the ropes, Unar probed inside her own body with such a minuscule amount of power she hoped neither Oos nor Frog would sense it.

They couldn't have sensed it, or Frog would have been there already, berating her. The child nagged like an old woman. Like a Servant of the Garden. Unar's body was only a few days away from bleeding again, and she could feel, with her thin thread of magic, the thickening that preceded it. She shouldn't have to accept the mess and aching of the whole ordeal. There had to be a better way.

Yes. The extra thickness could be reabsorbed. The body would resist, she sensed, but it could be forced. Tiny layer by tiny layer, each one of them invisible to the naked eye, could be returned to the body, to the constituent nutrients that ran in the blood, like thatch being torn apart and its constituent reeds returned to the river.

Unar thought irritably, *I shouldn't have to suffer what ordinary women suffer!*

And she drew, hard, on the thread of magic. Much more than a thread. She forced her body to obey her, and it obeyed. The extra thickness was gone. Even the egg was returned to the nest of eggs that lived inside her.

Then she realised that Oos's part in her duet with Marram had been completely muted by the surge. Now that the magic was over with, it seemed the musicians had stopped playing altogether, no doubt confused by the sudden silence of Oos's instrument.

Frog rushed into the room, snatching up a length of rope and whipping Unar's arms with it.

"You slow grey mould!" she cried. "You one-fingered worm!"

Unar tried to grab the rope. She opened her mouth to say that she was finished, that her experiment had worked, that she wouldn't do it again for another month, when she realised Oos stood in the doorway, wide eyes pinned to Unar's face.

"You did magic," she said in astonishment, just as Frog hit her in the side of the head with the metal weight from the rope jig. Oos crumpled to the ground. Unar leaped to her side.

"You've hurt her!"

"We must go right now," Frog snarled.

"Go where?"

"Out, out! Before the brothers stop us, you fly-catching stink-hole!"

"It's still raining out there, and Marram's the only one, he says, who can fly in the wet."

Frog pushed her, hard enough that Unar almost joined Oos on the floor. Crying out, using the sound of it to reach out to Oos, Unar found a healthy body temporarily unconscious. Frog had bruised but not broken Oos's skull. Unar sighed with relief.

Then she allowed Frog to drag her by the wrist into the hearth room. Bernreb lounged by the fire, eyes closed, with the baby asleep on his chest, Issi's fingers gripping his beard. Esse wrapped portions of smoked fish and meat in layers of dried leaves to stow in storage crates.

Marram filled the doorway to the fishing room.

"Where is Oos?" he asked.

"Fixin' 'er flute," Frog said. "Can you move? My bladder is full."

Marram slid into the hearth room with a smile on his lips. Unar didn't look up or speak to him; there would be plenty of time for that later, after he found Oos's body crumpled in the storeroom and went outside to find Unar still standing stupidly with Frog on Esse's platform, wet and helpless.

Frog placed Unar's hand on the rope that ran out through the vertical river.

"Hold it tight," she said. "Sing the godsong."

Unar obeyed, resigned, but no sound came out of her mouth. Magic flared around them, and the rope came to life, jerking her through the river as though a falling millstone had been tied to the other end.

By the time she'd sluiced the water from her face and blinked at the thin, grey, natural light, which was dreamlike after the golden, glowing confines of the hunters' home, Frog stood beside her, small hands at the railing, showing her teeth to the relentless rain. Heavy droplets of spray from the still-growing river struck Unar's back and black breeches. She hadn't finished the black jacket that would have replaced her Gardener's garb.

"I cannot do this part," Frog shouted. "You must. Feel the sap in the tallowwood. Feel the life in it and make it stretch out. Grow us a branch to the next tree."

Unar gaped at her.

"Grow a branch to the next tree? That's two hundred paces away. I can't even see the next tree!"

"Do it!" Frog shrieked, sawing through the rope with a small, serrated knife Unar hadn't known that she carried. "Marram will be here in seconds. Sing as loud as you can."

Unar sighed again. She began to sing. The first hoarse, untuneful notes jarred her ears before she could catch the source of Understorian magic and sink it into the side of the great tree. With the sensation of splitting into weightless, floating pieces came the feel of sap flowing, and water, too. She *could* make it obey her.

A shock went through her as she drew on the life of the tree and a full awareness of it blossomed in her mind from the crown, throbbing with pain where it had been cut to form the bed of Audblayin's holy Garden, to the roots, where power swirled in murky, unpredictable patterns.

She touched her face; it was wet, but not only from the rain. The song faltered.

"I'm sorry," Unar said to the great tree, "for causing you pain. I'm sorry!"

"Keep singing, imbecile!" Frog climbed down from the platform onto a branch, and Unar saw with another shock that it was the branch she had started to grow, right below them, stretching into the grey screen of rain.

Unar climbed down behind her, uncertainly, singing and urging the branch on as she went, so that Frog, clinging like a sloth to the leafy end of the shoot, was propelled ahead of her, laughing, encouraging Unar to send it further and further. Soon, they couldn't see the main trunk behind them. Unar sensed a slowing. She was straining the resources of the tree.

Tiny specks of life within the new branch began to die, too far from the tree for the flowing sap to reach them. Even as fresh green wood beneath Unar's feet turned brown and hard, she felt the junction where the branch joined the tree decay and turn brittle.

"It's going to crack and fall," she shouted at Frog as the other tree trunk abruptly loomed ahead. Unar plunged her magic into that tree instead. It was a greenmango, the sour fruit fit only for birds and slaves. Unar thought she'd seen its crown in daylight, made rainbow-coloured by parrots and toucans. A new branch erupted out of the side of it, arching to meet the one they held on to. Frog leaped across the gap between branches before they could cross. Unar followed close behind her.

When she turned to look back the way they had come, she saw Marram, running barefooted along the tallowwood branch, without ropes or chimera-skin wings. Without the bow and arrows he usually carried.

"Go back, Marram!" Unar shouted. "The branch is breaking."

His face looked grim. He could feel it, magic or not, but he kept coming.

"I will kill 'im if 'e does not go back," Frog said, crouched at Unar's heels, holding her little knife in a white-knuckled hand.

"Oos will wake soon." Unar's voice was haggard. The futility of Marram's determination broke her heart as surely as the tallowwood branch was breaking. "Go back. You love her. You should be there when she wakes." A twinge pulled at her even as she said this. She loved Oos too, but for now she had to follow Frog and find out more about her powers.

"You took me in." Unar tried to convince him a third time. "You fed me. Protected me from demons. Go back, Marram. *Please.*"

The tip of the tallowwood branch, which had been perfectly horizontal, silently slanted towards the forest floor. Marram sprang at the greenmango branch, hands and spines outstretched, but it was four or five body lengths away from him.

He fell into darkness. Unar watched his flailing arms and legs with horror until she couldn't see him anymore.

# FORTY

Dizziness threatened to send Unar over the edge.

She sat down abruptly on the greenmango branch, her gorge rising, still staring into the space where Marram had vanished. The wet bark felt unreal beneath her palms. Rainwater ran down the back of her collar and along the curve of her spine.

"It's your fault," she said, and there was no magic in her broken voice at all. She felt as empty as the day Oos and Aoun had drained her. "You killed him."

"If you wanna blame me for it," Frog said, "I do not care. Just grow us a big bracket fungus to lie down on and rest, and another one to keep the rain off. In the mornin' we can go on to the next tree, and the next."

Unar hardly registered the words. Marram had been kind. He'd been banished from his society for refusing to help strike at gods he didn't even serve. Now he'd fallen just as surely as if he'd made that attempt and failed.

*The only one who can fly.*

Minutes later, Unar heard them calling across the void. Bernreb's voice, and Ylly's. Even Hasbabsah's. They called for Marram and Unar and Frog. Unar bit her lip to keep from calling back to them. Oos wasn't calling. Maybe she was dead. Maybe Frog had killed her after all. As for Esse, he would be too angry to call, but busy putting together some contraption capable of coming after them, even in the monsoon.

Frog's small hand landed on Unar's shoulder and shook her impatiently.

"I can't grow anything," Unar said.

"Yes you can. Of course you can. If your voice is tired, use this." The hand tapped her back with something round and hard. Unar twisted to take it from her, a white rock the size of her two hands, shaped like a wishbone stuck into a flatcake.

"What is it?"

"The ear bone of an Old God."

Only when Unar turned it did she see the hole bored into the long end of it.

"There's only one hole. Where does the sound come out?"

Frog hesitated.

"It comes out in another world. In the place where the Old Gods dreamed while they were sleepin'. Just blow into it."

Unar blew. It seemed that the whole forest vibrated, yet the long, dark leaves of the greenmango didn't move. Not a single gemlike bead of water fell that hadn't been about to fall already. There was no moss on the new branch and no spores had had time to fall, but back at the main tree trunk, life surged, and the sheltered beds that Frog had asked for sprang, smooth, orange and gleaming, into being.

"Come on," Frog said, leading her by the wrist again. They lay against each other, wet but warm, and waited only a little time for first the urgent, calling voices and then the pale Understorian day to fade completely away.

# FORTY-ONE

It was still dark when Unar woke.

She peeled the leeches off her skin and rubbed the sores they left behind. Then she lapped a drink of rainwater from the edge of the enormous bracket fungus that unyieldingly took their weight.

"Are you ready?" Frog asked, proffering the ear bone, which glowed a gentle green. She had a leech sore on her eyelid, barely discernible.

"I'm ready," Unar said. She breathed in life and breathed out magic. The greenmango stretched a new-grown arm in the direction Frog indicated, and a fig, like the one at the great crossroads on the border of Ehkisland in Canopy, reached its new arm out until the branches crossed. Unar hesitated. This was more a crossroads than the other. If she made this crossing, it was one she could never return from, and she didn't know whether to feel anticipation or fear.

Then she remembered how she'd jumped off the head of the dayhunter. How she'd left her parents' home. That seeds were ambitious, desperate, single-minded, and strong.

Audblayin favoured boldness.

She and Frog stepped off the tree behind them just in time for it to slough the dying overextension of itself.

Fig branch met myrtle. Myrtle met sweet-fruit pine. Sweet-fruit pine met false palm. False palm met quandong, complete with ripe blue fruits that they ate for a morning meal.

"If you had been patient," Frog said reproachfully as she spat a seed into the rain, "and not alerted them until we were ready, we would have supplies with us. Proper food, rope, nets, and knives. Tinder and firestarter and sand."

"How far are we going?" asked Unar, who had never crossed more than one or two niches, never travelled further than she could walk in a day.

"To the far edge of Canopy. It would take a week in the dry. Maybe five days in the monsoon. To make a new branch, most of all a great tree needs water."

"You can't teach me about trees. I'm a Gardener. Teach me something else, sister." A thrill went through her when she said it. Why should she be afraid? She had done the impossible and helped two slaves to escape certain death at Servant Eilif's hands, while eluding the punishment of denying her power. Confident in her destiny again, she straightened her back and lifted her chin.

Nothing could deny her. She would be the greatest Bodyguard Audblayin had ever had. When she found him. After all, not even a season had passed in Understorey, and she had already found her sister.

"The Master will decide what you are to be taught," Frog muttered.

"Who is the Master?" Unar demanded, but Frog didn't reply, only pointed in the direction they had to go. Quandong crossed branches with metal-stone tree, metal-stone tree with bloodwood, bloodwood with floodgum, and floodgum with ironbark.

"I'm tired," Unar panted, hours later. Using the song-magic of Understorey didn't seem to deplete her the same way as using magic in Canopy had; there, she could never have raised so many mighty branches before exhausting herself. Here, the power came from the sounds. A person singing didn't tire as quickly as a person digging ditches.

Still. A person singing grew hoarse eventually, and concentration faltered. Frog looked unimpressed.

"So make a bracket fungus and sleep."

"Now? It's barely midday."

"We can travel in the dark if we must. If you are tired, rest. I have no more stolen bones to help you."

"Stolen?"

Frog's little mouth tightened again. When Unar lay down on the shelf between orange fungi, feeling her body heat sink into the velvet surface of it and hearing the rain strike the upper bracket softly, Frog stayed crouched on the edge, staring into space between the great trees.

"What's your earliest memory?" Unar asked. *My earliest memory is of you. Do you remember it? Do you remember me? We looked into each other's eyes.*

"My first foster parents fightin'," Frog said. "My foster father asked for fermented greenmango juice to drink. We call it bia. 'Gimme some bia, wife,' 'e said. She said, 'I given it for taxes.' You see, the villagers usually pay tax to a Headman. My foster father knocked 'er down and cut 'er in the face with 'is spines. There was blood everywhere."

It wasn't funny, but Unar wanted to laugh.

"If you'd stayed in our house," she said, "it would have been the other way around. Mother hitting Father with a stick, so that his legs looked like striped snakes. I'd run to him and hug his legs, kiss his bruises, and he'd pretend that I hadn't hurt him."

"You should have pushed 'er out a window," Frog said.

"Not me. I don't serve the god of death." Unar thought of Marram, and the urge to laugh died.

"I tried to kill my foster father," Frog said, unmoving where she squatted at the edge. "'E was a big man, though. Bigger than Bernreb and with a stomach like a barrowful of melons. 'Is job was to set the bridges. In daylight, 'e set them, when most demons are sleepin' and it is safe to cross and to trade. But most of the time, 'e just stayed home and drank bia. 'E drank some of the poison I put in 'is bia, but not all of it, and I had been wrong about how much I would need. Then 'e knew I had done it, and I had to run away."

Unar tried to glance at Frog's face, but could see only the back of the girl's head from where she lay. Frog had apparently not been bluffing about using Unar's power to kill. There was no squeamishness in the child. Nor any sense of loyalty towards the man who presumably had made the choice to take her in of his own free will. Frog, like her big sister, was desperate, ambitious, and single-minded as a seed. Unar could hardly judge her for it.

"If you ever decide to kill me," she said, "you'll tell me what I've done wrong first, won't you?"

She was joking, trying to lighten the mood, but Frog's slight shoulders shrugged.

"If it is my decision, I will. If it is an order from the Master, probably not. The first thing you will learn, if you wanna perfect your magic use, is never to disobey an order."

Unar didn't ask again where they were going. She didn't ask who the Master was, or what sort of orders she might be expected to carry out. To perfect her magic use, she knew she would do almost anything that Frog's superiors asked of her. Anything but damage the Garden or hurt her friends. There was no sense in freeing Ylly and Hasbabsah only to have them come to harm, and certainly no reason to involve Oos in anything. Oos had Ylly to take care of her now. She didn't need Unar.

"You're my sister. I trust you. You came to fetch me for a reason."

Whatever the reason was, Frog was not forthcoming.

*You want my advice, do not love anyone. Or anythin'.*

Unar sighed, closed her eyes, and wished she were dry. Her stomach grumbled, but a benefit of having nothing to eat, she supposed, would be not having to dangle her bare arse over the edge of a mushroom and defecate into the dark. Whatever Frog said, Unar shouldn't have had to put up with the added indignity of blood everywhere, not if she could do something about it. Frog wasn't old enough yet, but when she found out for herself what a mess menstruation made, she would apologise and beg for Unar's help.

Just like Aoun would, when he realised she had returned with Audblayin.

Behind her eyelids, Unar imagined the look on his face when she led Audblayin to the Garden Gates. Frog at her side. Aoun four or five years older, like Unar. He would gasp, *But nobody has ever found Audblayin so young, before.*

Unar would say, *There's never been a Gardener like me, before. Open the Gates.*

Aoun would open the Gates. A Servant—not Servant Eilif, most likely she'd be dead of old age—would fall to her knees and wail for Unar to become the god's Bodyguard at once. They'd take her to the night-yew. They'd perform the ceremony. Aoun would find her, later, alone in the Garden, and beg her to forgive him for pulling away from her kiss. The neutering magic of the Servants had severed him from his true heart, but now he knew that he and Unar were a single spirit with separate flesh. She would do with him what she had done with Edax.

And at last, laughing with the joy of it, Unar would fly.

# PART III

*Drowning Season*

# FORTY-TWO

It was near dusk on the fourth day since Marram had fallen.

"Will I make a shelter for us for the night?" Unar asked, hiding a yawn with the back of her hand.

The skin she pressed to her lips was wet and wrinkled. She could barely remember what being dry felt like. Frog had made a tiny fire, two days ago, to cook a roosting fish-owl. Owls were poisonous in large quantities, but birds in Understorey were rare enough that the travellers couldn't be choosy. Unar had trapped the owl's feet with a sudden growth spurt in the branch it rested on, trying not to think of Edax, and Frog had wrung its neck, suffering a bite right through the palm of her hand for her troubles.

Unar healed the bite almost at once, but Frog still plucked the feathers with a vengeful sort of violence. The fatty flesh had been rank, and the warmth from the smoky flame negligible.

"No," Frog said, staring in the direction they had been travelling. "We are close. We should keep goin'. We are almost at the dovecote."

"The dovecote?"

"It is what we call it. The place where we meet. Where the Master rules."

"You're sure you can find it in the dark?"

"Yes. Over there. That way."

Unar lifted the ear bone and blew. Her body lifted with the freedom of it. She knew the ear bone, at this point, better than she knew her own bones. Every unseen filament. Every concealed coil. There were gaps in and around it that should have been filled with living tissue, and it was these spaces where inaudible sound echoed and magic answered, as though a great being of spirit answered the cry of its naked child.

It was more powerful, more resonant, in the last several hours. Either Unar was growing stronger the more she flexed her magical muscle or there was something linking the bone with the location.

"Where are we?" Unar asked as the spiny plum they stood on sent softly uncurling spearhead-shaped leaves thrusting towards the gap-axe tree across the way. Rain wet down the new leaf fuzz as it grew. "What part of Canopy lies above us?"

"Airakland," Frog answered absently.

The realm of the lightning god. Unar had heard that the trees here, mostly floodgums, were taller than the rest of Canopy, even the emergents that housed the Temples, and their bare crowns were blackened from absorbing the lightning strikes that might otherwise set fire to the forest.

Frog left Unar's side, then, running lightly through the rain along the branch, and Unar followed, lifting the ear bone again, calling the gap-axe tree to meet her in the middle. The leaves meshed in patterns of dark greeny-black against pale pink.

Soon enough, with the sun fading, it was too dim to make out the colours of the leaves. Frog didn't hesitate to take Unar's hand and indicate direction in the dark. Seven crossings later, Unar thought she could see something glowing, like the moon behind clouds.

"That is the dovecote," Frog said. Unar was too tired to answer her. Wordlessly, they crossed again, floodgum to myrtle, myrtle to another floodgum, and then there was no need to grow any new branches, for a branch level with them, old and with a flattened top like a low road in Canopy, led from the trunk to a wide, round, flat-roofed building perched at the intersection of five roads.

Four of the roads were lit, each with one of Airak's blazing, blue-white lanterns. The lanterns were topped with wide, gleaming golden cones to keep the blaze from being directly visible from above. Unar realised that the fifth road, the one without a lantern, was broken.

If that was where they were going, there was no point standing around in the rain. Three tiny windows in the building, close to the roof, flickered with firelight, and she wanted to be where those fires were. Unar was halfway to the lantern before Frog cried, "Stop!"

Unar stopped. A door opened in the building, and a tall, narrow-shouldered silhouette with spreading skirts emerged, standing for a moment, fingers flexing, in the orange rectangle of the entrance.

"It is Frog," Frog called. "Frog the Outer. I have brought 'er, Core Kirrik."

"I felt her coming, Frog the Outer," the woman called back in a high, musical voice. "Strong enough to wake me from a future-searching. Wait and I will quench the lamp. The Master will see you right away."

Unar looked at Frog, whose eyes were wide and her grimace anxious. Neither demon attack nor Marram's fall had disturbed the girl so much. She was afraid of something.

"If there's some test to gain admission," Unar told her, "I'll pass it."

"The test is of your ability to serve," Frog said softly without taking her eyes from the dovecote, "and I am not so sure of that."

Now it was Unar's turn to grimace. Ungrateful child! If she had ever served anything, it was her desire to find her sister. She would hardly endanger this chance for them to be together. How bad could these people, this so-called Master, possibly be? No worse than Servants who threw worn-out slaves off the edges of Garden beds.

The image came to her, again, of Marram falling, and she shook her head to rid herself of it. She'd told him to go back. Three times, she'd begged him to go back.

The woman that Frog had named Kirrik emerged from the dovecote, holding something like a blackened, upturned bowl on the end of a long stick. As she came closer, towards the light, Unar saw black hair with a silver streak swept back from a pinched and pointed face, as cooked-fishmeat-white as the hunters' faces had been, with bloodless lips and a cleft chin. Her coat and full skirts were black, too, but finely woven, and she carried something on a second stick, leather stretched over a basket frame, to keep the rain off.

"We're already wet," Unar told her, and would have stepped forward, but Frog grabbed her by the seat of her pants and yanked back.

"Do not go into the light," she hissed.

"Why not?"

Frog stripped a piece of bark from the side of the road and tossed it contemptuously towards the lantern. Immediately, lightning crackled out of the lantern and set the bark on fire. It fell, smouldering, for a few body lengths before the rain quenched it.

"The lanterns keep the demons out," Kirrik said, smiling at Unar, and lowered the black bowl over the top of the golden cone like a slave snuffing a tallow candle. The blue-white light vanished. Unar could still see in the light from the other three.

"Go," Frog said, her fist now striking Unar in the lower back, and Unar walked forward until she stood in front of Kirrik, the black bowl between them, the rain diverted by the tilted, stretched leather making a river to one side of them. Unar was much shorter than Kirrik and didn't like having to look up at her.

"You people are my sister's protectors?" she asked. "Her adopted family? She owes her life to you?" Her questions were ignored.

"If you come into the Master's domain, you will be called Nameless the Outer, until the Master chooses to give you a name. You will call me Core, or Core Kirrik."

Unar grimaced. Even the Servants hadn't taken away her name. But Frog had said the test would be of her ability to serve. She mustn't make a mistake simply because she was tired.

"Yes, Core Kirrik," she said, more humbly than she'd ever been able to say Servant Eilif's name. Her eyes went to the firelight in the little windows. She imagined she could feel the warmth already. The Master would see them right away, Kirrik had said. Unar must maintain her humility until that meeting was over.

"Come past me, Frog the Outer," Kirrik said, and Frog led Unar until they both stood well behind the taller woman. Kirrik lifted the black bowl. The deadly ring of blue-white sprang up again across the road. Kirrik followed Frog and Unar towards the doorway of the dovecote. Frog opened the door. Kirrik remained silent until Unar tried to pass through the doorway.

"You will stay outside with me tonight, Nameless the Outer. We stand watch until dawn. It is Frog the Outer, alone, that the Master wishes to see."

Unar looked at her. Was this a test, too? She looked at the building. It had no eaves. Five days in the downpour, and she was still not to be permitted shelter.

"Yes, Core Kirrik," she said. "Can I have one of those?"

"You are already wet, as you said. What use would an umbrella be?"

Unar considered growing herself a shelter out of bracket fungus.

"Give the bone flute to Frog the Outer," Kirrik said, as if she'd guessed Unar's thoughts. "You will not use magic here without the Master's permission."

Unar hesitated. Frog grimaced. Kirrik's eyes narrowed, and Unar finally bowed her head, holding the ear bone out to Frog.

"Yes, Core Kirrik."

She could always sing, if she had to. Nobody would take her magic away from her again.

Frog pulled the door of the dovecote closed behind her.

# FORTY-THREE

Unar's stomach growled.

"Will we be eating, while we're on watch?" she asked.

Kirrik, hands clasped over the umbrella's handle, jerked her head in the negative.

"The Master is fasting. It helps him to see the future more clearly. While he fasts, so do we."

"And what is the Master looking for in the future? What is it that you do? What do you hope to achieve?"

No reply. Unar pressed on.

"Core Kirrik, you said I woke you from a future-searching. In Canopy, only the goddess of wind and leaves can speak prophecies that come true." *Although unspoken prophecies can come true, too.* "Will I be taught to see the future?" She was aware she sounded too greedy, too eager. But how much faster would she find Audblayin if she could see into the future? Pretending nonchalance, she murmured, "I don't need to see it, anyway."

But Kirrik heard her.

"No? You are so certain of your destiny? And what is that, then? Tell me."

Unar floundered for a moment. *The test is of your ability to serve,* Frog had said. Should she say that her destiny was to serve the mysterious Master? Unar needed to learn everything that these Understorian sorcerers and sorceresses could teach her, the better to equip her to leave them behind. But what if they caught her lying? They wouldn't teach her anything.

"There are five paths leading to this house, Core Kirrik," she said. "Should I watch the other side, so we can see in both directions?"

Kirrik's smile only deepened at the change of subject.

"In the rain, vision is not our most valuable sense. Did you not serve Audblayin? Can you not discern the approach of living things without using your eyes?"

"I could. When I was in Canopy. I could try, here, but you said I wasn't to use magic without the Master's permission."

Kirrik laughed softly. There was magic in her laugh, darker and different from the power in Oos's voice, or Unar's.

"If you cannot use your ears without opening your mouth," she said, "I will watch for both of us until you learn."

Unar's whole body ached. She was famished. Core Kirrik stood and stared into the rain like the legs hidden beneath her black skirts were made of wood. Unar looked for a flat part of the branch to sit on.

"You will stand and watch," Core Kirrik said.

Unar had never wanted to disobey an order more. Fragments of speech beat about her exhausted brain. *The Master will decide what you are to be taught. You are so certain of your destiny? And what is that, then? The place where we meet. Where the Master rules. What is it that you do?*

*This is anyone's home who would fight for justice.*

It dawned on Unar that the justice Frog referred to was the freedom for Understorians, perhaps even Floorians, to walk in direct sunlight. Could that be part of Unar's destiny, something she could be truthful about? Was it something that she should help fight for? It was the logical extension of her abhorrence of how slaves were treated. If there were no slaves, though, who would do the work? The poor would. Stricken and out-of-nichers. Canopians, like her own mother and father.

Unar thought, *Let them do the work. I don't care about Understorians, Floorians, or Canopians. I care about my sister and about finding Audblayin, proving that the Servants were wrong about me. Proving that Aoun was wrong.*

He had said, *You've breached wards that have been impenetrable for four hundred years, Unar. I can't imagine a true disciple of the Garden would ever do such a thing.* And also: *Only banishment to Understorey could make you safe.*

How could he have ever thought she would be a danger to him? No matter how he always sided with the Servants against her, she could never do anything to hurt him. Not much, anyway.

*Only another adept could do this to you. Break your bonds this way. Who was it? I'll kill them.*

Unar sighed.

*I'll break your bonds, Aoun.*

She resisted the urge to sit.

"Very well. I can stand and watch. What exactly are we watching for, if the lamps keep demons out?" Even as she asked, Unar realised she knew the answer to her own question. She had seen Bernreb, Esse, and Marram use ropes and gliders to overcome all sorts of obstacles.

Not in the rain, though. They didn't fight in the monsoon. The five-month monsoon that would not end for another two months, unless something drastic happened to Ehkis, the rain goddess.

"If you had met the Bringer of Rain's Bodyguard," Unar said, "you wouldn't be worried about the monsoon ending early."

"Oh," Kirrik said scornfully, "is he fearsome, indeed? Is he a ruthless killer? Does he stay by her side every moment? Is that how you were able to meet him, in a great meeting, a council of deities?"

"No," Unar admitted. "Our deities don't meet. They stay in their own niches. Edax was . . . He is . . . His goddess sleeps at the bottom of a deep pool. Anyone would find it boring, to stay by the side of a sleeping goddess at the bottom of a pool. He could, if she commanded it. He showed me. It's not by the application of magic, but by a permanent change to his body. He can stay down for days without air if he has to. Like the goddess. But nobody else can, so why bother? She's safe there."

"Except from the treachery of her adepts. Everyone knows that Canopians are deceitful. Do not think you will get close to the Master until you have been deemed trustworthy."

"I'm not treacherous! And the goddess Ehkis doesn't need to fear the treachery of her adepts. She's well loved. Rain makes life."

"Bria's Breath." It had the sound of a curse, and the air around Kirrik seemed to ripple; the closest of the lamps momentarily dimmed. "Eggs and semen make life, girl. What does your fool mistress teach you? Can you not think of anything the goddess Ehkis has to fear?"

"You don't mean to suggest that Ehkis fears Audblayin," Unar blurted, but abruptly she realised something else: Kirrik appeared to be in a position of seniority over her, but here she was, outside in the rain, right beside Unar, the lowest of the low. "What did you do to offend the Master, Core Kirrik? What fool question did you fail to answer?"

At last, Kirrik took her eyes from the darkness beyond the death-lamps.

"I am here because my future-searching showed that I must be here. Something is coming. Would you meet it alone, Nameless the Outer?"

Unar felt a chill.

"What is it?"

"Something that threatens the Master's plans."

"And what are the Master's plans?"

"How do you find the barrier from this side, girl?"

It seemed a non sequitur; Unar struggled to make the connection. Did the Master mean to destroy the barrier? That was impossible. And why? There was a way through. Otherwise Hasbabsah couldn't have become a slave.

"How do I find the barrier? I haven't seen it. I haven't touched it since I fell."

*But I'm sure it has a weakness. Somewhere. The window of the Odelland palace opened for me, and so did the wards of the Garden.*

"And if you desired to feel the sun, what then? If you needed fresh fruits to cure a child's illness? What if you had fallen and your family remained above, and they were forced to watch while demons ate the flesh off your bones?"

"That would be my misfortune." *If I hadn't been born gifted.* "The barrier is to keep demons out of Canopy. Without it, chimeras would grow fat, and it would be the end of us all. The gods use more than half their strength maintaining it. Each one spends power on the section that protects their niche." That was what Unar knew for sure. What came next was guessing. Thinking aloud. "They can't fashion one that lets Understorians in but keeps demons out. Any large, warm body—"

"Lies. Chimeras live in Understorey, and yet we thrive. And Canopians pass through the barrier. Why them and not us?"

"Canopians are born under the gods' protection. It's your misfortune, as I said."

"Why can they not protect everyone? Are they so weak?"

"No! That is, I don't know—"

"One Forest," Kirrik said. "One people. That is what the Master seeks in the future. That is what we hope to achieve. We believe the gods can and should protect everyone. And if they cannot, they are not true gods, and should be killed to allow the Old Gods to return."

The Old Gods cared for everyone, Hasbabsah had said. Now Kirrik seemed to be saying the same thing. Yet Unar had seen a neck bone in the bedchamber of a princess, and an ear bone in Frog's custody. And those had not been small bones. They had not been human bones, and in her experience it was rare enough for humans to care about other humans.

From which distant country would the Old Gods come, if their souls were to be reincarnated in the bodies of giants? And why did the Canopian gods have to die for it to happen?

# FORTY-FOUR

THE THREAT predicted by the future-searching did not materialise; nothing menaced them in the night.

By morning, Unar had stopped turning Kirrik's One Forest speech over in her mind. She was so tired she could barely think or speak. Imagining Frog, snug inside the dovecote but no doubt restless with anxiety that Unar would fail the test, was all that kept Unar's eyes from closing and her cheek from sinking to the branch.

The notion that she still owned the energy to somehow get her breeches down and urinate off the edge also faded. She'd let loose, uncaring, and the seat of her pants had felt warm for a moment. Eventually, the relentless monsoon had washed the warmth away.

Now songbirds flew down from the bright treetops, entering into the tiny windows of the dovecote. The death-lamps of Airak burned steadily, neither flickering nor waning, though they seemed dimmer as cloud-scattered daylight infiltrated as far as it ever would in Understorey, where the sun never warmed anyone.

Contrary to what Kirrik had said about fasting, cooking smells and men's voices came from the closed door of the dovecote. More tiny birds fluttered down, wet and bedraggled, to enter the windows, and some of them left, again, flying up towards the light.

At last, the heavy door swung back and Frog's big eyes peered out at Unar and Kirrik.

"The Master says you may enter and break your fast. But be quiet. 'E is upstairs. Sleepin'."

Core Kirrik passed the umbrella to Frog and swept immediately past Unar, through the open door. It took Unar's fogged mind a few more moments to absorb what was happening. She still didn't move until Frog took her hand and tugged.

"This way."

"I did what she told me," Unar said, too loudly, but the world was weird and tilting. "I passed the test."

"That was not the test," Frog said. Unar felt as though she'd been flattened by a broken bough. That was terrible news. And the world was tilting even more. Unar lost her balance. Stumbled through the doorway. Her hands and knees found polished floor in place of rough, wet bark.

She had tumbled into a cloakroom. Lit by an Airak-lamp of the non-deadly variety. Unar slowly raised her head to see not only heavy fur cowls and rows of strange boots with separated toes, but unfamiliar weapons with spikes and multiple curving blades.

"Let me help you up, Outer," said a voice like a belling ox, and Unar realised that one of those pairs of boots was occupied. A man's broad black hand was extended towards her.

*Somebody else from Canopy. Somebody else who has fallen.*

"Warmed One," Unar gasped, grasping the hand, and as it drew her to her feet, she absorbed the rich layers of embroidered silk that covered the man from neck to knees, the way his priceless outer coat was cut off at the elbows to leave his forearms bare, and the scar-like seams where his climbing spines were hidden.

"My One Forest name is Sikakis," he said. There was grey in his black hair and beard, but his grip was strong and his dark eyes unwavering. "I was Acis, once, a prince of Airakland, but those days are far behind me."

"You will leave Core Sikakis alone," Kirrik snapped, unseen, from beyond the cloakroom. "He has no time for you, Nameless. Come here!"

Unar went, stumbling a little. The floor was uneven where the five branches beneath joined one another. Kirrik waited in a room with a round table and sixteen chairs around it, none of them occupied. In the centre of the table, the blue-white light of another lantern overpowered the yellow light from a hearth fire on the right-hand side. To the left-hand side, a writing desk was covered in scrawled-on parchments and the droppings of tiny birds, who sat on rows of perches pecking grain from wooden feeders. Shelves on every wall held leather-bound books, stacks or rolls of skins and paper, and row upon row of stoppered ink bottles and feather quills.

"Is this a library?" Unar asked, bewildered. "A school?" She had expected more weapons. Space for fighting men to train. Cooks to feed the warriors and seamstresses to repair their armour. From the outside, it was a large building.

She had expected something similar to, but on a grander scale than, the three hunters' abode. Nets, traps, and stored supplies. Was this how the Master and his servants would seek justice? How they would kill the new gods and bring back the old ones? With only one old prince and his black-skirted hag, one clever child and an army of pink parrots and blue wrens to do his bidding? No wonder he had sent Frog to fetch a fallen Gardener.

And no matter how she thought on it, Unar couldn't see a way for the Master to kill deities who were almost instantly reincarnated. Kill them all at once, and the Old Gods will return, Hasbabsah had said, but gods didn't stay dead. Everyone knew that.

The Master was mad. But even madmen had tricks that could be learned.

"You are wetting the carpet, Nameless. Stay away from the writings. Stand by the fire."

Unar obeyed, still uncoordinated and aching. Three pale Understorian men—*so there are a few more fighters*—came from beyond the bird room, glancing at Unar and dismissing her before saluting Kirrik with their fists to the left side of their chests.

"We will not fail, Core Kirrik," one of them said.

"So Core Sikakis has already assured me," Kirrik said drily. "Follow him, now. The Old Gods' blessings go with you."

"Shall I quench the lamp for them, Core Kirrik?" Frog asked. Kirrik lifted a finger in assent, and Frog hurried after the men.

Kirrik stared at Unar for what seemed like a long time.

"Well. I suppose I must feed you if the Master's orders are that you are to be fed. Clearly you are in no condition to feed yourself. Everyone knows Canopians are weak, but I hadn't expected this."

*You called me strong,* Unar thought, not realising she'd spoken aloud until Kirrik answered her impatiently.

"Your magic is strong. Your body is pathetic. A weak body cannot sustain even the strongest magic for very long."

Kirrik's expression changed then. Unar was so tired she wasn't sure what she was seeing. Was it lust? Was it the hunger with which Oos had looked on Unar's bare breasts, all those endless hours and days and years ago in the Garden when Unar had expected to become a Servant of Audblayin?

Before she could be sure, Kirrik's face closed over again. She opened a brown earthen pot and took out some speckled, grainy bread. Another jar held a bright blue jam that Unar didn't recognise; at some point she found the jam-smeared slice in a bowl before her and tasted it, sour and strong.

"You will sleep by the fire for now," Kirrik said. "The Master will not be pleased if you become ill."

"Frog," Unar said. She meant to say, *Frog can heal me, if I become ill,* but then she remembered that it was her own power that Frog used, and perhaps if she became ill, Frog would not be able to use it. Frog said love was needed for healing. And Frog's advice was never to love.

*Frog's lying. She's good at it. She's cunning.*

Yet Unar actually had no idea what Frog's magic was capable of; for all she knew, Frog had shown her a lie when she had shown her by magic that they shared a blood mother and a blood father.

"Yes, yes. You will see Frog the Outer again soon."

Kirrik stripped away Unar's clothes. She hung them on the fire screens to dry. Unar, who had no way of knowing if more strangers would come out of the corridors, did not resist. Couldn't resist. The strange expression on Kirrik's face returned. Perhaps it was envy. Perhaps the pale woman wished her skin were darker, sun-warmed; perhaps she wished for Unar's youth.

No, she had called Unar's body pathetic. It couldn't be that.

"Go to sleep, Nameless," Kirrik said.

WHEN UNAR woke, she couldn't be sure how much time had passed. The great dovecote, sheathed in the sound of rain, was quiet but for the flutters, pecks, and toenail clicks of birds. The fire had been banked, and there was no sign of Core Kirrik.

Unar went to the side table where the brown earthen pot rested and was disappointed to discover there was no more bread. A scroll on the writing desk caught her eye, and she unrolled it.

Her parents had rarely allowed her to go to the school, and she'd never learned letters, but the page had some ink drawings on it, not just the tooth marks she knew were words. A black human silhouette with a silver-blue halo around her head was linked by fine lines to three more silhouettes. One had a silver-blue orb hovering above his palm. One had silver-blue tears tracked down his cheeks.

The third figure had owl feet and was linked by another tenuous ink line to a recently drawn figure with a green leaf growing out of her mouth.

Tooth-mark letters covered both sides of the line, still powdery with paper-bark residue from being blotted.

"Can you read, Nameless?" Kirrik asked from right behind Unar, and she jumped, letting the scroll roll up of its own accord.

"No, Core Kirrik."

Kirrik's lip curled.

"Pity. You could have helped with the correspondence. You are too old to learn letters."

"I'm not too old to learn anything."

"You appear too old to learn to hold your tongue. I have had enough of your whining, Nameless. It will not do. From now on, you will speak when spoken to, is that understood?"

"Yes, Core Kirrik." Unar gave the scroll a last, regretful look. The Master, the apparent leader of these One Forest people, must be writing letters to Canopy to try and set up a meeting of gods such as Kirrik had described. Probably demanding to know why Canopians could pass freely through the barrier and return while Understorians could not.

Servant Eilif surely would have answered thus: that Understorians were monsters, violent and simple, fit only for slavery. That they must be kept out of Canopy for the same reason that demons were kept out, to protect the civilised people of the city. Unar knew this to be untrue, and if she knew it, then the gods must know it, too. Perhaps Servant Eilif would also say, as Unar had once believed, that Understorians had their own supernatural protectors. But that was also wrong—the dark parts of the forest held no gods, only their old bones. *There must be another reason.*

Yet Audblayin would not meet, or correspond, with someone like Core Kirrik. The Servants would not allow it. Maybe that was why Unar was important to One Forest. She would be the link between those above and those below the barrier. Core Sikakis, though he had been a prince of Airakland, clearly had no wish to return to Canopy. That had to be why they were willing to teach her what they knew.

"Why do you think you are here, Nameless?" Kirrik asked, catching the glance at the scroll, seeming to read Unar's thoughts a second time.

"To be used, Core Kirrik."

Kirrik's laughter, this time, was so wild, beautiful, and powerful that it was all Unar could do not to grasp it and weave it into something, anything. Yet at the same time, she recognised that nothing of Audblayin could be fashioned from Kirrik's voice. Branches could not be brought to life. Seeds could not grow. Unar could gain no inkling from the sensation of it of what Kirrik's magic was good for.

"Perfect," Kirrik said. "How perfect you are. And gifted, as Frog promised you would be. Even considering the bone, you travelled here quickly. I will use you, Nameless. It has been a long time since I had a Canopian adept of my own to use. Greatly preferable to lurking by the border and snatching whatever song or speech I could."

"A long time, Core Kirrik? May I ask what happened to the Servant of Airak who made these lamps?" Unar hoped she wouldn't be chastened for speaking out of turn. Kirrik only smirked.

"Oh, yes. He was the last, before you. Not a full Servant of Airak, only a Skywatcher. Just as you are only a Gardener, but he was weaker. The Master had to use him up, all at once, and it killed him. That is what happened to the maker of the lamps and why we could not replace the fifth one when it failed."

Two birds quarrelled over a spray of seeds. Unar concealed her shock. How much worse could these people be? A great deal worse, as it turned out. She had foolishly offered herself for use, only to now discover that she could be used up, like a gourd full of monkey oil or a knife sharpened into nothingness.

It wasn't too late. She could leave. It was only Kirrik, here and now, and Unar thought she could overpower her. From what Frog had said, Kirrik would not be able to kill using Unar's power, and seeing the future or feeling the approach of adepts would surely be no protection against Unar's fists and teeth, not to mention a club or two of living wood. There were even five kinds of tree for Unar to choose from.

*They will not take my magic from me again.*

But how would she learn if she left the dovecote? Kirrik had asked her, *How do you find the barrier from this side, girl?* Without the secret, despite her confidence, Unar had to confront the possibility that she could bang her head against the barrier for a hundred years and not get through, since the magic of Canopy had faded from her skin. The Master might be her only way back. And she couldn't leave Frog. Not again.

"I see," she said. "Thank you for explaining, Core Kirrik."

Kirrik turned away. Took a few paces towards the table. Her fingers traced the surface grain contemplatively.

"If the Master used you up all at once," she said, "he could grow an entire great tree, I think. Grow it through the centre of the Garden and break open Audblayin's egg. The goddess would fall into our waiting arms, Body-guard or no. What do you think of that?"

Was this the test? Kirrik must know that Audblayin was dead.

"The egg is empty," Unar said. "Besides, Audblayin is only one deity. Your Master needs to speak with all thirteen."

Kirrik laughed again.

"He does need all thirteen," she said, "and he'll have them, Nameless the Outer. You will be allowed to help us, once we can be sure of you."

So. Unar had guessed right. Help them to gather all the gods and god-desses of Canopy together? Perhaps to murder them if they proved argu-mentative or incapable. Bring the barrier down. It remained as impossible today as it had been yesterday. It was ludicrous.

"I owe a debt to you. For my sister. I'll help you. I'll pay the debt."

*I'll stay until I've learned as much as I can learn. But Frog can't have re-alised that the Master's path leads nowhere; I'll convince her of the truth.*

"Not enough. You must come to know, as we here know, that the city of Canopy is a defilement that must be torn down."

"How shall I come to know that, Core Kirrik? I've heard of the Old Gods. They may be brought back to the forest, but how do you know they'd have greater care for Floor and Understorey than the new ones do?"

"Do the gods and goddesses of Canopy have a care for Understorians and Floorians, then? I have not noticed them! I have not seen the flowers of Irof or tasted the bounty of Ukak's bees! After you have lived with us for long enough, you will wonder why you ever wished to crawl and kiss Audblay-in's hand."

Unar forced herself to gaze patiently at Core Kirrik, who'd worked her-self into something of a frenzy.

"And until then?"

"You will require supervision. Tiresome as that may be. You have chores to do, Nameless. The Master breaks his fast this evening. You can be trusted to make a meal for him, I think. Follow me."

Kirrik led her away from the wide room with its round table and writing materials, along a dim corridor. Open doors lay to left and right. Each room contained a blue-white lamp, four bunks to each wall, with each bunk bear-ing a bundle of bedding, and a washstand. Here, where there was neither magic nor wood smoke to deter uninvited guests, the tiny, high windows had insectivorous plants smothering the sills. The last room on the right was a kitchen of sorts, with four hearths, clay chimneys, and pots dangling from hooks on the ceiling. To the left, another open door showed a primitive privy: two holes in the floor and two water barrels.

At the very end of the corridor, a spiral staircase led upwards. Unar had put her hand out to point at it, to ask what was at the top of it, when her fingers rebounded from an invisible surface.

*Like the barrier. A smaller version. What can be created can be destroyed. They practice replicating it so that they can determine its weaknesses and tear it down. Or perhaps they plan to help the gods and goddesses, to make a better, stronger barrier. One that can protect everyone. One Forest.*

*The Master's quarters must be at the top of this staircase.*

"Here," Kirrik ordered, marching into the kitchen. All the hearths but one were cold. Beside the lit one, enough cut wood to last the whole of the monsoon and then some made a wide stack from floor to ceiling. On a wooden bench top, a single white egg rested in the bottom of a deep basin of water. Kirrik looked at it, then looked at Unar. "The Master will have four eggs. And three birds. You have permission to use magic for this. Begin."

# FORTY-FIVE

Unar blinked. She swallowed.

She thought she understood what Core Kirrik expected her to do, but she'd never tried anything like it before. As Frog had shown her, Unar began singing the godsong, using it, tentatively at first, then with greater confidence as she located the spark of life within the egg and it broke open to reveal a hatchling of a type of bird she'd never seen. Long-legged and with splayed toes, it stood belly-deep in the basin, regarding Unar with a startled brown eye ringed by bright orange down. The rest of its fluffy body was yellow and grey.

When Unar pressed it with her magic again, it made a soft, grunting sound. Then it was abruptly taller, with sleek black feathers on its body and a bald, colourful head and neck.

The level of water in the basin had gone down. Unar stopped singing, startled that she'd somehow incorporated it as a raw material without even knowing. But why should she be surprised? She'd grown crops in the Garden and fruit for herself and Frog, as late as the day before yesterday.

"Go on, Nameless," Kirrik snapped.

The bird began panting, beak distressed and open, as Unar pressed it again. It laid two white eggs in quick succession, one of which hatched almost immediately into a second, identical bird. Core Kirrik had said that life came from eggs and semen, but Unar had already learned from Issi's healing that any part of the body could act as a seed. The new bird laid two eggs, one of which hatched and grew into a third bird, whose pair of eggs brought the total to four.

Unar fell silent, again, astounded and confused at once.

"What is it?" Kirrik demanded. "Why do you look like a poleaxed tree-bear?"

"It's just . . . Core Kirrik, when I was in the Garden, women came for increased fertility. They went away again. Sometimes they got with child. Other times they didn't. If this is Audblayin's power, then why can't her Servants do this? Why don't women leave the Garden with babes already in their arms?"

Core Kirrik's expression turned smug.

"You could make people. If you wanted their corpses for food. These birds are blank, mindless; it is life and learning that shapes brains, not quickened growth, and you have made them from air and water, as plants are made. But that is not how animals are made. Minerals are required, from Floor. Look at them."

Unar did look at them, really look. The birds lay helplessly on their breasts or on their sides in the empty basin. They could barely coordinate their breaths, much less stand, peck, or fly. Their feathers flaked and flew away, turning to dust. The very first one that Unar had made stopped breathing and turned blue. The shells of the eggs trembled, jelly-like.

Overextended, like the branches of the trees. Dead because of her inexperience.

Unar released a long, drawn-out breath.

"I see."

"Skin them and cook them, Nameless. Grow some mushrooms to go with the eggs. Grow them on the living wood at your feet. They derive their minerals from the tree. Make sure they are more nutritious than these birds. After that, your next chore is to make bread."

Kirrik took something from a shelf; it was a single grain. She placed it on the bench before Unar.

"Grow the grain in the flooring, too. Make as much as you can. Make enough for a hundred men, and then a hundred more. There is salt in the pantry. You will find yeast in the air you breathe. Choose wisely, or the bread will not rise. Fuel for the ovens is in the box behind the door. Do you have any questions? Speak up. I am busy."

Unar didn't have any questions about the bread making. After her failure with the birds, she would use more caution. Focus her awareness. Yet she hadn't forgotten the fact that she and Kirrik had been on watch together. Kirrik had brushed it off, but she must be afraid of the Master, too. *The source of her malice is fear.*

"I have a question. Not about the bread."

"Willful wretch! What is it?"

"Who is your patron, Core Kirrik? From which goddess or god do you derive your power? Is it Ulellin? Is that why you can see the future? Aren't you afraid that the Master will use you up, too?"

Kirrik stared at Unar again in the odd way Unar couldn't read.

"I have no patron," she said at last. "Only those born above the barrier can forge a link with a Canopian goddess or god. You said it yourself. People born in Canopy are under the gods' protection. But there are other alliances we can forge. I fear no one. My skill is that I cannot be killed."

Unar's jaw dropped.

Frog came into the kitchen then. Unar almost didn't recognise her; she wore a fresher, finer black tunic and trousers, and her hair, oiled and combed back, gleamed.

"Core Kirrik," Frog said.

"You have come to supervise Nameless the Outer," Kirrik said to Frog, "while she prepares the Master's supper."

"What? Oh. Yes, Core Kirrik. The Master's supper."

"Do not let her waste the salt." With that, Kirrik swept away, leaving Frog and Unar alone.

They stared at each other for a moment.

"Where have you been—" Unar started to say, at the same time as Frog said with astonishment, "You 'ave not refused any orders? You 'ave not attacked Core Kirrik?"

"No. I haven't attacked Core Kirrik. Why would I do that?"

"The Master wants to destroy Canopy. You care about Canopy."

"I care about you."

Frog scowled. "Well, stop it. I told you not to."

"There's something odd about the wood for the oven." Unar picked up a piece from the stack beside the fire. "Have you noticed? All these pieces are identical. Down to the wavy splinters where there was a knot in the branch. I used to watch our father cut wood sometimes. It never looked like this."

Frog looked uncomfortable. She took the piece from Unar's hands and threw it onto the banked coals.

"They are from Eshland. The wood god takes payment of human blood, and 'e multiplies piles of firewood in return. Just as givin' blood weakens people, givin' wood weakens the great trees. Fair exchange."

"How have you traded with people of Eshland? How is it that your Master breaks through the barrier, Frog?"

Unar took up the poker and prodded the fuel into position.

"Always the same questions from you! There is no breakin' through! I toss pebbles up to a boy I know in Eshland. Pebbles from Floor, you understand? These messed-up birds you made are wild flowerfowl, kin to the eatin' kind in Eshland. Flowerfowl need stones in their stomachs. I toss up the stones, the boy tosses down the wood. No livin' thing passes through the barrier."

"But how did you meet him?"

"I heard 'im cryin' one night. 'E was cold. I told 'im if 'e came down, I would give 'im a blanket."

"Why were you there, beneath Eshland?"

"Watchin' our father." Frog gripped both sides of her face as if her skull ached. "Do you not know anythin', Unar? Our father crawls between Airakland and Eshland now. 'E lost the strength to cut wood with 'is arms. 'E drains himself of blood to get enough wood to sell to stay alive. 'E should throw 'imself off the edge. It would be kinder. I should roll 'im off while 'e is sleepin'."

Unar's face grew hot. Frog had admitted their mother was dead, back at the home of the three brothers. Unar hadn't asked about the fate of their father.

*We'll get another,* Father had said when they discovered Isin was gone. Frog had done the same, finding another father for herself, before trying to kill that father and running away to find Core Kirrik and her Master.

But Frog had slipped. Admitted there was a way through.

"Roll him off while he is sleeping? When will you do that, Frog? When you go to Canopy?"

"When it is time," Frog grumbled, giving her customary grimace.

"Time for what?"

"Why are you using your voice for talkin' rubbish while the Master is waitin' for 'is supper? Show me you can manage a loaf of bread without burnin' yourself before you ask for the way to unravel the greatest magical structure the world has ever seen!"

Choking on her impatience, Unar picked up the single grain from the table.

"The Master's supper," she said. "Will I be permitted to meet him at last, then? Will I carry the serving tray up that spiral staircase?"

"No," Frog said.

Unar let the grain fall to the floor. She sighed and started to sing.

In the night, Unar served another watch with Core Kirrik.

"Have you given thought to what you have learned so far, Nameless?"

Kirrik asked, staring into the downpour yet again, her wide stance undaunted and her umbrella unmoving.

"I have, actually. You asked me if there was anything for the goddess of rain to fear."

"And?"

"I suppose, if there was an emergency that fell under another god's jurisdiction, the people of Ehkis's niche could be convinced to pray to someone else. To take their offerings from Ehkisland to other niches, other kingdoms. She might fear that. The loss of their faith and their tribute. Such an emergency might even be contrived. To turn her people against her."

"Yes. How? Think!"

"Maybe . . . maybe if there was too much rain. Or maybe if the monsoon storms brought a lot of wind, or lightning. If it was wrecking people's houses, they might pay tribute to the lightning god, instead. Or the wind goddess. To make it stop. Then Ehkis would be weak. Her section of the barrier might become weak. Or the monsoon might end early."

Unar waited for some indication that she was right before it struck her that she didn't have to wait for confirmation; what she'd described was the same situation that had seen Aoun's parents executed for disobeying the king of Ehkisland. No wonder Frog was always calling her slow.

Core Kirrik glanced over her shoulder, and her laughter, this time, was low and delighted.

"You see, Nameless? It does not take much to make a traitor of a Canopian. Oh, do not make that offended face at me. You are a traitor. To mortals, you are. To others like you, with only the . . . what word did you use? . . . misfortune . . . to be born below the barrier, you are a traitor. You consider your current disadvantage to be temporary. Your sister's disadvantage too. You show loyalty to Canopy when it shows no loyalty to you."

Unar tried to make her flared nostrils relax, to make her jaw unclench.

"That is better," Core Kirrik remarked. "You can learn to hold your tongue, after all. I will reward you. Speak."

"If your Master hates Canopy so much," Unar spluttered, "why take my sister in? Why protect her, when she has no patron deity whose powers you might use?"

Kirrik massaged her brow with thumb and forefinger as though withdrawing reminiscences by hand.

"The monsoon was just beginning when Frog the Outer came. She was soggy. Frightened. Furious. I guarded the paths then, as I do now. I could have allowed her to run into the light. Instead, I quenched the lantern. Allowed her to pass. A great, fat man, a village Headman, came snorting and pawing behind her. When the lantern killed him and he fell, Frog put her face in my skirts and shook. At first, I thought she was crying because the fat man was her father." Kirrik smoothed those skirts, seeming to see Frog still crouched there. "But she was laughing."

"Why did you save her? And why did the Master agree to keep her?"

"Once, the Master had a son. Taught him to hate. Hate is safety, for sorcerers and their sons. It was too much hate, in the end, and the son was driven away. But Frog reminded me of the Master's son. Her gift *is* hate. Even those without magical gifts may have mundane ones. The Master knew from his future-searchings Frog would lead him to something he needed. Something he had been searching for."

"To what?" Unar was aghast. She didn't understand the strange prohibition against affection shown first by Frog, now by Kirrik. She tried to think what Kirrik's Master needed and had been searching for. The guess escaped her lips before she could stop it. "Bones."

*Stolen bones,* Frog had called them. Stolen from where? From whom? Did the Old Gods need them, if they were to rise again? Did the Floorians act as custodians of the bones? Unar still did not know what a bone woman was.

"Hush," Kirrik said.

For a moment, she seemed to be straining to hear some distant music.

Then she turned an odd, triumphant rictus on Unar. The ear bone that Unar had used before was in her outstretched hand.

"Take this, now, Nameless. The danger we have been waiting for is here at last. Oh, and there is something else. You must wear this." She dug in a damp, black pouch at her waist, drawing out a strip of colour-shifting fabric Unar recognised at once. "Chimera skin. While you wear the blindfold, you will not be able to magically perceive the patterns I will make of your power. You will breathe out into the bone flute. You will supply me with raw sound. Whenever I command you to spin, you will draw it like a spider drawing silk, but I will be the weaver."

"You want me to fight blindly?"

"I will do the fighting. Are you afraid, Nameless?"

Unar's heart thudded. "Of course I am, Core Kirrik. You intend me to be. You won't tell me what is coming."

"Put the blindfold on."

Unar obeyed. The chimera skin was light and supple. It didn't hold water. It had no smell.

"Tighter," Kirrik said, pulling the knot painfully. Unar felt the wind of the abandoned umbrella falling, just as Frog's voice came shrilly from the direction of the dovecote.

"Marram! Stop!"

Something crashed into the building, making the branch beneath Unar shake.

*He isn't dead,* Unar thought, dazed and indecisive. The ear bone was smooth and cold in her hands. Kirrik's icy fingers sent a shiver down the back of her neck. Unar was bodily turned until she, too, faced the dovecote.

"You will play when I squeeze my hand, Nameless," Kirrik said, low and cutting.

*I must pass the test. I must stay with Frog. I must learn how to break through the barrier from this side.*

Yet she couldn't let Kirrik kill Marram.

# FORTY-SIX

"Who are you, to come into my place without seeking guest-right?"

Kirrik's voice half deafened Unar. She flinched away but not too far, mincing steps where it seemed the other woman had stepped, not wanting to step off the edge of the path and break with the umbrella on the forest floor.

Marram's voice, when it came, sounded weary. It floated down from a height, as though he stood on the flat roof of the cylindrical dovecote.

"The child you shelter, called Frog, is some sort of sorceress or Floorian bone woman. That Gardener you keep a prisoner was under my protection. I will have her back before I go."

"Will you? Where will you go, and how? It is the monsoon. You are at death's door yourself. What safe refuge will you take her to?"

Unar had no choice but to surreptitiously push up one edge of the blindfold so that she could see. She bit her tongue, hard, to keep from crying out. In the cold blue light of the death-lanterns, she saw dark, bruised stripes across Marram's face, neck, and chest. He stood, swaying, close to the edge of the roof, wearing a bone amulet she hadn't noticed him wearing before.

One of his arms was knotted with vines in a way that suggested his collarbone was broken. But the worst was the front of his left leg; some kind of creature had eaten away the flesh from knee to ankle, so that the shinbone where the spines were grafted was exposed to the air.

Unar let the blindfold drop. Everything was black, but she could still imagine Marram there, a living corpse. Only the magic that maintained his grafted spines could be keeping him on his feet.

"Marram, I'm safe here," Unar called. "Please, go back."

Kirrik spun to face her.

"I did not give you permission to speak, Nameless," she said, and pushed Unar backwards. Little hands caught her as she stumbled. Frog had somehow crept around behind her.

"Fly away, Marram!" Unar tried to scream, but no sound came out of her mouth, and Kirrik used her magic in some way that she couldn't see. Vines grew around her, pulling her backwards by the throat. Frog moved away from her, and Unar found herself roped to the road, vines holding the ear bone against her mouth so that when she breathed out she couldn't help but breathe into it. When she breathed through her nose, she felt Frog's little hands again, this time pinching her nostrils shut.

Marram made no sound. Was Kirrik choking him with vines, too? Unar tried to take control of her own gift, but something struck her in the place in her belly where her control came from, like a mother slapping a child's hands away from a pot of honey, and the only thing she could think of to do, to deny her power to Kirrik, was hold her breath.

*Curse you, Core Kirrik. What's happening?*

Trussed and blind, she listened to the blood pulse in her ears, straining for a hint of Marram's movements, but Kirrik wasn't even breathing hard, and Frog was silent, too.

Unar couldn't hold her breath forever.

She twisted so her lips were to one side of the bone flute, though the vines cut off the blood flow to her head.

"Frog," she gasped, light-headed almost instantly, "he helped save you from the demon!"

Then she had to relax back into position and her breath flowed through the bone, giving more of Audblayin's life force to a woman who wanted to use it for death. How could it obey Kirrik? Why would it not obey Unar herself?

"May I speak, Core Kirrik?" Frog said at last.

"Speak."

"The man did 'elp me escape a dayhunter. 'E gave me food and shelter."

"How can that be? A fool such as this. He comes all but naked into the forest. It is obvious he has fallen from a height. Only the chance of vines in his path has saved him, and yet, instead of crawling home, he has come here, without so much as a pair of bracers to keep the spotted swarm at bay."

"Is that not courage, Core Kirrik? Could you not use 'im? Could you not put 'im with the others? Nameless the Outer can be used to heal and slow 'im. I am sure Audblayin's power will work as well as Atwith's, and she has affection for 'im. I would have slowed all of them, if only we had not left so suddenly."

Unar tried to follow the conversation, limp and useless in her outrage. Her breath was being stolen by a woman who would have been a slave in Canopy. Her own sister was helping that maggot-faced witch. Kirrik and Frog had been worried they couldn't use her to kill enemies, but any green, living thing could be used to choke a person!

Kirrik didn't answer, not right away.

"'E is almost dead, Core Kirrik," Frog said softly. "Without air, 'e will not wake, and we will have one less warrior when the time comes. Better than any heightsman I ever saw, I swear."

"I will indulge you this one time, Frog the Outer," Kirrik said tightly. "The next favour you ask had better be for me to cut your throat for disloyalty."

Unar struggled to understand the change in the dynamic between them. Only moments ago, Kirrik had been telling her how Frog reminded her of the Master's son. How she had saved Frog's life. Now there was a coldness about her, a bloodlessness, as though her body had been taken over by another. Or an act she had been making an effort to maintain, now unnecessary, had been dropped.

"Yes, Core Kirrik."

Again, Unar's breath transformed into some shape she couldn't see.

"Take him, then. Put him with the others. Take the bone flute from Nameless the Outer. The very sight of her angers me. It would not do to lose my temper and kill her accidentally. Let her sleep outside. Do not bring her food until she begs to obey."

"Yes, Core Kirrik."

Frog took the ear bone and the blindfold away. Unar couldn't turn her head because of the vines still across her throat. She blinked away the rain that fell into her eyes. Kirrik had already gone back into the dovecote.

"You are failing," Frog hissed. "You must try harder!"

Unar didn't say anything. Words could be stolen and used against her. She gave as much of a nod as she was able. Frog pulled the knife at her belt and cut the snug vines around Unar's throat. Yet she couldn't do it without cutting Unar's skin.

"Core Kirrik told me not to heal you," Frog muttered, "but say something, and I will close the wound."

*You'll close the wound? Not if you don't love me!*

Unar would rather bleed than be faced again with the reality that her ability now belonged to these women. She shook her head, jerking her chin in the direction of the doorway, hoping that Frog would understand that Unar intended to obey.

"So you are a little bit afraid of 'er," Frog said. "Good. You should be. I am."

She went back inside, and Unar was alone.

When morning came, the door opened.

Unar watched black skirts approaching from her facedown sprawl on the wet walkway. She supposed she should beg to obey. She supposed she should beg for food. But she couldn't even make herself feel hungry.

Kirrik stared down at her.

*I won't ask what happened to Marram. I will stay. I will learn.*

"Did you sleep well, Nameless the Outer?"

That chill. That inhuman quality.

"Yes, Core Kirrik."

"You have not used Audblayin's powers. You make no move to strike me, though you know what vines can do. Can you be trusted to meet the Master now, Nameless?"

Unar crawled in an awkward scrabble to kiss the hem of Kirrik's skirts.

"If you think I should, Core Kirrik."

Kirrik laughed.

"Yes, I think you should. Come inside. Follow me."

Unar went on hands and knees after her, as far as the long, dark corridor, where she used her hands against the walls to gain her feet and stagger after Kirrik towards the blocked spiral staircase.

Today, there was no barrier.

Kirrik led Unar up the stairs to the second storey of the dovecote. Unar kept her eyes lowered; surely they would be met by the sight of a carpet even finer than the ones below. The upper apartment must be spacious and luxurious, if the Master lived here all alone. In the time since Unar had arrived, she didn't think he had left it.

Or maybe he was a monster in shape as well as deed. Maybe he lived in a morgue, surrounded by the body parts of men butchered to feed him.

Unar wanted to laugh. She and Frog would have to leave Kirrik as soon as possible, and the humour came from knowing Frog must've had the same thoughts on arrival at the three hunters' home. Yet Frog hadn't hesitated when Unar precipitated their early departure. She'd had a plan. Unar would have to formulate a plan, too, in case she was forced to flee before learning what she needed to know, gaining what she needed to gain.

*Spines. A way to pass through the barrier. A way to guard my own strength. Three things. Then I'll take Frog and go.*

Then she saw what was in the single, long room that filled the second storey. Packed into turpentine shavings like clothing being protected from pests were the bodies of men. Some were bundled for cold weather or wet, and some, like Marram, nearly naked. His wounds were healed, and the flesh of his chewed leg regrown, and he lay, supine, as if sleeping, though his chest didn't rise or fall. His bone amulet was missing.

Hundreds of men, as many as two or three Canopian kings might command, stored as thoughtlessly as Esse stored coils of rope. Waiting.

*Where's the Master?* Unar almost asked before remembering she must speak only when spoken to. Keeping her eyes lowered, she stared at Marram.

"Touch him," Kirrik commanded. Unar put her hand obediently to Marram's wrist and found it warm, but with no pulse. *Wait.* She felt a single, slow beat. The youngest of the hunters slept as a tree bear sleeps through the monsoon. Kirrik hadn't killed him, after all.

*One less warrior,* Frog had said, *when the time comes.*

But Frog and Unar knew the three brothers had gone into exile because they wouldn't fight against Canopy. Upon waking, Marram would refuse to serve and would die as quickly then as he would've before the dovecote, if Frog hadn't intervened for Unar's sake.

*Four things. Four things I need before I can leave. Spines. A way through the barrier. Magical defences. The spell to wake Marram. I can't leave him behind.*

"You look tired, Nameless," Kirrik said, smiling unpleasantly. "Will you not lie down beside him and rest?"

"Core Kirrik, will I wake again, if I do?"

Was the room enchanted, or perhaps the wood shavings? Unar could have extended her magical senses to find out, if she dared. Her throat remained raw from the strangling vines and still stung from the kiss of Frog's knife, however, and she didn't know what would trigger Kirrik's cruelty.

"I can wake any of them, at any time," Kirrik said, "but of course you are not a block of fish fat, to store with my other supplies for war. You will be my trained chimera, unless I find that you cannot be tamed."

"I can be tamed, Core Kirrik," Unar said, horrified to hear a whine in her voice she hadn't put there intentionally. "I can."

"We will see," Kirrik said, gliding away back down the spiral stairs.

Unar looked down at Marram.

"I can," she said again.

*I don't care about Floorians, Understorians, or Canopians. But I won't leave him.*

"What was that, Nameless? Did you say something?"

Kirrik had halted with her hand on the banister.

"No, Core Kirrik. Only . . . what about the Master? Where is he?"

"Where, indeed." Kirrik's mouth opened wide with glee. She howled with a flaying laughter, the sound of which penetrated Unar's magical senses, dissolving her body and tossing the soul that remained up and down on the waves of it. Realisation struck Unar: Kirrik was a woman somehow fused with a demon. The soul of the chimera, accustomed to floating nearby while the desouled fleshy shell transformed, was bound to Kirrik's soul, keeping it in this bodily plane even when she was fatally wounded. Teacher Eann's lesson, previously disbelieved, popped into Unar's head. *A female chimera lays two eggs into her own mouth, then transforms into a male. During the transformation, the creature's soul hovers; it does not go into the ether. It waits until its new body is ready to receive it again.*

Kirrik's laughter cut off. Unar returned to herself.

"You are the Master," she whispered. "Your skill is that you cannot be killed."

*Attacking you will do no good. Your soul will wait until your body is healed, ready to receive it again.*

"Return to your chores, Nameless. There will be no more standing watch. The enemy I saw approaching has been turned to a harmless thread in the carpet beneath my feet. Work hard and learn fast. The time will come when you will be a thread or a tool, and while tools are oiled to keep them sharp, carpets are beaten."

"Yes, Core Kirrik."

*There can be no half measures. I must destroy your body so completely that your half-demon soul can never return to it.*

# FORTY-SEVEN

Unar was allowed to use her magic in small ways.

With the blindfold off, she healed the messenger birds when they were injured. She coaxed eggs out of even the smallest of them, bringing tears of laughter to Kirrik's cold eyes. She made bread from replicated grain and grated fresh-grown aerial-tubers to make porridge. The nonmagical tasks of washing and darning clothes returned some of her old calluses to her hands.

With the blindfold on, she brought great rivers of power into Kirrik's grasp. She poured her breath into not only the ear bone, but also a cracked tooth and a tailbone as long as her arm. All of them for outcomes that pleased Kirrik; Unar was not permitted to see.

"The bones work best for different purposes," Frog whispered as Unar used a fragment of broken jaw to sprout seeds for the birds.

Unar nodded grudgingly. The hints Frog slipped to her when Kirrik was out of the room usually made sense. "I felt that. The ear bone is best as a simple amplifier. The tooth works best for splitting and breaking. The tail-bone for balance and for healing."

Frog would not, or could not, answer her questions about breaking through the barrier, but she had healed all of Unar's sores with Kirrik's permission. They hadn't given back the clothes she'd arrived in, but put her instead in loose skirts and shirts with long sleeves that covered her hands and fell to the floor. Unar recognised their function. They were garments unsuited to climbing.

"So," Frog said softly, with a rare smile, "not so dank and dunderheaded as I thought."

"The men that went from here, fourteen days ago, with Core Sikakis. Are they bringing back a bone? Or a god?"

Frog's smile faded.

"You should not—"

"I know. I shouldn't ask questions. Only remember what I am told."

Frog swallowed. She looked over her shoulder. Core Kirrik had gone up onto the flat roof to release two birds that were too big for the tiny windows.

"They went to find a claw of the Old God whose essence was stolen by Airak. They say it will work as the lamps do, only the lightnin' can be directed, and it will not harm the one who holds it. They call it Tyran's Talon."

"Who was—"

"You must never say the name of one of the Old Gods," Frog interrupted, her eyes bulging slightly as if startled by how much she had said. "Core Kirrik would feed me to piranhas if she even guessed that you knew it. Promise me you will not say it, not ever!"

"I promise," Unar said, but she suspected the name held power; more power than singing the names of the gods and goddesses of Canopy. Could it be her path through the barrier? Or the secret of stealing the power of another? *Tyran. The god whose essence was stolen by Airak.*

She wished that she knew how to read, for Kirrik might have all of the Old Gods' names listed somewhere, and if they were forbidden, then they must be a danger to Frog's mistress somehow. Unar wished she had asked Hasbabsah. The old slave seemed to have known all sorts of things, but it was too late now.

"This tooth, that's best for splitting and breaking," Unar murmured. "Couldn't it be used for war? Couldn't it be used for breaking a person's bones into tiny pieces?"

"One person," Frog admitted. "You could focus its power on a single enemy. It would be time-consumin'. You would be defenceless while you did it. Other soldiers might slay you." She glanced sharply at Unar. "You must not attack Core Kirrik, Un—I mean, Nameless."

Unar threw up her hands. The motion, she hoped, concealed the fact that she had slipped the Old God's tooth into a pocket of her black skirt, wrapped in her blindfold to keep Kirrik from sensing it.

"Why do you keep accusing me?"

"I am not accusin'. I know. You want to kill 'er, but you would not like what would happen if you tried."

"She told me she can't be killed. I believe her." *She can't be killed by an ordinary person, but I'm not ordinary.* "I don't need to kill her." *Only to make Audblayin safe from her.*

"Good."

Kirrik threw open the door to the corridor.

"Enough of that. Men are coming. Four of them. They will need feeding. Go to the kitchen, Nameless."

Unar was trusted enough to boil oil and cook long slices of aerial-tuber for Kirrik and her frequent visitors without supervision. Men and women came to relay reports or receive instructions, all of them wet, muddy, and injured, and went away again with repaired weapons and full bags of food supplies. Their wounds couldn't be healed, since Unar didn't love them.

*One day,* Kirrik had said, laughing, *you will love me enough to heal me, Nameless the Outer.*

Once, a boy had been brought to have his snake spines put in. Unar hadn't been allowed to watch, but she'd spotted the leather bag in which the live snakes were stored, hanging by a rope from a roof beam, and some of the women brought identical leather bags with them when they came.

Unar exited the kitchen, balancing four plates of fried tuber, to find that Core Sikakis and his three pale henchmen had returned. They glanced at her as she passed the room where they slung personal belongings, stoppered gourds of drink, feathered talismans, and fire starters onto their bunks. Then they followed her back to the writing room and sat down at the table.

"Will you take bia?" Unar asked as she put plates in front of them.

"No," Sikakis said, inclining his head in apparent thanks at the offer. Two weeks of new growth around the edges of the previously neat beard had shaped a sharp doorway around the bemused set of his lips. His eyes were bloodshot.

"You do not have it," Kirrik surmised.

"One who walks in the grace of Airak does not have it," Sikakis agreed between bites of fried tuber. "As you guessed, the Talon is kept in the Earth-House of Hundar. It's unguarded during the monsoon, but only because the entire structure is flooded. We are all swimmers, but even Garrag could barely set his fingers to the lintel of the gate before being driven back to the surface to take a breath."

The man he had indicated, robed in linen with long arms and hands like plates, lifted his eyes from his fried tuber long enough to mutter, "Magic is needed, Core Kirrik."

"But not the magic of Audblayin," Sikakis added, glancing at Unar.

Unar froze in place, petrified by the treacherous thoughts whirling in her head.

*Kirrik needs Edax.*

"You need the magic of Ehkis," she heard herself say distantly. "You need a Servant of the Bringer of Rain."

"The Servants of Ehkis can't be pushed from the roads of Canopy," Sikakis argued. "They stick to branches like snakes. Our people in Canopy would have no chance to get near them, much less shake them down here for us to gather like fruit. Ehkis's adepts do not stay in her emergent, either. How would we find one to snare?"

Kirrik massaged her forehead. Her eyes, when they fell on Unar, glittered. "Nameless, you show improvement, but you are not yet one of us."

"With respect, what do you mean, Core Kirrik?" Sikakis asked her.

"Nameless has associated in the past with one called Edax, the rain goddess's Bodyguard. She has boasted about his ability to stay underwater for extended periods, without the use of magic."

"I haven't boasted—" Unar said.

"Now she seeks to trade."

"Dank," Frog mouthed from her place behind Kirrik, holding a pitcher of water. "Dunderhead!"

"What kind of trade?" When Kirrik didn't answer, Sikakis turned to Unar. "Well, Nameless? What are your demands?"

Unar first looked at Kirrik and then back at Sikakis.

This was a trap. She couldn't reveal her ambitions.

Or an opportunity. Maybe the only one she would have.

"I want the spines of a warrior," she said. "I want every question about magic answered that I care to ask. I want my sister's custody, to go where I please, when I please. Core Kirrik will show me how to overcome attempts to steal my magic. There must be a way. When she wishes a magical task to be completed, she'll ask me, and I'll decide whether to comply. Everyone here will call me by my name, Unar, which my mother gave to me." Unar addressed her final lines to Frog as much as to Kirrik. "She was not much of a mother, but she gave me life, and she gave life to my sister, who is mine to protect now. Not yours."

Kirrik stared at her with disdain.

"Core Sikakis has listened to you. Now you will listen to me. Do you really think I will let a Canopian child wreck my home with magic she can barely control on the chance that she can deliver a live Bodyguard of renowned alertness and agility? How do you propose to call him? Do you claim to be loved by the formidable Edax, Bodyguard of Ehkis?"

"You pretend to scorn the idea of love," Unar said, "but even blindfolded, I see what's between you and Core Sikakis. I served the Waker of Senses, the Giver of Life. The prince has been your lover, and these three men are your sons, though not by him." Frog's chin jerked slightly, but Sikakis and the three men showed no change in expression. "You've had quite a few children for a woman who claims there is safety in hate. If you hate them and they hate you, why are they here? They have no connection to the gods for you to manipulate."

Kirrik showed no sign that Unar's discovery of her relationship to the men around the table disturbed her. Perhaps she truly didn't care for her own kin. Perhaps she was like Wife-of-Uranun, and weighed other humans purely by their potential uses. Yet she'd adopted Frog and cared for her, teaching her to deploy stolen magic, when Frog had admitted she was no adept, with no inborn gift of her own.

"Frog the Outer," Kirrik said, "whom you will never remove from my side, by the by, has told me of a Servant of the Garden, higher in rank than a mere Gardener, who also survived your fall. You are not the only source of Audblayin's gifts that I can use."

*Oos. Leave Oos out of this.*

"She may be higher in rank, but she is weaker. And it's Ehkis's gifts you need right now."

"Core Kirrik," Sikakis said, "with respect, Nameless's demands are reasonable. Besides the one about dividing you from your body servant. You were going to teach her the ways of a sorceress, anyway. You were going to give her spines. If we're able to fetch the object before the monsoon ends, much may be accomplished."

Nobody spoke for a long while. One of Kirrik's sons cleaned the last crumbs off his plate. Kirrik stared at Unar without blinking.

"Bring me the leather bag," she said at last over her shoulder to Frog. "The one with the snakes inside."

Unar hid her triumph. The bag with the snakes. They were giving her spines. She had won.

As soon as Unar had a means of climbing and control over her own power, she'd lead the escape with Marram and Frog, too, no matter what her fool sister wanted. She'd warn Oos. Perhaps even fetch her along the way. Return her to Canopy, to safety. May Ehkis drown Core Kirrik and One Forest like she'd drowned Aoun's brother.

Frog looked at Unar. She looked at Kirrik. "Core Kirrik."

"What is it? We have already determined that you will stay with me, Frog the Outer. You are not part of the bargain."

"It is not that, Core Kirrik. I have been watchin' my sister very closely. Forgive me, Unar. You have no intention of betrayin' that Bodyguard, Edax. You wish only to observe how to break through the barrier. Once that happens, you will return to the Garden. Findin' the reincarnation of Audblayin is your only care."

Unar would rather her sister had stabbed her.

Kirrik frowned at Unar.

"This is disappointing news, if true, Nameless. Despite all you have learned, despite the whole of the city having cast you out forever, why you would still defend your own humiliation and utter subordination?"

Unar didn't answer. She swallowed the lump in her throat and waited for what was inevitable. Kirrik might decide that she couldn't be her trained chimera after all. She'd use Unar all up, at once, to wreak destruction on one of the emergents, in the hope that other adepts would fall down like rain.

Remembering Odel's Bodyguard, Unar managed to smile at Kirrik. Maybe whoever she brought down would make even more trouble for Kirrik than Unar had. Whatever happened, Kirrik would be no closer to her goal. She would not capture thirteen gods. The Old Ones would not return. They'd never return.

Her vision blurred with tears. Frog had betrayed her. Frog loved Unar's tormentor more than she loved her own flesh and blood. Wife-of-Uranun had been Frog's flesh and blood, too, but Frog had showed no emotion when admitting that their mother was dead.

*Our mother fell, Unar. She was not with child, nor will ever be again.*

In that moment, Unar was gripped by the certainty that Frog had been behind their mother's death.

"I forgive you, Isin," Unar said. "The debt between us is cancelled. I loved Mother too much to see she was a monster at first. You love this woman, who is as a mother to you, too much to see the monster in—"

But Unar couldn't finish the sentence without her words being snatched away. Frog stole her voice. Vines grew up and across the floor, binding Unar's wrists to the back of one of the chairs. Oh, yes. Frog was a fast learner.

"Do you still wish me to fetch the snakes, Core Kirrik?" Frog asked earnestly in her childish voice.

*Oh, Isin. You advised me not to love. I thought you loved me, and you must,*

*or you couldn't have healed me, but not nearly as much as you loved the plea-
sure, the power you knew I would give her.*

"Yes," Kirrik said.

"Frog the Outer is loyal," Sikakis said as Frog left the room. "You will
give Nameless the spines, knowing her intent?"

Kirrik steepled her fingers.

"Nameless will keep her word, regardless of intent. She will bring us Edax,
Bodyguard of Ehkis. But she will do it from below the barrier. She will lure
him down. You will go with her, Sikakis."

"As you say." Sikakis inclined his head. "And if she cannot bring him? If
she cannot lure him?"

Kirrik's smile tightened.

"Then we must return to the great tree that is Audblayin's emergent. We
must take captive the Servant of Audblayin that Frog spoke of. With
Nameless and her friend, we can bringing down the emergent. It is hundreds of paces across, but they can do it, I think, with the tooth to help tear
it apart. If they tear it in the right place, and lengthen it as it falls, the crown
of it will reach here and my woken warriors will be waiting. Not just one
Servant for me to keep, but all thirteen of them, with some twenty-eight
Gardeners as well, and no goddess to help them escape back to Canopy."

Unar saw it in her mind's eye: Kirrik destroying the Garden. Forcing
Unar to bring down her own Temple and die in the process. The building
at the heart of the moat cracking like a real egg. Moat water, bulrushes,
and rainbow-coloured fish falling. Loquat trees, leaves down, naked roots
skyward. The Gates off their hinges and Aoun's bronze lantern lighting the
destruction.

*Aoun.* Kirrik would use him. Thirteen Servants, one to bring down each
of the other Temples, with twenty-eight Gardeners to hand as well. Kirrik
might even succeed, with that number of adepts under her thumb.

*Edax, you showed me a thing that Audblayin had hidden from me. You
showed me that life comes, not just from Audblayin, but from fire between two
willing pieces of kindling. But I lied to myself when I thought I didn't care for
what it was that I left behind. Aoun. The Garden. Audblayin.*

"I can bring Edax to you, Core Kirrik, Core Sikakis," Unar said. *I already
agreed to it; your threats aren't necessary.* "They stick like snakes, you said.
You said nobody can get close. I can, and without leaving Understorey."

Frog returned to the room with the leather bag that Unar had last seen
hanging from the rafters.

"What of your desire to search for Audblayin?" Sikakis asked.

"Core Kirrik said if I stayed here long enough, it would fade."

"It will never fade," Frog scoffed.

"I wanted to search for you, too, when you fell!"

"But you did not. You knew it was hopeless. You were wiser, then, than you are now." Frog raised her palm and with the forefinger of her opposite hand, impersonated an inchworm. "So dank. So doltish, Unar." Her fists flashed to her hips and she grimaced. "You want answers, but you do not even know which questions to ask."

# FORTY-EIGHT

HOURS LATER, rain drummed once again on Unar's head and shoulders.

She shivered. It trickled into the raw wounds where her spines had been implanted, where her own magic still hummed, setting up a resonance that interfered with anything else she might try, which was why she'd been set outside to cool off, as Kirrik called it.

She had expected the magic would render the procedure painless. The boy who had come before her hadn't screamed.

Unar had screamed, and her screams had been used by Frog to force the snake-jaws deeper into her marrow.

Hasbabsah, no doubt, had received her spines without screaming. Frog, too, and the three brothers Esse, Bernreb, and Marram. Thinking of them firmed her resolve. She'd done what she had to do, to get what she needed. She would undo the terrible consequences at the first opportunity.

*I have spines. Next, I need a way through the barrier.*

She thought carefully about what Kirrik had said, that the adepts of Audblayin would have no goddess to help them escape back to Canopy. Was the direct application of power by an incarnated god or goddess the only way to open a door in the barrier once a Canopian's innate magic had faded?

*Understorians do not always raid Canopy,* Hasbabsah had said. *In hungry times, they trade. In prosperous times, they buy back captured slaves.*

Kirrik gloated over the fact that the Gardeners couldn't return because their god was a mewling babe, somewhere, and could not open a door for them. But perhaps other gods could be persuaded. Unar had spoken to the god Odel, held a conversation with him as if he were a mortal man. What about Ehkis? Could Edax carry a message to her? Would the rain goddess help a Gardener to escape a house suspended in the arms of Airakland, to foil an Understorian plot aimed directly at the gods?

Unar rubbed at her forehead as if by rubbing she could untangle her thoughts. The movement of her tendons seemed to set her arm aflame. She couldn't cradle her arm, for the new spines were extended and razor-sharp. Instead, she howled and stayed as still as possible until the pain ebbed to a deep throbbing.

Frog poked her head out of the dovecote.

"Core Kirrik says to be quiet."

"Can't it be healed right away, Frog?"

"It has been."

"I don't feel healed."

"If your bone is healed too quickly and the snake bones are healed too quickly, they will heal separately and fall out. Is that what you want?"

"You don't know what I want," Unar snapped. "And I don't know what you want. I don't know who you are. You're probably not even my real sister."

Frog slammed the door shut.

More hours passed with Unar distracting herself from the pain by remembering the smell of loquats and the taste of pomegranates, the feeling of her bore-knife going into bark and the sound of Oos's thirteen-pipe flute.

The door opened again, and there was Frog, emerging with a plate of porridge.

"Eat this," she said. "I am your real sister. I wish that I was not. Do you want to know how I imagined my real sibling?"

"No," Unar said, but Frog told her anyway.

"I imagined a fighter. A warrior. Perhaps a soldier of the king of Audblayin, yet imprisoned, tortured, for the belief that the barrier is cruel and must be abandoned. Sikakis intuited the truth, even while surrounded by lies. But not you. Eat this."

Unar glared up at her. "Are you going to stay and watch me?"

"Of course."

"Of course," Unar said bitterly. "It's what you do." She stared at the porridge, knowing that when she moved her hand to grip the spoon, pain would shoot through her again.

"Do you want me to feed you like a baby?"

"No." Another scowl. "I want you to tell me how you and Core Kirrik can take my power away from me as if I'm a baby."

Frog laughed.

"Not how to get through the barrier?"

Unar gritted her teeth as she reached for the spoon. The pain wasn't as bad as before.

"If I'm so dank and doltish, it can't hurt to tell me, can it? You can always outwit me, can't you, my sister?"

"That is right," Frog said, sitting easily on her haunches. "I can. You wanna know why Core Kirrik is able to use you so easily? I am not surprised you could not work it out. Just as you can only heal someone you love, you can only steal power from someone you hate. You will not get control of your own power from Kirrik until you hate yourself more than she hates you, and that will never be. It was Servants of Audblayin who killed 'er parents."

*Good,* Unar thought angrily.

She ate another spoon of tasteless porridge, resisting the urge to rub her forehead again.

"So . . . so you hate me, too, Frog?" *Hate me and love me, because you healed me.*

"Just a little bit. Just enough."

"Like I had to hate Oos, just a little bit. I stole her power."

"Because she had what you wanted."

*True enough.*

"What did I have that you wanted?"

Unar expected Frog to answer, *A real mother and father.*

"The gift," Frog said, eyes gleaming. "If I had it, we would not need you. It would just be the two of us. Core Kirrik and me. That is the treasure our parents gave you. Not your dank name."

"The gift? Is that why she doesn't care about those three sons of hers? Because they were born without the gift? Or is it because of her other son, the one who hated her, who ran away? How can you love her, Isin?"

*How can you love her so much more than you love me?*

"Dunderhead! She does not care about them because it is dangerous to care. I will tell you somethin', and then maybe you will stop makin' stupid assumptions about me." Frog gestured with her chin towards the closed door of the dovecote and lowered her voice. "Core Kirrik had a daughter too, once. Before she had any of 'er four sons. That daughter was gifted, and Core Kirrik loved 'er, but bein' close to a sorceress means bein' burned by the flames. She killed 'er own daughter. By mistake, but it could not be undone. I do not want Core Kirrik to love me. Why would I wanna end up dead? If you love me, and you learn from 'er, you could kill me, too. So stop it."

"What do you want, if you don't want her to love you?"

Frog's smile echoed that of the woman in the black skirts. The woman who had accidentally killed her own daughter and deliberately driven away a hate-filled son. The woman who did not love.

"I want revenge."

THEY LET Unar back in at nightfall.

Core Kirrik sat at her desk, writing, seemingly oblivious. Sleepy birds perched above and around her. The men's voices rumbled in the corridor, though the door to their bunkroom was shut.

"Dry off by the fire," Frog said. "Change your clothes if you must. Hang your wet things by your bunk. Then go and make supper."

"No," Unar said. "Things have changed. My obeying your orders was before. This is now. We have an arrangement. I'm not your slave anymore."

Kirrik didn't look up from her work.

"You never were," Frog said. "You jumped out of the Garden to save a slave who held 'er tongue for seventy years, and you could not even hold yours for two weeks. Not even for me."

She went into the corridor and Unar followed her, furious. She had held her tongue. This past fortnight she'd let Kirrik treat her like dirt, when Unar was the one with the power. Unar was the one who deserved respect and obedience.

"Aren't you coming to watch me? I might poison the supper."

"Go ahead. You poison everythin'. Our parents' hearts, so they didn't want more daughters. Audblayin's Garden. You were the poison in the home of the three hunters, and you are the poison between my mother and me." Frog slammed the door again, this time to the bunk room they were supposed to share.

*She's still a child,* Unar reminded herself, *and she's wrong.* Wife-of-Uranun wanting Frog to fall had nothing to do with her. The Garden wasn't poisoned, it was healthy and strong. Its strength would only increase when Unar returned with Audblayin. As for the three hunters, she had begged Marram not to follow. But she couldn't help feeling uneasy about Frog's heated words.

*And Frog called Core Kirrik her mother. She does want to be loved, no matter how she denies it.*

Instead of going to the kitchen, Unar went up the stairs, alone, without a lantern. Now that the Master deception was over, the barrier wasn't needed. Marram was where Kirrik had put him, sleeping the sleep of the almost dead, surrounded by Understorian warriors. All of them had the spines.

*I'll wager none of you screamed,* Unar thought, ashamed.

She used the quietest possible sound, the tiniest wheeze of her breath, to send a filament of magic into Marram's chest. There was no injury there for her to find. Nothing for her to pull, to draw his waking mind back into his body.

Well, she'd gotten some information out of Frog by pandering to her vanity. She could do it again. Frog would tell her what she needed to know. Unar moved away from Marram, examining the next man, and the next man. They were all the same. There was nothing to find. It seemed a healthy sleep, except for the interminable slowness of their beating hearts and all-but-absent breath.

The next rag-shrouded figure seemed a little small for a warrior. When Unar probed the body, she gasped. Beneath the swathe of cloth lay the gangling form of a girl about the same age as Frog. When the thread of magic touched her, it vanished.

"She is Ilan," Kirrik said softly, and Unar spun on her heel. "Protector of Kings."

"How have you done this?" Unar cried. "How have you captured a goddess and kept her secret?"

Kirrik made no retort about Unar only speaking when spoken to. Instead, she gently stroked Unar's forearm, sending pain through Unar's spines.

"Her body is a girl's body," Kirrik said. "I was able to put her to sleep with all the rest. It is eighteen years since the old incarnation of Ilan died, only eight since I captured this one. She was not self-aware. Her powers had not manifested."

"Her Servants must be frantic not to have found her."

Kirrik smiled.

"They have started starving themselves to atone. Other Servants will take their place, and may those fools starve, too, for all the good it will do them."

"Is this how you'll do it, then? Capture them one by one, and keep them here, until you can kill them all at once? Between sunrise and sunset of a single day, is it? Does she dream? Are her powers manifest now? How do you know she won't wake?"

Kirrik waved a dismissive hand.

"She cannot age, and so she cannot manifest her powers. While she sleeps here, the strength of kings' rule fades. Disorder and injustice reign. It will help to keep them from organising against us when the time comes."

Unar stared at the sleeping goddess and felt afraid for Audblayin. Kirrik must not be allowed to find him first while he was vulnerable.

"Try to wake her," Kirrik commanded, and Unar jerked with surprise.

"What do you mean?"

"Try to wake her, I said. You gaze at her. You wish you could wake her and age her with your ability to manipulate the stuff of life. You wish to watch her destroy me. Is it not so?"

Unar blinked.

"Core Kirrik, you've given me these." She raised her forearms where the spines were still extended, ragged and bloody as though she had used them to kill. "I will give you what I promised."

"Frog tells me that your face heats when you mention this man, Edax, Bodyguard of Ehkis. She says you will never betray him."

Unar remembered the upside-down kissing. The animal sounds she had made in Edax's expert hands. She remembered how careless he had sounded, telling her about the foot bones of would-be assassins he had fastened to the bottom of a fig-tree lake, careless of anything and everything but the need to keep his goddess safe.

She looked at the small form of the child on the floor.

*I will keep my god safe.*

"There is a place," she said, "where we used to meet."

THE BROAD myrtle branches that had formed the rim of the pool spilled water like thin sheets of crystal.

Unar gazed at the place that had seemed safe to her while she dallied with Ehkis's Bodyguard. She and Edax had met after dark. This was the first time she'd seen the myrtle pool during the day.

Trapped fragments of scarce, grey light from the clouds above Canopy gave body to the vertical river. It twisted like a woman's waist seen through a window. The air was cooler, perfumed by summer blooms and fresh foliage.

Sounds Unar had half forgotten wove in and around the fall of water. Monkeys howling. The *too-woo, too-woo* of amorous fruit doves. Silvereyes *pip-pip-pipp*ing. Lorikeet trills, bowerbird wheezes, and the high-pitched chatter of fantails. Toucans croaking and manakins warbling, birds of paradise stuttering and catbirds screeching.

"You swam here?" Core Sikakis shouted into Unar's ear over the animals and the roar of rain and river.

"It was smaller," Unar shouted back. Streams from Canopy pounded the pool in five places, feeding the surge that fell from the lowest edge. The patter of fresh droplets, small sticks, dead leaves, fruit, and insects was relentless.

Three and a half months of the monsoon were past. There were one-and-a-half still to come. Ehkis was at the height of her power. The tributes and prayers to her this year must have been mighty. Last year's monsoon had been feeble in comparison.

"What makes you think he'll come? Won't he have heard you're dead? Your own people confirmed your fall."

Kirrik had shown Unar a note she hadn't been able to read. Apparently it was news that Servant Eilif had announced Unar's demise, along with the deaths of Oos, Ylly, and Hasbabsah. Eilif had raised a new Gardener, a new Servant, and had purchased four new slaves in the face of Wife-of-Epatut's refusal to return Sawas and baby Ylly to the Garden.

If not for the pronouncement of names that Kirrik couldn't otherwise have known, Unar might not have believed her. Who was sending messages to Kirrik from inside Audblayinland? Sawas had mentioned birds, and the slaves were taught to read and write so they could tally the produce of the Garden, keep track of the tributes, and maintain calendars for planning and planting, but Unar didn't think it could be Sawas.

"It's just a feeling I have," she told Core Sikakis, looking up at him. Here, Edax and Unar had broken the rules together, and she also had a feeling Sikakis knew much more than she about breaking rules. By Frog's account, the former prince had found out about his family's rise to power in a carelessly shelved volume of secret histories. He'd gone to the Temple of the lightning god and demanded that Airak open up his section of the barrier to allow Understorians to come into the sun.

Then he'd been forced to flee for his life before his father's soldiers could murder him; he'd fled into Kirrik's cold embrace. Unar made a face at the thought.

"The barrier is close here," Sikakis said. Unar knew, but said nothing. "Core Kirrik asked me to stay out of sight. This friend of yours may be skittish if he sees you're not alone. You know what to do, but know this also. If you try to run, we *will* bring you down."

Unar kept her face blank. *You'll bring me down? The three brothers could not bring me down, and they've brought down demons.*

Core Kirrik had given her the ear bone to augment her strength. After they'd reached the myrtle tree that held the pool, the pool where Edax had taught her to love both the water and the feeling of male and female parts together, Core Sikakis had confiscated the piece of Old God that Unar had used to grow the pathways.

Nobody had noticed, yet, that the tooth was missing.

"How can I run?" Unar's shrug, palms upwards, encompassed their surroundings. "Even if my spines were fully healed, there's nowhere for me to go but straight upwards. Nobody can glide from tree to tree in the monsoon."

*Hold on, Marram. I will find a way to free you.*

Her promises to herself had never felt so empty. She'd never felt so alone.

Sikakis nodded. He put his larger spines, gleaming magically clean and eternally razor-sharp, into the trunk of the myrtle tree and began to lower himself to the bracket-fungus platform that Unar had grown for him and the others.

Unar waited from midday until midnight.

Edax didn't come.

On the fifth day, at sunset, Unar hummed to pass the time.

She sat cross-legged by the pool in her dangling sleeves and long black skirts, wet and bored. They'd warned her not to use magic. It would arouse suspicion, and besides, she might need her full strength to capture Edax. In the meantime, despite the warning, she'd found a way to make fish come to the surface of the pool by making sprouted seeds wriggle on the edge of the pool's bank. She was so sick of porridge, even the taste of fish would have been welcome.

She thought of Esse handing her roasted fish portions on a stick. His long limbs. His grey eyes. He'd follow her, she knew. Punish her if he could. She remembered Aoun, passing her the fish with the spines on its back, and how hard she'd slapped it away.

"Who are you?" a man's voice exclaimed, not Edax's, and Unar sprang to her feet. The Canopian who stood there, dressed in only a short, silver-coloured skirt and sandals, was shorter than she, but muscular, wiry, and covered in scars that looked like burns. His skin was as velvet black as the depths of Floor, but the left half of his parted, braided hair was white, and he had one white eye.

A Servant of Airak.

"What are you doing in Ehkisland?" she demanded, but she knew. Oh, she knew. What else was the Servant doing here, below the barrier, but meeting a lover? One who couldn't be trusted not to take advantage of his powers?

She realised, quick as lightning, that Core Kirrik would be as pleased, perhaps more pleased, by the power of the lightning god in her hands.

"We were meant to meet," she said, taking a step towards him. *Some providence has spared me the pain of betraying Edax. Whatever god or goddess has done this, I thank you, from the bottom of my heart.* "What is your name?"

"Aforis," the man said warily, taking a step back. "But I've no intention of sharing him with a woman. Tell him—"

"Tell me what?" Edax said, all dexterity and strength, upside down with his owl feet gripping a rope. He was as she remembered him. The tear-shaped scars on his cheeks. The smile-lines around his eyes. Only, it was strange seeing the long sleeves of his robe. Men in Understorey didn't cover their forearms.

Unar lost her breath in an exhale like the aftermath of a punch. She was not to be spared, after all. She felt glad of the ridiculous long sleeves of her shirt. Her spines couldn't be seen.

"Little Gardener," Edax said, his brows raised, only he was upside down, so they were lowered. "You're alive."

"Devastated by my death, were you?" Unar said crossly, forgetting her traitor's errand for a moment.

"Your heart wasn't set on me. I knew it as I took you. You wanted me for teaching, as I recall."

"Come here," she shouted. *Come here so I can drag you down.* "Come and talk to me properly, the right way up."

He dropped lightly to his taloned feet. But he didn't go to her. He went to Aforis, kissed him, and murmured, "I'm sorry."

Unar went to them, looked each of them in the eyes in turn, and said, "I'm sorry, too."

But the words made no sound. Vines leaped up around the three of them. Twisting. Binding. Edax might have torn free, in the first instant, if he hadn't seemed entranced by her sorrow and regret. While he hesitated, trying to read the emotion in her eyes, the trap closed. His puzzled expression turned to alarm.

"What—"

Three of them, trussed together, fell, but not far. Nets grown almost instantly between branches delivered all three of them to Core Kirrik's men. Unar didn't hate Edax, nor Aforis, but it didn't matter that she couldn't steal their shouts from them, for they had no notion of using the sound themselves.

As Sikakis pulled her free and put the ear bone in her hand, she almost didn't use it. Almost. Edax and Aforis might be without magic, but they still had the power of their flesh, and might have been a match for Sikakis if not for her. Aforis seemed astonished at the sight of Sikakis, squinting at him in the last of the daylight.

"Prince Acis?" he said as Unar caused the vines to coil tightly around his wrists, trapping them behind him. "How can it be?"

"Never call me that," Sikakis answered, stuffing rags into the prisoner's mouth. "That is no longer my name."

Edax looked shrewdly at Unar. His eyes went from the seams in Sikakis's forearms to the long sleeves that she wore.

"And you, little Gardener?" he said. "Have you taken a One Forest name?"

Unar could only mutely shake her head, the beginnings of tears in her eyes.

Kirrik emerged to quench the lantern.

It was hours before dawn, but Unar didn't think the Master, the Mistress, the ruler of the dovecote, whatever she called herself today, had been sleeping. Kirrik moved slowly and carefully along the path from the doorway of the dovecote with the rod in her hands, the bowl of the instrument hovering before her. Before she could lower it over the lantern, she took in the sight of the two prisoners and breathed deeply with satisfaction, as though inhaling the smell of a delicious feast.

"Nameless the . . . Unar . . . kept her word," Sikakis said.

"So it would seem."

"Will you quench the lantern? We are tired."

Kirrik stared at Aforis. She seemed not to have heard what Sikakis said.

"Push him through," she said. "Push him to me, through the light."

Sikakis exchanged glances with Garrag, the long-armed swimmer, who had the prisoners' charge. Sikakis nodded. Garrag shrugged. He pushed Aforis into the circle of blue-white light.

Spears of white, so bright they left afterimages in Unar's eyes, struck from the lantern into Aforis's chest. Unlike the branch, Aforis didn't catch fire. He didn't stop breathing, and he didn't fall.

On his knees, he crawled through the light, being struck constantly as he went, until he passed out of the circle of light on the other side.

Unar saw his skeleton glowing, faintly. She felt the buoyancy of Understorian magic in use nearby.

"The surest way," Kirrik said, smiling, "to wake the bones of a Servant of Airak. I could have used him while his bones slept, but he would not have been able to use any tools of amplification, and amplification he must have, if he is to strike down the armies of your father, Sikakis."

"Yes, Core Kirrik," Sikakis said gravely.

Kirrik licked her lips as she gazed down at Aforis. Gingerly, as though trying not to wake a sleeping demon, she removed the rags from his mouth and the gag that held them there.

"You may speak," she told him.

Whatever he said, it made no sound. Lightning leaped from Kirrik's fingers and she shrieked with glee. Edax made a low growl in his throat, and Kirrik's greedy eyes came to rest on him.

"This one is to pass through the lantern light, too?" Garrag asked, shaking Edax's shoulders, but Sikakis put out a hand across Garrag's chest.

"No, Garrag," he muttered. "This one would not survive the light."

Even as he finished the sentence, Kirrik quenched the lantern and beckoned eagerly for the second prisoner.

"A Bodyguard of Ehkis," she breathed. "I can feel the music of the monsoon in him, so close does his soul lie to that of his goddess. We must use him quickly, before she can replace him. Now, today. Frog the Outer will go with you. Her hate for this Bodyguard is strong. You must fetch the Talon at once, Sikakis."

Sikakis gave a weary sigh. All the men were weary. They'd barely stopped to rest. Unar stared at the quenched lantern. It was her chance to seize Frog and run, while Kirrik was distracted by her prizes, but what about Marram? And the barrier? She bit her lip to keep from repeating what Sikakis had said, that she had done as she was bidden, and that her questions must be answered now, and as she tasted blood, Sikakis spoke.

"We've spent several days returning to you, Core Kirrik. How can you be sure Ehkis hasn't already replaced him?"

Kirrik's fingers laced around Edax's throat, her thumbs pressing his windpipe.

"I am sure."

Edax jerked defiantly out of her grip.

"And how," Sikakis asked, "does one wake the bones of a Servant of the rain goddess?"

Kirrik put her fingers to her chin.

"If he can be made willing, he will sing for me. The right song will wake the bones of any disciple. If not, we will wake them with water and fire. Will you sing for me, Bodyguard of Ehkis?"

In reply, Edax threw himself off the edge of the platform.

"No!" Unar shouted. She saw Aforis's lips shape the same denial, hearing nothing but Kirrik's hiss; vines hauled Edax back up into the light by one owl foot, and lightning crackled over his skin. Kirrik let him writhe and scream for only a moment, but when the vines peeled away, Edax's clothes were charred into bloody, raw seams.

Kirrik looked at Unar.

"Sing again, pretty bird," she said. "I will allow you to heal him."

Unar closed her eyes and sang.

# FORTY-NINE

INSIDE THE dovecote, half a day later, Frog sat on the edge of her bunk, projecting the lie of the distracted child, swinging her legs while practicing her letters.

Unar knew all her attention was on the two men, each bound to their respective bunks. If Aforis so much as reached for his own magic, Frog was instructed to give him a dose of it, and let Unar heal him afterwards if the punishment turned out to be too severe. As for Edax, he had until sundown to decide to sing for Core Kirrik. Unar didn't know what would happen, then, but she was afraid for him.

"Edax. Please."

He wouldn't even look at her.

"You heal 'im better than anyone you healed before," Frog said conversationally. "I thought Core Kirrik had killed 'im, that last time. With the hot coals and the poker."

Unar flinched.

"I've brought food and water for them. Shall I call the men to untie them?"

"I do not need the men," Frog said scathingly. "Untie them yourself. I promise not to let them hurt you."

Frog would steal Unar's magic, too, if it seemed like Unar might help Edax to escape. When Unar had asked Kirrik to fulfil her side of the bargain by answering her questions, Kirrik had laughed and said Unar could wait until Edax had retrieved the Talon.

Unar's hands shook as she unlaced the leather bindings that held his wrists to the support post of the bunk above his. She tried to pull him into a sitting position, with his ankles still bound, but he resisted, and when she put a goblet of water into his hands, he threw it down.

"I don't need water, Gardener," he said. "I am the rain."

"Feed the other one," Frog sneered. "This one will die of pride."

Aforis, whose failed escape attempt several hours ago had ended with him setting fire to his own internal organs, took the porridge and water with hands that shook even more than Unar's.

"You think what she's doing is right, then?" Unar asked Frog.

Frog sneered again.

"When you have lesser numbers, you must do things the other side has no need to do."

"That doesn't answer the question. This isn't right, Isin."

"You call me that when you want me to take extra notice of what you say. But when you say it, I hear only the wind. You speak to the dead. Maybe the dead will take notice of you. Maybe the god of the dead will hear you, loyal Canopian that you are."

Was she a loyal Canopian? A loyal Canopian wouldn't have attacked a Servant of Airak or the Bodyguard of Ehkis. Yet she'd done it so she might win free, to protect Audblayin. She had spines like an Understorian now, but being in the dovecote repulsed her. It was a place of pain, a container of suffering.

"I fell while trying to save a slave," Unar pointed out.

"And now you are one. But at least you are a slave to the cause of justice."

"She promised to tell me what I wanted to know."

"I heard no such promise from 'er lips."

Frog used Unar's next words to tie the two men up again. She didn't even look up from her ink and parchment.

"Go to Core Kirrik," she said. "Tell 'er the Bodyguard will not change his mind."

Unar looked at Edax again.

"Edax," she said with the same hopelessness with which she had called out to Marram. "Please!"

She might as well have been talking to the dead. He didn't understand what kind of a woman Kirrik was. Her cold ruthlessness. Just like Unar's mother. The day little Unar had spilled the expensive lantern oil, kicked it over because she was chasing butterflies, she had begged Father not to tell his wife. *Please, Father!* Her short little arms had gone around his knees, to try to stop him from going to Left Fork, where a strike that Airak hadn't prevented had killed one of the trees. Fuel-finders from all over would be going to take it apart, cutting charred homes away from under the feet of the families of the departed, but she hadn't cared about that. She'd only cared about not being alone when Mother came home.

Uranun had looked down at her, she'd thought then, with the eyes of the dead. He'd taken one stride, breaking apart the grip of her little hands, and left without a word.

Here, now, Edax didn't stir.

Unar went to Kirrik. Waited until the older woman finished placing the rolled parchment in the clutches of a small green parrot and sent it on its way. When Kirrik turned her ghastly, pale, mad expression on Unar, it was easy to imagine the wrathful Old Gods had taken possession of her woman's body, that there was nothing of reason or compassion left at all.

"Frog says to tell you that the Bodyguard won't change his mind."

Kirrik steepled her fingers. She took the god's ear bone from the table, unfolded her leather umbrella, and led Unar outside.

"Spin, my spider," Kirrik said, and Unar blew on the bone flute.

Out of the path, a wooden barrel began taking shape. It was all of a piece and part of the living wood. Bodiless, Unar rode the wave of unheard melodies, yet at the same time, she smelled the tacky floodgum sap, as she would have when performing magic in the Garden, and was distracted by the combination, as though two opposite ends of her nature were finding a way to knit together. Almost as soon as the continuous walls of the barrel rose, rainwater began to fill it. Kirrik stopped when the vessel was chest-high and just as wide.

They stood together silently while water fell around them.

"Not fast enough," Kirrik mused. "Fetch water in a bucket and fill it."

Unar bowed her head and went inside. Rainwater from the dovecote's flat roof was channelled into a holding tank behind the bathroom and kitchen. She trudged back and forth for an hour or two, filling a pair of buckets on a frame, carrying them on her shoulders and then tipping them into the new pool Kirrik had made.

When it was full to the brim, Kirrik sent Unar to fetch Frog, Sikakis, and the two prisoners. Frog and Sikakis took Aforis with them from the bunkroom first, leaving Edax alone with Unar for a brief interval.

"I have to help her," Unar said. "I have to help her, to win my freedom and save Audblayin."

"The moment you stop helping her," Edax said, meeting her eyes at last with his pain-emptied ones, "you'll become her. If you want to save

Audblayin, you'd better cut your own throat with those spines, before they heal and you become a fit shell for her black soul to crawl into. The gift goes with the body. Only godhood goes with the soul."

Unar didn't understand him. She stood, mystified, while Frog and Sikakis returned to untie Edax from the bunk.

"Keep up, Unar," Sikakis grunted as he dragged Edax down the corridor.

Outside the dovecote, the sun was almost down. The grey cloud-light seen high above in tiny patches between the trees had turned bruise-yellow, and the blue-white lanterns that kept demons away were too low on their branches to light the surface of the water in the pool. There, raindrops made small gilded circles before fading so that Unar couldn't see them at all.

"Put the Bodyguard in the water," Kirrik ordered, and Sikakis moved to comply.

Edax came to life, thrashing, straining for the edge again. There was fear in his eyes that Unar had never seen before, and it was contagious. She turned to go inside, but Kirrik's hand flashed out and seized a handful of her shirt.

"Stay. There is a thing about Bodyguards that you do not know. Every one of them has a private means of communication with his mistress. For the rain goddess, whenever she is immersed in water, her Bodyguard feels whatever she feels. It is so he can sense that she is safe while she sleeps. Most often, she feels nothing. She is rarely wakened at the bottom of her lake. What fool would disturb her rest?"

Sikakis wrestled Edax over the edge of the pool. Once he was in it, Kirrik motioned for Unar to spin again. Unar's knuckles whitened on the ear bone, but she didn't raise it to her lips.

"What are you—"

Kirrik seized her words and the rim of the water-filled pool began to grow closed, stopping just short of a complete seal, holding Edax by his neck in the water. He lifted his desperate gaze to Unar.

"Jump," he said. "Jump, now!"

"What my little birds have discovered," Kirrik went on, smirking, "is that this bond between goddess and Bodyguard goes both ways. When he is immersed in water, in her element, in turn, the Lady Ehkis feels what he feels. Did he tell you she was ignorant of his little excursions? Did he tell you so while he took you under the water, so that she could share in all those delicious sensations?"

"No," Unar said. They hadn't been together underwater. Only in the open air. But Aforis stared in horror at Edax.

"Jump, little Gardener," Edax said again, clearly. "Please!"

Unar remained still. She refused to abandon Audblayin, but she couldn't see any other way to stop what was about to happen. Kirrik planned to reach through Edax to harm his goddess. He wanted Unar to sacrifice herself to protect Ehkis. Just as Unar had sacrificed him to try to protect Audblayin. If Unar jumped, Kirrik wouldn't be able to use her.

"You are talking to the wrong tool," Kirrik informed him, just as Frog seized Aforis's power. Aforis's lips moved, making no sound as he attempted to speak to Edax, and Frog did something to the water that Edax was trapped in.

Edax gritted his teeth. An agonised sound still escaped him. Unar heard the muffled thuds of his clawed feet kicking the inside of the wooden vessel. He twisted, and the skin of his neck tore and bled. Aforis shouted in dismay, but the louder his objections, the more power Frog had to use.

It wasn't until Unar saw the steam rising that she realised Frog was boiling Edax alive. Trying to hurt him so badly he would agree to be their tool. Trying to hurt his goddess so badly that he would agree to be their tool.

"Sing," Kirrik shrieked at him. "Sing, wake your bones, agree to fetch the Talon for me, and your goddess will feel no more pain."

Clouds of steam erupted around Edax. Aforis clawed at his own face in an attempt to hold the sound of his involuntary shouts inside himself, to keep Frog from using them. Unar found herself screaming, too, though nobody bothered to use her screams. Her magic couldn't be used for boiling water. Only the magic of the lightning god was good for that. When the steam cleared, Edax's eyes were glazed and his head lolled to one side.

The rain stopped. There could have been no surer sign that the rain goddess had endured a terrible hurt. Edax was not resting. He was not unconscious.

"You killed him," Kirrik cried, and whirled to strike Frog, hard, across the face.

"Not I, Core Kirrik," Frog protested, sprawled on the path, nursing her cheek. "There was a surge from the prisoner, I lost control for a moment, and 'e—"

Kirrik struck Aforis, too, though he was not thrown to the ground by the force of it. Nor did he grin at her, or show any sign of triumph. His shoulders heaved, but Unar thought he was crying, not laughing.

She might have been crying, too. Was it tears, or rain? No, the rain was stopped. It stopped. *Is the goddess dead, too? Is that how closely they are connected?* Her face felt hot, but maybe that was the steam, the heat from the human cauldron.

*Cut your own throat with those spines. Before they heal. A fit shell for her black soul.*

At last, she admitted to herself what Edax had been trying to tell her. Kirrik would never reveal how to get through the barrier or how to keep her power to herself. The spines she had given Unar were intended for her own use; Unar was her backup body, spare parts, a vessel to hold her soul when her present body became too old or injured.

Frog's multiple warnings about attacking Kirrik flashed through her mind. *You want to kill 'er, but you would not like what would happen if you tried.* Unar put her hand into her pocket and squeezed the tooth through the chimera-cloth blindfold. Now was the time. Unar could break every bone in Kirrik's body. Destroy her. Rend that body beyond healing.

*But Kirrik would take my body. Push my soul into the ether. Wear my face and lull my friends into lowering their defences. It's no use. I stole this bone-breaking weapon for nothing.*

"What is your plan, now, Core Kirrik?" Sikakis asked in a low, troubled voice.

"My plan, Core Sikakis? My plan?"

"The monsoon is over." Sikakis gestured in the direction of the empty sky. "You've weakened the rain goddess. Your informers spoke true. You could take advantage of this. No Canopian army will be prepared for an assault more than a month early. They'll be dozing in their barracks. Of course, we're also unprepared. It will take time to train the men you have to work in units, to gather and secrete in strategic places the supplies they'll need to sustain repeated assaults. And we don't have the Talon."

Kirrik stared at him, mouth open and chest heaving, the umbrella cast aside, her fingers crooking like claws and her spines extended from their sheathes, quivering.

"We still have these two," Frog pointed out shakily. "The man got the better of me, but 'e is a sharper weapon than any old bone, if Kirrik wields 'im. If the rain goddess is injured, let us go and capture 'er right now!"

"We should wait," Sikakis said. "Consolidate our new gains. Explore our—"

"I am tired of waiting," Kirrik screamed suddenly. She seized Unar, turning her, kicking her in the back of her knees to force her down. "Frog, where is the blindfold?"

Frog's tiny hands dipped into the pocket in Unar's skirts. They pulled out the chimera-skin cloth and unwrapped, not the powerful tooth of the Old God that Unar had stashed there, but the useless amulet that Marram had been wearing when he arrived at the dovecote.

"Did you think I did not see you take it?" Frog whispered. "I took it back. So dank, Unar."

"Give it to me!" Kirrik snatched the blindfold from Frog, letting the amulet fall; it snagged by its cord on the rough bark of the branch. As soon as the chimera cloth tightened over Unar's eyes, the residue of the magic that had killed Edax became invisible to her. Kirrik's spittle flecked her ear. "Play as you have never played before, tool."

Unar had not jumped to her death. She had no choice but to play. Whatever it was that took shape in Kirrik's hands, she couldn't see it. She couldn't sense it. Only feel the powerful flicker of her weightless mote-self, between hot and cold, up and down, swiftly accelerating heartbeat and silence. Perhaps Kirrik was killing everyone around her. Perhaps she was killing no one.

Perhaps she was waking all the warriors in her house, preparing for war.

# FIFTY

EACH OF Unar's laboured breaths felt as if it might be her last.

As the vestiges of her strength ebbed, Unar's weightless motes coalesced into a body again. She lay facedown on the wide branch, her left hand embracing the bark, her right hand holding the ear bone to her lips. Kirrik's bare foot, with all her weight behind it, pressed between Unar's shoulder blades. Her skirts slid through Unar's hair and over her shoulders.

"More," someone exhorted. "More!"

*She is killing me. This is what it is like to be used up. To be drained to death.*

Another heave of her chest. Another rush of power through the bone flute and Unar's body flying apart. Sounds of something enormous breaking. The whole world split in two by lightning and water. But neither were Unar's domain. It was a monster's spine that was breaking. Or maybe Unar's own spine, ground beneath Kirrik's hate.

*She can't kill me. She needs my body. Edax said so.*

The forest roared as though a thunderhead had turned to stone and fallen on it.

"She did it." Frog's small, frightened voice. "It is finished. Core Kirrik, she is finished. Please, let 'er go."

*Frog loves me.*

Weight lifted. Small hands dragged at the blindfold. Unar had no energy for opening her eyes. Her body felt like it would stay limp, forever. She didn't want to know what she had done.

"Let her go." Kirrik's voice was mocking. "Very well. Rest here awhile, Nameless." No more pretence about calling Unar by her name. "Recover your strength. And have no fear for Audblayin, I will fetch her for you. You want to know where she is? Not long before you came to us, a slave and her child were sent from the Garden to the House of Epatut. That child is your reincarnated goddess. If only you poor fools had known."

*Impossible.* Unar wheezed. She hadn't the strength to lift her head.. *Audblayin is not a goddess. Not this time.* "Audblayin is young. Too young for you to find."

*He is a boy child. He must be a boy child, if I am to guard him. That's why I was given the gift. That's why Audblayin called to me, waking my powers in my parents' home, before I knelt beneath the night-yew.*

"Birth screams hold a powerful magic." The mocking voice floated closer. "I heard them, in my future-searching, and I saw the mother's face."

*No. It is what I am for.*

"I would have known," Unar mumbled into the bark. "I stood by the cradle of that slave child. Ylly. Baby Ylly. I would have felt the soul inside her!"

*It's what I was born to do.*

"Would you? Your bones were sleeping. You were untrained in song-magic. I felt the power in the baby's cries, but you who are deaf search only with your eyes."

*It's why I killed Edax.*

"Isin. Is it true? It can't be true. You would have told me."

Frog's lips, kissing her cheek. Kissing Unar good-bye. Was she dying, after all? Would Aforis make a better tool for Kirrik to use? A better body for the Master to steal?

"You speak to the dead." Frog sighed. "Well, the dead will answer you, this one time. It is true, Unar. Audblayin sleeps in the House of Epatut, child of a slave. Twice, our people have tried to take 'er, tossin' 'er out a window, and twice she has floated out of our reach."

"Someone," Kirrik said, sounding aggrieved, "made a powerful gift to Odel in that slave child's name. But it does not matter. We will bring her below. I will carry her in my own arms. This road now leads across all of Canopy. Audblayinland waits at the far end, and Ehkisland lies along the way."

"The rain goddess first," Sikakis suggested.

"Yes. Lest she recover quickly enough to fend us off. Then, we will take the Waker of Senses, while her soldiers scramble and her adepts do not know her. Frog, take the man-tool and wake every warrior who can be instantly useful to us. If you can manage that much without losing control of him."

"Yes, Core Kirrik."

"Fetch the goddess we already have, Sikakis. You are strong enough to carry her. She will get us through. No need to wake her."

"Yes, Core Kirrik."

"And you, Warmed One." Kirrik's breath was suddenly hot in Unar's ear. She pulled the ear bone out of Unar's grip. "If I thought I could get one more scrap of magic out of you without killing you, I would take you along. As it is, as I said, you must wait for me here. Resting. Recovering. Be mindful of the lanterns. Forgive me if I do not leave you the means to quench them."

# FIFTY-ONE

UNAR WISHED that Kirrik had killed her.

*I was wrong about everything.*

*Edax died for nothing.*

*Audblayin's Bodyguard will be a man, again, since she is born a woman. Not me.*

*Kirrik recognised Audblayin, baby Ylly, before I did.*

*I have no destiny.*

Never before had she been able to see the selfishness of her own actions so clearly. She didn't always behave in the way that the gods said a person was supposed to behave—showing kindness, consideration, obedience, humility. But the criticisms of her elders hadn't touched her. Not while she did what was no more than necessary for her to meet her glorious fate.

Now that there was no glorious fate, she looked back on recent events as though examining the life of a stranger, and she could not love what she saw. Nobody could. No wonder Frog had chosen Kirrik.

No wonder Aoun had pushed her away.

Unar kept her eyes closed and covered her ears with her hands. She didn't object when Sikakis dragged her by one leg off the path, to make room for the pounding bare feet of Understorian soldiers. They poured out of the dovecote as though emerging from another world, hundreds of heavy-breathers who smelled of decades of sleep.

"The Servant of Airak," Frog panted, somewhere close by. "'E tried to kill the sleepers, too, Core Kirrik. Then 'e tried to wake the goddess. You should take control of 'im. 'E keeps gettin' away from me, as if 'e hates 'im-self more than I hate 'im."

"Do you need more motivation than to save your own miserable life?" Kirrik said, and Unar knew from the cutting edge to her voice that she spoke to Aforis, not Frog. "I could claim a different god today. Your god. Whether he fell or not, I could use you up to find him. I could spend my men's lives fetching him here."

"The other Servants of Airak would kill you," Aforis said, meeting malice with malice.

"Not if I put my soul inside your dead bones. I could walk right up to him. He would embrace me."

"Pah! You cannot switch bodies and souls. That is the death god's domain!"

"I could do it. But it would be wasteful. The time is right to take the others today, not Airak. Airak's body is a young man's; he is early in his cycle. I am patient. I can wait until age slows him." And she petted Unar fondly with her foot as if imagining herself in the younger woman's skin. "I can wait until his mind begins to decay. Will you obey me today, Servant of Airak?"

"I will." Aforis sounded shaken.

"Lead the way, Sikakis," Core Kirrik said.

When they had all gone, the branch beneath Unar stopped vibrating. Everything was still, even the wind.

No rain fell on Unar. Moisture seeped into her from the wet bark, but that was all. With her hands still over her ears, she heard her own pulse against the nothing noise of trapped air in her ears, or perhaps that was the flutter of feathers. Kirrik's winged messengers came whatever the time; whatever the weather.

*Time to roll off the edge. Time to fall. All the way to Floor, this time. No nets. No more thinking. No more thoughts.*

Hands lifted her, gently. They peeled her palms away from her ears. Too big to be Frog's hands, and Frog didn't really care about Unar, anyway. Nobody did.

"Are you hurt?" Marram asked.

Unar opened her eyes. Marram's fingers were covered in scars, like tiny teeth had torn into them, over and over.

"I'm hurt in my heart," she said.

"Aside from the fact that Oos begged me to go after you, I knew you had not gone willingly."

*Oos begged you to come after me? Oos cares. But she doesn't know how worthless I am.*

"You were wrong," Unar said, eyes still lowered. "I would've gone anywhere, done anything, to learn the secret of wielding magic when the gods ordained that I shouldn't. My heart is bad, Marram. It's rotten inside. That's why it hurts."

"We do not have time for that. We have got to go after them. They have cut down Airak's emergent. They will cut down Audblayin's emergent. The tallowwood. Our home."

Unar raised her head. When Kirrik spoke of a path that stretched all the way to Audblayinland, Unar had imagined an extension of the great branches that held the dovecote. Nothing prepared her for the sight through the trees of a great floodgum, as thick through the trunk as the Garden was wide, sliced through a thousand growth rings and fallen, forming a road wide enough for fifty barrows to pass in each direction.

The great, creamy circle of the severed tree seemed to glow in the gloom.

"Was that Airak's emergent?" Unar asked.

"Yes."

"With his Temple in the crown of it?"

"Yes."

"Did the god fall?"

"He did if he was home. Unar, stand up. We must go. I do not care about Airak. I care about my brothers."

But Unar couldn't care about anything except the pain that hollowed out her middle. She could no longer see the broken tree. The world was blurred by tears. Her body felt too heavy to ever stand or walk again.

"You go," she said.

"And have that evil woman put me to sleep again?"

"She can't. Not without me."

"Then I need you to help us fight. We do not have magic."

"Me neither. Not anymore."

Marram sat back on his haunches at that.

"Is there something that will help?" he asked eventually. "Something she might have left behind in the hut? Birds? Bones? Any kind of tea that Hasbabsah might have taught you about?"

*Nothing will help. Except to let me fall.*

Unar wished she had been hit on the head. She wished she had amnesia. In the corner of her eye, she saw the living barrel where Edax had boiled to death. He was still in it, in memory too close to the present. Unar closed her eyes and shrank away, gasping for breath in between sobs. She wished she knew how to put the hibernating spell on herself, and even then, she couldn't be sure that those in hibernation didn't dream.

Death waited over the edge. She shifted her weight in preparation.

"You do not want to go down there," Marram said quietly, catching her as she rolled. "I was only in the water down at Floor for a few minutes, but I almost did not make it to the closest tree. The ripples, you see. The water-dwellers can tell the difference between a river and a living thing falling in."

Unar cried until her ribs hurt too much to keep heaving.

"I'm no use to you," she croaked. "I'm no use to anybody."

"Now, that is not true, is it? Esse said you made only the second-worst rope he has ever seen. Come on. Lean on me. I am not Bernreb. I cannot carry you if you will not walk."

Unar leaned on him, but only because he wouldn't leave her alone. He took her inside the dovecote, and she made no move to help or to hinder, even though the place made her sick. He found fresh fruit for them both, killed several of the birds for them to cook and eat. They tasted better than the owl. Marram put the parchments the birds had carried into the flames.

"Now," he said when he had taken her to toilet and back to the fire, "I want you to describe to me, in detail, what the process is for passing through the light of those lamps. I can see they are no ordinary, light-giving lamps."

"They keep away demons," Unar told him dully. "Lightning strikes whatever wanders into the circle of light. Although they seem not to burn the branches that they rest on. Kirrik had a thing like a basin on a stick for putting over them, for quenching the light."

He left her for a while, then, ransacking the writing room and the other rooms in search of the bell-shaped bowl on its long rod. Unar stared at the flames.

"It is not here," Marram admitted hours later.

"She's taken it with her," Unar agreed.

"If I cut through the branch, will the lantern fall? Or will it float, like the bones do?"

"I don't know. What bones?"

"There were little pieces of bone, no bigger than grape seeds, wrapped in chimera skin and stowed under her bed. When I shook them out of the cloth, they floated, forming a shape like a dream of half a giant's skull in dust. Can you use magic like that?"

"No." Unar shook her head. "I told you, my magic is gone."

"I will try to make something to replace the basin and stick, then. Maybe the bathtub. Can you help me to carry it?"

Unar shrugged and went to help him.

They dragged and pushed the copper tub all the way down the corridor. Its feet tore up the wood and its weight fell on Marram's instep once; he shouted an oath loud enough to wake whatever poor souls still slept in the storey above.

"How did you wake up, Marram?"

He lifted his end of the tub again, and hobbled forward with it, turning it to fit it through the doorway to the writing room. Unar backed slowly away with her end, staring into the gleaming curve of its full belly. The thing was expensive. No Understorian, denied the metal-seeded fruit of Akkad's niche, should have used such wealth in metal simply to hold water. Obviously Frog had friends in all parts of Canopy. Perhaps the bath could contain the power of Airak's lantern. Perhaps.

"It was a mistake, I think," Marram said. "Or the work of the Servant of Airak. I pretended to be still sleeping until the other wakened ones were gone, but the sleepers lay on the other side of me like corpses. It reminded me of a joke my brothers played on me when we were children. Left me crying because I could not wake them. Gave me a preview of their deaths."

"What do Understorians do with their dead?"

"We seal them into the wood of the trees that give us life. Surely you do the same?"

*No.* Unar wanted to close her eyes again. *We let them fall.*

"When Audblayin died," she said, "her body was wrapped up and kept in the Temple. They keep it there until a new god . . . goddess . . . comes to the Garden. Then they grind up the old bones and brush them onto the body of the new god . . . goddess. When he . . . she swims through the water to reach his . . . her new home, the bone-dust goes into the moat. I guess."

"It is strange," Marram said, grunting with the effort of shifting the bath. "When I fell asleep, there was a sort of cold feeling in the base of my skull. I was instantly convinced that it was the shadow of the first storm of the monsoon. I fell down. It felt like my skin was shrinking in on itself. When I woke up, I thought my own skin was a coating of moss. Then I realised it was still summer, even though the rain had stopped. I could not understand why I had woken early."

"Maybe the rain stopping helped you to wake, even though the spell was still on you."

"Maybe. Then I thought it was my amulet, but the amulet was gone. I guess it was just superstition, then."

"What superstition?"

He laughed.

"That a pendant of bone from the Old God whose essence now belongs to Audblayin protects the wearer from sorcery. Floorians find the bones sometimes under the roots of Audblayin's emergent. The amulet I brought was given in trade for a bundle of furs. I snatched it up when I saw what Frog had done to Oos."

Unar frowned, trying to remember where she had seen the amulet last.

"Maybe it's not superstition," she said slowly. "Maybe it does protect you. From having your body stolen. Frog put it in my . . . Frog betrayed me a second time. She thought she'd replaced my weapon with something ineffective, but she didn't know that Kirrik wanted to steal my body." *Didn't she?* "Kirrik can't have told her. The amulet is outside. I'll fetch it."

But when she tried to give it back to Marram, he wouldn't take it.

"You put it on," he said. "If it is your body the sorceress wants to steal, you had better be the one to wear it." And Unar acquiesced, not believing that the long curve of bone had any power. It felt inert to her, as it had before. Most likely it was not the bone of an Old God at all.

The bathtub wouldn't go through the front door of the dovecote. Marram set to with a hatchet, enlarging the opening. Unar couldn't make herself care whether anyone might come, whether messengers or wounded soldiers returning.

Nothing really mattered.

Marram sweated as he worked. Unar watched his strong, slender body in motion and felt nothing. Yellow hair fell over his young face and his odd, pomegranate-pink, Understorian mouth was pinched in concentration. She should have been relieved that he was awake. Saving him, bringing him away from the dovecote, had been one of her important goals. Vaguely, she remembered that before Frog had put him away like winter clothing, his collarbone had been broken and his leg had been all but chewed off. Nothing of those wounds remained, though the scars on his hands and feet remained. She didn't remark on it.

Soon enough, he tossed the hatchet aside. Unar applied herself to her end of the tub. It scraped through the splintered edges of the newly widened doorway and out onto the path. Together, they wrestled it to the very edge of the circle of blue-white light, where Marram manoeuvred it so that it stood upright on two of its four legs.

"Now," he said, "Unar, stand back."

She obeyed and he heaved the tub so that it fell forward, encompassing the lamp, dousing the light.

For an instant, it seemed as if they had succeeded, and would be able to walk over the top of the copper tub and away from the dovecote. Then, the gleaming metal flashed white hot.

Unar might have stood there, gazing at it, until death came, but Marram had the presence of mind to seize her arm, throw her into the dovecote, and push her down among the coats and boots of the cloakroom.

The blast turned her deaf for a few confusing moments. Everything was white, and then black, and then Marram's lips moved in front of her face, making no noise. She sat up, and realised half the wall behind her was missing.

A hand-sized piece of jagged copper pinned Marram's hand to the floor.

She pulled it out. It was embedded deeply and she needed all of her physical strength. Marram didn't shout, or maybe he did and she was still deaf, or maybe his words had been stolen.

*No. She's gone. She's gone, and I do not hate Marram.*

"I'll find something to bind it," he said. "Something to stop the blood."

Unar sat alone for a while.

*Baby Ylly. Your mother tried to teach me to dive like a duck. And I paid for that lesson in chimera skin.*

"Chimera skin," she murmured to herself.

When Marram returned, she made herself look at him. Really look at him. He'd dressed in odd bits of armour that he'd found inside the dovecote, leaving his shins and forearms bare. His demeanour was confident, but his eyes said he was afraid for his brothers' lives. They were in danger because they lived in Audblayin's emergent, but also because they had given shelter to two fallen, gifted women, two escaped slaves, and a little girl running from a demon.

"I know how to get past the lantern," she said.

The piece of chimera skin that had held the floating fragments of bone was barely big enough to drape the lantern. Marram took a slew of already-deformed weapons from the cloakroom to nudge the colour-shifting cloth into position. When it covered the lantern, only a tiny circle of escaped light remained.

"I'll go first," Unar said, brushing past him. Holding up her black skirts, she leaped over the little circle, half expecting to be speared by lightning, but she passed by it unharmed. Marram came a bare step behind her.

"I wish you had thought of that before the bathtub," he said, grinning.

"What are you doing?" Unar sucked in a sharp breath as Marram grasped the top handle of the lantern through the cloth.

"Bringing it with us."

"What if it can't be—" Unar fell silent as Marram proved that the lantern could be moved.

"It could be useful," Marram said, and his smile turned grim. "If we encounter that charming friend of yours, I will throw it in her face before I let her cut our tallowwood in half with Esse, Bernreb, and Issi inside."

# FIFTY-TWO

Night came.

There was no sign of Kirrik or her soldiers. Unar and Marram had gone quickly, but Unar suspected the gap between parties had neither widened nor narrowed. They trod the same path, and Kirrik had half a day's head start.

Marram set the lantern down behind them and uncovered it so that nobody could creep up on them from behind while they were sleeping.

"I'm not tired," Unar said, but mostly she was afraid of her dreams. Upon waking, stiff and uncomfortable from being wedged between branches, she felt more tears on her cheeks and the gut-wrenching aftermath of a nightmare whose lingering images she didn't care to examine.

"We will need to leave the lantern," Marram said softly in the dawn gloom, and when Unar twisted around to question him, she saw the demon crouched on the other side of the blue-white light.

Only its eyes, huge, round, and glowing yellow like twin suns, remained fixed, Unar's height above the branch. The rest of the body flickered through umber, emerald, and sooty grey, but the shadow stretched behind and puddled beneath it betrayed its basic form: a four-legged predator with a sleek, muscular, long-tailed body. If it had ears, they were invisible, and its scaly legs were tipped by curved black claws.

The chimera tested the air with a forked tongue.

"I agree," Unar said, shivering. "Unless you think the demon's skin will protect it from lightning the same way the dead piece of its hide protected us."

"I think it would have crossed already, if it could."

"Yes. I wasn't thinking. Should we go on?"

"We cannot go back," Marram pointed out, passing her a curled leaf that carried water. Unar watched the chimera while she drank. Its glowing eyes didn't move. When she got to her feet, she thought its tail might have twitched, and then she was following Marram down the trunk of the fallen floodgum, hunching her shoulders but not looking back.

In the middle of the day, Marram paused to squint through the forest at something indiscernible to Unar.

"What is it?" she asked. "Is it the chimera? Has it found a way around?" At her feet, a lateral branch of the floodgum vanished into the distance. Marram knelt and touched the bark, as if to detect damage from the passage of boots. "Do you think Kirrik and Sikakis might have gone down the side branch? Is that the way to Ehkis's emergent?"

"No," Marram said, straightening. "It is the way to Odel's emergent. The placement of the branch is convenient. Why were they not tempted?"

"Marram," Unar said, feeling sick, but unable to keep back from him now what she should have told him straight away. "Kirrik can't cut down any more emergents. She almost killed me to cut down this one. She used all of my power, do you see? Even if she captures Oos, Oos isn't as strong as I was. The tallowwood where your brothers live, the tallowwood that holds the Garden, is safe. Kirrik can climb it, or perhaps burn it, but not bring it down."

"Perhaps burn it," Marram repeated emphatically.

"She still has Aforis, Servant of Airak," Unar allowed. "But she was going to get . . . they were going to get Ehkis first. Ehkis first, and then Audblayin. If you can sneak past them while they're busy invading the Temple of Ehkis, you'll have time to warn Esse and Bernreb of the danger. The three of you can make sure Oos isn't captured."

He eyed her.

"Me? If I can sneak past them? The three of us? Where are you going? Back to feed the chimera?"

*Baby Ylly. Odel's power protects you for now, but whose power protects Odel?*

"I need a way through the barrier, Marram. Your brothers, the ones you need to protect, are down here. Mine are up there."

Marram made an exasperated sound.

"Whatever it is that lets you pass through the barrier to Canopy, you need to steal from Kirrik," he guessed. "You are going to wait for me to sneak past and then try to take something valuable from two hundred Understorian warriors, and you have no magic to protect you?"

Unar shook her head slowly. Trying to take the sleeping goddess away from Sikakis would be impossible.

"What I need is in Odelland."

"And what is that, exactly?"

"Thank you for saving me, Marram," she said, and wouldn't say any more.

Sighing, he took the rolled-up chimera skin from behind the strap of his shoulder guard and pressed it into her hands.

"Thank you for saving me, yourself. I hope we will meet again. If you are going to try to climb up through the barrier, at least let me help you with those."

He pulled out a knife and cut away the front of her skirts at the level of her knees. Her bare feet were blistered from running along the rough bark and there was muck between her toes.

"I've never used them," Unar said, staring at the crease in her shins where her spines were hidden. She hadn't had time to practice. Now she must climb, or die.

"Pull them in before you lift from the knee," Marram advised, "or before you lift from the wrist. Have them out before impact."

"I'll try."

They clasped forearms. Marram smiled encouragement at her a final time before turning to continue along the main trunk. Unar knew she shouldn't stand there watching him. She had little time herself if she was to reach baby Ylly ahead of Kirrik and Sikakis.

It was important, though, that she watch him. She needed to erase the image of him falling and replace it forever with the vision of him lithely leaping along the toppled abode of the lightning god.

When she couldn't see him anymore, she turned to the lateral branch and began making her way along it. As night began to fall on the second day since leaving the dovecote, her nostrils brought her the smell of sweet-fruit pine.

The branch of Airak's emergent was wedged tightly against the sweet-fruit pine trunk. Unar could only goggle at it for a moment, wondering how it could possibly be the precise tree that she needed, at a time when she had no magic, no means of growing a pathway.

*There must be other sweet-fruit pines in Odelland. This might not be the one.*

When she put out her spines and drove them into the sapwood, she realised it wasn't the one. Odel's emergent was ancient. This tree was too young and new. Somehow, she could taste its age through the snake's teeth that jutted out of her forearm.

It didn't matter. Who was to say Odel was in his Temple, anyway? He hadn't been, the last time Unar had climbed the steps cut into the spongy, white wood.

*Pull them in before you lift from the knee, or before you lift from the wrist.*

Pain shot through her bones as she took her full weight on her forearms. It should have frightened her. Nobody had mentioned pain. Maybe the spines were still not properly healed, or maybe they hadn't been properly set, so that Kirrik could laugh if Unar tried to escape and instead plunged to her death.

*Have them out before impact.*

When her shin spines were set, the pain eased a little. She willed the spines in her right arm to retract, and they obeyed. She willed them out again. This wasn't yet instinctive for her. She had to concentrate on each agonisingly sluggish shift in her weight and placement of her next cutting, downward stroke.

She was getting higher. Sunlight reached her. The beam was only a finger's width, and horizontal with the sinking of the sun, but she stopped to cry some more, with her face turned to the tiny trickle of light.

Licking tears from her lips, her shins and forearms on fire from holding her to the tree, she turned her focus back to the climb. She climbed when she couldn't see the bark in front of her face anymore. She climbed when night insects landed lightly on her nape to drink her blood.

At last, her head hit something hard and unyielding. It was a thousand times stronger than the princess's window. It was a thousand times colder than the magical wall around the Garden.

She'd reached the barrier between Canopy and Understorey. There was no sleeping goddess in her arms to bore a way through. There was no artefact and no incantation.

Unar pressed her lips to the sweet-fruit pine and used the barest breath of magic, the feeble speck that had regrown in her over two days of travel, to send the word she spoke into the heart of the tree, the secret word that Frog had ordered Unar to forget lest Kirrik discover she knew its power.

"Tyran," she whispered.

The cold, hard barrier rippled.

# FIFTY-THREE

UNAR HUNG from her spines, in a half daze, waiting.

It seemed like hours before the Bodyguard with the brindle-striped back appeared on the other side of the barrier, gazing with black eyes down at Unar, hands in the claw-tipped gloves.

"I need to speak to Odel," Unar pleaded. "His life depends on it."

The Bodyguard didn't step onto the barrier. It was insubstantial for her. She came down through it and searched Unar for weapons without a word, rifling through torn skirts and hacked-off sleeves.

When she whisked away, agile as a lizard, Unar couldn't be sure if the woman was returning to fetch the god she served, or simply evacuating in the wake of determining the nature of a threat.

"Gardener Unar," Odel's voice said. "You return to us much changed."

He stood on a wooden platform in the shape of an orchid, its four corners pierced and threaded with rope, holding a lit taper in his left hand as he had before. Unar looked up and could barely make out the shape of the Bodyguard, stretched panther-like along the branch where the end of the rope was secured. The lights of Canopy were above her, illuminating roads out of Unar's reach.

"Understorians, Holy One," she told Odel. "They want to kill you. You and the others, thirteen gods and goddesses, between sunrise and sunset of one day, to bring back the Old Gods. They have Ilan. It may be that Airak is dead. They've killed the Bodyguard of Ehkis and have gone to capture the rain goddess right now. That's why the monsoon is over. They'll go after Audblayin next."

"Come through the barrier."

"I can't. That's why I had to call you. Please, open it for me."

Odel cupped his chin in his gloved right hand.

"You told Aurilon that my life depended on speaking to you. She owns the power to read truth. My life *does* depend on what you've told me. The question is, will I die if I open the way for you, or die if I do not?"

Unar knew what she looked like: a spined Understorian coming to invade Canopy. Yet she had no weapons. Her clothes were torn, and her skin was dirty and scratched.

"There isn't much time," she said hopelessly. A flicker of movement from above suggested that the Bodyguard, Aurilon, grew impatient. So she began to tell her story from the beginning. She told Odel of being passed over at the choosing, of Sawas and Edax teaching her to swim. She told him of how she'd leaped from the Garden while roped to Ylly and Hasbabsah, of the home of the three brothers and of the arrival of Frog.

She spoke of Kirrik and her imprisonment at the dovecote. Without sparing her part in Edax's betrayal, Unar told of Kirrik's capture of him, and of Aforis. She told him of the sleeping warriors, wakened, and Marram's flight towards his home.

"Gods grant that he reaches it safely," she finished gruffly.

"Gods grant that," Odel said, and sighed.

He put his hand into empty air, curled his fingers, and made a pulling motion. There was a sound like cloth tearing.

"Come to my Temple, Gardener Unar," he said. "You gave tribute to protect the child Audblayin while you were there, though you did not know that the child you prayed for was she. Putting your hands on that tribute will allow you to speak across the distance between us and Audblayinland. You can warn the girl's guardians of what comes."

Unar had been stuck in one place for so long that she forgot to retract her spines, and gasped as she tried to raise an arm that wouldn't move. Then she remembered. The points slid back into her, springing out as she drove them towards a higher section of the tree. She lifted her knee, her body moved upwards, and she didn't strike the barrier.

As she dragged herself fully back into Canopy, she shuddered. A familiar sensation filled her. Earthy smells. Juicy roots. Fruit sweet and sour and bitter. It was Canopian growing-magic, life-magic, returning. Her magic, as powerful as it had ever been, and more. And at least half of it flowed from Marram's amulet, the bone seeming awakened by the mere act of crossing the barrier.

Strength flowed through her arms and legs. All the weariness of her heartbreak, the flight and the climb were gone. Part of it was the lightness that came from musical magic, the two inner sources now completely meshed, sound and sight and smell working together. Unar paused to wonder.

Then, with new energy, she scaled the sweet-fruit pine as far as the winding Canopian road where Odel and Aurilon waited for her.

Unar knelt before him and kissed the ground in front of his sunset-hued boots, careful not to seem like she was even thinking of touching him.

"Thank you," she whispered. "Oh, thank you."

The heartbreak was still there, after all; returning power could not redeem her. In the pit of her stomach, despair still lay in place of desire. Her final obligations were to secure Audblayin safely within the Garden and ensure that Oos was out of Kirrik's reach, that no Servant could be used to sever the trunk of the great tallowwood.

Then she would do what she had been going to do before Marram put his hands out and caught her.

"The Temple is this way," Odel said. "Put those spines away. The king's law forbids them, and you may need them before the sun rises. The amulet is forbidden, too; I should hide it beneath my shirt, if I were you." Unar obeyed him, tucking the bone amulet out of sight. Odel hesitated before turning towards Aurilon and telling her pointedly, "Ehkis is vulnerable without her Bodyguard."

Aurilon bared her teeth at him. "No."

"You must do as I say, Aurilon."

"I must stay with you. My duty is to protect you."

"You know where she sleeps. You're faster than they can ever hope to be. Go, before it's too late and we end up forced to trade for rain with One Forest. They'll demand we abolish the barrier. If we refuse, the monsoon will never come again, and children will not be the only ones to die."

Aurilon's nostrils flared. She quivered. Then she was gone.

"Come, Unar," Odel said.

For a moment, Unar was afraid to enter the circle of blue-white light that emanated from the closest of Airak's lanterns, but then she remembered these ones were safe and produced only light. The fish-shaped Temple was twelve trees away, the spiralling planks that had seemed perilous no longer frightening to a Gardener with spines to catch against the sweet-fruit pine if she lost her balance.

Unar stood in the room, laden with tributes, where the bronze dish, blazing, floated in the shallow pool, and swept her eyes across the tangle of offerings.

"Where is the cloth, Holy One?" she asked. Odel, behind her, didn't reply, and when she turned to face him, she took an involuntary step back.

The chimera filled the doorway to the Temple.

# FIFTY-FOUR

The demon rippled and flexed its claws.

"How has it come here?" Unar asked without thinking; it was obvious how the chimera had come into Canopy. Odel had torn a hole in the barrier because she had asked him to.

"Forget about finding the tribute," Odel said without taking his eyes from the mesmerising glow of the chimera's twin bulbs. He stood between her and the beast with the taper in one hand, the other hand relaxed at his side, and he'd sent his Bodyguard, his only real protection, to Ehkisland.

"I can use Audblayin's power to—"

"I forbid you to use Audblayin's power in my realm. In any case, other than the barrier itself, magic will not affect a chimera."

"Airak's lantern held it at bay."

"Did it? Did you see it turned back by the lantern? Or did you see a demon playing with you, as a monkey plays with an injured bird? You carried chimera skin on your person and your magic was spent. It couldn't be sure what you were. But now it knows."

"But the lanterns protected the dovecote from demons."

"Other demons, perhaps. Not chimeras. They are ancient creatures, close kin to the Old Gods. You said the woman, Kirrik, was a sorceress; a soul-switcher. If she spoke true, it's likely that she gained that power by merging her bones with those of a chimera; the stench of that foul deed would be itself enough to keep other chimeras away."

Unar wanted to laugh. If chimeras could smell past deeds, it was a wonder this one wasn't repulsed by her, too. She scrabbled in the mound of tributes for a tasselled spear and a costly, inscribed sword with an ivory handle, hefting them in her hands.

"I'll distract it," Unar said. "You can go to the king of Odelland. Order his soldiers to go after Kirrik."

"You can't kill it, Gardener Unar," Odel said sadly, "and this king would not spare a single soldier for the defence of a niche not his own. You must go after Kirrik. Perhaps we'll meet again in my next life."

And he blew out the taper with a gentle breath, just as the bunched chimera leaped at him, teeth bared.

Odel staggered backwards a quick dozen steps with the beast's jaw closed on his shoulders and neck. The chimera followed furiously on its hind legs, tail lashing the floor. Unar circled sideways around them, sword and spear still feebly raised, watching with dismay as the god crashed backwards into the pool and burning branches tipped from the bronze bowl over both of them.

"Holy One!" she cried.

"Go!" Odel shouted as he and the beast both began turning the white-hot colour of the bathtub right before it shattered. The chimera had let go of him, god's blood on its black teeth, trying to back away, but Odel's arms were locked around its neck and he whispered fiercely in the place where its ear should have been.

Unar dropped the weapons and ran.

She ran through a night that beat with the overwhelming percussion of frog song until her bleeding feet screamed. Odellanders stared at her as she pushed past them, but nobody hindered her flight from the Temple. She was crying again.

*Another god, dead because of me. Everything I touch turns to poison. Everyone I try to save turns to dust.*

Would Odel's power still keep baby Ylly from falling, if the chimera destroyed him? Or was Audblayin made even more vulnerable by his imminent death? What if Kirrik's people threw Audblayin out another window, with nobody waiting to catch her this time, and she did not float?

Unar stopped to rip more sections of her skirts away and bind her feet in them as best she could. She'd gotten turned around somehow. This wasn't the road she'd travelled before, and this late at night, only a few unlucky slaves still laboured along the lower paths.

She tried to control her breathing. Tried to feel her connection to the Garden. She couldn't, immediately panicking that despite everything, Kirrik had managed to cut the emergent down.

There.

There it was.

Unar took another deep breath. The Garden was still there. She knew which way to go. Ignoring the pain in her feet, she flew along the streets of Canopy, across the border into Ehkisland. There was an autumn market there, being unshuttered and stocked in the dark by slaves and the stricken, which shouldn't have opened until the true end of the monsoon. Unar didn't stop to speak to them.

Seven trees later, she found the place where Kirrik and Sikakis had come through the barrier.

At least, bodies whose throats had been slashed by serrated spines lay around the turning that led to Ehkis's emergent. Unar froze, indecisive, at the junction of wide, flat lateral branches. Her ears felt sharpened to points.

She could hear only the frogs and the wind in the leaves.

Kirrik had been far ahead of her, but how much time had she lost during her incursion into Ehkisland? Was Kirrik still battling in the rain goddess's domain? Did Aurilon defend the submerged goddess at this very moment? Was Odel's Bodyguard also dead? Or had Aurilon found Ehkis already missing, kidnapped, and Kirrik's soldiers moved on into Audblayinland? There were too many possibilities, most of them awful.

Unar stepped out along the path to Ehkis's sacred pool, then backed up and took a few steps towards the Garden. Her magic was returned to her. She would grow a new branch through Kirrik's black heart, before the woman even knew she was there, if only she could find her.

Or Kirrik would use Unar's power to triumph again. Steal her body, smash the Garden, and snatch Audblayin. She shrank from that thought as she shrank from the road to the Temple. The amulet was more than it had seemed, but could she trust it? Could she trust Understorian old wives' tales? The amulet hadn't saved Marram from Kirrik's sleeping spell. Yet he had woken early. And his soul remained firmly embedded in his body.

*I can't risk meeting her. The consequences of her soul in my body are too terrible.*

With stars wheeling overhead, Unar went away from Ehkisland, choosing the other road, over the border into Audblayinland.

# FIFTY-FIVE

WITH THE crossing, Unar felt as though she doubled in size.

She blinked. One hand went to Marram's amulet. The other hand went to the place below her ribs where her magic resided; her body hadn't grown at all, but the well of power within had deepened, and now it pulsed, exerting pressure on her to be used.

*No. I am not worthy of this.*

*I was wrong about everything.*

*Edax, Airak, Aurilon, and Odel died for nothing.*

*Audblayin's Bodyguard will be a man. Not me.*

Yet it was like nothing she'd felt before. It had to be something that Kirrik had done to her. Some wicked power entering her. Audblayin's gift somehow twisted. She wouldn't use it.

"Boy," she said, grabbing the elbow of a dirty child who scampered along the road with his arms stretched as if to catch the stream of flat-faced white bats overhead. "Which way to the House of Epatut?"

"Maybe I know!" He tried to pull angrily away from her. "What'll you give me?"

Unar put her hand up and caught one of the creatures, ignoring the razor-teeth that it drove into her thumb.

"I'll give you this."

Eyes shining, likewise enduring the creature's gnawing, the boy paused to wrap the bat in his jacket before scampering off again.

"This way!" he shouted back to her, and Unar followed with her palms pressed to her sternum, as if she could keep the magic from oozing out. It had wanted to come out. It had wanted to make a cage for the bat from vines and leaves.

*It doesn't want anything. Audblayin doesn't want anything, except for milk and arms around her. She's only a baby!*

Only a baby, and because of Unar, that baby had been sold away from the safety of the Garden. If Wife-of-Epatut had lost the baby she'd been carrying before the monsoon, she might have decided to love baby Ylly instead. Or, in a fit of jealousy, she might punish Sawas with hard labour.

If only Wife-of-Epatut knew that the daughter she'd dropped in the silk market now had an Understorian name. Rescued from the mouth of a chimera, Imeris lived with three huntsmen, below the barrier, in Audblayin's emergent.

Old Ylly, grandmother of the child that Wife-of-Epatut knew, cared for Issi in baby Ylly's place, while baby Ylly was cared for in the House of Epatut.

Unar felt dizzy just thinking about it.

*Is this what you wanted, Audblayin? Was this your plan, when you chose to enter baby Ylly's body with her first breath?*

But Audblayin couldn't hear prayers until she became self-aware at puberty and her memories merged with those of the body she had taken. Odel had said he might see her in his next life, but he couldn't know for sure. His domain was neither birth nor death. Anyway, Unar wouldn't survive him long. She had one last task to carry out before she joined him, maybe in the same chimera's jaws. The demon could very well be following her.

"There it is," the boy said. "In the gobletfruit tree. The whole crown, it's his, isn't it? My pa catches songbirds. Sold some in a cage to the wife. But if you need cloth, and obviously you do, he's not open till morning. I'm going home."

Unar didn't answer him. She stared at the gobletfruit tree. Ruddy, skin-soft arms were twisted into a labyrinth of hollowed burls each as big as most men's houses, connected by small bridges to a hollowed bulge in the wide main trunk. Fluffy white flowers that would open with the sun and bell-shaped nuts hung everywhere. If Wife-of-Epatut had caged songbirds inside, it would be a wonder if she could hear them over the screeching of parrots that would arrive at daybreak to feast on those nuts, and daybreak was not far away.

Unar marched up the front ramp and beat her fist on the heavy door. Smoke to keep insects out oozed under and around the oval-shape; the wheel and cocoon of the silk merchants' guild were carved over the more humble loom symbols of the family of weavers from which Epatut had come. Unar beat on the door a second time. When it was finally thrown back, the short

and dumpy human-shape that answered was too smoke-wreathed to iden-
tify for a long moment.

"Sawas?" Unar said, coughing.

"It's you," Sawas breathed. She'd gained a great deal of weight since Unar
had last seen her, and without her duties in the sun, she'd reverted to a lighter
golden-brown. One of her enormous breasts was shoved into the greedy
mouth of a boy child black as char against her brown bosom. It couldn't be
Epatut's son. Unar hadn't been away for long enough. An adopted nephew,
maybe. Sawas's other, covered breast made a wet spot on the front of her
fine robe; the sight of the leak made Unar press her own chest even harder,
determined that none of the evil she had brought with her would enter
Epatut's House.

"It's me," Unar agreed.

"Where's my mother?" Sawas asked. "You stole her. You killed her."

"She's alive in Understorey. I didn't steal her. I freed her."

"Only a fool would believe you!"

"Sawas, listen," Unar said urgently. "Your baby is Audblayin reborn. She's
in danger. Haven't there been attempts to steal her? You must take her back
to the Garden, right now. Where is she?"

*Can I beg for her forgiveness?*

*No. She's only a baby. She can't hear me.*

"She's not mine to take," Sawas said venomously. "She's the property of
the House of Epatut, and you are a runaway thief who couldn't pass through
the Gate of the Garden if you tried. If you have no fear of exposure or
arrest—and I would fear both, if I were you—then come back when the
sun's in the sky and ask the mistress for the babe yourself."

Sawas closed the door in her face. Unar heard the bar dropping into place.
There was no time to argue. There was no time to explain. Reluctantly, she
took her hands away from her sternum.

"Wake, friend," she whispered, feeling the great gobletfruit from its top
shoots brushed by cloud-filtered starlight and the first suggestion of sunrise
to the roots that fed on fish corpses, pressed beneath the restless weight of
swirling monsoon water.

The House of Epatut came to life. It had no mind of its own, but it borrowed Unar's mind while they were merged, and the creatures that had
nested in its skin and kept the wounds open made its sap quicken with re-
sentment.

"Be gentle with them," Unar said softly. "They haven't given you burdens you could not bear. Only give me the child."

A man started screaming. His voice was soon joined by a woman's. More screaming voices joined in.

Branches moved. The tree groaned. Windows widened and narrowed like talking mouths. Leaves entered cavities and brushed woody corners, searching. Unar shook her head; there was no need to search. She felt every human life within the tree. She knew each one of them intimately. Sawas was with both children in the farthest room of the house, body folded protectively over body, as she and Ylly had been before birth.

There was no question about that baby being Audblayin. The power that animated the tree flowed directly from the diminutive form, not to the Garden and then to Unar, but on the shortest path, from one to the other.

Wood bent into wave patterns. Sawas was tossed mercilessly into the air. Ylly was carried out from underneath her mother by undulations that brought her through previously solid walls, out the door and down the ramp.

"As you were," Unar said sharply, and the tree contorted itself back into shape. The screaming didn't stop, but Unar knew no one had been harmed. She pressed on her sternum to stop the flow of power, as wonderful as the connection felt. The gobletfruit became separate from her, and she became separate from the child, even as she bent to pick her up beneath the armpits.

Ylly gazed at her with enormous eyes. She was not a baby anymore, not really. Unar had forgotten how quickly children grew. Ylly's feet, which had been doughy, club-like, and ineffectual, now bore calluses from leather shoes, and her hair was long enough to braid.

"You're big," Unar said.

"I want Mama," Ylly answered.

"Mama will come later. Let's go to the Garden."

She wasn't a thief. The Gates would open for her, though not in the way she dreamt. Nothing she could do would be enough to redeem her. Aoun wouldn't welcome her with his arms around her. She would not be a Bodyguard, and she would not fly. *But Audblayin will be safe.*

Then she smelled it. Ozone in the air. She heard the crack of lightning. Felt the flow of a different river of power, this one coming all the way from Airakland.

*Aforis.*

Clutching Ylly to her chest, she began to run again.

Drawn to the screams of the occupants, people had come to stare at the House of Epatut. Perhaps they'd seen her pick up the baby disgorged by the house itself, but none of them got in her way. If they whispered to each other in her wake; if they reported to the king that the runaway Gardener had been seen; if soldiers came, then that was to her advantage. A heartbeat later, she began to shout at strangers in passing.

"Summon the guards! Rouse the army! Understorians are here!"

She didn't stay to see if any took heed, nor did she angle towards another, taller gobletfruit which held the palace and its associated outbuildings; it must be in mimicry of the King of Audblayinland that so many wealthy merchants wanted gobletfruit crowns of their own.

Only the Garden mattered, and the blue-white blaze before its Great Gate, distant but growing larger as Unar approached.

She saw armoured Audblayinland soldiers in brown skirts and tunics wielding weapons against bare-limbed Understorians. The king's men were here. She had rarely seen so many. Two hundred or so, and that was two-thirds of the soldiers that he commanded, with only a third left behind to protect the palace. Metal made dull sounds against bone. Some that fell screamed, but others fell in silence.

It was a battle like none the Garden had seen in Unar's lifetime.

Unar thought the closeness of death in this moment made all the warriors' lives blaze brighter to her magical senses. She sent threads out along the web of wooden paths, searching for Frog and Kirrik, the ones she must avoid until she could reach the Gate. If Kirrik sensed her, she might snuff her life out, stealing her body, to keep her from interfering, and then make off with Audblayin.

If only Unar had learned from the sorceress to see the future. Or some-how earned her sister's loyalty. Two enormous men swung swords at one another right before her. Unar tried to take another path, but fighting blocked that way, too.

Lightning struck the brown-clad soldier. His skeleton glowed blue-white as he fell. The other man turned towards Unar, his sword turning with him. She skipped backwards to avoid the gleaming blade.

Only, there was no more path beneath her feet.

# FIFTY-SIX

Unar looked down at nothing.

It occurred to her to try and heave the child back onto the branch, even as she tipped back and any attempted action became futile. She moved her arms briefly to throw, but the baby's weight didn't shift. The child wasn't falling. Instead, under Odel's protection, the baby bobbed like an empty barrel.

Unar clung to Ylly for her life, gasping. Another soldier had already engaged the Understorian man who had swung the sword at her. Nobody seemed to notice them floating there, to one side of the renewed battle. The men were too busy fighting for *their* lives. Unar's kicking shin, spines extended, finally found the path. Writhing, she used the anchor point to draw herself and Ylly back to safety.

*Thank you, Odel,* she thought sacrilegiously.

Lightning struck, again and again.

Kirrik's work, or Frog's. There was no way for Unar to fight back without attracting their notice. She had no choice, though, and so there was no more need for her to stick to existing paths. Her power flowed in the trees, and the trees were in her. *She* was the pathway.

Merging her will with the tallowwood, Unar knew several things simultaneously. One, the home of the three hunters was sealed against intruders. The fishing room was flooded. Oos's life force moved restlessly within the breathable space, a pale blob of tenuous power in Unar's awareness. Esse, Bernreb, Marram, Hasbabsah, Issi, and the older Ylly were there, too. The bones of the lizard-like dayhunter had settled to the bottom of the trap that Esse had made, while other traps held the fresher corpses of warriors whose snake-tooth magic still lingered. Those, Unar presumed to be Kirrik's men.

Two, Kirrik and Frog, stood with their backs to the Gate. Unar found the eyes of all the fighters, all the unguarded lives, abruptly available to her.

In the vicinity of the Garden, she could see what she wished. Visions spun around her, answering what it was she desired to see. Frog and Kirrik must have sensed Unar's magic in motion, but they had neither a clear line of sight to attack her with lightning, nor any melody to steal from her lips. The danger was an attack to displace her soul. How was such a thing accomplished? *Audblayin, protect my soul.* Aforis, a rope around his neck, knelt between Kirrik and Frog, his head bowed and his breath wheezing through a bone of the Old Gods.

Unar hugged Ylly close as she walked forward, using the eyes in her own head once more, new path bursting to life beneath her feet. Kirrik would have no fear of the Great Gate at her back. She would know that any Servant or Gardener emerging from its protection would be easy prey for her, or for Frog. But Unar would not be her prey.

"Stand aside, Kirrik," Unar called when she was close enough.

The tall, maggot-white, black-skirted woman met her eyes and showed her teeth. Lightning didn't immediately stab down at Unar, which meant that Kirrik supposed she still had some hope of controlling her.

"Stand aside," Unar demanded a second time, with no fear that her voice would be stolen and used.

Neither Kirrik, nor anyone else, would be able to borrow her power again. Seeing Aforis, kneeling and humiliated, Unar knew she would have to kill him to deny his power to Kirrik and Frog, this poor man who had loved Edax. The thought of Edax's memory being lost with Aforis's death fostered her own self-loathing.

Kirrik tried to intercept the flow of Unar's magic, Understorian meshed with Canopian, through the branch beneath her feet. Unar easily fended her off.

Kirrik's eyes widened.

Unar continued to grow her inevitable path towards the Great Gate. She saw Servant Eilif standing beneath the beautiful, ornate archway, Aoun at her right hand, other white-robed Servants around them. Unar could hardly believe her childish self had wanted to kill Eilif once. That seemed so far behind her.

Frog, too, tried to take control of Unar. When she failed, she tried again, growing visibly angrier.

"How are you resisting? What bone of the Old Gods have you stolen?"

Unar didn't bother to tell her.

*I hate myself more than you could ever hate me. You don't really know me. True knowledge is required for true hate.*

At last, when Unar and Ylly were mere paces from the Gate, Kirrik said, "Nameless commands no bone of the Old Gods, Frog. Somebody has let the secret slip. I shall have to take her before this body's time."

Whatever else Kirrik said, with her mouth wide and her throat vibrating, it made no sound. Her dark power coiled and struck at Unar. It felt like the first time Unar had heard Kirrik laugh with a vibration that was opposite to joy, seeming to form a tunnel to a time before trees; to draw from a formless but magnificent primordial rage. It smelled of old blood and sounded like the hiss of a chimera.

Unar had once wondered what such magic was useful for, and now that use became plain: It was intended to convey Kirrik's soul from one body to the other.

Kirrik's power rebounded from the bone amulet Unar wore around her neck. Marram's amulet. They had guessed true. While Unar wore it, Kirrik couldn't steal her body, could not displace her soul.

"Core Kirrik?" Frog asked Unar, her little face bent by rage. "No, you cannot *be*'er, you cannot *take*'er." Kirrik's tall body swayed, and Frog leaped towards Unar, beating at her with fierce fists. "I cannot serve you if you look like 'er. I hate 'er. I hate 'er!"

"I am Unar," Unar said angrily, turning her shoulder to protect Ylly.

"I am still here, Frog," Kirrik said from behind Frog, sounding shaken. "Very well, if you hate her so much, destroy her. We cannot use her anymore."

Frog stepped back quickly, standing at Kirrik's side again as if pretending she'd never left it, gripping the sorceress's skirt in one hand like a much smaller child. "Gladly," she seethed.

The lightning turned on Unar.

Unar was struck. No, Ylly was struck. Unar's hair stood on end. Her teeth clenched and her muscles spasmed, but it was Ylly who was burning, dying. Unar flooded little Audblayin with desperate healing, reflecting the tiny goddess's strength back into the blackened, breathless body until Ylly's eyes opened, her skin unblemished and whole.

"Is that a slave's child?" Frog's expression was ferocious. "Have you bought your way back into Canopy with human lives? You would still rather serve this unholy Temple on your belly than be free?"

Another strike fell. Audblayin died again, and lived.

"Stop it," Unar shouted. "Stop it, if you care so much for human life."

More lightning. More burning. This time, a more powerful bolt, and Unar was dying, too, in too much pain to heal herself. She staggered. Fell to her knees. Something touched her, causing more agony. Another lightning strike? Blows from a sword? Was her head split?

No, it was a pair of wrinkled old hands. They were very like Hasbabsah's, only as richly brown as the soil of the Garden; they belonged to a Canopian, not a colourless Understorian. And there was dirt from the Garden under the nails. Unar could sense the spores.

*Servant Eilif.* The burnt sticks that had been Unar's fingers were returned to flesh and blood by the old woman's skill. *She has to love me to heal me.* How could she love one who had wished to kill her? Unar tried to push Ylly into the curve of the other woman's body.

*Take her into the Garden, please. Heal her. Protect her.*

Eilif's arms began to close the circle.

But then the lightning fell again, and Eilif fell with it. Into the dark, before Unar could do more than snatch at her sleeve. Ylly floated. Unar gathered her. But Eilif was gone.

A half-formed thought, of branches like spears piercing Kirrik's heart, entered Unar's head, but she couldn't concentrate on it for long enough to make it happen. The branch behind her was burning. Her clothes were burning.

Everything was burning.

Then it started to rain.

# FIFTY-SEVEN

UNAR HEALED the child and held her.

"You have until the count of five to crawl back down where you belong," boomed the thunder.

*I forbid you to use Audblayin's power in my realm,* Odel had said. But he hadn't said that it wouldn't work. Only that he had forbidden it, and Ylly, who ruled this realm, could barely speak, and so could not forbid anything.

Soldiers covered their ears, but the sound was everywhere. Unar looked into Ylly's eyes. The child goddess and her would-be protector curled up together a mere body length beyond Kirrik's bare feet. Raindrops darkened the enemy's black skirts. Kirrik's fingernails cut into her palms. Frog had eyes only for her mistress and Aforis let the bone fall while they weren't looking.

Unar watched the bone plummet, wondering if it would land on Eilif's broken body. She looked at Ylly again. The child should have been terrified, but she reached out to pull a yellow leaf out of Unar's hair.

"I want Mama," she said.

Unar kissed her, pushed the warm little head whose wounds she had healed so recently, and in rapid succession, into her armpit, and craned her neck to try to see what Kirrik was staring at.

A woman stood at the far edge of the fighting, dressed in robes so luminously kingfisher-blue that Unar could hardly bear to look at them. Her skin was blue-black, but her eyes were as sky-pale as the gleaming silk she wore. Like most goddesses and gods, her hands were gloved and her feet booted. A high collar studded with sapphires stood up around her long neck, sheathing a head of grey and indigo hair twisted into ropes like rivers running down ironbark.

*Bringer of Rain.*

Audblayinland soldiers who had cowered at the sound of Ehkis's first command straightened and looked at their opponents, giving them space, clearly expecting them to flee back to Understorey now that all the rules had been broken. A goddess had trespassed in another deity's niche. It was unheard of. The Canopians couldn't imagine that the enemy wouldn't be as shocked as they were and obey the very voice of the storm. In the separation of combatants, Unar finally spotted the king of Audblayinland, a fat fighting man whose belly protruded through his vest. Spines from slaves he'd captured rattled on a chain around his neck.

"One," the thunder rumbled. The blue-clad figure's lips had not moved. Unar saw, with her magical sight and sense of smell, the connections between the woman, the sky, and every drop of rain that fell around them.

"Ehkis," Unar whispered. She looked for Aurilon and spotted her, camouflaged, in the shadow of a bent branch.

"Put her to sleep, Frog," Kirrik murmured above Unar's head. "I will divert her."

Then everything happened at once.

Aforis twisted away from Frog. He would have fallen, taking the leash and its holder down to Floor, if rain hadn't seemingly solidified around him. Wind howled through the trees, lifting Aforis high into the sky. Unar watched him fly upwards, and then fall with the rain towards some distant part of the forest.

Ylly, after everything that had happened, finally started crying.

Frog, who had let go of the leash, stood motionless, staring after Aforis, for a full second before seizing Ylly's cries from out of her mouth.

"You cannot steal a goddess's power, Core Kirrik," Frog said, meaning Ehkis, but making a liar of herself as she prepared from Audblayin's power the pattern of something encompassing and smothering, suited to putting everyone outside the Great Gates, besides Kirrik and herself, to sleep.

Unar soaked her senses into the tallowwood tree, and a branch erupted upwards, directly through Kirrik's body. The sensation of the woman's heart muscle squirming around the living wood, trying to keep beating, sickened Unar, and she heaved nonproductively over the silently screaming, struggling little girl in her arms.

And Kirrik's soul hovered for a moment over the body that Unar had destroyed. An intangible essence, sucking light and warmth from the air, it crossed the space like an arrow and plunged into Ehkis's body.

The rain stopped, again. It wasn't just that no new droplets fell, but that water which had been suspended vanished as if it had never been.

"It is my power, now!" Kirrik cried triumphantly from the lips of the blue-robed goddess, but her voice didn't boom like the thunder. Confusion crossed her beautiful features in the time that it took for Aurilon to leap out of the shadow and onto her back, curved blade in hand, already beginning a line of red across the slender throat.

*The gift goes with the body. Only godhood goes with the soul.*

Frog turned such a rictus of hate towards Unar that Unar knew she could no longer pretend that Frog could be redeemed. Had she really thought Frog would give in, just because her tool, Aforis, had been taken away? Had Unar really thought there was any way to keep Audblayin safe without spilling her sister's blood?

"I love you, Isin," she said, and the first flush of her magic through Frog's flesh healed the cuts and scrapes Frog had received while climbing. The second flush urged even healthy tissues to begin replicating madly. *Repair. Change. Grow,* Unar's magic ruled.

In Frog's eyes, Unar saw the confused, unfocused eyes of the baby Erid had brought into the world, so different from the angry child who had tried to poison an adopted father, who had hoped to find a sister wiser than Unar had any hope of being. *If only you hadn't fallen. We could have protected one another. I could have protected you from Kirrik, and you could have protected me from my own selfishness. It wasn't Audblayin that I was supposed to guard.*

*It was you.*

Frog's body was torn apart by ripe explosions of obscenely distorted muscle and bone.

Unar realised she could hear Ylly's crying again. It was audible because nobody remained to steal the sound of it. Kirrik and Frog were dead. Murdered by her.

She kissed the cradled head, again, and whispered that all would be well. Kirrik's men, still stunned by the appearance and apparent assassination of Ehkis and flinching from droplets that fell from the trees, began surrendering all around her, new slaves for the king of Audblayinland. Servants emerged from the Garden, willing to heal soldiers outside of the grounds, another thing unheard of, but Unar didn't care.

Unar crawled to the Gate and set her hand against the wards. There was no need to summon the Gatekeeper. She was home. Aoun had showed her how to open it. He had given her the key. She did what he had shown her, sowing the seed, taking a piece of it inside herself, but strangely, the wards didn't soften against her hand. Instead, they accused her, in her head.

*Have you stolen food?*

*Have you stolen the sovereignty of another's body?*

*Have you stolen human life?*

"No," she said listlessly. It wasn't supposed to accuse her. She was home. There was some mistake. It had to be Ylly who was keeping her from entering. Children stole things all the time. She let go of the incarnation of the goddess and beat against the wards with both hands.

"Unar," Aoun said soothingly, shifting through the Gate to stand beside her. At his feet, Frog's mutilated remains had left a shallow splash of blood, fat, and gristle. With one hand, he held Ylly back from the dangerous edge, ignorant of the fact that Odel's power prevented the child from falling. With his other hand, he squeezed Unar's shoulder. "Unar, you're alive, you saved us, but you killed the woman and the child. You cannot enter."

"I can," she shrieked in his face, flecking his cheek with spittle. She beat harder against the wards, this time with her magic as well as her fists, feeling the shields made of Aoun's magic begin to bend under the mighty, unmatched pool of power she now possessed. If he had tried to stop her, to drain her as he and Oos had once done before, she might have killed him.

Instead, he waited calmly by her side. Over and over, she planted the seed, the key, in the gateway, watched the tendrils curl out of it, only for those tendrils to wither under the weight of her crimes.

*I can't break them. I can't force my way through.*

"Who is this child, Unar?" Aoun asked.

*I have stolen human life.* Unar didn't answer him.

"Is she another orphan?"

*I am no orphan. The Garden is my mother. The Garden is my father. I must go home.*

"The Garden cannot use a slave so young." Aoun's face was earnest. He thought he was speaking reason. He hadn't shared her journey. For him, nothing had changed. "We can't care for her, not yet. Not until she's old enough to serve."

*I must go home.*

Unar gazed into Aoun's dark, deep-set eyes. *No tears.* He could see that she was searching for something and not finding it; the frown lines between his heavy, knitted brows deepened. Why wasn't he more distraught about their impending separation? Why not euphoric at discovering she was still alive? What was wrong with him? Couldn't he feel anything? Didn't he know anything?

*So dunderheaded, Aoun.*

Unar was made speechless by the depths of her failure, the heights of her absurd expectations.

She could have told him that the child was Audblayin. She could have told him where to find Sawas. Slave mother and slave child would be reunited and readmitted to the Temple. But Unar had fallen in the first place to free a slave. And now she realised what her true destiny had been, all along.

*After you have lived with us for long enough, you will wonder why you ever wished to crawl and kiss Audblayin's hand.*

It was not to bring Audblayin to the Garden, that she might grow surrounded by the same ignorance and isolation of Gardeners and Servants that had always surrounded her. It was to answer the questions that Kirrik had posed Unar, back at the dovecote during their first night on watch: *And if you desired to feel the sun, what then? If you needed fresh fruits to cure a child's illness? What if you had fallen and your family remained above, and they were forced to watch while demons ate the flesh off your bones?*

Maybe the gods and goddesses didn't care for the people of Understorey because they didn't know them. Had never lived among them.

*Why them and not us? Why can they not protect everyone? Are they so weak?*

She would return Audblayin to the Garden. Yes, she would. But not now. Not yet. The Garden was no place for children, and there was no place that was a good place for slaves. Let baby Ylly stay with her mother, and below the barrier too. Then, perhaps Audblayin in her next life would have a proper answer to give, when asked why everyone couldn't pass through the barrier, why everyone could not live in the sun.

It was a good decision, Unar thought, but it also robbed her of the triumphant moment she'd dreamed of for so long. She wiped her nose on her torn sleeve. The motion drew Aoun's attention to the seams where her spines were hidden. His handsome face showed revulsion.

"Unar, those cannot be . . . you cannot . . . the rules have been bent, this day. I don't believe there would be objections if I . . . Unar, do you want me to . . . I could remove those. I could heal them."

"No, Aoun." Unar gathered Ylly to her again. She reached out to unfasten the sash that held his robes closed. He allowed it, but she took no pleasure in the sight of his muscular chest. The sash was for binding the child safely, and his bore-knife she took because the Garden made good tools. She might not again have the opportunity to take one. "I'll need them."

She slashed at the branch beneath her feet with her forearm. Her spines bit deep. She lowered herself over the edge, meeting Aoun's gaze for what felt like the last time. He could have called the king's men to imprison her, a traitor whose only place was as a slave. Instead, he shifted his position slightly so that his body shielded her from their line of sight.

Neither of them said good-bye.

# FIFTY-EIGHT

As UNAR dropped through the barrier, her magic faded.

Not all of it, just most. Ylly cried continuously, calling for her mother. Unar would go back for Sawas, but she had to see Oos first. She moved gradually around the great girth of the tree, until the river lay to her left. Down and down, into the rainless gloom, her final task incomplete.

*Not yet. I cannot join you yet, Isin. First, I must have an answer to your Master's question.*

At one point, she became aware of three men with hatchets, trying to chop their way into the tree. Tallowwood was extremely hard, and they hadn't made much progress. They couldn't enter the huntsmen's home through the flooded front entrance beneath the river, so they were attempting to enlarge one of the ventilation holes that supplied the storeroom. They'd torn off the mesh that kept insects out, and splinters flew.

Some kind of poisonous smoke made them cough. *Esse.* He must have been burning something beneath the hole, up on the ledge where the tallow candles normally sat, but it wasn't poisonous enough to kill the would-be intruders, who still searched for Oos, not knowing that their mistress, Core Kirrik, was dead.

Three white faces looked up and saw Unar. Before they could reach for weapons, she murmured the godsong to herself. Her chest vibrated, relaxing the baby who squirmed there, but there was no sound.

Instead, the three men simply dropped off the tree, their snake-tooth spines dissolved into nothing, eaten by the healing of their own human bones. Aoun had given her the idea.

Unar had loved the three men for their urge to find freedom, their hunger for justice, even as she killed them. What did killing matter anymore? She couldn't enter the Garden. There was no difference between two deaths and five. She climbed down further, until her face was level with the ventilation hole.

"Esse," she called down the hole, coughing. "Stop burning whatever it is you're burning. I have Ylly's granddaughter. I'm coming inside."

The living wood flexed and shivered. It opened for her, transforming into a stairway, the arched opening a smaller replica of the Great Gate. She swung herself down into it, withdrawing her spines from the tallowwood, and walked down two dozen steps to stand in the small room where she'd slept with Issi, Ylly, Oos, and Hasbabsah.

They all stood there, now, Issi in Ylly's arms, gaping at Unar. Esse stamped distractedly on some ashes, but Bernreb and Marram held long knives, showing no signs of recognition.

"Are they controlling you, Unar?" Marram asked softly.

"No," Unar said. "Your amulet protected me. Thank you. You should take it back now." She lifted the cord over her head, handing the bone amulet back to Marram, and also held out the younger Ylly for Bernreb to take.

Bernreb looked to Esse, who nodded briskly, before putting away the blade and lifting Ylly's small body away. Unar sagged immediately, sitting down, hard, on the steps she had made.

"What happened?" Marram asked, slipping the amulet over his head. "Is that really Ylly's granddaughter? Did you catch her? Did she fall?"

"She didn't fall," Unar said. "She can't fall. Odel protects her, even though he's dead now. Ehkis, the rain goddess, is dead, too. I don't know what happened to Ilan, goddess of justice, Protector of Kings, whom Kirrik had captive. I didn't see her, or the man, Sikakis, who carried her."

"Two gods." Hasbabsah deliberated. "Maybe three. It is the most they have managed in some time."

"But still futile," Esse said, stamping.

"We know, Esse. It is why we left them," Marram said.

"They wanted Oos," Ylly said, sharing a glance with the younger, darker woman.

"To keep her captive," Marram said. "To use her, as they used Unar."

"Is that true, Unar?" Oos asked. Her long hair, gleaming and springy, hung in two cord-gathered bunches over her breasts. Her neckline was embroidered with seedlings that Unar thought were symbols of the Garden, but as the smoke cleared, she recognised as night- and humidity-loving Understorian epiphytes. Her huge eyes were fearful, and her voice quavered. "Did they use you? Or are you with them? How did you get through the barrier? Where is that little girl, Frog, who went with you?"

Unar stared at her. She didn't answer. Couldn't answer. *She was my sister, and I killed her.*

"Oos," she said, "I'm going back to get Sawas. She's at the House of Epatut."

*Thank you for sending Marram after me.*

"Mama," baby Ylly said.

"Yes," Unar said. "I'm going to get Mama and bring her here."

"This is my house," Esse said loudly.

"We have room," Bernreb grumbled, peeling a black grape for the younger Ylly, clearly already taken by his newest guest.

"We have room," Marram said, his grey eyes sparkling, "if Unar will consent to form some added rooms, just as she has formed this magnificent staircase."

"I can make more rooms," Esse scowled. "That's not the point."

"Oos," Unar said, ignoring him, "I can take you back up through the barrier. I know the way through, but you must come now if you're coming. Servant Eilif is dead. Once they choose another to take her place, there could be no room left for you."

Oos exchanged glances with the older Ylly again.

"My place is here, Unar. My place is with Ylly. My feelings are for her. I couldn't give her up, any more than I could give up music a second time."

Unar shrugged. She abruptly felt too tired to do more than mumble. Oos, who had once accused her of having feelings for Aoun, would be the one to find love and happiness. Oos, who came to the Garden because she liked butterflies and flowers, not in search of the greater things Unar had craved.

"If that's what you want."

"Somebody help Unar to the hearth room," Hasbabsah said sharply. "She needs food and rest."

"No," Unar said, struggling to her feet. "I have to go back through the barrier before the residues of Canopy fade. Just get me some new clothes. Please." She could pass through the barrier, alone, if she didn't wait. Otherwise, she would have to carry Audblayin back through it, tearing another hole. Who knew how many demons might pass through this one? Could the Garden's wards keep a chimera out?

"You're going to fetch my daughter?" Ylly asked. "You're going to bring

Sawas here? What about her slave's mark? How do you know it will vanish, as mine did? What about the sickness that almost killed Hasbabsah?"

"You don't need to worry about that," Unar said. "I don't have Audblay-in's soul, but the goddess and I are very close now." She had hardly noticed when her healing of the child outside the Gate removed the mark pressed into Ylly's tiny tongue.

"I thought you said Audblayin was a god," Oos said gently. "You were convinced he would be a man this time, Unar."

"I was wrong," Unar said. "Take care of little Ylly until her mother gets here. Mothers and daughters shouldn't be apart for long. I hope you can forgive me. I hope you can forgive us all."

# FIFTY-NINE

DAYLIGHT SEEMED to pierce her.

Unar couldn't remember it being so bright. Colours of dyed cloth. Scarlet fruit in baskets. Yellow birds so illuminated by sun that they might have been small suns themselves. The House of Epatut was raucous with the chattering of macaques. Disregarding the movements of humans on the roads below, they feasted on nuts and threw the empty casings at passers-by.

Two hired guards who hadn't been there before dawn flanked the ramp to the front door. One of them yawned behind his hand. The other asked, "What is your business with the House?"

"I'm a healer, come to see Wife-of-Epatut," Unar said.

The yawning one went inside. When he returned, Wife-of-Epatut was with him, big-bosomed and frog-eyed, but so was Sawas. She threw herself at Unar at first sight, her fist smacking Unar in the eye.

"Where is she? Give her back!"

"Sawas," Wife-of-Epatut said in a low, acerbic voice, and Sawas retreated behind the woman who owned her, cringing yet trembling with rage at the same time.

"Good day, Wife-of-Epatut," Unar said. "I knew your slave, Sawas, when I was a Gardener in the Temple of Audblayin. I come to offer you healing and new life, if you will accept it, in exchange for Sawas."

"That will not be possible," Wife-of-Epatut said, folding her arms. "Even if you are the adept who turned my house inside out as I slept this morning. Sawas makes milk for my nephew, who has come to live with us. His mother suffered an accident. If you take her, he'll go hungry."

"Let him eat nut paste. Fruit mush. Insects trapped in sap and boiled in monkey oil. Or bring his distraught mother to live with you." It was a guess, but the widening of Wife-of-Epatut's protuberant eyes told Unar she had hit on the truth. "The healing I offer is a healing of your husband's mad desire to have a son. Without one, he is afraid that you believe he is less. You are a better weaver than he is. A better trader and a better human being. I can heal his envy. I think I know how."

Wife-of-Epatut struggled visibly to hide her shock.

"My husband isn't an envious man," she said, "but even if he were, what healing could I accept from you? You're cast out, worse than a slave, and you're a thief. You wrecked my house."

"Do you refuse my help, then?"

Her lip quivered.

"I must refuse it," she said.

"If that's what you wish," Unar said, exactly the same way she had said it to Oos. She had no need to sing the godsong here. Seizing power from Canopy itself, she ignored Wife-of-Epatut's astonishment when the merchant's already-large breasts became heavy with milk. "I'll give you this gift instead. Feed your own nephew from now on. Come with me, Sawas. I'll take you to your daughter."

"No!" Sawas howled, touching her tongue, which no longer bore her slave's mark. "Little Epi is like my own child, too. I've been closer to him than anyone! You must bring my daughter back here, or, I warn you, my mistress will go to the king!"

Unar sighed. For a moment, she was tempted to leave Sawas where she was. Did Audblayin really need this fool to raise her? Surely she would be better off raised by those who were older and wiser, like Hasbabsah and Ylly the elder.

"You promised to teach me to swim, Sawas," Unar said. "Somebody else needs your lessons now. Whatever those lessons are."

*However unworthy I may think them.*

"You're a liar," Sawas cried, clinging to Wife-of-Epatut. "You're not taking me to Ylly. You're taking me to drink my blood and steal my soul."

"What have you done?" Wife-of-Epatut babbled. She patted ineffectually at her erupting bosom. "What have you done to me? Undo it at once!"

Unar didn't use her magic to seize Sawas with vines. Instead, she marched up to her, plucked her by the collar, and began dragging her down the ramp. The hired guards looked uneasily to the otherwise occupied Wife-of-Epatut, but didn't try to stop them.

"You were named so you could travel up and down, Sawas," Unar said. "Down you'll go. Whether you come back up again is up to you."

Once they were out of sight of the House of Epatut, Sawas seemed to give in. She allowed Unar to push and prod her along the now-crowded streets of Audblayinland. Everyone who had emerged from their homes—everyone but the occupants of the House of Epatut, it seemed—spoke of the battle that had raged at the Garden Gate that morning. About how the king had defended them, even in the absence of the goddess Audblayin, and that perhaps some of the tribute that had been reserved for the deity might find its way to the palace, instead. Maybe some of their second sons could be spared to serve the royal family.

Meanwhile, marketplaces that should have stayed closed for another two months had become bustling and noisy, the signs still wet with paint and the ropes that kept people from falling from platforms pale green and freshly knotted.

At the Great Gate of the Garden itself, lines of grateful citizens, from stricken to internoders, waited to press material goods upon the Gatekeeper. Aoun ushered them in towards the egg and moat that Unar would never see again.

Tears blurred her vision in her uninjured eye as she stepped out onto the branch where she had planned to descend. Before she could crouch down and order Sawas to climb on her back, Aurilon stepped out of a shadow, tall and scarred and graceful and deadly.

Sawas whimpered and clung to Unar's clothes the way she had clung to Wife-of-Epatut's.

"Odel is dead," Aurilon said without preamble.

"I know," Unar replied hesitantly. "At least, I didn't see how he could have survived. I'm sorry."

"I do not want you to be sorry. I want you to find him again."

"Find him again? But he must be just born, and besides, I've had enough of taking babes from their mothers. I won't do it."

"I will not take him. I swear to you on his soul. Only watch over him. Wait for him. You found Audblayin. Do not pretend that you did not. You can find Odel."

Unar was so tired. So close to being allowed to rest.

"I can find him," she said. "What happened to Aforis? Do you know?"

"Ehkis returned him to the second-tallest tree in Airakland. Airak did not die when his Temple fell. His Servants have approached the wood god to help build them another Temple. When Aforis tells his story to the other Servants, I cannot say whether he will be punished or rewarded." Aurilon's expression showed little concern.

"Let's hope for a reward. He's been punished enough. What of Ilan?"

"She was a casualty of the fighting in Ehkisland."

"So. Three gods did die at once. I'll come with you in just a moment."

Unar gathered her magic. Seeds sprang to life, soaking up water and sunlight, infiltrating the bark with their roots. Vines writhed along the tallowwood's branches and then fell away, forming a rope ladder that led down; a long way down.

Unar stood at the edge, looking down at the ladder, not moving. She had planned to escort Sawas down, but after agreeing to help Aurilon, it seemed she had a Canopy-wide search to accomplish first.

"Thank you," Aurilon said. "I would not ask it of you, but I still fear the soul-changer. This is what the Lakekeeper conveyed to me of the One Forest henchman, prince of Airakland. He was by the lake at the Temple of Ehkis. Ilan had been cut from the straps on his back by one who did not recognise her true nature. She was dumped into the lake, sleeping even as she sank into the water. The prince slew the man who had cut the straps, and turned as if to dive and retrieve her, his best key to unlocking the barrier. But then his body shuddered. He fell to his knees. He lifted his hands and gazed at them. The whites of his eyes showed. 'No! Sikakis, no!' That is what he screamed, over and over."

"Core Kirrik," Unar said flatly.

"Indeed. He was no longer the prince Sikakis but the sorceress, Kirrik. She saw the Lakekeeper skirting the lake, coming to kill her again, and she dropped, climbing with her spines down the side of the tree. By the time the Lakekeeper reached the place where she had begun to descend, she was gone, and the child, Ilan, drowned."

All Unar could think was *If Ilan is dead, Kirrik can't come through the barrier again. Even if she has taken Sikakis's body.*

True, Unar had sent Audblayin below the barrier, but nobody else knew of Ylly's true nature besides Aurilon; perhaps Sawas, if she'd been listening closely, but Sawas was even less likely to jeopardise her daughter than Aurilon was to endanger Canopy.

"Sawas," Unar said. "Go down the ladder. It will take you home."

Strangely, with Aurilon staring at her, Sawas didn't argue. She climbed down nimbly until Unar couldn't see her anymore. When she passed through the barrier, Unar's sense of her life force faded.

"Three hundred boy babies were born in Odelland last night," Aurilon said.

"Lead me to them," Unar answered thickly. She drank water from a gourd that Aurilon put to her lips, and let the Bodyguard take some of her weight. "I'll listen to them cry. And then I'll find the goddesses who died. You must watch over them, too, Aurilon."

"It will be my pleasure. They will not even see me. I have a new chimera skin, and this one I do not intend to mount for display."

THREE DAYS later, Unar parted ways with Aurilon and went into Understorey.

Aurilon was content. She'd knelt at the feet of an out-of-niche woman who was beatific in her status as a new mother at the age of fifty-two. Odel's newborn head had been spotty and squashed-looking. He'd had hair on his forehead that the midwife assured them would fall out soon enough.

The Lakekeeper, one of the rain goddess's Servants, hadn't been best pleased to see Unar, but she'd forced on him every detail she could remember of Edax's fate. Aurilon's mildly threatening presence had convinced him to come with them to the House of Itit, where a jeweller's daughter, only one day old, already preferred blue gemstones to green.

*How can you be sure she's Ehkis?* the Lakekeeper had asked, fists on hips.

*Unar is the Godfinder,* Aurilon answered. *She crosses into all niches. Canopy is hers now.*

It wasn't the title Unar had yearned for, but the Lakekeeper had repeated it with bafflement and a little awe. His respect meant nothing. He wasn't Aoun, or Isin, or Audblayin.

He was nobody. Unar would have despised him if she hadn't been numb on the inside. She would have flung the undesired bestowment back in Aurilon's face.

*I'll find one more goddess,* Unar had said. *Then I'm done.*

She found that child, the child that would be Ilan, goddess of justice, in a prison cell in the queen's palace in Ilanland. The child's mother, Ear, despite being heavily pregnant, had been arrested for insulting the royal heir, and had given birth that night in her cell.

*I would have protected my baby anyway, goddess or no,* Ear said earnestly. *I would have bought Odel's protection if I'd had to lie with the jailer to earn it.*

*You don't have to,* Unar had said. *Aurilon, can't you—?*

*I can,* Aurilon sighed, and filled Ear's cupped hands with coins of silver and gold. *This is for you. We had it from the Servants of Ilan, when we brought them the body of their drowned goddess. The Servants are no longer starving*

*themselves because they cannot find the one they serve. Call on me in Odel's*
*Temple if you need more. You are free to go.*

Unar rolled up her sleeves and carefully set her spines in the side of the tallowwood tree.

She, too, was finally free to go.

The much-reduced river sang to one side of her, and the autumn wind made the forest moan. Gods died and returned to life, but Unar was seventeen years old, significantly older than the girl child who would be Audblayin. Unar would die before Audblayin was reborn a man. When Unar was born again, unlike Audblayin, she wouldn't remember anything of her past lives.

With the finding of the last deity, she was set adrift. How strange to feel, while not performing Understorian magic, less solid than the trees that turned the wind. To have felt for so long that she was a tool constructed for a single purpose, only to discover she was as fit for being a Bodyguard as a frog was fit for flying. But there was still the question.

She would have an answer.

The opening she'd made into the brothers' home was now neatly fitted with a door. It opened when she pushed against it, and she walked down the stairs into light and warmth. The new addition had been modified to accommodate candle niches. A second fireplace had been built in the en-larged storeroom-turned-permanent-bedroom. Unar smiled at the candles. The bear that had died so that its fat could produce that smoky, flickering light; the grasses whose twisted fibres had made the wick and the trees, not pillars of the world as the emergents were, but smaller, unnoticed in the dark, that had provided the wood for fuel for the hunters' dwelling; those tran-sient things were her kin, unmourned and unremembered, interchangeable as individual breaths.

"You are back," Hasbabsah said, sounding surprised and pleased, a knit-ted cap pulled down over her almost-bald head. She looked up from the rope jig with its metal weights, where she and Oos formed uniform lengths that must have pleased even Esse the perfectionist.

"I'm back," Unar agreed. "How is Sawas settling in?"

Hasbabsah grunted.

"She will take some more time to adjust. You kept your word. You have done what you promised to do in the Garden and more. You do not need to worry about Sawas anymore."

*I have not done what I promised,* Unar thought, *because the Garden has not kept its promise to me, to raise me into the sun.*

But the Garden hadn't made that promise. Unar didn't know why she'd promised herself something that could never come true. Nobody else had stood over her, insisting that she take what she deserved; it had been her own inner voice, all along, and she had trusted it. But why not? Who else in the world was trustworthy?

"Where's Esse?" she asked. "I must make more rooms."

"He is sleeping," Oos said. "He has been making more defences around the tree, further down. He said that those men should never have reached as high as they did."

Unar walked through the brothers' house. She smiled at faces that smiled at her, but didn't speak to any of them. Ylly and Issi fought over a floppy black hat that had golden imitation chimera's eyes sewn onto the sides of it. Sawas sat in Bernreb's lap, picking bones from her plate of roasted fish.

The brothers' bedroom was cramped. Unar pushed back the curtain to enter, and tried to straighten once inside, but her head brushed the curve of the spherical ceiling, and the three free-standing bunks in the centre of the room looked like a stack of rough-cut, storm-felled debris. Esse slept on the top, covered in an itchy-looking fur.

Unar sang the godsong to herself as she reshaped the bed into a thing of elegance and added space, waking up the last still-living cells at the timber's rim. They'd been part of a sweet-fruit pine tree, once. The tallowwood walls of the room were easier to flex and widen. The great tree told her which parts of itself were safe to hollow and which must remain sound, which carried the sap and which carried the incredible burden of the weight of the top of the tree.

Before she had finished, she saw Esse's grey eyes, open and watching her. He didn't move a muscle of his long body.

"I'm sorry for disturbing you, Esse," she said. "But there's one more favour I need from you. Not monsoon-right, this time, but a right to sleep here, in the new part of this room, for fourteen or fifteen monsoons, or however much time passes before the younger Ylly feels in her bones it's time to wake me."

"Is this Canopian double-speak?" Esse asked. "Is it death that you want?"

"Not yet," Unar answered. "I must deliver the goddess Audblayin to the Garden first. Help me to get up there, please."

Esse sat up. Before she'd changed his bed, he would have struck his head, but now there was room for him to stand on the top bunk, if he wished, without touching the domed ceiling. He examined the niche she'd made, high in the wall, with its brackets shaped like loquat trees, and a hammock-sized space that a large human or a small dayhunter could have crawled into.

"How will you breathe in there?" he asked.

"I've made a small, hidden, ventilation hole. The mesh over it is magic. Nothing will crawl down it, I promise you."

"That is good. I would not want cockroaches gnawing on you while you are sleeping. Mind your spines, Canopian. You still do not use them very well."

Esse lifted her to kneel on his shoulders. From there, she was able to use her forearm spines to pull herself into the space. It was cold, but her body heat would soon be enough to keep her warm. Esse took a few steps back and peered in at her.

"What if Ylly dies?" he said. "What if she never decides it is time to wake you?"

*Unspoken prophecies can come true, too.*

"Good night, Esse," Unar said, forming the pattern that she had seen Frog form outside the Great Gate. She wrapped the deep, hibernating sleep around herself like a blanket, being careful not to let it touch any of the other lives nearby.

And she closed her eyes.

# PART IV

*Season for Growth*

# SIXTY

UNAR HAD hoped it would be dreamless.

*I love you, Isin.*

Edax died over and over again in a world made of steam.

*I love you, Isin.*

Frog's body fell apart into blobs of muscle and bone.

*I love you, Isin.*

Unar beat against the wards that protected the Garden, with no hope of passing through. Not unless she sabotaged her own memory, and if she did that, her desire to enter the Garden might be lost, too; her memory of how to do magic, how to find goddesses and gods. What if she died, was reborn, and walked into the Garden as a supplicant, with no power of her own?

It would be better to sleep until Audblayin grew as old as Hasbabsah and died. Sleep until he was born a man. But, no. She must wake sooner than that. She must ask the question.

SOMETHING PRESSED down on her.

The ceiling had collapsed. Kirrik had returned and was cutting down the tallowwood tree.

No. Not that. It was two small, muffled, giggling bodies. Sitting on her. Crushing her so she couldn't breathe.

"Ylly! Issi!" Oos was a threatening presence below and to one side, outside the sleeping place. "Come out of there, right now!"

Hands scrabbled around in Unar's clothes, catching dirty feet and pulling hard. Wailing children's voices receded. Unar slept again.

*I LOVE you, Isin.*

BREATHING BESIDE her. Sharing the air.

It was Esse. His long legs didn't fit. They hung off the edge of the ledge.

"Move over, little tree bear," he muttered, and squeezed her deeper into the crevice, so that he could fold his limbs in beside her. "It is cold outside, even if Sawas and Bernreb do not feel it."

Quiet for a while. Sharing the air. Heat, from Esse's body. Moaning, from the main part of the room.

"Let Marram pretend he does not mind the cold and wet," Esse growled. "This is my house. I am not leaving just because she says she cannot relax if people are listening. She should be quieter, then, should she not? I brought us here. I made the very first mark in the bark."

Esse, breathing. Bodies in Bernreb's bed, breathing. High above Canopy, the leaves of the great tree, breathing.

*You speak to the dead*, Frog sighed. *Well, the dead will answer you, this one time.*

A boy's piping voice.

"Great-Grandmother is dying." He was close. Inside the crevice with Unar. No, outside of it, standing on something to make him taller. "She said to tell you. She said to thank you."

"She will not answer, boy." That voice was Bernreb's. "She is sleeping. Here. I will set you down."

Not a ladder. Bernreb. Holding the boy up to Unar's hollow.

Who was his Great-Grandmother?

*Maybe it's me. Maybe Audblayin will never be a man, and I'll sleep for eternity.*

*You slow grey mould!* Frog cried. *You one-fingered worm!*

"Wake up, Godfinder," Audblayin whispered in her ear.

Unar opened her eyes.

The lanky young woman who pressed her hands into Unar's hands had a Canopian's dark skin, an Understorian's long, straight hair, and a Warmed One's soulful, sepia eyes. She wore a yellow silk robe. It was cut off at the elbows. Unar saw the crease and sensed the magic of the spines. She smelled quince blossom and wood fern.

"I'm awake," Unar tried to say, but her mouth felt adhered shut. Another young woman of about the same age—Unar's age—with a rounder face, short hair, snub nose, and mischievous grin, stepped forward with a leather cup. She helped Unar to sit up and moisten her mouth with water.

"I am Imerissiremi," she said. "You can call me Issi." She had spines, too, and armour of overlapping metal scales that slithered as she moved. Weapons hung about her, as they had hung around Edax. "Ylly says it is time to go to Canopy."

*Edax.*

Imerissiremi's eyes glittered with excitement.

Unar heard weeping and lifted her head, blinking in the firelight. She'd been pulled out of her recess and into Bernreb's bunk, the lowest one; at least, it smelled like him. She imagined she didn't smell particularly pleasant herself. Her nostrils flared, perhaps expecting to find the smell of Edax's broiled flesh, or Frog's violated innards.

She'd thought time would heal her, but it seemed to her as if no time had passed.

"Is that what Ylly says?" she wondered. She looked into Audblayin's eyes again. "Have you had a good childhood, Holy One?"

Audblayin's smile was very kind.

"I have. I had more time, I think, because I'm down here. It's been very different from my usual style of childhood. Enlightening, you might say."

"You told them you were a goddess?"

"Only a few hours ago. I've been myself, properly, for a week, I think. The memories came slowly. I had to wait, to be sure. To remember everything that happened with you and Kirrik."

"How could you remember that? You were a babe in the House of Epatut."

"I remember everything that is done with my power. Every spell. Every new life. Every person the gift passes through. What you, Frog, and Kirrik used was my power, Unar."

Unar's hands, which had lain quiescent under the girl's slender fingers, now seized Audblayin's wrists, grinding them, before she could remember not to lay hands on a goddess.

"Do you mean to say that you could have stopped it?"

"Not at all. I was as helpless as you were at your worst, when you felled the great Temple of Airak. Let go of me."

Unar let go. "Forgive me, Holy One. Please. I have a question for you, if you care to answer it. Long ago, when you took power from the Old Gods, why did you and the others fashion a barrier that would allow Canopians through, but not Understorians or Floorians?"

Audblayin's large, dark eyes grew solemn.

"There are things I cannot share with you," she said, "but trust this to be true. The barrier must stay the way that it was made until the Old Gods are forgotten."

"That can't be the answer, that you are afraid of the resurrection of the Old Gods," Unar said, despairing. "Couldn't you just make people forget?"

"No. To change people's minds, to force them to forget, is to cut off their arms and legs. It is to cripple them. The barrier was my idea. I am the Waker of Senses, not the diminisher of thought. The death god, Atwith, suggested that those of Understorey and Floor who remembered the old ways should simply be killed. I opposed him."

"But, Holy One. Now you've seen what it's like to live down here. In the dark. Do Understorian children deserve to fall to their death because Odel isn't here to protect them? Must Marram risk his life in the monsoon because there are no safe roads between villages, no defences against demons? Couldn't he be allowed through the barrier, even to trade? Wouldn't he be grateful to the new gods then, and more inclined to uphold your rule?"

"The barrier isn't intended to be cruel to Understorians, Unar. It's to protect Canopians, whose tribute gives us the strength to defend them. Unfortunately, the two peoples must remain apart. If the barrier were open for folk to freely trade, ideas would be exchanged as freely. Ideas that must be left in the dark to die out. Canopy could be contaminated. The risk is unacceptable."

"But owning humans is acceptable?" Unar burst out angrily.

Audblayin smiled and shook her head.

"That's something that may be changed. In my own niche, at least."

Unar looked around, at last absorbing the tear-tracked faces of Ylly, Sawas, and Oos. Ylly's hair was white, and her cheeks age-spotted. Sawas was even rounder, with crow's feet at the corners of her eyes. Oos had lines on her neck and pouches under her eyes which hadn't been there before, but her weak, endearing, watery smile was the same.

"You've said your good-byes, here," Unar surmised. "That's why everyone's crying. You're ready to see the sun in a place where your own mother can never walk free."

"So much bitterness, Unar."

"I saved you," Unar said, pleading. "I saved you. Can't you force the Garden to let me in?"

"No."

Unar put her face in her hands.

"Maybe it would be better if you went without me."

"I don't think so. Aoun is waiting for you."

"For me?" Unar barked a laugh. "Aoun loves the Garden."

"He loves the Garden," Audblayin agreed. "But he hasn't changed the key."

*I will not cry.* Unar disguised her sorrow with rage. "So he hasn't changed the key. So what? It will never turn for me!"

Audblayin's smile deepened.

"No. I don't suppose it ever will. But he gave it to you, and he hasn't taken it back. It means something to him. A bargain. A promise. He's very powerful now. I am the living goddess Audblayin, and I can't force the Garden to let you in. But the Gatekeeper could, if he were ever to choose you over me."

Unar took a deep, shuddering breath.

"That day will never come."

"I agree," Audblayin said simply. "There is too much honour in him. The Servants chose well, when they chose him."

# SIXTY-ONE

UNAR WENT into the hearth room.

It was discoloured with age and smoke, and the tapestry hangings were faded, but the great table was the same, even if it hosted extra chairs. Esse hung fish over the fire as though he hadn't moved for seventeen years. The back of his head looked the same as it always had, but his ears looked bigger and there was a stiffness in his crouch that hadn't been there before.

"Good morning, sleepyhead," Bernreb said gruffly from his chair. His beard was salted with grey, and the snarling animals that covered his arms and chest were faded, the flesh beneath slightly sagging, but he still looked as though he could split a chimera skull with a single blow of a cleaver.

Unar stared at the red and green vest that he wore. It was made in the colours and the cut of a Gardener.

"My middle-father will be my Bodyguard for a time," Audblayin said. "Until I can find another to trust. Canopians are strangers to me, though I have fuzzy memories of Canopian men and women that I have trusted before. Still, they're like tales told at a fireside that I vaguely recall."

*Your Bodyguard? But the Bodyguard must be an initiate. An adept.*

"Take care of yourself, madwoman," Marram told Audblayin warmly. Of all of them, he seemed to have aged the least. Unar thought he still looked boyish, but she couldn't concentrate on what he was saying. Bernreb preoccupied her. "It cannot be easy having a goddess in your head."

"I am the goddess, Youngest-Father. Do not fear. I'll take care of this body. I'll take care of little Ylly."

"You can't think they will let Bernreb into the Garden," Unar said. She pointed to the depiction of a headless man etched into the burly hunter's pale skin. "He's a murderer, the same as me."

"As for that," Audblayin said, "I don't intend to stay in the Garden all the time, as I have done before. When I'm in the Garden, I won't need a

Bodyguard. The strength of my Gatekeeper has seen to that. When I'm outside the Garden, that's when I'll have my middle-father with me."

"Understorians can't walk free in Audblayinland. Unbroken spines are not permitted."

"Then I'll have to see the king," Audblayin said calmly, "about what is permitted and not permitted. Refresh yourself as needed, Godfinder. I mean to reach Canopy before high noon."

"Not without me," a child's voice said with determination. Unar turned to face a boy who couldn't have been older than nine or ten but who was almost her height, white as churning river water but with something darker in the sound of him. It was something she recognised with her magic sense, the same sense that had told her about Kirrik's kin.

"Frog's soul," she whispered, stunned.

Bernreb's giant hands massaged her shoulders, or perhaps he was holding her up by the shoulders like giant pegs holding up a drying shirt.

"This is my son," he boomed proudly. "Leapael."

"I am Leaper," the boy said fiercely, and grimaced the way that Frog had grimaced. "Not Leapael. I will go one way, and that way is up. I want to see the sun, all day, every day. You cannot make me stay down here, Middle-Father. Issi promised to take me with her."

The mischievous-looking girl's grin slipped, and Sawas pinched her.

"That is not Issi's decision to make. I should have whipped her for helping you to get spines so young."

"It is my decision," Leaper said loudly.

*My sister's soul.*

"Why couldn't you wait?" Unar accused Audblayin. "Why couldn't you let me share in the joy of it, this time? First you separate us by distance and now, again, by time?"

"I had no part in Frog's fall," Audblayin said. "You saved me, Unar. You said so. Ylly's life was your gift to me. Now I give this gift to you."

"Too late! Frog didn't love me. She was already half grown. This boy is the same. He doesn't know me."

"He thirsts for the heights. That much is the same. The rest is up to you."

"Do not talk about me," Leaper said crossly. "Do not talk about me! Tell Middle-Mother that I can go to Canopy, if you want to talk!"

Sawas sighed. She shared a long look with Bernreb.

"You can go," she said. "So long as you obey your middle-father and your sister, you can go. Thank Audblayin I'll be rid of your complaining." And then she seemed shocked by what she had said, covering her mouth and looking at Ylly.

Unar went to the fishing room to wash herself and her clothes. There were fewer storage racks and ropes in there now, more benches and buckets for washing, and ointments and sweet-smelling tinctures. She opened the stopper of one gourd of wood fern and another of distilled quince, marvelling at how strongly they brought back her earliest premonition.

She restoppered them and put them away, wiping her hands uncomfortably on her cut-off skirts. The river was a thin trickle, parting the smoke-screen that kept the opening closed to biting intruders.

Oos arrived with Unar's old green Gardener's breeches in hand.

"Do you want to wear these?" She touched Unar's cheek in the dim, greenish glow of the fluorescent fungi, and her eyes slitted a little with envy. "They'll fit you. You are still so young."

Unar took the breeches from her and traced the faded cloth.

"No. I have no right to them now."

"What will you do?"

Unar wanted to tell Oos that she had nothing left to do, once Audblayin was delivered, but to die, but she was overcome with giddiness at the realisation she didn't want to die anymore. *He thirsts for the heights.*

What could she do, in place of allowing herself to fall like a leaf?

*The rest is up to you.* Unar licked her lips.

"Become a fuel finder, I suppose," she said slowly. "My father may still be alive. Although I doubt it. Frog said he was bleeding for wood in Eshland. What have you done for sixteen years, Oos? Stayed here? Lived here? Without a thought for the Garden?"

Oos shrugged prettily and looked at her feet.

"I've become an accomplished musician, Unar. I've travelled the twelve towns of Understorey, playing with Marram, while Ylly and Hasbabsah tended the sick. Though I'm sure you noticed Hasbabsah is gone." *Yes.* Unar remembered Leapael's voice. *Great-Grandmother is dying.* "We couldn't go to Gannak, because of the history that Marram has there, but you'll see when you go outside, Unar. It's only in the summer that the great trees stand apart. In the dry season, there are ropes and bridges connecting all of these people in a vital, beautiful web. They have so little, but they all work together. And what is the Garden but the place where the goddess resides? All this time, we've had her here, with us. We'll miss her."

"The Garden is more than that," Unar muttered, dunking her hair in a bucket and shivering as she worked out the soapleaf lather with her fingers.

"What is it, then?"

"I don't know." But she did know. It was the place where Aoun waited.

*I will not weep.*

AUDBLAYIN OPENED the barrier for the diverse little party.

Leaper climbed the fastest, scuttling up the vertical surface like a skink. The snake-tooth spines seemed large on his lithe body, compared to Bernreb's, but Unar supposed hers were proportionally the same. Third in line after Leaper and Bernreb went Issi, with a swiftness and stamina that made Unar think, with another pang, of Edax. Seventeen years since he had died, and who still mourned him? *Aforis, perhaps.* Perhaps even the goddess Ehkis. The old acquaintances of a deity might seem fireside tales, but the heroes of tales could be as close as kin if the tales were told with conviction.

Issi would want to meet her real mother, Unar supposed. She wasn't sure she could remember the way to the House of Epatut.

Fourth was the goddess Audblayin herself, less sure of her climbing skills than the others. Or maybe her mind was on the task ahead, of claiming her rightful place while keeping her father and siblings from harm.

Fifth, and last, came Unar. To be higher than a goddess was disrespectful, after all, and she would have to be careful not to touch Audblayin anymore. It might have been an aftereffect of her long sleep, or simple reluctance to confront her failure again, but she climbed through the barrier almost wishing it would close on her.

Magic rushed into her lower belly as she returned to Canopy, swirling invisibly around her, welcoming her like an old friend. Audblayin gasped and went limp, hanging from the tree like a piece of fruit, until Unar climbed up to her and kissed her cheek.

*One final touch.*

The aroma of quince and wood fern was overpowering.

"Wake up, Holy One," she said.

Audblayin's lashes fluttered.

"What's wrong with her?" Leaper called down the trunk of the great tree.

"Nothing," Unar called back. She lowered her voice. "Can you keep climbing, Holy One?" She knew what was wrong. She had gone to merge with the tallowwood, only to find Audblayin already merged with it.

"I think so," Audblayin said faintly, and struck out with her forearm at the tree. She followed up with the opposite knee. "It hurts her, when we climb."

"She doesn't mind," Unar said, hovering, waiting to catch Audblayin if she fell. "Pain reminds her that she is alive."

They reached the platform in front of the Great Gate before noon, as Audblayin had wished. The carved doors themselves were open. Aoun stood outside them with a shaven-headed Gardener, now a white-robed Servant, whom Unar vaguely remembered.

Aoun carried the lantern of his office in smooth fingers that had never been scarred by fighting. His handsome face carried a little more flesh around neck and jaw, he wore a short, tidy beard and his eyes seemed slightly more hooded, but the steadiness, the solidity of him, had not changed.

"Are you the Gatekeeper?" Bernreb asked him.

Unar made a choking sound.

Aoun looked at her and frowned, slightly. He opened his mouth as if to speak, said nothing, and pressed his lips closed again.

"Only devotion to wickedness," the shaven-headed Servant said, her eyes wide, "could have kept you so young, Gardener Unar."

But Aoun directed open astonishment towards Audblayin, now, and his hand holding the lantern trembled.

"It's not wickedness, Iririn," he breathed. "Audblayin has come home. It was she whom Unar brought to me in the middle of the battle. Wasn't it, Unar? But I didn't know her. I didn't take her."

"It's well that you did not," Audblayin said, as the two white-robed Servants sank to their knees. "New life does not need love to grow, but I have felt it, stronger this time than ever before, and I will grow it too, wherever I can. There will be no more slaves in the Garden. Adepts will serve by their own free will or not at all. Stand up, you two who have pledged yourselves to me. I go to see the king, and I require formal robes and a suitable retinue."

"Of course, Holy One." Iririn jumped up and went into the Garden. Unar thought she might vomit with envy at the way the wards parted for the woman.

"Aoun, my Gatekeeper," Audblayin said, and another spasm went through Unar's body at that. Aoun belonged to this woman, body and soul.

*She would never use that body for what I would use it for,* Unar thought, her treacherous body aching in a way she had never thought it would ache again.

"Holy One," Aoun said, his composure recovered.

"This is my middle-father, Bernreb. I wish him to be my Bodyguard. He cannot enter the Garden. He cannot go to the night-yew tree. I wish a house to be built for him, here, outside the wards."

Aoun inclined his head.

"I'll send a message begging the wood god for his assistance with this task, Holy One."

"There's no need. The Godfinder is suited to the work. I will move away so that you may speak together. She will be allowed to use my power." Audblayin gave Unar an unreadable glance. "For this undertaking alone, Unar. Do you understand?"

"I understand, Holy One," Unar said. Oh, she understood. She was not to try to force her way into the Garden. She was not to try to extract any secrets from Aoun. Like Bernreb, she would loiter outside the wards, but that didn't mean she was not bound to serve and obey.

She laughed, darkly, as the goddess turned away, leaving her with a man who still made her skin prickle and her hands clench to keep from touching him.

"What is your desire, Gatekeeper?" she asked distantly, pleasantly. "What design shall I sculpt for you with the limited magic I am to be permitted?"

"Unar."

"Yes, Aoun?"

"How is it you haven't changed?"

"But I have changed, Aoun. Just not where anybody can see."

He nodded. Unar felt his magic gently touching her bones where the spines had been set. For a moment, he stood back, appraising her, and then he closed the space between them and folded his arms around her. Dependable as living wood. As pricked by the pain of Unar's spines as the tallow-wood had been, and as forgiving.

Unar couldn't speak. Her face flushed and she dared not move. She must still be sleeping inside the tree. It couldn't be real. Aoun did not hold people. He stood apart, as aloof as a god.

"Audblayin would grow love," he whispered into her hair. "Grow a house up around us, Unar."

She cooled her heat and urgency by melding with the tree, drawing on water seven hundred body lengths below, in the darkness of Floor. The bodies of Servant Eilif, Kirrik, Frog, and fifty unknown soldiers were part of the soil that sated the great tree's hunger. River, sky, and sun all came together to form the wooden shelter that sprang up around them, shutting away the light.

Aoun let go of her. She staggered. He was laughing softly, relighting the lantern.

"Is this much like the place where you've lived?" he asked, the lantern light revealing a room not so very different from the hearth room of the three hunters' home.

Issi came in through the open door and beamed at them.

"My father will be happy," she said at once.

"But not you?" Unar asked, silently cursing her for intruding.

"I am not staying here." She lifted her chin, a proud huntress, daunted by nothing. "I am going to Odelland. There is a warrior there, called Aurilon, who has never lost a duel. If she will teach me, I will learn from her."

The fool whisked away and was gone. Bernreb and Leaper replaced her. The boy immediately began to howl.

"This is just like home. What did I even climb up here for?"

"You won't live here, Leaper," Audblayin said, passing through the doorway behind him. She was robed in cloth that seemed made of dewdrops, her spines covered and her feet booted. Unar realised the robe was covered in cut diamonds. The goddess's gaze went from Unar's face to Aoun's. When it returned to Leaper, her expression firmed. "You will live with the Godfinder in Airakland, far away, at the other end of Canopy."

Unar felt as though she had been slapped.

"You don't trust me to stay close to the Garden," she said.

"I'm trying to make it easier for you, Unar," Audblayin answered. "It will be easier for you if there is no temptation."

Unar looked at Aoun. She looked back at Audblayin. Her heart felt heavier than stone, and for a moment some of the old self-loathing, the old anger, swept through her. It would be easier if she did let herself fall. For Aoun. For Audblayin. For everyone.

"The god of lightning," Leaper said with awe, already seeing through the sister he hadn't known was a goddess, but whose power over new life clearly failed to capture his imagination. "Yes. Airakland. Yes! Have you been there before, Godfinder?"

*Godfinder.* There it was again. A little piece of a less glorious destiny. A clue to why she had been born with such a powerful gift and sent to the Garden.

Unar forced herself to take Leaper's hand. Moving away from Aoun was more difficult than making tallowwood walk. For an instant, she could hardly breathe. There he was, in the corner of her eye.

No, she wouldn't look at him. She would look at Leaper. His face shone with eagerness. There was plenty of light still left in the day. Plenty of time to cross the border.

"No," she said, feeling the lives, bright with power, behind her. Bernreb, wry. Audblayin, decisive. Aoun, obedient. "I've never been there." *Not to the Canopian part of it, anyway.* "But I hear tales of towering floodgums, black from being struck by lightning, and houses that blaze at night like moonlight poured through the veins of a giant leaf."

"And what about Airak? Is he as tall as one of the great trees? Does lightning shoot out of his eyes?"

"I never met Airak," she said, "but I met one of his Servants. A brave man, and strong. Let's find out together."

Outside the house, there was a patch of sunlight. It wasn't as wide as the glorious sunlit spaces of the high heart of the Garden, but it would have to do from now on. The boy pulled free of her, put his arms into it, and shouted with joy.